Christmas with the
Rushbrokes

Christmas with the Rushbrokes

Caroline Akrill

Published by Jane Badger Books 2025
First published as *The Last Baronet* by The Fane Press, 2016
© Caroline Akrill

Author's Note

My father had a dance band in the forties and I grew up with the music of the age. Although I have had my pop, rock and classical favourites since, my heart still belongs to the music of the forties, to the age of Hoagy Carmichael, Jerome Kern and Irving Berlin.

Although this book is set in the 1980s, I so wanted Lavinia to sing these evocative, sentimental, yet heartfelt songs, and to speak to you through the lyrics, but I was utterly defeated by the complexity of the copyright and permissions jungle surrounding the music industry. In one case a search for the copyright owner revealed almost 3,000 entries that I could examine ten at a time. I was referred to companies who charged hefty fees for researching and obtaining permissions. My attention was drawn to terrifyingly complex legal cases over copyright that had been dragging on for years.

In the end I wrote my own lyrics and, believe me, you only realise how clever these deceptively simple lyrics are when you try to match them.

So if you are minded to look for the music to *I*

Remember You, try *I've Forgotten You, Just Like I Should*. Similarly, for *It's a Brand New Day Tomorrow*, try *It's a Lovely Day Tomorrow*. I believe *Silver Threads*, published in 1873 (lyrics by Eben E Rexford, music by H P Danks) is out of copyright. If it isn't I had better get myself a good lawyer...

Orchard Cottage, Semer, 2016

Disclaimer

This is a work of fiction.
The author would like to stress that no character
in this book relates to any person living or dead
and that all incidents are entirely imaginary.

For James

Chapter One

'...and so, not to put too fine a point on it,' said the representative of the National Westminster Bank, 'the Rushbrokes of Rushbroke are no longer considered a viable risk, and the bank want their money back.'

In the ensuing silence, Francis Hercules Sparrow, recently assigned to the branch expressly to identify and resolve myriad difficulties left in the wake of a devoted, long-serving, but overly sympathetic (Francis would have used the word gullible) predecessor, tapped at a keyboard on his desk. A pound sign appeared on a screen, followed by a sum running into six figures.

Sir Vivian Valentyne Rushbroke of Rushbroke, family motto *Prudence Before Valour*, looked away hurriedly. He didn't like this new man or his new-fangled computer thing. He concentrated his attention instead upon the carpet between his cracked, but well-polished shoes, hand made by Lobb thirty years ago when life had been less complicated. It was good carpet, thick and springy, the colour of old port; still red, but faintly brown at the edges. Observing that his shifting feet had produced a foam of loose fibres Sir Vivian supposed it to be new; its purchase probably made possible by the bloody scandalous interest on his overdraft. There had not been new carpet at Rushbroke within living memory, nor was there port in the cellar, which was fifteen inches deep in stagnant water and colonised by newts. The situation was dire, the prospect dismal, and there was bugger all to say. Yet some response was evidently expected, and so a few appropriate words had to be found.

'Wanting is all very well,' Sir Vivian said. 'Wanting is easy. *Getting* is a different kettle of fish altogether.'

Francis Sparrow frowned. In his rather too shiny pinstripe, with his sleeked-back hair, his bead-bright eyes, and his brown, bony fingers, an ornithologist would have considered him more starling than sparrow, but bird-brained he was not. Many interviews had taken place since his arrival; each had been conducted with practical, hard-hitting efficiency; every single difficulty had been resolved to the board's complete satisfaction. 'The bank do have ways and means of obtaining payment,' he said in a sharp tone.

'Ways and means?' Sir Vivian looked up from the carpet in a vaguely startled manner, glancing round the office as if half-expecting thuggery to emerge from the filing cabinets. *'Ways and means?'*

'We could force you to sell. There is a legal charge. We do have the power.'

'Power, eh? As well as ways and means.' Sir Vivian raised his untrimmed eyebrows as if in admiration at such a display of verbal omnipotence. He lifted his tweed-clad shoulders in a gesture which might, or might not, have been intended as apologetic. 'Won't do you any good though. There's nothing left to sell.'

'Come, come, now; there must be *something*.' Francis

Sparrow forced a note of optimism into his voice. 'Some valuable little painting hanging in a gloomy corner; a stack of old porcelain in the back of a disused cupboard. Is there no family silver tucked away?'

'*Silver and gold have I none; but such as I have I give thee.*' Sir Vivian shook his head. 'The silver went in the fifties. After that we were down to plate. We did find a good epergne that brought in a tidy sum a couple of years ago. Thought I'd done rather well until it turned up in a sale catalogue with a reserve of six times what I'd been paid for it. You can't win, you know. They're all crooked in the antiques game; dealers; sale rooms; even the big auction houses. Untrustworthy, the lot of them. All tarred with the same brush.'

'Quite,' said Francis Sparrow swiftly. 'What about the pictures?'

'Gone.' Sir Vivian looked glum. 'All gone. There's absolutely nothing left at all. Nothing of any value, anyhow. Anything worth selling went years ago.'

Francis was rather afraid that this might be the truth. He had, after all, perused the Rushbroke file. He had already noted how, particularly over the last two decades, periodic attempts had been made to reduce the debt by stripping the estate of its assets. Several quite substantial sales had indeed arrested the rise of the borrowings for a while but, inevitably, had failed to resolve the underlying cause of the problem, which was that Sir Vivian's income, apart from the bare minimum of statutory pension, was practically zero. Now, as Francis contemplated his latest client, his frown deepened.

In the 1980s the elderly country landowner fallen upon hard times was hardly a new phenomenon; it had become so familiar it was almost a cliché. The manifestation always took the same form wherever it was encountered: inevitably male, the once upright frame spare and slightly stooped, the cavalry twill trousers threadbare, the ancient shoes buffed to a fierce shine. There would be a Norfolk jacket in an indeterminate mud-coloured tweed, a Jermyn Street shirt frayed at the neck and the cuffs, and a neatly trimmed moustache tending to yellow like the tail of an old grey horse. Below sprouting eyebrows, faded blue eyes would be watery and vague.

It seemed to Francis Sparrow that there was a similar difficulty waiting for him in every posting all over England, wherever his trouble-shooting travels took him, sometimes more than one. Men who had never known what it was like to have a job, who had never needed employment. Men who had no business acumen, no professional qualifications, and no comforting company pension, steadily sinking into a quagmire of failed investments, dwindling capital and crumbling assets; men with no prospects and no future, who had outlived their era and were, according to their temperament, bewildered, infuriated, contemptuous, or frightened, of the new. Inevitably in such situations no solution could be entirely painless, and now, obliged to confront the even more than usually catastrophic affairs of Sir Vivian Valentyne Rushbroke of Rushbroke, Francis Sparrow, for once, was not confident.

'Perhaps we should be looking towards the disposal of some of the remaining furniture?' he suggested. 'Might there be one or two interesting pieces left? Would there, for example, be a few dining chairs of early Chippendale you could bear to part with? A choice oriental lacquer cabinet? Could there be a particularly fine long-case clock ticking away in the hall?'

Sir Vivian made a sound which might have been a snort

of mirth, but then again, could just as easily have been derision. 'Not a hope! Talk to Pendleton Antiques across the road if you don't believe me. Old Pendleton lived off Rushbroke furniture for years. Now the place is stripped to the bone he's reduced to selling imitation brass fenders and nasty little leather-topped tables. Reproduction, the lot of it, light as a feather and no use to anybody. Knocked for six the minute the dog wags its tail; absolute bloody rubbish. No, I'm afraid you're out of luck. Anything half way decent would have been sniffed out by Pendleton years ago. Went though the place with a bloody toothcomb. Didn't miss a trick.'

Francis did not doubt it. After all, the Pendleton Antiques account was also handled by the National Westminster. Nevertheless he eyed his client steadily. He was perfectly aware that it was possible to underestimate the aged in situations such as this. Nothing should ever be assumed. Nothing could be taken on trust. The air of distrait might or might not be authentic. The client could be either a genuinely hopeless case, no longer capable of managing his affairs, or he could be a cunning old fraud, trading on his years, cleverly concealing irresponsibility and indifference behind a facade of wool-gathering senescence. 'I don't suppose there is any more *land*?' Francis enquired in a careful tone. 'Some little pocket you may have overlooked?'

The question was followed by a silence which lasted rather too long to be comfortable. 'I asked you if there was any more land,' Francis said eventually. 'I was wondering if there might be a few acres left, a few *disposable* acres? A modest plot?'

Sir Vivian sat like a stone. His silence seemed to gather around him, thickening and expanding until it filled the room, until the very air was swollen with expectation, but still he said nothing.

'Sir Vivian,' said Francis, 'I need your cooperation. I must have an answer to my question. I do need to establish whether or not there is any remaining land.'

Sir Vivian was reluctant to answer but the question could hardly be avoided. Indignation overcame his resolve to sidestep this most mendacious and emotive issue by meeting it with a contemptuous silence. 'How the *devil* can there be any more land?' he exclaimed. 'How, in God's name, can there be *any more land* when you and your blasted cohorts have sold the entire estate piecemeal from under my feet!'

Irascibility was always a promising development. Francis, feeling he might be getting somewhere at last, welcomed it. He inclined forward on his perch. '*All* of it? The *entire* estate?'

'You mean you don't know?' Sir Vivian was outraged. 'When you are responsible for it? When every last acre of my estate has been sold to a madman? On your advice! At your instigation!'

Francis Sparrow uttered a small chirrup of condolence but his gaze sharpened. '*Every* acre? Am I to understand that there is nothing left at all? No small parcel of land you could sell?' He met Sir Vivian's glare with equanimity, noticing how his client sat stiffly upright in his chair, observing the fierce expression in the old blue eyes which, quite suddenly, appeared neither watery nor faded. 'Sir Vivian, you are quite, *quite*, sure there is no more land?'

'Of course I'm sure! The land's gone, I tell you! If you want to know where it's gone ask my cretinous neighbour, ask Williamson! You do realise the man is stark staring mad? That he's a bedlamite? You know he's deranged? Has nobody bothered to inform you that all of my land, the whole of my estate, is now in the possession of a raving lunatic? Haven't you read the blasted files?' Sir Vivian demanded contentiously. 'Don't the bank keep any bloody records? Haven't you done your homework!'

'I am aware,' Francis said smoothly, 'that parcels of land have been sold off at intervals over the years.'

'Then you know damned well there's nothing left, so what's the point in banging on about it? *There is no more land!*' Sir Vivian declared with explosive emphasis, '*and that is all there is to it!*'

'I see.' Francis folded his arms upon the desk and assumed a grave demeanour. 'In that case...' he leaned forward in a deliberately confidential manner as if to ensure that his words were heard exclusively by his client, as if the office might be alive with eavesdroppers, although they were quite alone. 'In that case, I very much regret to inform you that the National Westminster Bank will have no alternative but to call in the overdraft and arrange for the remaining estate to be sold in order to defray the debt.' Francis paused for a few strategic seconds to allow the full import of his words to take effect, then, 'I'm talking about the house and garden now,' he added. 'I'm talking about Rushbroke Hall itself.' As he had hoped, reaction was immediate and vigorous, banishing all traces of senility.

'The *hell* you are!' Sir Vivian reared up in his chair like a startled warhorse. 'The hell you are *not!*'

'Regrettably, I can see no other solution.' Feeling no regret whatsoever, Francis leaned back in his chair and regarded his client with satisfaction masked by a bright-eyed severity. 'For your own sake as well as our own we cannot afford to allow the situation to become any worse. The overdraft has been increasing at the rate of thirty thousand pounds per annum, without taking into consideration any interest, commissions, or management charges. Soon it will have outstripped the value of your equity; equity which, as you will surely agree, is not as substantial as it once was.' Beadily confident, skilfully assured, Francis moved in upon his prey. 'I don't suppose there *is* any more land?' he enquired again in a more conversational tone. 'A few remaining acres? Some saleable little plot you may have been reluctant to relinquish?'

Sir Vivian, breathing heavily, cheeks dangerously reddened, sank back into his chair, inwardly consigning Francis Sparrow to the banked fires of hell, and that too comfortable an end for him. But at the same time, sportsman that he was, he could not help but feel a sneaking regard for him as an opponent; he was a sly little devil this one, and clever with it. All his talk of ways and means; for your sake as well as ours; the damnable suggestion that Rushbroke Hall should go under the hammer—it was all bloody hogwash! The oily little bugger had known about the home paddock all the time! The banks were certainly recruiting a different type these days. There had been no slick city tactics employed by the previous manager; no threats, however fraudulent, no nonsensical talk of force and power, of ways and means. Old Langham may have been a duffer in many ways; couldn't shoot to save his life, for all his much-flaunted ownership of a Game Conservancy Holland and Holland, but he had been a decent enough fellow for all that; the sort of chap who had been ready to concede that nobody was to blame for the situation, that little could be done; that one was simply a casualty of the times, like the victims of inner-city muggings and the long-term unemployed.

But this cocky little smart-arse was a different sort of

animal, and, *Prudence Before Valour* being bred in the bone, one had to tread carefully if one was to successfully circumnavigate this particular issue. Sir Vivian was not about to part with the home paddock. On this he was resolute. He knew that if he was persuaded to strip the estate of its only remaining land he would have diminished and devalued the property entirely. For what was the use of a manor house without any ground to call its own? And there was another, a more important reason why he was determined not to sell. On these last five bald acres, Nicola, his only child, schooled delinquent equines for a meagre living. The pittance she received for her painstaking, dangerous, and (it had to be said) sometimes fruitless, labours, only just covered the running costs of the stables. If he allowed himself to be pressurised into making this final sacrifice, what then for Nicola? And what difference would it make anyway? Any proceeds would be swiftly appropriated by the bank, and after that? No, he was not going to sell. There had to be another way. 'There is no more land,' he said calmly, but with finality. 'So we shall have to look for an alternative.'

Francis Sparrow raised a sceptical and questioning eyebrow.

'There's always an alternative. Always has been.'

'Until now, perhaps.' Francis favoured his client with a thin smile. 'I am aware of your previous enterprises. I have *done* my homework; I have studied your file.'

'*He that hath pity on the poor lendeth to the Lord,*' Sir Vivian pointed out.

'I believe the Old Testament also states that *the borrower is servant to the lender,*' Francis replied smartly. 'Perhaps you could enlighten me as to what manner of alternative enterprises you have in mind on this occasion?' Francis endeavoured to fix his client with a steely gaze, but

Sir Vivian was evasive. In lieu of a reply the old man averted his eyes and, through the discreet grey slats of a venetian blind behind his interrogator, observed Lady Lavinia Rushbroke of Rushbroke crossing the street in a purposeful manner carrying a shopping basket.

'I understand that you have already attempted to cultivate mushrooms in the cellars with quite disastrous results,' Francis said in a severe tone. 'There was also, I believe, an ambitious scheme for the manufacture of organic apple juice, and yet another catastrophic project involving the purchase of hives and bees.'

Sir Vivian was mute. Over Francis' shoulder he watched his wife walk through the entrance to the Supersave Supermart.

'I think I need hardly mention the rabbit breeding enterprise, or the extensive and expensive plantation of spruce trees intended for the Christmas market.'

Sir Vivian shifted uncomfortably in his chair. He looked uneasy.

'But I would be failing in my duty if I neglected to remind you,' Francis continued, 'that every single one of the aforementioned ventures was unsuccessful. That all served only to plunge the Rushbroke estate deeper into debt.'

Still Sir Vivian made no reply, although he looked deeply troubled.

'Sir Vivian,' Francis was not cad enough to kick a man when he was down, 'I can see that you do fully comprehend the perilously vulnerable position you are in, and I would not like you to think that we at the National Westminster are in any way unsympathetic to your predicament. I can assure you that the very fact the bank have not elected to take any precipitate action until now is *entirely* due to our very *real* concern for your welfare.'

With an expression of mounting anxiety, Sir Vivian watched as Lady Lavinia emerged from the supermarket. She was followed by a blonde woman in a green tabard. The blonde woman in the green tabard was immediately followed by a dark-haired young man in a suit. After a short but urgent consultation they followed Lady Lavinia across the road. Sir Vivian jumped up out of his chair and made for the door.

In a remarkably swift and quick-witted manoeuvre, Francis Sparrow managed to get there first. 'Sir Vivian,' he said hastily, 'the situation is indeed grave, but I hope I have not been guilty of overstating the case, of inducing panic.'

Sir Vivian made no reply but reached for the door handle.

'There are, as I have indicated, always ways and means,' said Francis in a conciliatory tone.

Sir Vivian was not listening. He pulled open the door.

'And so what I am about to *suggest*...' having managed to insinuate himself between his client and freedom, Francis was now most anxious to conclude the interview on his own terms, '...was that I should arrange for our valuations officer to make a *renewed appraisal* of the estate.'

But Sir Vivian appeared to have lost interest and, brushing Francis off as if he was a minor irritant, of no more importance than a horsefly, he walked quickly away across the crowded floor of the bank towards the entrance.

Ruffled and a not a little disorientated by the unexpected turn of events, Francis ducked back into his office noticing with a little dip of dismay that his next client was another elderly man with well-polished shoes, cavalry twill trousers and a Norfolk jacket in a particularly disagreeable tweed the colour of pond slime.

* * *

'Oh, Vivian, *there* you are! Thank goodness! I had no idea where you might be. You could have left me the *keys*.'

'Lavinia, I didn't leave you the keys because last time you drove home without me and I had to catch a taxi.'

Standing beside the ancient Rover in the Park and Pay (the Rover being conspicuous as the only vehicle bereft of a ticket attached to the windscreen; it being Rushbroke policy to park but not to pay) Sir Vivian cast an apprehensive eye over the contents of his wife's shopping basket.

'Well, now that you *are* here, are you going to open the car, Vivian? Or are we both to stand here indefinitely, I wonder?'

Sir Vivian felt in his pockets, produced keys and unlocked both front and back doors of the Rover. 'Lavinia, I suppose you did... er... you did...?' He gestured towards the shopping basket.

Lady Lavinia smiled. Taking up her accustomed position on the back seat, she placed her basket by her side, folded her hands in her lap and began to hum softly.

Sir Vivian sighed heavily as he climbed into the driving seat. He slammed the door. Almost immediately a face appeared at the window. Sir Vivian wound it down with reluctance.

'I hope you won't mind me mentioning it, Sir Viv, but...'

'How much?'

'Well, two pink candles, a bunch of watercress, a jar of apricots in brandy, and the pickled dill cucumbers; just twenty-one pounds ninety-five, if you wouldn't mind.'

'Take a cheque?'

'I'd prefer cash, if it's all the same to you.'

'I suppose you would.' Sir Vivian produced a dried and

flaking wallet and proffered three notes with resignation. 'Better keep the change until next time. Very decent of you to keep an eye and all that...'

'Don't mention it, Sir Viv. All part of the Supersave service.'

Sir Vivian wound up the window and jabbed the key into the ignition. 'Ingratiating little fool!' The Rover wheezed into life. 'All part of the service; ways and means; for your sake as well as ours...' The Rover coughed and jumped forward out of the parking space causing a passer-by to leap sideways in alarm. 'A few dining chairs of early Chippendale; some little pocket you may have overlooked...' Sir Vivian, looking thunderous, drove straight out of the Park and Pay without a glance to the left or to the right, directly into the path of a Royal Mail Parcel Force van. The driver, standing on his brake, his rightful progress arrested in a welter of squealing tyres accompanied by the smell of burning rubber, slid back his door in a fury. 'Ever fucking well considered looking where you're going, you geriatric old turd?'

> *'Darling I am growing old*
> *Silver threads amongst the gold...'*

Lady Lavinia waved graciously from the back seat.

Chapter Two

Without any warning at all, the grey horse burst through the hedge, bringing with him a good deal of dry blackthorn, half falling, half leaping down the bank onto the lane and landing almost, but not quite, on the bonnet of Rupert's precious Porsche 924. He was wild of eye with flaring nostrils showing red inside, and trailing reins, and dripping sweat, and exceedingly lucky not to be hit.

Rupert, whose reflexes were faster than one would expect from knowing him, stamped on the brake pedal and, braced against the back of his seat, hung onto the steering wheel whilst the car bucked and stalled and skated on its locked wheels across the modest verge, made slippery by its long, flattened grasses. The brakes shrieked, the horse wheeled, and a stirrup swinging out on the end of its leather smashed into a headlight. The car lurched sideways as its nearside front wheel sank slowly, but inevitably, into the bramble-filled ditch.

Anna had often doubted the efficacy of safety belts, but hers saved her from a violent confrontation with the windscreen, slapping her backwards in an uncompromising way she could only in retrospect feel grateful for, temporarily depriving her of speech. In the breathless, shocked interval which followed, Rupert uttered a string of obscenities, somehow managing to end with '...merciful *God in Heaven*' (which He certainly had been to save them from catastrophe by a hair's breadth) but already Anna had released her safety belt and was out of the car and through the brambles and had taken the horse by the rein. She had always loved a grey and was sick for horses and he seemed to her to have been sent by providence.

The rider appeared almost at once, running down the lane towards them in old-fashioned jodhpurs with a garter strap and a tweed jacket worn to the thread. Her cheeks were flushed, her pale hair flew, and the slate grey eyes that Anna was later to know as being calm and steady in almost every circumstance, were wide with anxiety. Good manners clearly bred in the bone, she held out a hand to Anna. 'Nicola,' she gasped. 'Please say you didn't hit him! Do tell me he isn't hurt! He doesn't belong to me and I don't have any insurance!'

Anna was ready to sympathise at once, but Rupert raised his head from the steering wheel and his expression was painful to behold. With difficulty, he managed to force open the car door in order to inspect the damage to the paintwork and headlight that must now be paid for out of his own pocket. He was assistant manager at the small, quayside hotel in Orford, where Anna had worked since leaving catering college, and his wages were not large.

'Never mind the bloody *horse*—just look what it's done to my fucking *car!*' Directing a savage glare towards Nicola and the grey horse he reached into the well of the driving seat and retrieved his mobile phone. After which, muttering the most bitter and violent invective against the entire

15

equine species, he clambered up out of the ditch and stalked off up the lane in search of a signal, his mobile phone clamped against his ear and trailing a wickedly long bramble attached to his trouser leg.

The grey horse (who could not have anticipated the explosive potential of his reception) would have set off to accompany him at once, his progress swiftly arrested by a restraining hand on his bridle. Nor was Rupert to know that Anna had already resolved to pay for the damage to his car herself since this jaunt in the country had been on her behalf. Rupert, tall, lean, with hair like a raven's wing and a worrying pallor from which no razor in existence (and he had tried them all) could quite remove the blue shadow, seemed to Anna to be constructed of some highly combustible material which required careful handling at all times and rendered him a tiring companion. By now accustomed to his mercurial temperament, she was unmoved by his departure and turned to his rider.

'Don't worry about Rupert—he'll get over it. We didn't hit the horse though, I promise you; the stirrup smashed the headlight.'

In relief, Nicola took the horse by the bridle and, in between examining a few superficial scratches occasioned by his encounter with the blackthorn, lamenting his broken rein and removing a briar from his tail, explained that the gelding was prone to hysteria in traffic, and described in graphic terms his consternation upon meeting an oil tanker in the narrow lane. The driver of the vehicle had been sympathetic and stopped at once, but the whoosh of his compressed air braking system had sent the horse straight up the side of the bank and through the hedge. Nicola had not so much fallen, as been swept out of the saddle, and there had followed a tiresome chase around a plantation of

Christmas trees which had ended only when the gelding had dived back through the blackthorn.

'The pity of it is,' said Nicola in a rueful tone, 'that he was coming along beautifully, and now all his confidence will be lost and we shall have to begin all over again.' On hearing this, the grey horse, who had obligingly lowered his head to enable Nicola to extract a thorn which had perforated his ear, gave a deep and gusting sigh, for all the world as if he was fully conversant with what had been said, and was utterly fatigued by the prospect.

Reassured as to the wellbeing of her equine pupil Nicola turned her attention to the rescue of Rupert's car. 'But here am I thinking only of the horse when both of you could have been badly injured and all of it my fault. You stay with the car,' she decided, 'and I'll fetch the Rover and pull it out of the ditch.' Gathering up the broken reins she mounted the grey gelding, who threw up his head and slid his front feet to attention. With typical equine perversity he now chose to regard the lopsided Porsche as a wild and dangerous beast, snorting and sidling and rolling his eyes at it before plunging round in a spirited volte and setting off along the lane at a rib-rattling trot. 'I'll be back in ten!' Nicola shouted above the crash of shod steel on tarmac. 'Don't go away!'

'As if we *could*!' Rupert, having gained higher ground and achieved a signal only to find his battery had run out, was not in the mood for conciliation. 'As if we're in any sodding position to go *anywhere*!'

But Anna stood watching until the grey gelding's tail twitched out of sight, listening as the hoof beats grew steadily fainter. 'She will come back?' she said almost to herself, and then 'Of course she'll come back. She wouldn't just ride away and leave us here.'

'And you would know about that, would you? You're quite familiar with the superior classes?' Rupert was now prepared to become properly incensed. 'The fact that she's the sort of person who rides a crazy horse on the roads with no bloody insurance, with no consideration for other road users, doesn't alter your opinion of her one bloody iota, I suppose? Well, if she thinks all she has to do is apologise and that's all there is to it, she's bloody well mistaken; she can bloody well think again, because when she comes back, *if* she comes back, she's going to pay for repairing my bloody car. Patronising little snob!'

'I'll pay for the repairs.' Anna said. 'Rupert, do you have to swear quite so much?'

'Yes, I bloody do! I'm upset. I'm *bloody* upset!'

'I appreciate that. But the car isn't badly damaged. There doesn't seem to be much wrong with it; nothing that can't be mended, anyhow.' But Anna knew that Rupert would not be so easily mended. That after stimulation would come recrimination; that the entire mishap would have to be endlessly and tediously analysed and, in the end, judged to be her fault. As indeed, strictly speaking, it had been.

'I *still* don't know why we had to come this way, why you were so bloody *insistent*. We could have gone to Lavenham or Woodbridge. We could have gone to South-wold, but no! You wanted to go *somewhere*, but you didn't actually specify *anywhere*, so in the end we finish up in the back of beyond with a bloody horse on the bonnet! You can see now where your bloody aimless meanderings have landed us—stuck in a sodding ditch God only knows where!'

Anna could have said that her meanderings had been anything but aimless, but from past experience knew it was futile to argue with Rupert when he was upset. Instead, she peered into the Porsche and saw that her beautiful fruit and vegetables were in disarray. She picked her way gingerly through dried and wickedly spiked brambles in order to rescue them. Opening the boot she placed tenderly back into their tray delicate pink sticks of forced rhubarb; a punnet of fat raspberries, a trio of perfectly round turnips, their deep purple tops fading to a bone whiteness ending with a surprising little tail like a mouse; huge handsome leeks, fresh and fragrant, tied up with rough, hairy twine. Under Rupert's disapproving gaze she rescued freshly dug Jerusalem artichokes, cool and moist and knobbly, still stuck with damp earth. Arranging them carefully on the tray, admiring them, Anna imagined herself turning them into sorbet and hearty soups for the staff of the Harbourmouth Hotel, none of whom could ever bear to eat the unrelenting seafood specialities they served to their diners; fish dishes which called only for the inevitable wedge of lemon, the token garnish of a handful of mixed leaves, the ubiquitous frozen pea.

There had been altogether too much fish in Anna's life recently. Those working hours not spent spreading mountains of ready-sliced brown bread with livid yellow catering margarine, were spent skinning salmon, decapitating prawns, sorting winkles and whelks, dropping live lobsters into a cauldron of boiling water (closing her heart to the waving of their banded claws and the whistle of their departing breath), dressing crabs, opening oysters, gutting squid (removing the spilling ink sac and the plastic backbone, searching out the sharp little beak from amongst the flaccid crown of tentacles), impaling scallops on skewers, de-bearding mussels. Working at the Harbourmouth Hotel

involved not so much cookery as oceanic crustacean geno-
cide and Anna had endured enough of it.

What she particularly disliked about it was that she was
never completely able to remove the smell of fish from her
clothes, her hair, her skin. In her cramped little room in the
eaves of the hotel even her bed linen smelled of fish. Anna
imagined that however often she bathed in floral, fragrant
oils, a piscine aroma must invisibly surround her like an
aura. She fancied that people sniffed the air as she passed
by, wrinkling up their noses, grimacing with disgust. Even
the Porsche, immaculate as it was, regularly shampooed and
valeted as it was, and now smelling blissfully of country
market vegetables, usually smelled of fish. I am impregnated
with fish, Anna thought, I am contaminated. One day I shall
look in the mirror and I shall see a cod's head wearing a
striped Laura Ashley blouse with a piecrust frill around the
neck, and I shall not be surprised.

Disturbed by the thought she negotiated her way back
through the brambles and made her way up the bank in
order to stand on a rise overlooking a vast field of stubble,
widening her nostrils and pulling into her lungs great gusts
of fish-free air. I have to *do* something about my life, she told
herself firmly. I have to list my priorities. I have to make a
plan.

On the way to this (according to Rupert) unspecified
destination, they had called at Framlingham, where there
had been stalls on the market square and, after a perusal of
what was on offer and the purchase of the vegetables, they
had called into the Crown Hotel for coffee. Anna had liked
the Crown; the market-day bustle of it, the scrubbed tables,
the Labradors flopped on the stone floors, the waitresses
threading cheerfully though the crowded rooms balancing
trays of latte and toasted sandwiches. She had warmed to

the murals of friendly cows in the ladies' and the unexpected luxury of hand cream from The White Company. She had imagined the guest bedrooms; heavily beamed with half tester beds, plump pillows and Egyptian cotton sheets; cold and smooth and as soft as rose petal. She had wondered if she should ask if they were in need of a chef, but then remembered that now she could quite easily afford (quite suddenly and unexpectedly she could *afford*) to have her own kitchen. She reminded herself that she actually *could* buy a restaurant of her own, and, for a few moments, she imagined herself in an ancient lime-washed building with pammets on the floors and original bread ovens in the brickwork, somewhere in a village like Lavenham, in a street full of crooked, half-timbered houses.

But there was something more pressing, something else she had resolved to deal with first. And when I have come to terms with *this*, she thought; when I have dealt with whatever it is I have to deal with *now*, then maybe I shall find the courage to do something on my own. And so that I might not be completely alone (the devil you know being generally a better bet than the devil you don't) perhaps Rupert might be persuaded to leave the Harbourmouth Hotel if I offered to make him a partner. Thinking of Rupert, she glanced back and down into the lane and saw him leaning against the tilted bonnet of the Porsche with animosity apparent in every line of his body. And then again, she thought, as she turned back to the altogether more congenial view of the cornfield, perhaps it might be preferable to be alone.

The stubblefield, hugely silent and blessedly peaceful, was scattered with great whorls of harvested straw like slices cut from a gargantuan Swiss roll, and whilst she waited, alert for the approaching sound of their rescue, she watched the clouds move across the enormous sky and thought of John Constable and how he must have watched these great East Anglian skies, noticing every nuance of light, of movement, of colour, of beauty.

Along the far edge of the stubblefield some movement caught her eye. A man, wearing what looked like plus-fours, had come into sight pushing a wheelbarrow with a palpably painful slowness, his shoulders bowed by the weight of it. Even from so far away, Anna could see that he was not a young man, and it struck her as being odd to see someone pushing a heavily laden wheelbarrow across a stubblefield in the country. Wheelbarrows, to Anna's way of thinking, were domestic things, more at home in yards and gardens or building sites, rather than in open fields, where it was surely more usual to use a tractor and trailer or a Land Rover to transport a heavy load for a long distance over uneven terrain.

After a goodly period of exhaustive travail, the man and his burden arrived at what appeared to be his destination; some kind of pond or quarry Anna was unable to see properly but was able to recognise as such by the fact that it was bordered by rough ground and fringed with rushes. Here the man dropped the handles of the wheelbarrow and, after an interval during which she supposed him to be recovering his breath, he leaned over and took something from it, uncoiled it with care and arranged it around his neck.

Anna watched him do this, and afterwards would be able to say that she saw him put the noose around his neck and tighten it, but that her brain would not allow her to believe what her eyes had seen. And so she continued to watch, still unbelieving, as the man leaned into the wheelbarrow once more and lifted, with the most enormous difficulty, and only at the expense of truly herculean effort, some tremendously heavy object which appeared to be fashioned of stone, and was round, with a hole in the middle. A millwheel perhaps or a grinding stone, with the end of the rope attached to it. Then, succeeding in one massive and final feat of exertion, the man somehow contrived to throw the stone into the quarry and, with a grotesquely jerking and peculiar twisting movement, his body followed.

There was an audible splash.

Anna ran.

Chapter Three

David Williamson drove into his farmyard like a madman. He felt, much of the time anyway, quite like a madman, but in his calmer moments realised that he was in the grip of an obsession.

These days, watching the Rushbrokes occupied most of his waking hours, and even when he slept, Rushbrokes were there, inhabiting his fevered dreams. Spying on them, tracking them, hating them was, he knew, not only damaging his health and ruining his life, but also threatening both his occupation and his sanity. Especially his sanity. It seemed to David Williamson that the Rushbrokes had somehow taken possession of his brain and must be lodged there like a terrible, malignant growth, like the manifestation of some unspeakable, incurable disease he could never be free of, never escape. He felt, (illogical though it was; there were, after all, only three of them) surrounded by Rushbrokes, swamped by them, hemmed in and persecuted. Even his farmhouse, situated as it was on a modest rise, on the only high ground for miles, seemed uniquely and conveniently placed to look down upon the Rushbrokes, enabling him to observe them walking, riding, driving over his land, shooting his game and stealing his crops, from a natural vantage point.

His latest confrontation with Nicola had left him trembling and anguished. Before it happened, he had been pondering the condition of his bullocks in Twenty Acre, considering their shining flanks and the gentle humps and hollows of their quarters. David Williamson liked bullocks and had been content in the midst of their moist curiosity, a willing recipient of their breathy, if somewhat pressingly claustrophobic companionship, until he had noticed the horse droppings.

There had been no possible mistake about it; they had definitely been horse droppings; not the distinctive flat black pools of grazing cattle, but quite unmistakably the glossy, oval, ginger-coloured droppings of a corn fed horse. David Williamson had stared down at them, feeling the familiar stabbing discomfort of chronic anxiety as he speculated on what new and indefensible outrage they could possibly represent. For he had realised at once that they heralded some form of deviation from the usual abuse of his pasture; there were far too many piles to be the result of a regular short cut across the land and they marked no particular line but appeared to be distributed at random. And the more he looked, the more he saw!

Prowling to and fro he discovered older evidence, darker in colour and scattered by birds, and some piles that were new, absolutely fresh and recently evacuated. He was both incensed by this and mystified. Surely Nicola could not have been using his pasture as a schooling ground for her obnoxious quadrupeds? Almost certainly his bullocks were too inquisitive to have allowed it. They would have become excited and gambolled about, obstructing any disciplined exercise, upsetting the horses. Not only that, but any unwonted activity on the pasture would have attracted his attention at once; yet horses had obviously been on this land for some time, for several hours at a stretch, regularly, and recently, and if not in the daytime, when he could hardly have failed to notice them, then at night, in the dark! Nicola had been stealing his grazing! Turning out her horses amongst his cattle at night!

The realisation had filled him with a passionate rage. At once, his heart had begun to race, he had begun to sweat, and he had felt the first swimmy, sickly stirrings of nausea. His bullocks had crowded around as if to show sympathy and support. One of them, more forward than the rest, had licked his arm with its warm, abrasive tongue, but he was not to be comforted, feeling that they had somehow betrayed him, that by their innocent involvement in the conspiracy they were partly responsible and must bear some of the blame. He had shouted at them to get off, waving his arms angrily and setting them shying away, lurching and capering, becoming clumsily frolicsome with a bovine insensitivity that he might, a few minutes earlier, have found rather pleasing.

As they regrouped around him, wary now, and at a more respectful distance, David Williamson had closed his eyes and forced himself to breathe deeply and slowly, filling his lungs to capacity and exhaling to maximum degree. He had recognised the physical symptoms as those of chronic stress occasioned by his obsession and knew that his anger must be controlled otherwise the Rushbrokes would succeed in damaging his body as well as his mind. He had resolved to make a determined effort to be calm so that he could decide, in a rational manner, (for David Williamson honestly considered himself to be a reasonable, rational, man), how to cope with this latest depredation, this new and appalling deceit, this subtle act of legerdemain, this wilful violation of his property.

And so, standing on his pasture, surrounded by his raptly attentive cattle, he had resolutely performed his respiratory exercises and, in due course, his heartbeat had slowed and become steady in his chest, his nausea had faded, and the sweat had begun to cool on his body.

But the anger had not faded. The anger had stayed and, staring venomously at a pile of droppings, David Williamson had burned with a desire to wreak vengeance. But how? He had considered making yet another complaint to the police, but abandoned the idea almost immediately. He had appealed to them on countless occasions in the past but, whilst listening to his lengthy catalogue of grievances with every appearance of patience and sympathy, they had displayed a curious reluctance to take any action. Trespass was a civil offence, they had informed him; it was something they would prefer not to get involved with. Of course, theft or criminal damage was a different matter, but where was his proof? If he wanted to bring charges he must provide proof of intent to permanently deprive, to wilfully damage; he must provide evidence. And even if such evidence were to be at hand, had he really thought about the consequences of prosecution, of instituting criminal proceedings against the Rushbrokes? Would he really want to have the whole sorry business dragged through the courts, reported in the newspapers? Had he considered how it might damage his reputation and social standing in the local community? And even if he won the case and was awarded damages, how would he manage to extract his compensation from the Rushbrokes when everyone knew they were already on their uppers?

No, David Williamson had decided, there would be no help forthcoming from the police. They had actually suggested that he should go away and quietly forget all about it. Given time, they had said consolingly, wouldn't the situation resolve itself? The old buffer must the pretty ancient by now; how old would he be? Eighty? Eighty-five? Wouldn't he be fairly certain to drop off his perch soon? And when he did, wouldn't the rest of the estate be coming up for sale, and wouldn't he, David Williamson, then find himself remarkably well-placed to buy it for a knock-down price? Well then, they had concluded, taking all this into account, wouldn't it be in everyone's best interests to turn a blind eye and exercise a little neighbourly tolerance? All of which might have been sound advice had David Williamson not been driven to a state of acute hypersensitivity by the Rushbrokes, from which there was certainly no prospect of any return to patience or tolerance, neighbourly or not.

Realising that any assistance from the police was extremely unlikely, David Williamson had decided that if the Rushbrokes were to be punished he must take the law into his own hands. He must turn vigilante. He must act! But how? What could he do? Threats against the Rushbrokes or appeals to their better nature he knew to be useless. Sterner measures were called for. He had kicked out at the pile of droppings, disturbing a small cloud of hideous ginger flies, revealing glistening dung beetles. What he *ought* to do was to catch Nicola red-handed just as she was about to turn her horses out onto his land. Catching her in the act would give him a great deal of satisfaction. And why not? Why shouldn't he lie in wait and catch her at it! Of course, the execution of such a plan would entail mounting a night watch. The idea both excited and alarmed him. The very prospect of apprehending Nicola in the dark made him quiver with trepidation, for what was he to do with her once apprehended? He could hardly wring her neck because in the event of a murdered Rushbroke he would certainly be the prime suspect. The thought of Nicola's soft, dead body was oddly disturbing; imagining it, picturing it, brought him a sharp thrill of pleasure, swiftly followed by feelings of disgust and outrage; largely directed towards his prospective victim. Why, the woman was turning him into some kind of monster! A murderer! A necrophiliac!

It was clear to David Williamson, walking up and down the pasture in an agitated manner in order to lose a certain wholly unwelcome and humiliating personal rigidity, that any close contact with Nicola was something to be avoided at all costs. It was out of the question. The plan had to be revised. What Nicola needed was a shaking up. She needed to be given such a fright that she would never again dare to set foot on his land in the dark, or in the light for that matter, with or without her loathsome equines. But how to achieve it?

Whatever scheme he devised, he had realised it was essential he was not recognised. This rather vital consideration indicated that some form of disguise should be adopted, but the wearing of a wig, a false beard or a moustache would surely require a certain theatrical flair which he feared was absent from his nature. He knew he could not be a convincing actor, even a mute one (for to speak would be to give the game away immediately) and must beware of being ridiculous rather than frightening. Clearly something more sinister than a simple disguise was called for. He considered pulling a stocking over his head like a bank robber, or wearing a menacing black hood with slits for his eyes and mouth, like the IRA or the SAS, but would either garment actually be sufficient to protect his identity? He doubted it. His shape and mannerisms would betray him. In fact, given the situation, any human shape might be assumed to be his simply by association. There was also the indisputable fact that Nicola possessed nerves of steel. She might not be frightened enough. David Williamson could imagine only too well the ignominy of being brushed aside or disregarded. Nicola was also physically strong and, unexpectedly encountering a threatening figure in the darkness, might be predisposed to violence. She might attack him! He would then be obliged to defend himself and he had already ruled out any possibility of intimate contact.

No, a disguise was not going to be sufficient. What he must do, he had decided, was to transform himself completely; not into *someone* but into *something*; he must somehow contrive to turn himself into something monstrous and inhuman, something ghastly! That was it! He must assume an entirely different shape and appear out of the darkness as something hideously malformed; a hellish apparition! He must take the form of some unspeakably awful creature out of the worst kind of horror film! Some evil and repulsive being out of the most hair-raisingly fearsome nightmare! He must appear as a ghoul!

The idea delighted him. Immediately he was filled with a feverish anticipation. His mind began to race. Putting the plan into operation would require stealth and planning. Somehow a terrible costume must be constructed; a costume designed to scare the living daylights out of Nicola; a costume to make her scream aloud with terror; a costume to ensure that never again would she venture out under cover of darkness; a costume which would present her with a sight so incredibly awful, so unbelievably shocking, that she would be forced to sleep with the light on for the rest of her days. Naturally, such a costume would not be contrived in five minutes. It would take time to achieve exactly the right effect. Sketches would have to be made. A prototype would have to be constructed. Great care would have to be taken if the desired effect was to be achieved. Patience would have to be exercised if this wonderful opportunity for revenge was not to be wasted.

In the meantime, he must say or do nothing which might alert Nicola to the fact that he was aware she was grazing her horses on his land. No accusations must be made. Cautioning himself thus, fired with excitement and quite dangerously over-stimulated, David Williamson set off towards the gate with a spring in his step followed, at a deferential distance, by two dozen bullocks. It was somewhat unfortunate that at that very moment he should have spotted Nicola riding across the next field, taking advantage of a convenient short cut through his beans.

In a trice, he had bolted for his Land Rover and was bucketing after her in a rabid fury with all thought of caution gone with the wind. '*Get off my bloody land!*' he had shouted. '*Get off! Get off my beans!*'

The grey horse had bucked and leapt and snorted in alarm at his approach, flattening its ears and shaking its head and splattering him with revolting brown froth as he drew alongside. But Nicola had remained undisturbed in the saddle, leaning forward in order to massage the loathsome creature's dripping neck in a reassuring manner; as if sitting on top of a crazed equine was the most natural thing in the world; as if there was nothing to it. 'I'm not actually on your beans,' she had pointed out, as the maddened beast had plunged about with its mane flying and its great eyes rolling round in its head. 'I'm on a tractor crossing, as you very well know, and I don't see how you can possibly object to my taking a short cut, especially when it's an emergency. There has been an accident in the lane and I have to get the car to pull somebody out of the ditch.'

He had not believed her. He had been infuriated by the fact that his rage had made no impression on her whatsoever; she had been impervious to his anger and, whilst he was anguished and filled with violent and passionate resentment, she was untouched by him. He had rubbed wildly at his face, feeling his skin contaminated by the horse's odious spittle. '*Get Off!*' he had yelled, his voice strangled by distress, and then, rendered almost inarticulate and hysterical, had bawled, '*Get off my bloody beans! You're trespassing on my bloody land! How many bloody times have I told your sodding family to bugger off; to bloody well stop using my bloody land as if it was still your bloody own!*'

Unfazed, Nicola had leaned over the horse's shoulder, the better to peer in at him through the window. Exactly at eye level, the soft fullness of her generous breasts strained the top button of her jacket. 'It's habit, I suppose. Quite possibly something to do with the fact that my family have owned this land for over four hundred years, whereas you have only owned it for three.'

The cheek of her! The sheer impertinence! He had felt about to explode; that she might actually have caused him to split asunder with fury. '*I don't care how many years your blighted family have owned the land!*' he had howled. '*It's MINE now! Paid for with MY money! This land belongs to ME!*' Tearing his eyes away from the mesmerising movement of her breasts as they rose and dipped in response to the cantering gait of the horse, fixing his gaze ahead, gripping the steering wheel as if his very life depended on it, '*I'm warning you, Nicola,*' he had shouted. '*I'm not standing for any more of this! I'm taking action! This time I MEAN it!'*

'Well, of course you mean it.' She could have been talking to an imbecile, or one of her maddened equines. 'But now, just at this very moment, shouldn't you be doing something about your cattle?' What did she mean? Distraught, he had put his head out of the window and looked back across the rows of beans, just in time to see the first group of bullocks shoulder their way through the gate from Twenty Acre.

* * *

Returned to the comparative sanctuary of his own farmyard, David Williamson clambered shakily down from his vehicle and leaned against the bonnet. It had been a bad morning. Nevertheless, he knew he must guard against depression for the sake of his health and wellbeing. He must look on the bright side. At least his bullocks, having enjoyed their adventure, were now safely back in their own pasture, and he now had his plan with which to comfort himself. Things were not as black as all that.

Below him, all appeared tranquil. Rushbroke Hall slumbered peacefully in all its ruinous glory. There was no sign of Nicola and the grey horse. But then, beyond the hall, at the far end of the big barleyfield, a movement caught his eye. There seemed to be some kind of activity on the mere; two coots possibly, squabbling over territory. No, it was more than that; it was some much larger disturbance. David Williamson opened the door of his Land Rover and reached for his binoculars. The next minute he was back behind the wheel and hurtling down his drive towards the barleyfield, looking remarkably like a madman.

Chapter Four

'Help me! HELP ME!'

Anna, near-blinded by a coating of pond weed, spurning the reluctantly offered hand and fastening upon the wrist as the safer option, was immensely relieved to find herself towed up the bank like a log across the dry blades of the rushes. She could spare but one hand for her own rescue as her other arm was locked around the drowned man's neck like a vice. She had bound the rope around her waist in a valiant attempt to ease the pressure upon his throat and now it bit into her flesh and threatened to cut her in half, but she barely noticed it. 'The rope!' she spluttered. 'Pull up the rope!' And as her rescuer hesitated, 'PULL IT!' she commanded.

David Williamson, his violent arrival fired to deal with trespass, unauthorised bathing, possibly nudity and even indecent exposure, now uncertain whether he was to be instrumental in the rescue of his avowed enemy, or a witness to his expiration, pulled mightily, heaved upon the rope, and caused the millstone to rise at last amidst a great cloud of syrupy mud, dragged by weed and rotting vegetation, to arrive on the bank with a thud accompanied by a deathly stench.

Anna, choking and wheezing, her hair and clothes plastered to her body, streaming water and trailing weed of a brilliant green hue, struggled free of the rope and threw herself at the rescued man, dragging the knot from his neck, throwing off the noose, snatching away the sodden tie. The collar of the shirt fell open of its own accord, having no button to secure it. 'Who is he?' she gasped. 'Why has he done this?'

David Williamson, looking down upon the blanched and sodden face of Sir Vivian Valentyne Rushbroke of Rushbroke, felt his stomach turn over in a sickening somersault, and quickly averted his gaze. 'He's my neighbour. He's a madman. They're all mad. The whole family. Every last one of them.'

Anna looked up at him, aghast. She saw a youngish man, haggard and pale, his dark, haunted eyes having great shadows beneath, his fair hair dishevelled. Heavens, she thought, is he one of them? Is he mad as well? Frantically, she felt for the old man's pulse, first at the bony wrist, then at the neck, and found nothing. His chest appeared motionless and when, offering her cheek to his mouth, she felt not the faintest whisper of breath and saw that his lips were blue, panic threatened to overwhelm her. 'Well, don't just *stand* there!' she shouted at David Williamson. 'HELP me!'

But David Williamson had no idea how to help and, having looked death in the eye (or so he believed) was now most thoroughly shaken by the encounter. A farmer through inheritance, through parental expectation, though not by inclination, he was unusual in that he was unaccustomed to death because he had always taken pains to avoid it. A combination of sound stock, careful husbandry, and large veterinary bills kept his bullocks in rude health until it was time for them to go to market. He never attended. He had never set foot in an abattoir, nor had he allowed himself to imagine it. At Christmas, hired hands killed his turkeys, swiftly and professionally, in his absence. There were small deaths, of course, amongst his chicks, his poults, and whilst he accepted that they were inevitable and largely unavoidable, even these tiny fatalities were a source of dismay to him. So that now, faced with a large death, albeit that of his enemy, far from experiencing feelings of triumph and gratification (as might reasonably have been expected), he was instead distressed and filled with dread, and turned away. 'I can't,' he said. 'I don't know how. I'm sorry.'

Mercifully, Anna was better equipped to deal with the situation, although the first aid instruction she had received as part of her training had been somewhat rudimentary and inclined towards common occupational hazards in the working environment such as cuts, scalds, burns and electric shocks. Whatever she did, she knew she had to be quick if there was to be any chance of recovery at all and, lifting the old man's chin, easing back the lolling head, forcing her fingers into the mouth and feeling for the position of the tongue, for lose dentures, for any possible obstruction to the passage for air, she searched her mind frantically for remnants of what she had learned about resuscitation, and all the time addressed herself to a God in whose existence, if pressed, she would have had to confess a deep scepticism.

'Help me, God! Don't let me be too late! Oh, God, don't let him be dead, *please!*'

For David Williamson, any prospect of escape vanished as he felt himself arrested by the leg of his trousers and yanked down onto his knees beside the drowned man. Never could anyone have been blessed with a more unwilling assistant, but Anna, laying hold of one of his hands and slapping it down upon the motionless chest, clamping the other hand on top, dragging him up by his shoulders, straightening out his arms, was not to be refused. 'Now,' she told him urgently. '*Listen to me! When I tell you, you have to push down *hard* on his chest; hard enough to compress the ribcage and it has to move *at least* a couple of inches to do any good. You have to *keep on doing it* and you have to do it quickly, *very* fast—we need to get his heart restarted!'

It seemed to him impossible, a vain hope; but, immobilised in his position, frozen, he waited and watched (although he would have preferred not to watch) as Anna twisted back her dripping hair, leaned determinedly over the lifeless face, took a deep breath and then, pinching together the beaky nose, and without even a trace of squeamishness, placed her mouth firmly over the cold, blue lips.

Nauseated, David Williamson looked on as one forced to observe an obscene act. In terror, he felt the ribcage rise under his hands, then, as she removed her mouth, subside. Petrified, he watched as she lowered her head again, then 'NOW!' she shouted, taking him by surprise, causing him to jerk involuntarily into action. 'PUSH!' she commanded. 'And *release*! PUSH! And *wait*!'

This time he waited, breathless himself with a mixture of revulsion and anxiety, as she sealed the mouth again with her lips, anticipating now the rise and fall of the chest, knowing what he was about, ready for the second exhalation, for her command. 'PUSH! Now! Again!' Impatiently he watched as she fumbled for the pulse, caught up in her desperation, as furiously, relentlessly, he pumped and pushed, compressing and releasing the old man's ribcage at her command, until suddenly the commands ceased and, looking up, he saw her face set in anguish, flooded with exhaustion and despair, the tears dripping off her chin falling onto the drowned man's face, and even he, who knew nothing about resuscitation, could see that it was useless, that it was over, and stopped.

It was hard to know what to say, hard to find words of comfort, yet anything seemed better than nothing. 'Nobody could have done more,' he said. 'We did our best. We were just too late, that's all.'

'*That's all?*' Inexplicably she turned on him in a fury, frantic and distraught, hitting out, knocking his arms away, pushing him, causing him to lose balance and fall backwards. '*We were just too late, that's all?*' In horror he saw her launch herself at the old man, battering at his chest, clawing at his clothing like a wild animal, pummelling him. 'We were *not* too late! I *saved* him! I *saved* him!'

Desperate to put an end to it he pulled her away, pinning her arms to her sides although she screamed at him, and kicked, although it took most of his strength, until finally she gave in and leaned against him, her body racked by sobs. David Williamson was amazed and humbled by such a display of grief for a perfect stranger and when, over her tangled hair, he saw a small roach, its rosy fins fluttering briefly in a sodden fold of the shirt where she had torn open the drowned man's waistcoat, he reached out a hand for it and tossed it back into the mere so that there had, after all, been one life saved.

He brought sacks from the Land Rover at her request and arranged them in the wheelbarrow. Together they leg-and-winged the drowned man into it. She had recovered now and seemed quite composed. Unbidden, she had assumed total responsibility for the old man and was determined to transport him back the way he had come, across the stubblefield; the way he had walked; the way she had watched him make his painful, laborious progress, only a few minutes earlier, when he had been alive.

David Williamson did not demur. Quite desperately he had not wanted to be the one to deliver back his vanquished enemy into the fold of his family. Standing beside the rope and the millstone and the flattened rushes of his mere, he watched as Anna set off across the stubble; the wheelbarrow bearing its incongruous burden lurching and bumping across the hard, uneven ground. With her dripping hair, her drooping shoulders, and her long skirt soaked and dragging in the dirt, she could have been a refugee fleeing some ravaged and war-torn country or some appallingly catastrophic natural disaster. She looked desolate.

No wonder the poor man had found it tough going, Anna thought, as she struggled to push the wheelbarrow across the corrugated, sun-baked ridges of the stubblefield. No wonder it had taken him such an age to reach the water. In fact, it was nothing short of a miracle that he had managed to get there at all, for she had noticed that the drowned man was lean to the point of emaciation, clearly much too light for his height, and this is spite of the added weight of the water.

'You may have been suffering from a terminal illness, I suppose,' she said aloud to the occupant of the wheelbarrow who, possibly due to the bumping and jolting, was now not nearly as blue, and lay quite peaceably spread-eagled upon the sacking. 'That would explain a lot. But I suspect...' here she paused for a moment as she negotiated a particularly rough patch of ground, '...that the simple truth is that you just didn't eat enough. Old people can starve themselves without knowing it, apparently. Because they don't feel hungry they tend not to bother about food. They forget that they need to eat to live; that food is the fuel of life. I expect that was it.'

Was it to enable her to offer such futile post-mortem advice that she had studied nutrition at catering college, Anna wondered, because a fat lot of good it would do him now; no disrespectful pun intended. Ahead, she saw with some relief an oak door set in a wall of crumbling red brick. As she drew nearer she noticed that the door (behind which she supposed would be found the drowned man's home and family) was weathered pale and dry and hanging open, suspended from its wasted frame by the merest thread of a grandly ornate but sadly rusted hinge. Obviously the family within were not inclined to occupy themselves with such unimportant matters as maintenance.

'And what, in heaven's name,' she asked of her passenger in anguish, 'am I to say to your family about all this? Do I just wheel you in and say, "I've brought back your husband/father/grandfather, but I'm afraid he's dead; unfortunately I was not quite quick enough to save his life?" Because I did do my very best for you, I would like them to know that. Furthermore,' she continued, 'as I seem to have been the only witness, I suppose I am morally obliged to inform them that you drowned yourself on purpose; that you meant to end your life! Have you any *idea* how they are going to feel about that? Did you even consider it, I wonder? You do realise,' she demanded of the drowned man, 'that this will be their last memory of you? *This*—delivered to their door, dead in a wheelbarrow!'

But then, she thought, indignation turning to sudden alarm, the neurotic young man in the Land Rover had mentioned madness and, on the assumption that the young man had himself been quite sane and speaking the truth, what if this man's family are indeed mad? What might I be walking into? What horrors am I going to find behind this ruined wall? What appalling scene of carnage might lie on the other side of this ancient door? For a moment, she faltered, picturing in her imagination a verminous farmhouse, a mange-ridden dog on a chain, and a family butchered with an axe, or blasted with a shotgun, minutes before this old man set out to drown himself with a wheelbarrow, a rope, and a millstone. Hesitating now, it occurred to Anna that the young man had not offered to accompany her. True, he had offered transport, but her refusal had been received with obvious relief. He had wanted no part in this. He had been afraid. Why? Well, whatever the reason, she could not abandon the drowned man now. Taking a deep breath, she forced the wheelbarrow resolutely onward towards the door in the wall, pushing it faster, allowing no time for further doubt or speculation.

'Whatever happened,' she told the drowned man, 'however it was, God has certainly not helped you. God, had He so wished, could have allowed me to save you; it would have been so easy for Him, another minute was all that I needed. But He, in his *infinite* wisdom, begrudged you even that. Oh, *bugger*,' this last exclamation as the wheelbarrow hit a particularly large lump of clay and leapt in the air, bouncing down again and lurching violently to one side, threatening to tip over, causing its occupant to be thrown upwards and to smack down again and almost fall overboard. As a direct result of this, there was a strangled choking sound, followed by a flood of pond water from the mouth, and the drowned man opened his eyes. He looked up at Anna in an unfriendly manner. 'Who the devil are you?' he spluttered.

Chapter Five

Anna dropped the handles of the wheelbarrow as if they were electrified; as if they had suddenly become red hot. Her hands flew up to her face. Afterwards, whenever she had cause to describe the incident, she would never be able to find words of sufficient intensity to explain how she felt. Words such as shocked, stupefied, dumbfounded and flabbergasted would, even after the passage of many years, always seem like understatement. For at first, sceptic that she was, unbeliever that she was, she thought she had witnessed a miracle and fell to her knees in relief and gratitude. 'Oh, God! Thank you! *Thank you!*'

At this, the drowned man struggled desperately to sit up, flapped his arms, coughed and gurgled in agitation: his face, no longer blue, turned to red, but all to no avail. He flopped back at length, defeated. 'Rescued!' he gasped in disgust. 'Not only rescued, but rescued by a damned religious maniac!'

Anna, struggling to believe the unbelievable, breathless, kneeling in the dirt, was nevertheless prompted to defend herself with indignation. 'I thought you were *dead*! I was *sure* you were dead!' She struggled to her feet, much hampered by the voluminosity of her wet skirt. 'I was just telling God what a rotten so-and-so He was for not giving me time to save you, and then *He...* or it seemed to me that *He...* not that I really *believe* that *He...* anyway,' she said finally, abandoning any further attempt at explanation, tugging at her skirt, having managed to recover her balance and most of her wits, 'I'm not a damned religious maniac at all and you, Mr Whoever-You-Are, should be grateful to be alive!'

The drowned man lifted his head with difficulty. He peered at Anna in disbelief. 'Grateful to be alive?' he wheezed, 'for what? For *what*, eh? And if you're not religious, what the devil were you thanking God for? I certainly wouldn't bother thanking him on my behalf; he's not interested in me! He's never bothered to send in the troops before, and it's too blasted late now! So if you think you've been sent as an instrument of divine intervention, young woman; if you see yourself as some sort of angel of mercy, you can think again! *I am not grateful to be alive!*' The outburst exhausted him. His face turned perilously white. His head fell back upon the sacking in a manner that was frighteningly abrupt; nevertheless, '*Saved*,' he managed in an agonising rasp. '*Blasted impertinence.*'

Whilst she had not considered that she might reasonably expect to be thanked for saving a life, Anna was somewhat taken aback to find herself abused on account of it. Nevertheless, noticing that the old man was motionless and that a froth had appeared on his lips, she snatched up the handles of the wheelbarrow and pushed on across the last few remaining metres of stubble and over a strip of rough grass in a final, determined burst of effort. Then, 'Oh!' she exclaimed as she reached the door in the wall, and on the threshold stood transfixed by the sight of a romantic and beautiful house standing behind a walled moat; a house built of rose brick, serene and majestic, with deep wings surmounted by turrets shaped like pepper pots, and long stone-mullioned windows set with leaded glass.

'Oh!' Anna said again in wonder, and '*Ho!*' gasped the drowned man, momentarily revived by being stopped short; 'Am I saved or am I not, because if I am, better get on with it.' He began to tremble violently. His face had regained a bluish tinge. His teeth chattered.

Alarmed, Anna grabbed the handles and set off at a run. Through the door, down a grassy incline she steered the wheelbarrow, regardless of the bobbing, wobbling discomfort of its occupant, across a sunken, overgrown lawn, down a weed-choked path she pounded, and on across a mossy bridge over the moat where the crumbling walls were thick with ferns and toadflax and where, on the deep, dark waters below, a pair of mallard sailed away swiftly and silently from the commotion of their passing.

In a courtyard formed by the wings of the house there was a mighty door with broken steps in a half-circle leading up to it, and at the top an iron bell-pull, but when Anna pulled with the utmost urgency, although there was immediately an answering clatter from within, nobody came.

Anna stood on the steps, desperate, helpless, indecisive. It was unthinkable that she should find such a house deserted. Even though the air of neglect and dilapidation was palpable, the prospect of it being abandoned was inconceivable. 'What now, God?' she asked aloud, and almost at once heard the distant sound of music; of someone singing and playing a piano.

Abandoning the old man at the foot of the steps, noting with apprehension his ghastly pallor, his convulsive shudders, Anna began to hop from window to window in an agony of impatience, following the sound, plunging through neglected shrubbery, her skirt snagged and dragged by firethorn, brambles and gnarled old roses. At length she reached a window longer and more imposing than the rest and to her relief saw within a grand piano and seated at it a slender, elderly woman, her greying hair secured on top of her head by a complex arrangement of pins and combs, playing a nostalgic love song which, had Anna been thirty years younger, she might have recognised...

> *'I remember you, of course I do*
> *Not just when soft winds blow*
> *Dearest, everywhere I go*
> *I remember you.'*

Anna knocked vigorously upon the window, although the glass, being exceedingly small-paned and old, made very little noise and the lead casings bent inwards in a disconcerting manner. '*Help!*' she shouted. 'I need *help!*'

> *'I remember you, of course I do*
> *Not just when stars are bright*
> *Sweetheart, every single night*
> *I remember you.'*

The pianist looked up with a delighted smile. A hand fluttered aloft in a graceful little gesture of acknowledgement, dropped in order to turn a page of sheet music, and resumed playing.

> *'I remember you, of course I do*
> *Not just when nocturnes play*

Darling, each and every day
I remember you.'

Anna hammered on the window. With her clenched fist she battered the glass, the lead casing and the metal frame until flakes of rust flew. '*Help!*' she cried. 'You have to help! *Please help me!*' But the pianist smiled and played on with a curiously serene and charming indifference, turning her extravagantly coiffeured head now and again in order to bestow upon Anna a gentle and affectionate yet totally impersonal glance, as if to reward her for being a particularly warm and appreciative audience.

'I remember you, of course I do
Not just when church bells chime
Dear, I miss you all the time
I remember you.'

Anna opened her mouth as a great bawl of rage and despair welled in her throat, but the sound died on her lips. She stepped back, her eyes on the pianist, hearing the young man say again, '*He's mad. The whole family are mad. All of them.*' Anna backed away from the window, stumbling over edging bricks, slipping on broken roof tiles.

'I remember you, of course I do
Not just when skies are blue above
Or when someone speaks of love
I remember you
Of course I do.'

Really, she could have fallen to the ground and wept out of frustration, fright and exhaustion but instead made her way back to the drowned man, inspecting every window on the way in the vain hope that one might be open, that she might somehow gain access to the house, to a telephone to call the emergency services, but these windows did not appear to have been opened for centuries. In the absence of any prospect of entry at the front of the house she decided to try the back and bent again to the handles, her palms by now red and blistered and the old man motionless— comatose or dead perhaps, it was impossible to know which.

The brick and gravel paths which ran alongside the house made haste awkward but, reaching the foot of one of the pepper-pot turrets and turning down the side of the house, Anna heard the unmistakable and most incredibly welcome sound of a vehicle door slamming. Stumbling and sliding on the gravel, she began to run.

The sudden acceleration roused her passenger. *'Thanks be to God. Praise the Lord,'* he announced unexpectedly and with surprising vigour. *'He that believeth in me, though he were dead, yet shall he live.'* He clutched at the sides of the wheelbarrow for support as it veered abruptly back across the moat in the direction of the sound and swerved in between two ivy-covered gateposts bereft of a gate, on the other side of which was a cobbled yard with three or four horses looking over half doors (one of which was certainly the grey gelding since he was still wearing his bridle) and parked in the centre, a corn-merchant's lorry laden with hay bales and sacks of animal food. There was not a single person in evidence but the door to the barn stood open and, abandoning her charge on the threshold, Anna ran inside.

In the gloom, Anna at first saw nothing but then, as stacked bales and galvanised corn bins materialised, she heard a familiar voice.

'Not *now*, Anthony! I can't! I have to go *back!*' Some

energetic scuffling was followed by the sound of something metal falling to the ground. 'Anthony, this is *serious*! I really can't! *I have to find the rope!*'

Anna did not know what she was interrupting, nor did she care. 'I doubt if you will find the rope, Nicola,' she said in a loud voice. 'Not if it is the same one your father was wearing round his neck when I pulled him out of the water.'

Chapter Six

There was a moment of absolute silence after which Nicola appeared out of the shadows and with her a young man with golden hair, furtively buttoning the fly of his blue overalls.

'*I am he that liveth, and was dead, and behold, I am alive for evermore,*' announced the drowned man from the threshold. '*I am tossed up and down as the locust. I am escaped by the skin of my teeth. I know that my redeemer liveth.*'

'Help me,' Anna said urgently. 'He needs an ambulance. He probably has pneumonia!'

'*I will lie with my fathers, and thou shalt carry me out of Egypt and bury me,*' said the drowned man. 'Pneumonia, eh? *There is death in the pot.*'

'He's also delirious,' Anna decided.

Nicola took in the situation without finding it necessary to utter a word. Abandoning the golden-haired youth without as much as a backward glance, she picked up the handles of the wheelbarrow and set off towards the house at breakneck speed. Her fair hair flew and her jodhpur boots pounded across the ground. Anna raced after her, holding up her wrecked and muddied skirt. Reaching the back of the house they heaved the wheelbarrow up three gracefully curved but calamitously worn stone steps and progressed speedily through various sculleries heaped with rubbish into a kitchen with a vast, stone-flagged floor, a line of butler's bells and an antiquated cooking range set beneath a wide chimney breast. A kettle sat beside one of the hotplates and an orange and red horse blanket was airing on the rail in front of it.

Without any need for consultation they stripped off the old man's sodden clothing, wrapped him in the horse blanket and laid him, for want of anywhere more conveniently accessible, back in the wheelbarrow.

'*Naked came I out of my mother's womb, and naked shall I return hither,*' intoned the drowned man. '*Moab is my washpot; over Edom will I cast out my shoe. Tell it not in Gath, publish it not in the streets of Askelon. I am a brother to dragons and a companion to owls.*' His cheeks had become unwholesomely red. His eyes glittered.

From a cupboard beneath a stained and miserable Belfast sink, Nicola produced two stoneware hot-water bottles. 'Fill these. I'll ring the surgery. Then we'll get him upstairs.'

Anna lifted one of the heavy lids and set the kettle on the hotplate beneath. She struggled to un-stopper the antiquated bottles and set them on a long, plank table, where they squatted on their flat bottoms, hideously expectant. Elsewhere in the house, oblivious to the drama; oblivious, it seemed, to anything, the pianist continued her performance.

> '*It's a brand new day to-morrow,*
> *To-morrow is a brand new day...*'

'*Cast me not off in the time of my old age; forsake me not when my strength faileth,*' pleaded the drowned man. '*I am fearfully and wonderfully made.*'

All this can't be happening to me, Anna told herself. It's impossible. It has to be a dream; a nightmare. In a minute I will wake up and be safe in my bed at the Harbourmouth Hotel with my alarm clock bleeping and the smell of yesterday's fish in my nostrils.

The spout of the kettle was so furred with limestone deposits that filling the hot-water bottles was a painfully laborious procedure. The kettle was not only perilously hot, but also exceedingly full and heavy. The water poured forth in so thin a stream that Anna was obliged to keep resting the kettle on the table in order to allow her aching arms some respite.

'*Let us crown ourselves with rosebuds!*' cried the drowned man, undeterred. '*Purge me with hyssop, and I shall be clean; wash me and I shall be whiter than snow. I was eyes to the blind, and feet was I to the lame.*'

From a telephone nearby, Nicola could be heard summoning assistance. 'No, it is no use at all telling me to call the emergency services, I want a *doctor*, and if Doctor McLoughlin is unavailable then it will have to be someone else, but whoever it is *must* come now, *at once*. It really is *most* urgent; a matter of life or death. Yes, Rushbroke Hall. Yes. Good. Thank you *so* much. I would be terribly grateful if you could. And do please tell him to *hurry!*'

Anna put down the kettle. Her heart had suddenly leapt up into her throat, making it difficult to swallow. She felt light-headed, as if her brain had been removed leaving a cavity filled with air. *Rushbroke Hall. Rushbroke Hall!* With shaking fingers she twisted the stopper on the first stone bottle. *Rushbroke Hall!* She picked up the kettle. Water splashed onto the table.

'How shall we carry him?' Nicola was now considering the patient, who was wrapped like a mummy with his arms pinned to his sides. 'I shall have to find something we can use as a stretcher.' She went away and returned after a short interval bearing a dusty oriental screen painted with elegant Japanese ladies, lush peonies and pale blue birds which she laid, unopened, on the flagstones. 'It's not ideal,' she admitted, 'but it's the best I can do.'

Anna was beyond speech. In her mind the refrain Rushbroke Hall, Rushbroke Hall, was beating like a drum. Together they lifted the patient by his legs and shoulders and placed him upon the screen with the two stone hot-water bottles at his feet.

'*Upon earth there is not his like, who is made without fear,*' said the drowned man in tones of deep anxiety. '*Can one go upon hot coals, and his feet not be burned?*'

Picking up the improvised stretcher was awkward because it involved the accommodation of three pieces of bamboo in each hand, but they managed it somehow, although when they raised the patient aloft there was an ominous crack. Anna froze, but, 'We don't have to go far,' Nicola said. 'Just to the top of the stairs.'

Cautiously they progressed out of the kitchen and along a gloomy passageway floored with brick, lined with bulging panelling and smelling of mushrooms. The passage led into great hall with an ornate plaster ceiling patched with mould and a massive armorial fireplace heaped with ash. There was no furniture. Light from a heraldic stained glass window flooded the wide, dusty treads of a magnificent carved staircase with colour. Nicola, electing to go first, began to climb the stairs.

'*Cast thy bread upon the waters; for thou shalt find it after many days,*' muttered the patient. '*Remember Lot's wife.*'

Anna, her eyes fixed on the hot-water bottles, willing them not to slip off the end of the screen during the ascent, followed as best she might, straining to hold up her end of the screen, unable to see the treads beneath, feeling with each foot the way up every step, painfully aware of the crackling protests of the bamboo. The patient was not himself heavy, but the combination of the patient, the stone bottles of water and the screen, made the burden excessively cumbersome and heavier than was desirable given the circumstances. Climbing from below, Anna found herself bearing most of the weight and whilst, as a rule, she would have been equal to the task, she was much hampered by the fact that her heart felt so constricted that it might have shrunk to half its customary size and, as if this was not bad enough, her lungs seemed to have lost most of their elasticity, making it difficult to breathe.

Nearby, the pianist began again with gusto.

> '*It's a brand new day to-morrow*
> *Tomorrow is a brand new day...*'

The patient began to struggle, flipping up and down like a chrysalis about to pupate.

'Stop that at once,' Nicola commanded. 'Keep still. You will do yourself a mischief.'

> '*If today is filled with pain*
> *Tomorrow you can start again...*'

Anna wobbled. Her arms felt as though they might

easily snap off under the strain, and still the patient struggled. '*Praise him with the sound of the trumpet!*' he
bellowed. '*Every beast of the forest is mine, and the cattle
upon a thousand hills.*'

> '*If today you feel forlorn*
> *Tomorrow there's a brand new dawn...*'

Just after the turn of the stair the screen gave out. There
was a resounding crack and the patient vanished in a welter
of tearing fabric and splintering bamboo. Anna threw
herself forward in a valiant but unsuccessful attempt to
break the drowned man's fall only to be struck on the
temple by one of the stone bottles.

> '*It's a brand new day tomorrow*
> *So let your heart be light and gay*
> *Pack away your worries and wear a smile*
> *Tomorrow is a brand new day!*'

Lady Lavinia Rushbroke of Rushbroke finished with a
flourish.

Chapter Seven

'And how is Sir Vivian, may I enquire?' Francis Sparrow looked a trifle apprehensive, as if anticipating an unfavourable response, adding, as Anna hesitated in order to formulate a reply not too greatly removed from the truth, 'In good health, I hope and presume?'

Never before had Anna seen a man with such round and shining eyes, nor such a curved and shortened upper lip, pouting forward slightly like a fish, or perhaps a beak, yes, thought Anna, *very* like a beak. How birdlike he looks; how appropriately named. 'There has been some cause for concern recently. The responsibility of preserving what is left of the Rushbroke estate has taken its toll.' Anna thought it best not to mention attempted suicide, delirium, heart problems, pneumonia.

'I am indeed sorry to hear that.' Guilt was not a permissible emotion by bank mandate but Francis Sparrow's regret was both genuine and allowable. 'And now, if I am to understand you correctly, you are here to repay the *overdraft*? May I enquire on whose *authority*?'

'Would I require authority in order to settle a debt?'

Anna wondered. 'In any case, I am not offering to repay any of the borrowings, not yet. First, I need to be sure I have enough money to invest in the restoration and conversion of the property.'

'And do I further understand that it is your intention to turn Rushbroke Hall into an *hotel*?' Francis looked incredulous and also somewhat nervous, as well he might, having had dealings with hoteliers before. Any dip in the economy hit the hospitality industry first; one didn't need to be a bank employee to be aware of that. 'Would you care to *elaborate*?'

'Not a hotel exactly—a restaurant with rooms perhaps, but beautifully done, *properly* done.'

Anna had rehearsed this part. 'I want to invest my own money in the conversion and setting up of Rushbroke Hall and, with your permission, keep the existing borrowings on an interest-only arrangement until I have a clear idea of how much the restoration will cost. The house, as you probably know, needs a great deal of attention, especially the roof and the exterior brickwork and chimneys, not to mention the windows, and as for the interior, the plasterwork is...'

Francis Sparrow held up a restraining hand. 'If you will excuse me, Miss... er...'

'Gabriel,' Anna supplied.

'...Miss Gabriel, would it be deemed permissible for me to enquire, at this admittedly extremely *early* and *preliminary* stage, exactly how much capital you have available to *invest* in such a project?'

Francis Sparrow's tone was courteous, respectful even, but how bright his eyes were; how sharp his gaze: he doesn't believe I have the money, Anna thought, but then I can hardly believe it myself. I don't *feel* like a person of substance and I probably don't look like one either. He probably sees me as some hopelessly naive and foolishly optimistic person, full of unrealistic ideas and has already dismissed my proposal out of hand. 'Almost a million pounds,' she said, and was gratified by Francis' obvious surprise and awakening interest; by the way he seemed to grow upwards in his chair and change shape, so that instead of resembling a round, roosting bird, he appeared quite sleek and elongated and altogether more predatory. 'It is a legacy,' Anna was moved to explain. 'My parents, both of them, died almost two years ago.'

'Leaving you a most respectable sum,' said Francis in an appreciative tone. 'A tidy sum indeed. A substantial legacy, if I may be permitted to say so. A most useful inheritance. But sad,' he added hastily, 'most sad and unfortunate to lose both parents together. May I enquire as to the circumstances? A tragic accident, perhaps? An aeroplane? An automobile?'

Anna thought it none of his business. 'A handful of barbiturates, actually. And two plastic bags. A suicide pact.'

Francis sank back into his chair with a small cry of distress.

Anna was instantly repentant. 'Mr Sparrow, the truth is that my father had motor neurone disease; it was fairly well advanced and neither of them could face what lay ahead. They were extraordinarily close.'

Francis opened his mouth to commiserate but no sound emerged. He had not married, but his sisters had taken husbands and had produced children toward whom he had proved surprisingly and devotedly indulgent, and whilst he remained unattracted to the marital state, he was enormously grateful for the opportunity to appreciate the pleasures and pitfalls of family life at second hand. How close, he wondered, would a couple have to be in order to disregard the possible effect of their actions upon their children?

'The whole thing was impeccably organised right down to the very last detail. A letter alerted the local police within twenty four hours and I was not called home from college until everything had been tidied away according to instructions. My parents left a lot of instructions. They were extremely orderly people. They liked everything to be tidy and immaculately arranged.'

But their daughter was not tidy and immaculately arranged. Francis surveyed with his unblinking gaze the pigtail of fair hair secured with an elastic band, the much-laundered shirt that might once have been described as blue, the faded jeans, the scuffed sandals such as a school-girl might wear. Most of the young women with whom Francis came in daily contact were of the business management school; girls who had learned to use clothing to project a favourable image, to create an impression of worth, diligence and efficiency. Women clients of the bank invariably dressed with some care for an interview, but not Anna Gabriel. Her garments looked as though they had been thrown onto her person as being the nearest to hand. Certainly they had not been assembled to impress a bank manager, or anyone else, for that matter. Francis pecked at his lower lip. Did this casual attitude to dress convey the message that here was a confident, positive young person who had no need of protective colouring, who could afford to dispense with the conventional camouflage of formal business attire? Or was it simply the outward manifestation of a careless and undisciplined nature? On the other hand, could it be a reaction to an impeccably restrained and painfully immaculate childhood? Had those extraordinarily close parents, those extremely orderly people, found their daughter an unsatisfactory child? If so, how unsatisfactory would a daughter have to be before a mother would choose to die rather than live for *her* sake?

'The house where we lived was not large, hardly more than a cottage really, but there was over an acre of garden and the situation was suburban; it was a valuable infill site. Outline planning consent for two more houses on the land had already been applied for and granted, and the agent had received his instructions; my parents were pretty keen on instructions, as you will have gathered. Of course,' Anna continued, 'I knew nothing of this; it had never been discussed in my presence. It was a carefully planned under-cover operation designed to ensure that I would be left well provided for.' And because Francis Sparrow said nothing, but regarded her in silence, motionless and watchful as a broody hen on a nesting box, she added, 'I was... I *am*... the only child. There is no other claim on the legacy. You can speak to my own bank manager. He will confirm that the money is available.'

But Francis, (professional though he undoubtedly was, and a National Westminster man to the core) was unusually reluctant to anticipate too soon the possibility that a solu-tion to a particularly emotive and tiresome problem may have presented itself, albeit in this somewhat unconven-tional and unprepossessing form. For he was not without scruple, even where the Rushbroke debt was concerned. 'Is it your considered opinion, Miss Gabriel,' he enquired in a careful tone, 'that it would be entirely sensible to invest this precious legacy; a sum which, if profitably invested could provide you with an appreciable income for the rest of your life, in a speculative venture such as you have described?'

'I am not sure if it is sensible,' Anna replied with candour. 'But it is what I intend to do.'

'I see,' said Francis. 'But whilst I applaud your resolve, I have also to ask myself if you have fully considered the fact that should you fail in this extremely ambitious exercise, you stand you lose a great deal of your investment; indeed, you may well lose everything you have.'

'I won't fail,' said Anna.

Francis Sparrow placed his brown, bony hands upon his desk and surveyed them carefully, subjecting them to a most thorough and meticulous examination. 'Miss Gabriel, I would be failing in my duty if I neglected to point out that the statistics for entrepreneurial success in the small business sector are, at the present time, not at all encouraging. The failure rate is alarmingly high. Statistics indicate that fifteen percent of new ventures fail within the first year. In the second year the current failure rate is twenty percent, and in the third year a further thirty percent fail. Of the survivors, in the present economic climate, less than fifteen percent will still be in business by the end of the fifth year.'

'I am not interested in statistics,' said Anna. 'I do not intend to fail, but if I do, I ask you to consider that it will be my investment that will be lost, not yours. Your investment will be safe because my money will have restored the property. At the end of the day you will have gained a sound and saleable asset on which to recoup the debt.'

'I am not,' said Francis with severity, 'looking at your proposal exclusively from our viewpoint. I am obliged to examine it from both sides. I may be employed to act in the best interests of the National Westminster Bank, but I also have a moral responsibility to consider the possible consequences for the second party.'

'I am not asking for your moral consideration,' said Anna. 'I'm simply asking for a year of grace on the Rushbroke overdraft.'

'And I am asking you to consider, Miss Gabriel, that for the sum of eight hundred and fifty thousand pounds, perhaps for considerably less, you could purchase a moderately sized hotel, already well established, in a satisfactory state of repair, with a track record of profitability, and by doing so, save yourself much anguish.'

Anna sighed. 'I could,' she allowed, 'but I most certainly won't.'

'Furthermore,' continued Francis is a severe tone, 'the conversion of a vast and ruinous country house into an hotel is a *mammoth* undertaking. It requires expertise and experience. A veritable army of builders, electricians and plumbers will have to be employed. You will need a clerk of works, possibly even an architect. Because it is a listed building, English Heritage will have to be involved. This is not a project to be tackled by an *amateur*.'

'I am not intending to do the work myself!' Anna protested. 'I shall employ *experience*! I shall pay for *expertise*!'

'You will need to organise the decor, you will need furnishings and catering equipment; you will need to engage staff. The grounds are exceedingly neglected; you will need gardeners. Have you considered the *responsibilities* involved? Do you have any idea of the *enormity* of what you are proposing to undertake? Have you calculated, with *any degree of accuracy*, how much this vastly ambitious enterprise will *cost*?'

'Not yet,' Anna admitted. 'I wanted to talk to you about the Rushbroke borrowings first.'

'You will need to obtain permission from the council for change of use. Your application may be refused. You will require a licence in order to serve alcoholic refreshment to your guests. It may not be granted.'

'I also require help and support from the bank,' Anna snapped. 'It looks as though I won't be getting that either!'

They faced one another across the desk, their body language signalling mutual dissatisfaction. It seemed to Anna that the interview was doomed to end in failure. In weary resignation she picked up her shoulder bag from the floor. She said 'Mr Sparrow, may I ask if this is a *gender* issue? If I had been a man and arrived in a pinstripe suit with a briefcase and good shoes, would the outcome have been *different*? Would you have taken a more positive view?'

Francis Sparrow sat back in his chair. He folded his arms. His expression was sombre.

'Without wishing to be in any way personal, you are not the only one to have formed opinions during this interview,' Anna said. '*I* am of the opinion that whilst you are almost certainly blinkered in your view, and unbelievably circumspect, you are not a *stupid* man.'

Francis found it necessary to rearrange himself in his chair. He opened a drawer in his desk and began to rustle about amongst the contents like a blackbird in a pile of leaves.

'In fact,' Anna was warming to the attack. 'You are obviously good at your job. You are intuitive, intelligent and sharp. You must *want* to recoup the Rushbroke borrowings, and I would hope that you would want to achieve it is a less painful manner than having to evict the family from a house they have owned through six generations. I must be correct in assuming that?'

'Indeed.' Francis produced from the drawer a pair of large, round spectacles and arranged them on his nose. 'Yes, indeed.'

Oh God, thought Anna, *I am a companion to owls.* Nevertheless, 'So you can hardly fail to recognise that what I have to offer is a virtually foolproof way to recover your money? A year of interest-only payments followed by a suitably negotiated repayment scheme, or alternatively, if things go wrong, the sale of a vastly improved and renovated property? It seems to me to be an entirely reasonable request.'

'It may be reasonable,' said Francis. 'But is it sensible?'

'Bugger sensible,' said Anna.

In the small silence that followed Francis had regarded her speculatively through the owl glasses. Now, somehow, a notepad had appeared in front of him, a pen was in his hand. He appeared, if not exactly officious, much more professional; suddenly, he looked like a man ready to do business. 'Then let us have your cards on the table forthwith, Miss Gabriel,' he said briskly. 'Favour me, if you will, with a brief outline of your proposal. Present to me the salient facts of the matter. Tell me, in as few words as is humanly possible, *everything* I need to know—and by *everything*,' he added severely, 'I do mean everything. Do I make myself clear?'

Somewhat taken aback by the turn of events Anna put down her shoulder bag. 'Haven't I already....?'

'No. You have not. Most *certainly* you have not. I need to be informed of your immediate plans. I need to know how you intend to set about this gargantuan endeavour. I need you to explain your *modus operandi*.'

'Well, I...um...' Having gained the upper hand momentarily, Anna now found herself wrong-footed. You sneaky little bastard, she thought, then, ' ...I'll renovate the central part of the house to start with. That will provide an entrance hall, a dining room, a lounge and a library for guests. On the first floor there will be four en-suite rooms for guests. I shall need to attend to the kitchen area of course, but the rest of the house, the two wings, I plan to refurbish gradually out of income. I need to be open for business as soon as possible, so that by the time the house is completely converted and refurbished, I shall already have an established reputation and a regular clientele.'

'Hopefully,' interjected Francis, making a note on his pad.

'*Definitely*. And speaking of expertise' (never mind that they were not, at this point, speaking about expertise at all) 'One question you have failed to ask, Mr Sparrow, is what particular skills I, myself, can contribute to the success of this enterprise.'

Francis made another note. 'And what are these particular skills that I have neglected to enquire about?' he asked.

'I'm a chef,' said Anna, and this being no time for false modesty. 'I am fully trained and qualified and I'm a very good chef, an excellent cook, and I truly believe I have the potential to be a brilliant one. I also believe that good food and extreme comfort in tranquil and beautiful surroundings cannot fail.'

Francis had no cause to doubt her qualifications, nor her sincerity, however, 'What of the Rushbrokes themselves,' he enquired. 'What of the family? Might you not find them slightly... problematical?' Francis chose his words with care, his bright eyes fixed upon her face. 'Locally, I am aware that they have an unfortunate reputation for eccentric behaviour and, should they remain in residence, might they prove something of an embarrassment? Might they perhaps constitute and actual impediment to your plans?'

Francis did not fail to register the time it took Anna to compose her reply, neither did he miss the rising flush to her cheeks, nor the slight edge of anger to her voice, try as she might to conceal it.

'Mr Sparrow, at this moment there is only one impediment to my plans, and that is yourself,' she said steadily. 'The family will not embarrass *me*. I want to do this, Mr Sparrow, for *my* sake and for *their* sake, and even, if you will only allow it, for *your* sake. But I will *not* be patronised, and I am *not* dependent on your goodwill! I shall not be stopped in this. I do mean to go ahead with my plans. *I shall do it!*'

'Will you, indeed,' said Francis in an interested tone, 'and may I enquire how you propose to proceed without the cooperation of the bank?'

'I shall take out my pen and here and now write out a cheque in full and final settlement of the Rushbroke debt!' Anna said furiously. 'And the first thing I shall do after leaving the National Westminster Bank will be to walk straight through the door of Barclays!'

'*Barclays*,' said Francis in a thoughtful voice. He adjusted his spectacles slightly. His mouth twitched. 'I *see*.'

'I don't think you see at all!' cried Anna. 'I don't think you want to see! I don't think you have the slightest intention of helping me, Mr Sparrow; I think you are wasting my time!'

'As *you* are most certainly wasting *mine!*' said Francis sharply. 'Because I *see* more than you realise, Miss Gabriel; and what I do see, is that there is more to this proposition than you have revealed; there is more to it than meets the eye; there is some other consideration, some *more important consideration*, that you have so far omitted to mention; there is, Miss Gabriel, *a raison d'être!*'

Anna sat back in her chair. 'I am not altogether sure that I know what you mean,' she said faintly.

'On the contrary, Miss Gabriel, I think you know *exactly* what I mean and, as neither of us is desirous of wasting even more of our most *valuable* time, I suggest you supply the missing information forthwith!' In one swooping movement, Francis removed his spectacles, replaced them in the drawer and banged it shut.

Anna contemplated him in silence. She had not intended to tell him. She had hoped it would not be necessary. But now she knew it was necessary and, rather to her surprise, now that it came to it, she did not mind nearly as much as she had expected. Somehow she knew, without any doubt, that this odd, clever little man would respect her confidence, that she could trust him. For the first time since the start of the interview, Anna Gabriel smiled, and Francis Sparrow relaxed into his chair and smiled his own beaky little smile and they had, at last, the measure of one another. 'Now,' said Francis with satisfaction. 'Tell me.'

Anna told him. And Francis gave her the whole of his attention, and whilst he listened he surveyed the young woman with the slate-blue eyes and the pigtail, warming to her steady gaze, aware of her rather sharp floral scent; Jasmine? Lily of the Valley? (Francis was a Floris man himself and quite at home with a fragrance, although he was, naturally, unaware of Anna's phobia about the smell of fish.) And as she reached the end of her story he thought that, reckless, idealistic and hopelessly optimistic she may be, and most probably doomed to failure and disappointment in so many ways; but brave, he thought admiringly, most uncommonly brave indeed and, God help her, she will need to be.

'And so, Mr Sparrow,' Anna said at length, 'now that I

have told you everything, now that my cards are all on the table, am I to be granted my year of grace?'

'Miss Gabriel,' said Francis with dignity. 'I am pleased to inform you that, subject to your concurrence with certain terms and conditions, the nature of which will shortly be manifest, you most certainly are.'

Chapter Eight

Mrs Maitland-Dell stood in the cemetery beside a hedge of shaved Cupressus leylandii looking at the newly erected polished granite headstone, dabbing at her eyes with a small handkerchief embroidered with a C for Clarissa.

Harry Featherstone, chauffeur, gardener, handyman, and wearing a black tie for the occasion, stood with his head suitably bowed and his peaked cap clasped in front of him in an attitude of the very deepest respect. 'Now, don't you go upsetting yourself again, Madam,' he warned. 'Otherwise you'll get one of your migraines and then where will we be? It don't do to take on so, and it won't make any odds to Freddie now, will it? It won't alter nothing at all. It won't bring him back.'

'Losing Freddie has broken my heart,' said Mrs Maitland-Dell. 'Freddie was my first and greatest love. He was my best friend. We understood one another, Freddie and I. No words can express how much I miss his devoted companionship; his warm, loving and generous nature.'

'We shall all miss old Freddie,' agreed Harry. 'It was a very sad day when he passed away, very sad indeed.'

Although he knew, of course he knew, that the recently departed had been cantankerous and bad-tempered and universally loathed by all who knew him.

'We were never apart, Freddie and I,' said Mrs Maitland-Dell, 'never; not for a single day. I shall never forget him. I shall mourn him for the rest of my life.'

'And so shall I, Madam, so shall I,' said Harry Featherstone stoutly. After all, it was hardly the moment to admit that he had distrusted Freddie, and had been somewhat afraid of him at times, and was most heartily relieved to be shot of him at last.

'This has been an extremely traumatic time for me, Harry. I am crushed and anguished by sorrow, and my poor, grief-stricken heart is broken in two. But I have the family to consider, and I must carry on for their sake.' Mrs Maitland-Dell swallowed bravely. 'I must count myself fortunate to have so many wonderful memories of Freddie; I must be eternally grateful that he left me so much to remember.'

'There is that indeed, Madam. Memories can be a great consolation.' In particular, Harry remembered the deceased's rotten teeth and halitosis and how, when he had his portrait painted, the artist had tactfully hidden away his mouth in his moustache.

'I do believe they have made a most skilful and artistic job of the engraving.' Mrs Maitland-Dell leaned forward to touch, with a small, black-gloved hand, lilies and acanthus leaves painstakingly carved out of the black stone and miraculously coloured in white and green.

'That's very nice indeed, Madam,' said Harry Featherstone warmly. 'A very beautiful touch, if I might say so. Very tasteful. Would you be wanting to place the wreath now?'

'I think that would be a very good idea,' said Mrs Maitland-Dell.

Harry stepped behind the Cupressus leylandii and reappeared bearing a small but exquisite wreath constructed of white freesias and miniature carnations. He stood back in a discreet and deferential manner as Mrs Maitland-Dell walked solemnly forward (only the slightest bit unsteady due to the rather high-heeled shoes she still favoured) and laid it reverently at the foot of the gravestone with all the sober dignity of royalty at the Cenotaph.

Harry found this little ceremony so extremely moving that a tear formed in the corner of his eye and he was obliged to brush it away. Madam had looked so small and round and sad, stepping forward in her black velvet coat with the surprising little hat shaped like a cone sitting on her fluffy hair, holding the tiny wreath that was so dainty and nice. Not that Freddie would have appreciated it. Freddie had cared not a jot for flowers, for all that he enjoyed a stroll around the garden, morning and evening, regular as clockwork. No, Freddie's chief enjoyment in life had been food; good food and plenty of it. But the food and the drink and the home comforts had done for Freddie, that and his laziness and his weight problem had done for him all right because first his wind had gone and then his heart and not even his expensive, customised Private Patients plan could save him.

'Thank you, Harry,' said Mrs Maitland-Dell, 'and now, if you would be so kind as to wait in the car, I would appreciate a moment of private contemplation before we depart.'

'Certainly, Madam.' With a final respectful and some-what relieved obeisance to the late departed, Harry Feather-stone was thus dismissed and walked off briskly along the row of shiny new gravestones, replacing his peaked cap with a smart, military flourish, although not a soul was visible above the ground in the cemetery, and those below it were in no condition to observe social niceties.

* * *

Losing Freddie had placed a great deal of strain on the Maitland-Dell household. Bereavement affected people in funny ways, and sometimes, Harry knew, they never got over it but carried their sorrow around with them like a heavy suitcase for the rest of their lives.

Harry was worried about Madam. She had quite lost her sparkle and her bubbly zest for life and had become pale and withdrawn. She was careful, of course, never to let Harry witness her distress, and did not allow it to affect the routine of the family, but Harry knew that in her private moments she gave way to grief. Harry saw the giveaway signs, the swollen eyelids, the puffy cheeks, the reddened eyes that no amount of D R Harris's Miracle Eye Drops and Elizabeth Arden face powder could conceal. Harry could understand grief at the loss of a loved one, he knew that a period of mourning was an essential part of the grieving process, but he considered that the weeping and wailing over Freddie had gone on long enough.

Since Freddie had passed on, Madam had lost interest in everything and everybody; even the family, heaven forbid, seemed to have lost its potential to charm. Harry could see that there was a very real danger of Madam becoming obsessed by Freddie deceased, and whilst in life Freddie had (by dint of some evasive action and a bit of smart manoeuvring) been manageable; in death, if Harry didn't watch out, he was set to become invincible. At this rate Madam would take to table-rapping, the house would be turned into a shrine, and Freddie would be canonised.

Something had to be done about it. But what? Harry Featherstone had absolutely no idea.

The sun had come out in time for Madam's little ceremony and, as a result, the Rolls Royce was a little steamed up. Through rivulets snaking down the windows the family watched Harry approach with their small flat noses pressed against the glass. When he opened the passenger door, the smallest Shih Tzu fell out into the gutter. Harry retrieved it and set it on the back seat where it was received with a great deal of snuffling and jumping up and down. When Harry got into the driver's seat, the grey and white Shih Tzu, who was rather more athletic than the rest, attempted to jump onto the back of his neck but missed and fell back with a yelp, displacing the others and causing some consternation and argument, but eventually calm was restored and the family arranged themselves in an orderly row on the back seat from whence they regarded Harry in an expectant manner with their marble-like eyes shining and their mouths slightly open showing crumpled pink tongues and rows of tiny bottom teeth like seed pearls.

'What Madam needs is something to take her mind off Freddie.' Harry turned on the ignition and lowered the windows to release an extraordinary and somewhat overpowering smell. That very morning, it had been his task to bathe the family in an expensive canine shampoo called Gold'n'Delicious (purchased by Madam from Town and Country Dogs in Knightsbridge, and manufactured expressly for long-haired breeds) which due to the family becoming overheated, now filled the car with the sickly aroma of rotting apples. 'What Madam needs,' said Harry, as soon as he had inhaled some fresh air, 'is a *diversion.*'

The family listened to this with the greatest attention and every semblance of cognisance (although a recently published survey of intelligence in dog breeds had unfortunately placed the Shih Tzu second to last, only fractionally above that well-known bonehead, the Afghan Hound, which had come out bottom).

'What Madam needs,' continued Harry ruminatively, 'is something to look forward to; what Madam *needs*,' said Harry in a sudden burst of inspiration, 'is a *holiday!*'

The family goggled a bit at this, showing whites of eyes. Noses twitched in anxiety and there was some paddling of front feet (a common sign of anticipation in the Shih Tzu) and even a couple of excited yaps, which precipitated a wholesale investigation of the spokesperson during which the golden and white Shih Tzu (a highly regarded and remarkably expensive member of the family due to his colour which, according to Tibetan legend, rendered him closer to Buddha) was inadvertently pushed off the seat and only managed to regain it after much difficulty; the intense interest of the rest of the family peering down at his predicament much impeding his ascent.

For as long as Harry had been in service with Madam, he had never known her to take a holiday. Day trips with picnics had been much enjoyed, but nothing of a longer duration. Of course, Madam would never agree to leave the family and that was the rub; it would be more than Harry's job was worth to mention the word kennels. 'So if Madam won't go on holiday without you,' said Harry thoughtfully. 'She'll have to go with you, won't she? We shall have to go somewhere where you can come as well, won't we? We shall have to sort out a holiday in a nice hotel in the country, somewhere with nice big gardens, run by people who like dogs. We shall have to find somewhere congenial.' Harry was pleased with the word congenial, but 'that might pose a problem, that might,' he allowed, 'there being so many of you. So I shall have to put my thinking cap on. I shall have to make a few enquiries. It might not be easy, finding the right sort of place, but we'll cross that bridge when we come to it. The first thing I've got to do is to sell the idea to Madam.'

The family, having reorganised themselves into a picturesque group that would have been the making of any aspirant chocolate box or jigsaw photographer, were all eyes and ears (although their comprehension was virtually nil as the words holiday and congenial had not hitherto been a feature in their limited vocabulary of recognisable words).

'A holiday, eh?' said Harry in delight. 'Now that *would* be congenial.' He was just setting his mind to work on how a suitable holiday hotel for Madam and the family could be located, when the younger of the two black and white Shih Tzus (being the most alert and observant member of the family and in this a true descendant of the sacred lion dogs whose task it was to alert the ferocious mastiffs at the slightest whiff of intruders in the temples of Tibet) spotted Madam's somewhat wobbly progress toward the Rolls Royce along the gravel path beside the sign proclaiming

EVENTIDE PET CEMETERY
(CREMATIONS ARRANGED)
Because You Care, So Do We

and caused pandemonium to break loose on the back seat.

Shelving his deliberations until a more opportune moment, Harry Featherstone climbed out of the driver's seat as a preliminary to opening the passenger door to admit his employer. The yapping, yelping and yowling of the family was almost, but not quite, enough to wake the dead.

Chapter Nine

'I've never heard anything so bloody ridiculous in my life! Have you gone completely out of your mind? Has the knock on your head affected your *brain*?'

'Not permanently. No, I don't believe it has.' After the catastrophe on the stairs of which Anna could recall very little, she had emerged from a rolling mist; a swirl of physical sensation, emotion and barely coherent thought, to find herself in a high, canopied bed, struggling to sit up, thwarted by an unfamiliar slippery silk nightdress and a pounding sensation in her left temple. A bearded face with small round spectacles and a wagging finger had appeared above her and she had felt herself pressed firmly back onto pillows grown heavy and dubious with age. 'Ah, ye'll no be going anywhere betides, young lassie. Ye'll be just fine given a day or three. Ye've just a touch of concussion, is all there is to it.' The broad Scottish accent had been strangely comforting and had brooked no disagreement.

'I'm not stupid, Rupert,' Anna said, 'if that's what you mean. I've made preliminary enquiries. I've discussed the current situation with the bank. I've talked to Nicola. I've approached the local council to see how they feel about change of use. I do realise it is a vast undertaking, but I think it will work. I think I can make it work.'

'You can make it work? *You?* With your vast knowledge of conversions, of building works, of running hotels, of starting a business from scratch? *You* will make it work?' In the empty dining room of the Harbourmouth Hotel, Rupert stared in incredulity across a table with legs stained to look like oak, whose raw, yellow chipboard top was hidden by a blue plastic tablecloth laid with tablemats decorated with fish, flanked with fish knives and forks, presided over by laminated menu cards decorated with the hotel logo of a grinning cod wearing a chef's hat and a striped apron. 'My God, Anna, you are *priceless.*'

'So you don't want anything to do with it?' Anna said. 'Well, I can appreciate that. I shall just have to find someone else, but I wanted to ask you first. I thought you might be ready for a challenge. I imagined you wanted more out of life than being an assistant manager at a smelly little fish restaurant that likes to call itself a hotel.'

'It may be a smelly little fish restaurant to you,' Rupert said angrily, 'but to me, it's a job! It's a safe job! It pays a regular wage, it provides me with somewhere to live, and it's secure. People like me value security, Anna. People like me don't have sodding great legacies to fall back on when the going gets tough!' On the fake black-painted beams above his head a prickly cluster of paternosters bloomed and beside them a dried puffer fish dangled like a petrified balloon covered with spikes, its tiny beak frozen for eternity into a little round "o" of shocked surprise.

'You would still have somewhere to live,' Anna pointed out. 'And I would pay you a wage, a decent wage. I'd pay you far more than the pittance you earn here.'

'And for how long, Anna? For six months? For twelve months? Until the money runs out? Until the bank forecloses on you? And after that? What then, Anna? What price security *then*, Anna?'

'You would find another job easily enough. It isn't as if I'm asking you to take any financial risk; I'm not asking you to invest in the place.'

'Good! Because I wouldn't! I wouldn't touch it with a bloody barge pole! Anna, it's a *crazy* idea! It's fucking *madness*! You'd be insane to do it! You'll lose everything! It won't *work!*'

'It will work.'

'It won't! It *can't*! It's too much of a risk! You don't have the *experience!*'

Anna rather felt she had covered this ground before. The door of the dining room opened and a young waitress arriving for her shift took one look at Rupert's face and backed out, wide-eyed, closing the door behind her with exaggerated care.

'But you have the experience, Rupert! You will be able to look at the structure and the fabric of the building with a trained eye! You are no stranger to building works.' Anna knew that Rupert had spent the first three years of his working life in the family building firm, working on site with the men, carting bricks, digging out footings, hammering down battening, levelling concrete, learning the trade from the bottom, until he had decided that the construction industry was not for him. His father, though bitterly disappointed, had managed to be philosophical about his subsequent decision to study catering and hotel management instead and, wise man that he was, seeing recession as inevitable and recognising that speculative builders such as himself would be especially vulnerable, had chosen to encourage, rather than remonstrate.

'Well, I'm sorry you don't want to be involved, Rupert. I'm honestly, genuinely sorry, because I had hoped you might be willing to take a chance with me on this. I mean it, Rupert, I really wanted you to be a part of it.' Because, unexpectedly, surprisingly, Anna *had* wanted him to be a part of it. When it actually came down to it; when the first absurd, ridiculous, wonderful idea began to harden into reality, it had been hard to imagine him *not* being part of it. It had been impossible, in fact, to imagine tackling a project like Rushbroke without him. And yet...

'You really expected me to be a part of it? *Me?* You wanted *me?*' Rupert stared at her in disbelief. 'Are you serious?'

'Of course I'm serious.' Anna began to assemble soothing words with which to explain just how much she needed him; his support, his skills, his experience, the familiarity of his tetchy, volatile companionship. She needed to say that without him the task she had set herself would be that much more daunting. She wanted to tell him how desperately she needed an ally in this because deep inside she was not nearly as confident, as positive, as she might seem. She was ready to confess that the previous night she had woken up suddenly and in fright, her body drenched in sweat, her heart racing away in her chest like a bolting horse, and to describe how she had sat at the open window, staring out into the darkness, forcing herself to concentrate on the regular, rhythmic rasp of the outgoing tide on the shingle, until at last there had been a degree of control, until the panic had subsided. She wanted to explain all of this but before she knew it, Rupert had moved around the table and pulled her close, into a ferociously tight embrace, so that she felt the very bones of his body pressing into hers. He said in a constricted voice. 'Anna, don't do this. If you don't want to stay here, we can find another place together. You know how I feel...'

Abruptly she turned her head away, struggling out of his grasp. 'Rupert... don't... nothing is different, not in *that* way. You have to accept it. We tried... it didn't work.'

'It worked for me.'

'It has to work for both of us.'

'So you don't want me then?'

'Of course I do!'

'Oh, yes! As the bloody hired help! As a paid employee in a venture that hasn't a sodding hope in hell of getting off the ground! That's what you *want!*' Rupert slammed his fist onto the table, making the wine goblets jump, the cutlery rattle.

There seemed no point in denial. Why was everything to do with Rupert so difficult? Why had she even bothered to mention it when she had known what his reaction would be? Anna walked across the room to the deep bay window overlooking the quay where cheerful young fishermen were sorting the morning's catch into orange plastic boxes, to where whiting and dabs poured in silver streams and mackerel flipped through the air, arching and flashing in the sunlight, still gasping, still beautiful, still alive. 'OK,' she said with a casualness she did not feel. 'I expect I shall survive without you. After all, you're not the only hotel manager in the world. You're not the only pollock in the ocean.'

In response, Rupert flopped down on a chair and put his head in his hands. Fervently, he wished he didn't love her. He wished with all his heart that loving someone was something you could turn off like a tap. He felt drained by his feelings, exhausted by them, and worse, he had begun to suspect that there was someone else. The unexplained absences; the lost weekends, the mysterious days off without any explanation, when even the most innocuous enquiry was blanked, had become a torment to him. He wondered if this tyrannical, uncontrollable insanity would ever leave him. He wanted it to stop. He wanted his life back. Now there was this. This bloody ludicrous, idiotic notion. He said in a despairing voice, 'I have never been able to fathom you, Anna. I don't pretend to understand how your mind works, but just lately you've been impossible. Ever since that crazy horse jumped out of the hedge you've been different; you've changed, Anna, you're weird. I don't know what it is; I don't know what's happened, but I do know you've become obsessed with that place, with those people. They've had some sort of psychotic effect on you. You don't seem to be here most of the time; it's as if you're in a dream.'

'This is not a *dream*, Rupert, this is real! It is what I have been waiting for! It is my chance to make a difference; to earn a place for myself. I know I'm not making much sense,' Anna said with a sigh. 'I don't expect you to understand.' She did not turn from the window but looked out beyond the quay, out to the harbour, watching the little boats move round on their moorings with the turn of the tide. She couldn't tell him any more, not now. And really, how *could* he understand, without knowing the facts; without being told the full story. Nevertheless, 'Rupert, I don't know how this will turn out. I only know that I have to do this, that I cannot *not* do it. My life may be better for it or it may be worse. Whatever happens though, it will be changed, as I am changed. Come with me, Rupert,' she entreated. '*Please.*'

He came and put his arms around her and laid his head

on her shoulder in what, in another person entirely, might have been capitulation or quiescence but, being Rupert, managed to be neither. 'Don't be naive, Anna. How can I? Why should I? If there's no future for us together, what would be the point?'

Anna lifted a hand and smoothed his hair, feeling it sleek and cold under her fingers. Rupert's hair was always cold, cold and black, as black as night. 'What about friendship?' she said. 'Surely we can have a future together as friends?'

He jerked his head away. 'You just don't have a clue, do you, Anna? You have absolutely no bloody comprehension of how I feel, of how sodding desperate I am, of what it feels like to have you calmly stand there and offer me your friendship! *I don't want your bloody friendship!*' he shouted. 'I don't want your friendship any more than I want to be your fucking employee! I could tell you what to do with your friendship and your gracious offer of employment, Anna! I could tell you where to stick your lunatic visions and your precious future, because I can see a few visions myself! I can see a vision of a bloody disaster! I can see a vision of bankruptcy for you, Anna! I can see your future and it's a sodding nightmare! For Christ's sake, show some common sense and drop this crazy idea of yours! Pull out before it's too late! For God's sake, Anna, *forget it!*'

'But maybe,' said Anna thoughtfully, not really knowing why she was saying it, not really knowing that it was even true, 'in a way it's for God's sake that I'm doing it.'

For a few moments Rupert was rendered speechless, then, '*What* did you say?'

'What I mean is, whatever you like to call it: fate, destiny, kismet, karma, God or whatever, well, maybe that's the reason I'm doing it.'

'I thought that's what you said. Now I know you're bloody bonkers! You never fail to amaze me, Anna. I don't know exactly how or when God came to be in your team, but it's a brilliant idea; it's a bloody master stroke! After all, if you're on a losing wicket it could be very useful to call in the Almighty to bat on your behalf! And why stop there, Anna? Why not recruit Father bloody Christmas, whilst you're about it? Why not ask the Man in the bloody Moon!'

'Stop it, Rupert. I've heard enough.' She turned to leave, but he forestalled her, taking her hands in his, reining in, biting his tongue, trying to be gentle now; now that he was losing her, and knew it. Looking at him she saw eyes dark with pain and frustration, noticing the familiar blue shadow on his cheeks and the stubborn line of his jaw, and the strained set of his mouth and she thought; how beautiful he is, how lovely, what a pity I can't love him. What a shame. What a waste. 'You might wish me luck, anyway,' she said resignedly. 'According to everyone I have spoken to, I am going to need an awful lot of it.'

'And what about me?' he demanded. 'What about *my* luck? What about *my* life? What about *my* future? How shall I bear it? How can I let you go away and risk never seeing you again when I can't even stand the thought of it, not even for a minute?' His voice was agonised, his expression painful to behold. He lifted one of her hands to his lips only to drop it again in a despairing gesture as he acknowledged the hopelessness of his situation. 'What you are going to do is *madness*, Anna. It's financial *suicide.*' But even as he spoke his tone betrayed the resignation he felt. How could he let her go ahead with this crazy project without him? Even if she didn't love him, she *needed* him, and that was a start, that should be enough; that *had* to be enough. For the moment. Wearily, he sat down on one of the dining chairs, the plastic seat of which was patterned with anchors. He pulled up beside it another chair patterned with shrimps. 'But if I can't persuade you to change your mind, perhaps you and I might be able to come to some sort of arrangement. Sit down, Anna. Explain to me your conditions of employment. Tell me about friendship.'

Chapter Ten

'Now, what do you think of this one?' With a flourish, the proprietor laid upon the counter a mask with many warts and a snout like a pig.

David Williamson liked pigs but did not particularly want to look like one. 'I'm looking for something a bit more... well... *evil*,' he said.

The proprietor beamed. 'Oh, I think we can help you there,' he said. 'Yes, I think we can definitely help you there.' "We" consisted of the proprietor of The Jolly Jape and Novelty Shop (Masks and Fancy Dress our Speciality), and an enormous white cat asleep on the counter which, not being very large to start with, was somewhat cramped as a result of it. The proprietor, who was himself not very large, but exceedingly neat and nimble, with a shiny bald head and bright, twinkling eyes, manoeuvred himself deftly into the window space, displacing a stock reduction offer on Barbara Cartland (all sooty eyelashes and candy floss hair with a shocking pink bow) in order to procure a distinctly unpleasant mask of a greenish hue turning to black around the eye holes, the purple mouth sprouting an assortment of rotting fangs, and the whole attached, via a veined and hideous forehead, to a hairless scalp like a skull.

'Count Orlok to the life, I promise you,' said the proprietor, easing himself neatly back behind the counter. 'Based on Klaus Kinski himself in the 1979 version of *Nosferatu*; an absolute masterpiece of the genre and never bettered, in my opinion. Now, why don't we try it on? I do believe I have a mirror somewhere.' He looked around without success until, lifting a portion of the cat and feeling around underneath, he managed to locate a small hand mirror with a polished wooden back. 'Good, now we can see what it looks like.' He edged out from behind the counter and, standing on tiptoe, placed the mask carefully over David Williamson's head. Surveying it with a critical eye, he made one or two adjustments before holding up the mirror. 'It really is magnificent,' he said admiringly. 'Quite marvellous in its way, and absolutely *Nosferatu*. Undoubtedly a wonderful piece of craftsmanship, a genuine work of art, and an incredible likeness; the ears are particularly fine. Herzog insisted on the rat-like ears apparently although Kinski is credited with having thought up the rest—the bald skull, the hollow eye-sockets, the fangs placed centrally in the mouth. I don't suppose you are at all familiar with the film in question, it being rather before your time, but I can tell you that all you need now is a black costume and some good fingernail extensions and Bob's your uncle. It really does look *very* splendid. I *like* it.'

The effect was certainly very evil and disturbing, but it was not quite what David Williamson had visualised. He felt rather hot and agitated inside the mask and was glad to take it off. He was relieved to be the only customer and fervently hoped to complete his purchase before anyone else entered the shop. Not that there was room for anyone else; the proprietor, the counter, the cat and David Williamson already filled almost every inch of available space. 'I think I need something a bit more... bestial,' he said.

'Bestial!' The proprietor was delighted. 'Ah, *now* we're talking! *Now* we're getting down to it!' He squeezed back behind the counter and restored Klaus Kinski to pride of place in the window. 'Bestial! Yes! Bestial we can do, can't we puss? Now then, let me see...' Removing Prince Charles from a shelf above the window space, he took down a box marked HORROR, placed it upon the counter and, rummaging inside produced a leprous mask with grey, peeling skin, half a nose, an empty eye socket, and tufts of bristly hair sprouting all over the scalp.

David Williamson shuddered and shook his head.

'No?' The leprous mask was followed by one upon which the features appeared to have liquefied and were streaming down the face in a wash of blood and gore. '*House of Wax,*' the proprietor said with relish. 'Do you recall the film? No? Well, never mind. What about this one?' He held aloft a mask consisting of half a face. The other half was just a raw, red pulp. '*Phantom of the Opera.* It comes in two parts, mask and prosthesis. I don't suppose you've seen the Lloyd-Webber production in the West End? Marvellously theatrical. Wonderful music. Very good tunes. The boy's a genius actually, no doubt about it.' He hummed a few bars of *The Music of the Night* with enthusiasm, as a result of which the cat opened one perfectly round, pink eye, surprising David Williamson who, due to the fact that it had shown no previous sign of life whatsoever, and because its fur looked ravaged by moth, had presumed it to be stuffed. 'I think I would feel a bit more comfortable with something furry,' he said. 'Something a bit more like an animal. Something hairy.'

'Hairy! Like an animal!' The proprietor rubbed his hands together in anticipation. 'Of course! Now, why didn't we think of that? Yes, I think we can help you there! I think we can find you just the thing, just exactly the right hairy sort of thing!' He replaced the cardboard box marked HORROR on the window shelf and took down another box marked W-WOLF/GOR. The contents of W-WOLF/GOR seemed infinitely more promising. 'Now, what have we here? What do you say to this?' The proprietor extracted a black gorilla mask having a large flattened nose with flaring nostrils, a pleated brow and a wig of thick, matted hair.

'That's nearly it,' said David Williamson, 'but not quite.'

'Nearly it,' repeated the proprietor, 'but not quite. Getting warmer, wouldn't you say? Getting within spitting distance now! Ah! Now then, let's take a look at this... *American Werewolf de Luxe with Latex.*' He took out what appeared to be a ball of verminous dark fur and inched himself out from behind the counter again in a purposeful manner. 'We really have to try this on in order to appreciate its artistry. It really is a consummate example of maskmanship. You will be amazed by this, I can guarantee it, but there is a certain skill involved in its application. It stretches like so...' he inserted both hands into the furry ball and stretched out the mask to its fullest extent, '...then you lower it carefully over the face like so...' Reaching up, he eased the mask over David Williamson's head and pulled it down over his face. When he removed his hands it contracted and settled into place. The smell of rubber was overpowering. The proprietor gave it a tweak here and a tug there before holding up the mirror. 'Now,' he said with glee. 'That is *bestial!*'

It was. Instantly, the mask had transformed David

Williamson into a nightmarish monster with a hideously hairy face, wild, bloodshot eyes and a mouth pulled to one side in a vicious snarl displaying realistic yellowing fangs. 'Oh yes,' he said. 'I like it. I'll take it. This is exactly what I had in mind. It's perfect.'

'Perfect! Exactly what you had in mind!' The proprietor was overjoyed. 'We knew we'd get there in the end! *American Werewolf de Luxe with Latex* it is then! A truly magnificent creation and possibly the most realistic mask on the market today. I don't suppose you are familiar with the films? No? Well, perhaps we should get you unmasked and, as before, there is a knack to getting it off, you have to roll it up from the bottom like so, and with one hand on either side of the head and using the palms, you continue to roll until you get to the top like so. It's so easy when you know how, don't you think? Now we have to unroll the mask by taking a very firm hold of the top like so and, inserting the fingers into the roll, pulling the mask down again like so; we can't afford to leave it rolled up and inside out because that would affect the lie of the pelt and that wouldn't do, would it? No that definitely wouldn't do at all, not at the price we have to ask you to pay for it because, sadly, *American Werewolf de Luxe in Latex* is the most expensive mask in the shop, very costly indeed, second only to *Elephant Man*. John Hurt played the title role in the film, if you remember? A thrilling and unforgettable performance, quite heartbreaking in its pathos. Yes, I am afraid we have to ask you to part with a great deal of money; one hundred and sixty eight pounds excluding VAT and more's the pity. We are almost too embarrassed to mention it, aren't we puss?'

David Williamson left the tiny, claustrophobic shop with a feeling of relief and in better spirits than he had been for some time. It had been a bitter blow to discover that Sir

Vivian had somehow managed to return from the dead. He had not been able to believe it at first. After all, he had been there; he had witnessed his demise; with his own hands he had leg-and-winged his old adversary into the wheelbarrow and watched as he was carried away, as dead as a doorknob.

Rendered magnanimous by the prospect of being rid of the Rushbroke family in their entirety (for how long could Nicola and Lady Lav hold out at Rushbroke? Surely it would just be a matter of time before they were forced out; everyone knew they were practically bankrupt and owed money all over the place) he had called into Rushall St. Mary's flower shop with the intention of ordering a wreath. But the florist had frowned when he had enquired as to the date and time of the ceremony. She had no knowledge of a funeral being arranged, neither had she heard that Sir Vivian had died. Was he, David Williamson, quite sure he had the correct information, she wondered, because if he had been the victim of a malicious joke, it was in pretty poor taste, if anyone cared for her opinion. And by the way, if he happened to be calling at Rushbroke Hall at any time in the near future in order to determine the true facts of the matter, and if he happened to see Sir Vivian, provided that he was still in the land of the living, would he be kind enough to mention that he had still to pay for the last wreath he had ordered despite several statements, the last one accompanied by a threatening letter from the proprietor? David Williamson had left the florist's shop a deeply confused and troubled man.

From the vantage point of his farmyard, he had watched Rushbroke Hall for days afterwards. He had seen the local doctor come and go on several occasions, likewise the boyfriend of the girl who had rescued Sir Vivian (recognisable to David Williamson because he had been the one who had eventually pulled his car out of the ditch) had visited; from which he surmised that the girl he had dragged out of the mere looking like Ophelia with her wet hair streaming and her soaking garments clinging to her body, had suffered some unfavourable reaction and was still there. Through his binoculars, he had observed Nicola going about her usual duties, tending and exercising her quadrupeds much as usual, but he had perceived no sign of grief, no undertakers, none of the usual activity associated with death and the subsequent arrangements for internment or cremation. It had been baffling.

Finally he had discovered the truth as relayed by the lad who manned the pumps at the Rushall Road Service Station where David Williamson, in common with the Rushbrokes and most of the inhabitants of Rushall St. Mary, purchased petrol and diesel. Sir Vivian had recovered! By some extraordinary chance he had not died at all. He was alive and was expected to be released from Ipswich Hospital within days. The Rushall Road Service Station lived in hope that he might even settle his account.

This knowledge had been a bitter blow. It had sent David Williamson into a black depression during which he had not even been able to draw comfort from the fact that he had managed to successfully incubate a record 90% of his Norfolk Black Turkey poults which, at just over three weeks old, were almost ready to be transferred from the brooder to the rearing sheds.

David Williamson's Christmas turkeys were a local tradition and something of a speciality in the area. By September his order book would be full and many would be disappointed. Soon, inoculated against blackhead, his turkeys would be roaming free across his farmland in a great black flock, wandering at will, settling to rest where they fancied until, disturbed by anything or nothing, they would pick up their blowsy skirts and noisily depart in search of a new resting place. Occasionally, being perching birds, a foolhardy soul would attempt to fly up into a tree and fall back in a swirl and tumble of feathers. Once, one exceptionally heavy bird had collided with a bough and broken its neck, but otherwise the flock came to no great harm and returned, sometimes after a little encouragement, to the barn for food and shelter as darkness drew in. Their life was pitifully short, but they were free and healthy and well-cared for whilst they lived and their death, when it came, was as unexpected as it was swift. David Williamson could live with that.

Nevertheless, it had taken the discovery of several more piles of freshly evacuated horse droppings on his pasture to dispel enough of the black depression to enable him to revive his plan to frighten Nicola off his property for good. Now, as David Williamson, clutching *American Werewolf de Luxe in Latex,* walked back towards his Land Rover along an Ipswich back street lined with shops selling mobile phones, musical instruments and aquarium supplies, interspersed with take-away food outlets of every possible variety plus a rather threatening tattoo parlour and at least two sex shops with blacked out windows, a Sue Ryder charity shop caught his eye and what he saw in the window stopped him in his tracks. Displayed on a plaster mannequin wearing a slightly lopsided orange wig was a vast and hideous black fur coat priced at twelve pounds and fifty pence. It was *exactly* what he needed.

Chapter Eleven

During the lengthy and meticulous tour of the property, Rupert had been scribbling furiously in the spiral-bound notebook that now reposed before him as he sat at the plank table with his head buried in his arms. Anna would have preferred to be optimistic but feared that this might be a bad sign.

Nicola had come in from the stables with a limp and a swollen lip, the result of unboxing her latest equine delinquent who had been inclined to stay within the hired conveyance that had facilitated his arrival. Strong drink was called for.

To accompany the cheapest supermarket brand of instant coffee, which was the best that Nicola could provide, Anna drew from her battered leather shoulder bag a half bottle of Armagnac and a packet of ginger biscuits extravagantly coated in dark chocolate in the hope that these small items would alleviate at least some of the gloom in the atmosphere. 'It's bad, isn't it?' she said. 'It's even worse than you imagined. Go on, Rupert; you can say it.'

Rupert lifted his head in order to partake of a small

eggcup of brandy; an eggcup being the best that Nicola could find in the circumstances, the good glass having long gone under the hammer and the plain tumblers vanished without a trace. (The glass regiment beneath Sir Vivian's bed had yet to be discovered.) 'It's every bit as bad as I had imagined and in many ways it's far, far worse. If you want my honest opinion, you would do well to reconsider.' Of course, she wouldn't reconsider; she wouldn't hear if it; nevertheless, he felt an obligation to recommend it. 'But if you really want to go ahead, if you are absolutely one hundred percent certain, then I have to warn you that this is going to be one holy devil of a job.'

'But it is possible?' Anna wanted to know. Her face was pale and her eyes were anxious. She was covered with cobwebs. Rupert looked at her across the table and felt a stab of longing so acute that it was like a physical pain.

'As I understand it, anything is possible with the help of the Almighty.'

Anna bit her lip. 'Please don't joke about this. It is too important.'

'Was that a joke?' Nicola winced and put a hand to her mouth; talking hurt.

'You should put something cold on that,' Anna said. 'I don't suppose you have any frozen peas?' As soon as she said it she realised the futility of the question.

'Frozen peas?' Nicola looked astonished.

'If you two could bear to give me the benefit of your undivided attention for a moment,' Rupert tapped his note-book impatiently, reminding himself of his resolve to keep calm, to avoid any suggestion of conflict, and to watch his language, 'we might perhaps discuss what we have seen.' For they had seen everything. Picking their way along dark, slanting passages and negotiating major and unstable minor staircases they had explored rooms that had not been entered for decades; rooms where the walls bulged, where the ceilings had fallen, where the stench of damp and rot and decay was sickly and pungent. They had inspected attic rooms heaped with the detritus of centuries, in some places thick with an accumulation of dust, dirt, and bat and mouse droppings and in others sodden and beslimed as a result of years of missing tiles and rotten beams. In one room, an ancient hip bath, positioned in more optimistic times to catch the drips only to be acknowledged as hopeless and abandoned, was hanging through the ceiling of the room below, the overflow running down its rusted sides having rendering the floorboards soft as a sponge. In the wings of the house some rooms boasted a broken chair or a square of mouldering carpet, with here and there a sad flourish of drapery at the windows, rotting and watermarked and home to a variety of insect life. Not just insects had taken up residence here, but pigeons, bats, rats, mice and even squirrels were the present occupants. The condition of the house had not really shocked him, he had expected as much, but the extent of it had; there was just so much of it. Even with his limited knowledge of restoration costs he could see that it would need the expenditure of millions, rather than thousands, to put it right and now his mind grappled with priorities; with what had to be done and what could safely be left, and how the necessary work could be carried out in an impossibly short time. 'I suppose it is absolutely essential that you open for Christmas?' he said. 'You couldn't persuade the bank to give you a six month extension so you could open in time for the summer?'

But Anna, remembering Francis Sparrow's watchful, beady eyes; the way he could unexpectedly change from benevolent to belligerent in the space of a second; the way he had slammed the desk drawer and made her jump, could not even contemplate it. 'I couldn't and they wouldn't. Honestly. I had enough problems getting them to agree to a year.'

Rupert fortified himself with another swallow of Armagnac. 'Somehow I knew you would say that.'

'I only need a few rooms to be ready. Just the central section of the house,' Anna said. 'I did explain what would be required'.

'You did.' Just a few rooms, just the central section of the house—the main section, naturally. As if it was not so much to ask, as if it was a perfectly reasonable request, which, in her own mind, it probably was. Time for some plain speaking: 'What is required,' Rupert said heavily, 'is the complete renovation of the roof. That is the priority. It is the most essential job and it's going to be incredibly, astronomically expensive; it's going to cost a bomb.'

'But do you have to renovate it completely?' Nicola wanted to know. 'Wouldn't it be possible to simply repair the patches where the rain comes in? Couldn't you just replace the missing tiles?'

Rupert looked at her in exasperation. 'Nicola, you can't patch up a roof when the main timbers have been eaten away by beetle. You can't relay tiles when the battening has rotted away because there would be nothing to fix them to. Nor has the roof ever been felted or insulated and without that, any attempt to heat the house would be useless.'

'I hadn't thought of it like that.' Nicola put down her chocolate biscuit and looked at it in regret, as if her ignorance had rendered her somehow unworthy of it. She did not, at this moment, care who Anna was, where she had come from, or what her motives might be. All she saw was the frightening state of Rushbroke Hall, its rotten, stinking beams and bulging walls, the heartbreak of its crumbling brickwork, its overgrown gardens, its broken fences. She saw the monster that was all that remained of the family estate; she saw the millstone and what it represented. Now, at this moment, all she wanted, quite desperately, was for this extraordinarily unexpected opportunity not to disappear. Because if it did, she knew there were no other options. If it didn't go ahead the future didn't bear thinking about.

Anna said cautiously, 'When you say incredibly expensive, what do you mean exactly? Can you be more specific?'

'I can, but you might wish you hadn't asked.' Rupert expected his rough estimate to shock, and shock it did, because when he said, 'at a conservative estimate I'd say it will cost around four hundred thousand,' both Anna and Nicola looked completely stunned.

'Just for the roof!' Nicola exclaimed in dismay. 'I don't believe it!'

'Rupert, that can't be right.' Anna was stricken. 'In any case we don't have to do the whole roof, do we? Can't we forget the wings for the present?'

'Anna, there is no way we can forget about the wings because we need to use them. We need one of the wings for family and staff accommodation, and the other will house essential services; the kitchen, laundry, storerooms and offices; we *need* to be watertight. All of the chimneys need attention, some can be repointed but others are in a catastrophic state and will have to be rebuilt. Whilst the roofing contractors are here with their equipment and scaffolding, it makes sense to do the lot; it would be false economy not to. You also have to remember that the bank will probably want to have their surveyor oversee the work, not to mention English Heritage who will certainly put their bloody oar in. They'll never agree to anything but a complete and authentic restoration of the roof, I would stake my life on that.' Rupert looked from one to the other. How little they understood. How clueless they were. How the hell had he got himself into this godforsaken enterprise? He took a large swallow of brandy. 'And another thing; I don't think either of you realise what it is going to be like once the work gets under way. The house will become a hellhole. Floors will be torn up, walls and ceilings will have to come down. There will be dust and rubble and plaster everywhere. The noise will be indescribable. We shall have to move Vivian and Lavinia out.'

'We are not moving them out,' Anna said sharply. 'This is their home. It will always be their home. Whatever happens, they stay.'

'When I say out, I don't mean *completely* out, there's no need to jump down my throat!' Already Rupert was struggling with his good resolutions. 'What I was about to suggest is that we move them out of their present rooms into one of the wings.'

'And I suggest you forget it; we have just looked at the wings; they are not habitable.'

Nicola jumped up ostensibly to put the kettle back on the hotplate. With her back to them she closed her eyes and put a hand to her swollen lip. She had opened her mouth to defend him. She had been about to say: Don't snap at him. Can't you see he's doing his best? He's only trying to help. But Nicola had learned diplomacy at an early age. Out of necessity she had learned to pick her way carefully across the surface of her problematic family life like a gnat on a pond, stepping neither too deep nor too far, ever ready to fly back to the orderly, comforting world she had created for herself in the stables where, even if other troubled souls awaited her behind the half doors, at least it was within her power (or almost always within her power) to improve the quality of their lives. Now this sixth sense told her she could not, should not, interfere. That it would not be diplomatic to interfere. Rupert's jaw tightened. 'They would be habitable if they were watertight,' he pointed out. 'They could be made habitable if the roof was sound. They could actually be converted into perfectly satisfactory accommodation. Anna, if you are going to slam the door on every bloody suggestion I make, we are not going to get anywhere.'

'Rupert is right.' Nicola turned back to the table. If she was not able to defend him, then at least she could speak for her family. 'My parents couldn't possibly stay in their present rooms with all the work going on around them. At their age they would not be able to endure it. Of course we shall have to move them.' She poured more Armagnac into Rupert's eggcup and moved the chocolate biscuits within his reach in an encouraging manner. 'Tell us what you have in mind.'

Rupert looked at Anna in a questioning manner. 'Shall I go on, or not?'

Anna had not yet recovered from the estimated cost of the roof. It had been a shock, although she was trying not to let it show it had frightened her. It was almost half of her inheritance. She did not trust herself to speak. She nodded.

Rupert flipped over a few pages of his notebook and showed them rough sketches of the ground floor of the east wing. Two pairs of slate grey eyes studied them. Either side of his shoulders, two heads of thick fair hair bent over them. He was aware of nothing but the benefit of their full attention and the need to explain what they were looking at. 'There should be enough room for a couple of bedrooms, both with a small en-suite here,' Rupert stabbed the suggested area with his pen, 'and a good-sized reception room here—we have to remember we need extra space for the piano so this room needs to run almost the entire length of the wing—then we still have enough room for a small study and a decent kitchen. There is already a door into the courtyard so the accommodation would be self-contained. We would have to give it priority because we can't start on the central section of the house until Sir Vivian and Lady Lavinia are moved, but we could tackle the roof of the east wing first. We have to start somewhere. I can't see any problems.' Not here anyway. Not yet.

They were impressed. 'Well, I think it sounds marvellous,' Nicola said. 'It will be luxury living compared to what they are used to. My father will adore it, it will appeal to his sense of adventure and mother will be easy to manage as long as she has her piano.'

Anna said 'Yes, I'm impressed you remembered the need to accommodate the piano.'

Briefly, their eyes met. 'I have thought this through, you know.' Rupert told her. 'I'm not a complete bloody idiot.'

'Did I say you were? Please don't start taking offence at things I have never said.'

How are they ever going to achieve anything if they can never agree? Nicola wondered. She had assumed they were partners. After today she was not so sure. She placed a mug of frighteningly strong coffee in front of Rupert. He winced.

'When the kitchen is done we'll have a proper coffee machine,' Anna promised.

'When the kitchen is done, I suspect we might even get proper meals,' Nicola said fervently. 'That will be a first as well.'

'Speaking of the kitchen,' Rupert continued. 'I have presumed that Nicola would want to live independently and I have included her in the staff accommodation above here, in this wing. We can't use it for guest accommodation because of the noise.'

'So the price of independence is being housed above the kitchen and serenaded by the crashing of pots and pans, is it?' Nicola said ruefully. 'Thank you very much.' She moved the biscuits back to her side of the table.

Rupert said, 'Well, if you are going to be fussy about it...'

'I am not fussy,' Nicola said hastily. 'I am definitely not fussy. Above the kitchen will be fine.'

'So can we get things moving?' Anna wanted to know.

Rupert considered. Whatever he thought, however he felt, he could not withdraw his services now. He was committed. Later, if things became impossible, *when* things became impossible, he would walk away. Perhaps. Maybe. But for now, for better or for worse, he was her promised henchman. What had she said? Call it karma, kismet, fate or God? Call it fucking insanity was nearer the mark. 'First of all, we need a good clerk of works, someone with a good knowledge of building and renovation works, someone with contacts; suppliers, contractors, workmen; someone with local knowledge. Without a site manager we can't really go anywhere. I'm capable of being a good second in command, but I don't have the experience to do the top job.'

'So how do we find this person?' Anna wondered. 'Do we advertise for someone?'

Rupert snapped the elastic on his notebook. 'No need for that. As a matter of fact, I already have someone in mind.'

Chapter Twelve

'And another thing,' said Penelope Lamb, 'all those old sale catalogues on top of the bookcase. They'll have to go. If you don't move them, I shall. I shall put them out with the refuse. I don't know why you keep them, you never look at them, they just sit there collecting dust and looking untidy. Well, I have had enough of them. I'm telling you, Henry, they'll have to go. I mean it.'

'Yes dear,' said Henry Lamb mildly. *Three bags full, dear,* thought Henry Lamb. *Touch those catalogues and I'll cut your tongue out. Put them out with the rubbish and I'll slit your throat.* 'I'll move them, my darling,' he promised. 'Don't give them another thought. I'll have them out of your way in no time at all.'

'I should jolly well think so too,' said Penelope Lamb. 'And whilst you are about it, there are those boxes of books cluttering up the utility room. I can't move in there. Every time I put in a load of washing I bark my shins. Those boxes are a danger and an obstruction and I want them moved...'

'Where would you like them moved to, dear heart?'

enquired Henry. 'Just say the word and I will move them to wherever you suggest.'

'Out,' said Penelope. 'I want them moved out. I want them out of this house. I don't care where they go as long as they are off the premises. If you are going to retire, Henry, we have to come to an arrangement. There are to be no more dusty old catalogues and no more cartons of mouldy old books in this house. I can't stand it. I hope you understand what I'm saying, Henry; I hope you're taking this in because I've quite made up my mind; no more sale catalogues, no more cardboard boxes, no more piles of musty old books.'

And no more Penelope, thought Henry. *String up Penelope. Drown her in the bath. Push her down the stairs. Shatter her skull with a candlestick. Pump her full of hydrogen and float her off into the wide blue yonder. Shoot an arrow from a bow. Pop goes Penelope.* With his round face, his large brown eyes and his mop of gingery grey curls, Henry Lamb resembled an ageing Raphael cherub. He smiled sweetly at his wife. Penelope looked away in annoyance.

'When we move into the flat,' she said sharply, 'we won't have nearly as much space. We shall have to dispose of some furniture. I'm thinking of the big bookcase, Henry. The big bookcase will have to go.'

Henry Lamb looked up from the latest issue of *The Bookseller*. 'Sell the big bookcase? I really don't think I can agree to that, my love. Whatever would I do with my collection?'

'There won't be room for your collection in the flat, Henry,' said Penelope. 'That's what I'm trying to tell you. We shall have to downsize. We shall have to dispose of some of our furniture and the big bookcase would be a start. The collection will have to be sold. You will have to send it to auction. Either that or I shall give it to Oxfam.'

'Give it to Oxfam? You can't possibly give my collection to Oxfam, my precious darling. The Arthur Rackhams are worth an awful lot of money now, and so are the Aubrey Beardsleys. I'm afraid I should be very reluctant to part with my collection, and as I need somewhere to put it, it does seem sensible to hold onto the bookcase. I feel sure we will be able to accommodate it somewhere.'

'Then it will have to be put in your bedroom,' said Penelope firmly. 'I won't be able to accommodate it anywhere else. It's far too big. It's monstrous. It doesn't fit in with my plans.'

'The bedroom it shall be then, dearest,' said Henry, who had a few monstrous plans of his own, all of them involving the disposal of Penelope.

'I would like it understood from the start that when you retire I shall not be doing lunches,' Penelope said. 'Breakfast will be served as per usual and dinner will be at the regular time but I definitely won't be doing lunches or tea. I have to draw the line somewhere. I can't be expected to spend all day preparing food.'

'Oh, I won't be needing lunch,' said Henry easily, 'and I never eat at teatime. You won't have to worry your little head about me, my treasure; I shall be no trouble to you at all.' *The dead have no worries,* thought Henry Lamb. *Why, one little dose of strychnine in the Earl Grey would only be a kindness. It would be an act of mercy. Lucky, lucky Penelope.*

Penelope gave him a sharp look. 'Now I have to say this, Henry, and I hope you won't be offended, but when you retire I can't have you in the house all day long. I'm not used to it. I do need my personal space. I need time to myself. I need to meditate. I need privacy. In the afternoons you will have to go out.'

'In the afternoons,' said Henry comfortingly, 'I shall go to the library.'

'Two evenings a week I shall be attending adult education classes. I shall be studying Italian and music appreciation. I shall take piano lessons. I may well join the University of the Third Age.'

'Goodness me,' said Henry admiringly. 'You will be busy.'

'The one thing I shall regret when we move into the flat will be having to leave the garden. I do so enjoy gardening and it will be a wrench. It will be my sacrifice. But it has to be said, Henry, that you have never pulled your weight in matters horticultural. The garden has always been down to me. It has always been my responsibility. You have never shown the slightest interest in my herbaceous borders. It has been purgatory getting you to mow the lawns, and as for clipping the hedge...'

'I'm not much of a gardener,' Henry admitted amiably.

'You have never shared my love of being out in the fresh air,' said Penelope. 'You've always spent your time fiddling about indoors with your dusty old books, wrapping up parcels, your nose never out of *The Bookseller*, talking to your weird collector friends on the telephone. I'm afraid that will have to stop, Henry, once you have retired. We won't be able to use the telephone *carte blanche*, not on a pension. We shall have to cut back. Economies will have to be made.'

'I was thinking I might take an evening class myself,' Henry said thoughtfully. 'Always supposing there is something of interest in the prospectus; provided there is something on offer relevant to my needs; some useful skill I could acquire.' *One Hundred Ways to Dispose of a Corpse, for example*, thought Henry Lamb. *Imaginative Ways to Murder Your Wife.*

'Evening classes? You?' Penelope looked at him in astonishment. 'Don't be ridiculous, Henry, you've never had an interest in your life other than in your mouldy old books.'

'Of course I haven't.' Henry favoured his wife with a gentle smile. 'What an old silly I am.' Of course, Henry could afford to be gentle because Penelope was not party to his plans. Penelope had no idea that she would not have to worry about the monstrous bookcase or about lunches and teas, or even breakfasts and suppers for that matter. Penelope did not know that she would no longer be troubled by cardboard boxes and sale catalogues and dusty old books, and that she would be in no position to mind leaving the garden but might easily end up beneath it. Penelope just didn't have a clue.

'If we are thinking of moving into the flat in the spring,' continued Penelope in a determined voice, 'and the agents seem to think that Ensleigh Gardens will be completed by then, we shall have to start getting things organised. We shall have to start thinning things out very soon. I'm talking about the furniture now, Henry. I'm talking about the bookcase. I really don't think it will fit into your bedroom. It's only a single room. It's very small.'

'Don't worry about the bookcase, my sweet,' said Henry soothingly. 'All you have to do is make a list of the items you want to dispose of and I shall see to it. I promise you won't have to give it another thought. I shall contact the auction house and have everything collected. You can leave it all to me. Only say the word and I shall arrange it.' *Only say the word,* thought Henry, *and I shall dispose of Penelope. Only say the word and I shall arrange Penelope under the floor-*

boards wrapped in vinegar and brown paper. Penelope neatly packed into seventeen cardboard boxes. Dusty old Penelope. Mouldy old Penelope. Henry Lamb smiled winningly at his wife. 'And whilst I am about it, I shall ask them to include my collection, the bookcase, my book stock and the sale catalogues. How does that sound? What do you think of that?' Henry enjoyed playing games. Henry beamed. 'I'm thinking of you, my sweetheart, I'm thinking of what you would like. I'm thinking that you really don't want your nice new flat cluttered up with my disreputable things, do you? You don't want my ugly old bookcase and my dirty books and my untidy cartons and my dusty sale catalogues, you really don't. They would make the place look untidy, wouldn't they? Of course they would. I *understand* Penelope, I really do. So if that is what you want, my dearest, my absolute treasure, that is what you shall have. I shall see to it personally. Trust me.'

Penelope stared. Henry,' she began in a faltering voice, 'I didn't mean... I only wanted you to...'

'No thinking allowed,' said Henry firmly. 'And as retirement looms, and as all these changes are shortly to take place, I have a surprise for you. I have decided that we shall go away for Christmas. We shall spend a few blissful days in a comfortable country house hotel. What do you think of that? No...' Henry held up a pink and cherubic hand. 'No objections please! This is my treat and I am going to arrange it. It will be our last little extravagance.'

Penelope was so taken by surprise that she sat down rather suddenly on the settee with her thick and rather shapeless legs stuck out in front of her like a jointless doll. For once, she was quite lost for words. Of course, she was not to know that what Henry termed "our last little extravagance" could turn out to be true in more ways than one might suppose. How could she possibly know? Only Henry knew that. Only Henry Lamb with the angelic face and the dark and murderous thoughts knew that, and Henry wasn't telling. Oh no, Henry wasn't saying a word.

* * *

Len Sparkes had been dozing in his conservatory and when he opened his eyes his son's fancy car was on the drive. 'What now, Sadie,' he said to his old black Labrador. 'To what momentous event do we owe this unexpected visit, I wonder?' Wearily, he hauled himself to his feet and made his way to the kitchen to put the kettle on. Sadie began to scratch at the front door in a way that, twelve months ago, would definitely not have been allowed.

Len had converted this cottage for his wife, Rupert's mother, who had not lived long enough to appreciate it. Now Len lived alone with the fruits of his labours. He had been self-employed all his working life, surrounded by clients, craftsmen and casual labourers. Loneliness was something he was still coming to terms with. He saw Rupert less often than he would have liked, but would not have admitted it. He may have thought it but he would not have said it out loud. Not to Rupert. He didn't want sympathy. He didn't want visits made out of obligation. He didn't want the few visits he had to be increased and compromised by guilt, by duty. 'What brings you to this neck of the woods then, son? Not your usual day of the week for visiting, unless I've read the calendar wrong.'

Rupert rubbed Sadie behind her ears and looked ruefully at the line of slobber decorating his trouser leg. 'She's getting too fat. It's not good for her. You should go for more walks.'

'I'm not much of a walker.'

This was true. Len was more of a worker than a walker. 'All the same, it's not good for her. She really is overweight.'

'Come to lecture me about Sadie, have you?'

'Not really. Good thing you've got the kettle on. I've come to ask a favour.'

'Funny you should say that.' Len reached for a tray and the sugar bowl. Not that his son would have any sugar. Sometimes Len felt he was the last person on earth who liked two spoonfuls in his tea. 'Get the milk out the fridge then. And get the biscuit tin out whilst you're about it. We'll have our tea in the conservatory.'

'Nice this, isn't it? Good bit of workmanship.' Rupert put the tea tray on the coffee table and fended off Sadie, who was eying the ginger biscuits. 'You've painted it again since I was last here.'

'Wasn't sure about the colour at first. It's growing on me now.'

'I like it. Farrow and Ball, I bet.'

Len sank back into his armchair and grinned. 'Farrow and Ball-ish. I had it mixed to match.'

Rupert poured the tea. His dad knew his trade. Whatever it was, tiles, timbers, handmade bricks, fancy ironwork, conservatories or paint, he always knew how to get the right effect for half the cost. That's why he, Rupert, was here. Unexpected. Unscheduled.

They sat for a few minutes looking out onto the neat lawn and the flower beds that had been planted by Rupert's mother and were now meticulously tended by Len as her legacy. Sadie flopped down on the tiles between them, her eyes still on the biscuits.

'So what's what, then?' Len took a sip of his tea from a

mug with a pansy on it. 'What's to do? Got the sack, have you? Getting married?'

'No to both of those. I came to ask you something. I want to know if you are enjoying retirement. I wondered how you are managing here, all on your own, except for good old Sadie, of course.'

Len thought about it. He didn't want to mention loneliness. Or depression. Or the aches and pains that were the result of giving up an active life to sit in an armchair drinking tea, reading detective novels, watching TV and doing Sudoku puzzles. 'It's too late to change my mind now. I've got rid of the business. I've sold up, and that's the end of it.'

'It might not be. I've got a suggestion to make. I might have a job for you, if you are interested.'

Len put his mug back on the tray. Was his son about to suggest he become a pot boy at the hotel? A kitchen porter, scouring dirty plates in the wash-up? Wheeling out the rubbish? 'A job for me? What sort of job? How come?'

'Anna, the girl I've told you about, the girl I work with, she wants to convert this old ruin of a house into a hotel. I've said I'll help. I've said I'd ask you if you would be the project manager; you know, a sort of clerk of works, organising the job. I wondered if you would be interested.'

Good God. This was a turn up for the book. Unexpected wasn't the word for it. Nevertheless: 'Interested is one thing. I may be interested but I'm too old now; too decrepit. Anyhow, I made my decision, I retired.'

'Then un-retire. You still have the expertise. You still have your contacts. And you're far from decrepit—you haven't been retired all that long, you would soon get back into it. And you have to be bored, sitting here on your backside all day. Look at you,' Rupert gestured at the puzzle books, the stack of novels, the conservatory painted again before it needed it, just for something to do. 'You could at least just come and have a look. See how you feel about the job. See if you fancy it.'

'What about your own job? I thought you were doing OK where you are, assistant manager and all that. I thought you were settled.'

'I am. I was. But I've made the decision now. If it works out, it could be good.'

Len knew his son well enough to recognise doubt when he heard it. *If*, not *when*. 'You don't sound so sure. Has she got the money?'

'Not enough. Not nearly enough. It's a big project.'

'So you don't know if it's going to work, and you don't think she's got enough money, so you could be on a loser and you're giving up a good job. Why would you do it?'

Rupert took a sip of tea from a mug with a foxglove on it. He supposed he had better come clean. 'To tell the truth I'm a bit keen on her, Dad. Not just a bit, I suppose. If I'm honest I have to say I'm really keen. I don't want her to go off somewhere else without me. I don't want her to find herself another manager. I don't want to lose her.'

'And this girl, Anna, is she keen on you?'

'Not yet.' As well as not yet, Rupert could have added maybe not ever. He would not mention that their tentative relationship had failed, nor would he mention the unexplained absences; his suspicion that Anna may have a relationship elsewhere, nor the incredibly agonising, gut-wrenching pain of hopeless, unrequited, longing. 'Well, you know me, Dad,' he said lightly. 'Your unpredictable offspring. Contrary as ever.'

'You're not kidding. It's bloody typical this is.'

'What is?' As if he didn't already know. As if he couldn't anticipate what was coming.

'Of all the girls you've had, of all the girls you could have had, you have to pick on one who doesn't care a fig for you.'

'I didn't say she didn't care a fig.' There had, of course, been many girls in Rupert's past. Far too many girls in Len's opinion. Not all had been treated kindly. Was Anna his come-uppance? 'She's a friend, and that's a start.'

'Not much of one, in my book. Not enough to leave a good job for. Still, I'll come and have a look. Only a look. No promises, mind.'

As Rupert's car drew out of the drive Len collected up the mugs and put them on the tray. He carried the tray into the kitchen. Was it his imagination, or did he suddenly feel better? Less weary, more invigorated? 'Well, it looks as if we've a bit of excitement in prospect now, Sadie. Property restoration, eh? Project management, eh? We weren't expecting *that* to land on our doorstep today, were we? Mind you, building works is one thing and love is quite another. Love can be the very devil. We'll have to watch our step there, Sadie girl, because you can guarantee that when love comes into it things can get complicated. Things can get messy. Oh yes, only one thing's certain and that is when love comes in the door, common sense flies straight out the window.'

Sadie, who knew nothing of love but a lot about devotion, loyalty and the desirability of ginger biscuits, thumped her tail on the kitchen tiles. Len patted her soft head affectionately and took the lid off the biscuit tin.

Chapter Thirteen

'Ah, the Angel Gabriel.' Vivian had tottered down the brick passage wearing an ancient dressing gown and dusty monogrammed slippers. 'Some woman to see you. Got a card out of the post office apparently.' He flopped onto a chair, wheezing.

'You should be in bed,' Anna said severely. 'Doctor's orders. You can't get up until next week.'

'Bloody doctor. What does he know? Can't do this. Can't do that. I want to see what's going on. My *house* you know. My *land.*'

'Of course it is.' Anna took him by the arm. 'And as soon as the doctor gives you the green light you will be in the thick of it. They have started to strip the tiles off this wing already. It's too cold for you to be wandering about in just your pyjamas. I'll take you back to bed. Would you like a hot drink?'

'Wouldn't mind a whisky.'

'You know you are not allowed whisky. It's bad for your heart.' Anna looked at his downcast face and her own heart melted. This was, after all, her own drowned man; the old man she had rescued from the mere; the man who had gripped the sides of the wheel barrow and quoted the Old Testament: *Cast me not off in the time of my old age; forsake me not when my strength faileth.* 'I tell you what, if you go back to bed, I'll bring you some brandy and warm milk.'

Vivian got up from the chair with what might almost have passed for alacrity in a geriatric patient. 'I'll tell her you'll be five minutes then. Fine figure of a woman, I must say.' He added hopefully, 'Nurse, is she?'

'In your dreams,' said Anna.

'You can forget about the warm milk.' Vivian tottered off down the brick passage. 'Just bring the brandy.'

* * *

'Mrs Sholto, if you will forgive me for saying so,' said Anna a little warily, when they were safely seated at the plank table and Sir Vivian was back in bed sipping brandy with honey and hot water. 'You don't actually *look* like a gardener. To be perfectly frank, you are not at all what I was expecting.'

Mrs Sholto, whose high-heeled sandals had barely survived the brick floor of the passage, wore a full-skirted floral print dress topped with a cardigan of breath-taking whiteness and three rows of fake pearls. Her extravagantly large spectacles had flamingo pink frames and the generous curls of her hennaed hair were held in check by two diamanté combs. She was about forty years of age with a trim figure and quite striking in her way, but it was true that she was nobody's idea of a gardener.

'I expect I've overdone it a bit, as usual,' she said apologetically. 'I did so want to look nice for the interview and I expect I've gone right over the top. I try too hard, Miss Gabriel, that's my trouble. I put in a lot of effort. My Arnold always said "Mavis, you never do anything by halves; with you, it's all or nothing," and he was right, he really was. I particularly wanted to make a good impression today because the stars are with me, Miss Gabriel, Mars being in Aries. I'm a great believer in the stars; we're all governed by the planets whether we like it or not, and when I saw your card in the post office it hit me like a bolt from the blue, it really did. Mavis, I said to myself, this is *it*. This is *you*. You've done all you can with your own little plot and this is fate giving you a chance to spread your wings. I put a lot of trust in fate, Miss Gabriel, although fate is determined by the stars, it quite definitely is. I'm a student of astrology, you've probably guessed it, and when I saw your little card I just knew it was heaven sent.' Mavis Sholto leaned over the plank table in a confiding manner. Her scent was overpowering and her lipstick applied with a lavish ferocity. 'I must confess to having a little potter round the garden on my way in and from what I've seen you certainly need a gardener to sort you out, Miss Gabriel, you really do.'

'We do,' agreed Anna, who had decided that plain speaking was the best way out of an awkward situation, 'but to be honest, Mrs Sholto, I was expecting a man. This garden needs restoration. Nothing has been done here for years and there is a lot of heavy work involved. I am not talking about a bit of light digging and planting, I am talking about cleaning out ditches, scything banks, repairing walls and rebuilding glasshouses. I am talking about earthworks, about mowing acres of grass with heavy machinery, about clipping yew hedges twenty feet high. I am talking about hard, physical labour. I am not talking about woman's work.'

'Oh, I realise *that*, Miss Gabriel,' Mavis Sholto said confidently, 'that's why I'll be bringing Barry.'

'Barry?' enquired Anna faintly.

'Barry from the village, Miss Gabriel. He's mute, I'm afraid, and not quite all there in the head due to being partially asphyxiated at birth, but put him in front of a mower or a pile of bricks and he's as happy as a lark. Oh yes, Barry will deal with all your scything and your earthworks and glasshouses, there's no problem about that and he's yours for four pounds an hour as long as it's cash in hand and no questions asked. He's ideally suited to the rough, Miss Gabriel, and the rougher the better; you'd be doing him a favour, you really would. He does love to mow and he's rather run out of work down in the village; well, you've only to look at the churchyard and the cricket pitch and the verges mown nearly into Earl Soham to appreciate Barry's work, and if you want a reference for my own gardening skills, number twenty-five The Glebe is all down to me and it's the show garden of the village, even though I do say it myself.' Here, Mavis Sholto paused for breath, but before Anna could utter a word, gripped her by the sleeve and looked at her imploringly. 'The thing is, Miss Gabriel, that since my poor Arnold departed, I've taken to gardening in a big way; I see it as my salvation; I'm very keen. I subscribe to *Gardener's Weekly* and I've been to Wisley and Kew. I never miss a gardening programme on the television. I know a lot about gardening, Miss Gabriel, I really do. My hanging baskets and my petunias stop people in their tracks, you can take my word for it.'

'But Mrs Sholto,' Anna struggled to find suitable words with which to explain the difference in scale and style between a modest plot in front of a modern bungalow and the large, formally landscaped ground of a grand country house without causing offence or sounding superior, and failed. 'Mrs Sholto,' she said in a gentle voice, 'these gardens are simply enormous. The gardens are *huge*.'

'I need a bigger canvas to work on, Miss Gabriel.' Behind the flamingo pink spectacle frames Mavis Sholto's eyes were beseeching and her words were heartfelt. 'I need something enormous. I need something huge. My Arnold going like he did was a catharsis for me. It freed a lot of repressed emotion. It released a lot of latent energy. These days I've far too much energy for my own good. I've got all this newly discovered talent and dynamism and I see your garden as a golden opportunity, I really do. I'm meant to come here, Miss Gabriel, you can believe me absolutely when I say that everything is predestined. I've drawn up my own astrological birth chart and you would be amazed at what it revealed about my future, you really would.'

'I probably would, but Mrs Sholto, without wishing to offend you in any way, I really don't think...' Anna's attention was momentarily diverted by the ringing of a telephone in the office next door to the kitchen, where Rupert had set up a makeshift desk constructed out of two bales of loft insulation material and a slab of chipboard.

'I'm afraid you will have to excuse me now, Mrs Sholto. I have to answer the telephone.' Anna made an attempt to rise from the table only to be forestalled by hands too pale and delicate to belong to any gardener, the perfectly manicured nails of which flamed with a deep vermillion varnish.

'I can see you're doubtful, Miss Gabriel,' Mavis Sholto said in a deeply understanding tone, 'and I don't blame you one little bit, I really don't. You don't know me from Adam, and if you'll forgive me for taking the initiative, I'll make a suggestion: we'll come for a week and work for nothing, Barry and me, and we'll see how we get on. That way, if we don't suit, there's no harm done at all. I think that would be the best way round it.'

'Well, I'm not altogether sure...' But Anna was hesitant,

the telephone caller was persistent, and the most unlikely gardener in the world had a will of steel.

'That seems to be settled then.' Mavis Sholto gathered up her immaculate little straw handbag and her white lace gloves and got to her feet. 'Now there's no need to show me out. I can find my own way. You go and answer your telephone and I'll make myself scarce, Miss Gabriel, I'll be on my way. We'll see you on Monday morning come fair weather or foul, it makes no difference to Barry and me, rain or shine, it's all the same to us. We'll start at eight, if that's all right with you; I've always been an early riser, six o'clock and I'm wide awake at the first stroke. My Arnold used to say, "I'll never need an alarm clock whilst you're around, Mavis," and he was right, he definitely was. I'm at my best first thing in the morning; ready to take on the world and a mind like a rapier. It's all to do with when the planets rise in your star sign, but I'll take you through it on another occasion when we've more time. Until Monday then, Miss Gabriel, and it's been a pleasure to meet you, it really has.'

As Mavis Sholto's high-heeled sandals clicked their way down the brick passage, Anna ran into the office and grabbed up the telephone.

'Well, it took you long enough, I must say,' said Henry Lamb amiably. 'I was just about to hang up. I've been given your number by the Crown Hotel at Framlingham and I would like to make an enquiry about a possible Christmas break. There would just be the two of us; just myself and my very dear wife, Penelope...'

Chapter Fourteen

'Hap-py birth-day to you, hap-py birth-day to you; hap-py birth-day dear Nor-man; hap-py birth-day to you!' To a small burst of applause, Yvonne trotted into the office on her spiky heels, in her tubular short skirt, bearing aloft a minis-cule iced cake with a single candle burning. There had been several Yvonnes, but the ceremony never altered. Now Elsie, with the usual huffing and puffing that accompanied any exertion on her part, leaned down and produced from under her desk a tissue-wrapped bottle of dark, sweet sherry, whilst Genevra fussed around, organising the glasses onto the tin tray decorated with a view of Balmoral Castle. (None of them, to Norman's knowledge, had ever been there.)

'There now,' said Elsie, as she always did, 'I bet you thought we'd forgotten you, Norman! Come on, admit it! I bet you did!'

'Never,' protested Norman, as he invariably did. 'I knew you wouldn't forget!' Although every year he secretly hoped they might and was inevitably disappointed. The ceremony progressed. Norman blew out the candle. The cake was cut.

Paper serviettes were distributed. It was Norman's privilege to be presented with the first glass, the first slice. Now came the worst part.

'For he's a jol-ly good fel-low; for he's a jol-ly good fel-low; for he's a jol-ly good fe-el-low, and so say all of us!'

Glasses chinked together. 'And how many years are we celebrating today, Norman? Well, *we* remember, even if you don't! Sixty-nine years to the day and you don't look a day older than sixty and that's the truth, isn't it girls? A very happy birthday to you, Norman, and many more of them!'

Carefully packaged gifts came next: a giant handker-chief with a few bars of music printed on it. ('Pity you haven't got your violin with you, Norman; we could have had a tune!') A box of continental chocolates from Thorn-tons. ('At least you've kept your figure, Norman! Slim as a willow, and straight as a die, isn't he girls? Not like me. Not like poor old Elsie!') A pottery mug bearing the legend OLD ACCOUNTANTS NEVER DIE, THEY JUST LOSE THEIR BALANCE. ('No offence intended, Norman, it just seemed appropriate for the occasion, don't you think?')

But old accountants do die, thought Norman, *and I have almost outlived my threescore years and ten. Next year I shall be seventy. I am old!* Norman didn't feel old. He didn't feel any older today than he had felt ten years earlier when he had been fifty-nine, and that had felt quite old enough at the time. Sixty-nine years! It didn't seem possible, but a birthday was a birthday, and a date on a birth certificate was a date on a birth certificate, whichever way you looked at it. There was no way of putting the clock back. Norman was sixty-nine; like it or lump it.

In the midst of the celebration, the shop doorbell pinged. The shop, with its sparse selection of stationery, its shelves of dusty box files and its racks of dog-eared greeting cards; most of which were beginning to acquire a genuine period charm, was separated from the office area by a low partition of frosted glass. Above this partition now appeared a long, sallow face with a drooping moustache.

Elsie heaved herself to her feet in greeting. 'Well, now, here's Mr Allison come to see us! Genevra, have you got Mr Allison's printing ready for him? Pardon the festivities, Mr Allison, but we're having a little tipple on the occasion of Norman's birthday; sixty-nine years to the day, and to look at him you would never believe a word of it. Come round, Mr Allison, dear; come round to the inner sanctum and join us in a glass of sherry, if you will. It's not every day Norman has a birthday, is it Norman?'

'No, indeed,' agreed Norman in a heartfelt voice. 'Once a year is quite enough.'

Mr Allison stood beneath a dusty Christmas garland, pinned up years ago by one of the Yvonnes and never taken down. From it was suspended a pleated paper bell which had once been red but was now faded to an unwholesome shade of orange. He was tall and thin and everything about him drooped; his moustache, his shoulders, his trousers, his tweed jacket and the forlorn little scrap of his bow tie. Even the few sad strands of hair he had arranged carefully over his scalp refused to stay in position and drooped forward over his brow.

'Good health to you, Norman,' he said in his whispery, apologetic voice. 'A very happy birthday. I must say you are wearing very well. I had no idea you were sixty-nine. You wear your years very lightly. I am amazed.'

'I'm pretty amazed myself,' confessed Norman. 'I don't know where all the years have gone and I don't want to be sixty-nine years old at all. I don't like it. It doesn't seem just cause for celebration as far as I'm concerned and I rather wish people wouldn't keep reminding me.'

'Now, Norman, don't be a spoil sport', admonished Elsie. 'You know you enjoy your birthdays just as much as we do.'

'All the same,' said Mr Allison hastily, 'I do understand how you feel.' Already his glass was empty and he looked longingly at the sherry bottle on Norman's desk.

Norman took pity on him and refilled his glass.

'Thank you, Norman. Thank you very kindly. This is an unexpected treat, I must say. Well, *tempus fugit*, Norman. The sands of time and all that, eh?' He drained the glass with one swallow. The Adam's apple in his throat barely moved.

I can't stand much more of this, Norman said to himself, as he had said to himself for the past thirteen years, I have to get out of this place. It's pathetic. We are all pathetic. I have to get a grip. I have to make a move.

Genevra, bustling and fluttering over the simple matter of obtaining Mr Allison's signature for the collection note, irritated Norman so much that he had to turn away. In despair, and in defiance of his usual custom, he poured himself a second glass of sherry. He disliked it intensely but felt it might have a numbing effect on his sensibilities. Yvonne, gathering up crumpled serviettes, winked at him in a conspiratorial manner. This Yvonne had only been in the job for a few months but already she had confided to Norman that she was looking for something else. 'Something a bit more demanding, if you know what I mean; something a bit more interesting; no disrespect intended to anybody here, Norman, you're all lovely people and its very cosy like, it's just... well it's just a bit stuffy, that's all.' The Yvonnes never stayed long. Who could blame them? This

Yvonne had a tiny waist and legs like a racehorse. Today she had piled up her mass of auburn hair and secured it to the top of her head with what looked like two knitting needles. They stuck out like two little horns with knobs on. These, and the extravagantly long false eyelashes she had attached to the lids of her large and rather languorous (Elsie would have said vacant) hazel eyes, reminded Norman of a giraffe he had once taken a photograph of at Dudley Zoo. Norman liked this Yvonne. He would miss her.

Of course, Norman had not intended to stay long either. In the early days he had tried for more demanding jobs, more interesting jobs, better paid positions. He had become a familiar figure at the job centre on his days off. He had scanned the situations vacant columns in the local newspapers, written letters, even attended a few interviews. But his age had been against him and gradually the constant rejections had nibbled away at his self-esteem. He had become discouraged and depressed. A feeling of hopelessness had seeped into his soul and he had stopped trying. Nobody would touch him with a bargepole now, not at almost seventy years of age. Yet, I can't stay here, he thought in despair. I can't put up with this for the rest of my life. My brain will shrivel to the size of a walnut. Yet, if he was honest, the alternative, the thought of retirement, frightened him. The prospect of sitting in his little terraced house just off the Mile End Road alone with his memories, giving the odd violin lesson to eke out his pension, warming up his Bird's Eye Dinner for One, terrified him. So I shall probably die here, he thought, bent over my desk, sitting in this very chair. I shall carry on entering up the invoices in the sales ledger, filling in the quarterly VAT return, balancing the totals in the analysis book, my head getting greyer and greyer and lower and lower until one day Elsie will say

'You're very quiet today, Norman. You haven't said a dickey bird all morning, has he, girls? Out on the tiles again last night, were we?' And then, a little louder, 'I said, you haven't got much to say for yourself today, Norman! Cat got your tongue, has it?' Then, as panic set in, 'Norman? *Norman!'*

'*Norman!'* Elsie's voice, interrupting his reverie, made him jump. 'Mr Allison was just asking how long you've been with us! I'm telling him it must be at least twelve or even thirteen years, because it's got to be fifteen years since Clark Strang folded. Oh yes, Mr Allison, our Norman was one of the lucky ones; he took the redundancy before the crash came; he saw the writing on the wall. Well, he would, wouldn't he, being an accountant. Now it's thirteen years he's been with us and it only seems like yesterday he walked through that door; such a nice, softly spoken little man I thought he was, a lovely manner with him and quite dapper in his way; we were lucky to get him; he was too good for the likes of us if the truth be told. I bet you didn't know our Norman was properly certified, did you, Mr Allison? Oh yes, quite a high flyer was our Norman in them days; a real accountant, he was, with all examinations passed and paper qualifications, the lot. Will you have another little tipple to help you on your way, dear? Well, why not? A little of what you fancy does you good, and so say all of us. It is Norman's birthday, after all, and he won't see sixty-nine again, and that's a certain fact.'

When Mr Allison had left, clutching the box of copying to his chest and colliding with the card racks on his unsteady progress towards the door, they settled back to work: Norman preparing the monthly statements, and Elsie, Genevra and Yvonne packing a promotional mailing for a charity Christmas catalogue.

'Now we've got Norman's birthday over,' said Elsie, when she was comfortably ensconced again behind her desk and engaged upon peeling address labels from a seemingly endless roll and slapping them onto polythene mailers. 'The next event on the social calendar will be Christmas. It might seem a long way off now, but it comes round quicker than you think; once we get past Halloween and Guy Fawkes night, Christmas will be on us before we can say Jack Robinson, just you mark my words.'

'If I was rich,' Yvonne said dreamily, 'which I'm not, as you very well know, but if I was, I'd fly off somewhere really exotic for Christmas every year. I fancy the Bahamas, myself, people do say it's ever so nice, all white sand and palm trees, but I expect it'll be just my mum and me again this year with half a box of crackers and a turkey breast from Tesco, killing time, waiting for the shops to open on Boxing Day.'

'Oh, I like Christmas,' said Genevra. 'I know it's got too commercialised, but I must confess that I always enjoy it. I like going home in the dark evenings with the shops all decorated and warm-looking, and fairy lights in people's windows. We always go to Elsie's for Christmas Day, Norman and me, and she spoils us something rotten with special treats and all her nice little touches. Elsie always does us proud, don't you, Elsie?'

'Well, I do make a nice mince pie,' Elsie admitted, 'and even if I say it myself, I've never tasted a better chestnut stuffing than my own. I make my own rich fruit cake with marzipan and last year I tried a new recipe for Christmas pudding with breadcrumbs and it came out a treat. Light as a feather it was, and Genevra had two helpings, didn't you, dear?'

Norman would never know exactly what prompted him

to say it; whether it was the result of his own resolve, or the extra glass of sherry; but, 'I'm glad you mentioned Christmas, Elsie,' he said. 'Because I won't be coming to you this year, I'm afraid. I've made other arrangements.'

Elsie stopped peeling labels. Genevra stopped pushing catalogues into the polythene mailers. Even Yvonne, who had been counting the packets into twenty-fives and snapping them with elastic bands before dropping them into the Royal Mail letter sacks at her feet, stopped work and stared at him.

'Other arrangements?' said Elsie in tones of the very greatest astonishment. 'What other arrangements?'

'I've been invited to stay with friends,' said Norman. 'I'm very sorry, Elsie, but every year they invite me to stay and every year I refuse, and I thought that just this once I should... that perhaps I should...' Norman heard his voice falter, felt his resolve weakening. He reminded himself of the stifling heat of Elsie's over decorated, over furnished house; the unutterably stultifying sameness of the conversation; the dry little mince pies, all pastry and no filling; the frozen turkey that somehow managed to taste of fish, the glutinous gravy, the tough roast potatoes, the truly horrifying colour and texture of the stuffing; the flaming horror of the Christmas pudding, full of pips and stalks and solid knobs of candied peel, everything pressed upon him with infinite kindness and generosity and a genuine concern for his comfort and enjoyment, and he knew that he would not be able to endure it, not this year, not next year, never again. But he was a poor liar and unaccustomed to being the cause of upset, and his new-found resolve deserted him completely in the face of Elsie's incredulity and the sight of Genevra's stricken face. 'On second thoughts, I think I shall probably write and tell them that I won't be able to make it this year,' he said. 'I feel sure I could manage to excuse myself again without causing offence.'

'You'll do no such thing!' Having overcome her astonishment, Elsie now decided that a change of surroundings was just what Norman needed. 'You've been looking a bit peaky of late, dear, if you don't mind me saying so, and a change is as good as a tonic at times. You go off and enjoy yourself with your friends and don't you give us another thought. We'll still be here when you get back, won't we girls? I must say, Norman, I would never have guessed that all the times you've been to mine you've been turning down a chance to be with your own friends,' she said warmly. 'I'm flattered, Norman, I don't mind admitting it. Not that you won't be missed, dear, because you will, but I'll see you don't miss out. I'll put aside a few mince pies in my Tupperware and you shall have them for New Year with a glass of my best sherry and a slice of my Christmas cake if it's successful; I'm trying a Delia Smith recipe this time for a lighter cake with crystallised fruit in it; I'm living dangerously this year, Norman; we oldies mustn't get too set in our ways which is why you should go off and have a good time with your friends and we'll look forward to hearing all about it when you come back. It will give us something to look forward to, won't it, girls?'

'We shall miss you though, Norman,' Genevra ventured. She turned a little pink as she said this, and kept her eyes on the catalogue in front of her, the cover of which featured an artist's impression of an Edwardian Christmas with a laughing family, a blazing fire, a tree with real candles, and a spaniel with a ribbon around its neck. In her imagination, Genevra placed Norman in the wingback chair by the hearth with the pile of beautifully wrapped presents at his feet. She tried to feel glad for him but could only feel her own disappointment. 'I shall miss your violin recital especially. It won't be the same without you.'

Norman felt mean. He was fond of Genevra. He had opened up to her once. Unusually, he had talked about his early life. He had been a professional fiddle player with a well-known band. They had played all over the country in dance halls before settling themselves in London, playing the clubs and the big hotels including the Ritz and the Savoy. They had played for a dance or two at Buckingham Palace. They even had a regular spot on the radio. He had been happy then, in the years before his life had fallen apart. He had been in love with their pianist and vocalist, Lilly Lamont, from the moment he first saw her. But Norman had been a humble and inexperienced third violin, obliged to worship from afar, watching enviously as the first violin played duets with his beloved, plotting and practising so that he could take his place, imagining himself sharing the limelight as an equal; respected, noticed. Norman had worked his way up to second violin when war broke out. To his dismay the band had been split in two. Norman's half were sent to entertain the troops. Lilly Lamont sang and played with the other half in town halls and barracks across the country and, as the war progressed, in convalescent homes, performing sentimental, patriotic songs that broke your heart. When the band reassembled after the war Norman had found himself, at last and deservedly, first violin. By now he was skilled and played with a passionate and artistic intensity. Through his playing he had wooed and won Lilly Lamont, and the painful desperation of it, the piercingly sweet agony of their affair, had haunted him ever since. It had ended when he had been loaned to another band whilst their first violin had his appendix removed. When he returned, the love of his life had gone; left to get married they had said; replaced by another vocalist. Just like that. It had felt as if his heart had been torn out of his chest. He had drawn a veil over that part, of course.

After leaving the band, he had trained for a new career as an accountant. Numbers rather than people. Rows of figures that taxed the brain but left the heart untouched. Norman was damaged goods. He avoided emotion. Now he was disturbed to find himself the cause of it. He opened his mouth to tell Genevra he had changed his mind, that he no longer wanted to stay with his friends but would much prefer to spend Christmas day at Elsie's house, but Elsie was having none of it.

'Now don't you go putting him off, Genevra,' she said sharply, 'not when he's been invited. At his age he's got to strike whilst the iron's still hot; he's got to take his opportunities whilst he's still got his health and strength. Take no notice of her, Norman. You're going, and that's all there is to it.'

'These friends you're going to stay with...' began Yvonne.

'The Fletchers,' said Norman, a little wildly. 'Fletcher-Smyth. Hyphenated. Spelled with a "y".'

'These Fletcher-Smyths that you're going to stay with,' said Yvonne. 'Do they live in London? I hope you don't think I'm being nosey, Norman. Tell me to mind my own business, if you like.'

'Oh no, they don't live in London. They live in the country, in Suffolk, actually; miles from anywhere and very rural, very quiet. I expect I shall find it rather boring.' Norman was amazed at his own inventiveness.

'My mum lives in Suffolk,' said Yvonne, 'and you're right, it is boring. I suppose it's all right if you like peace and quiet and that, and the views are very nice, just miles and miles of nothing with a few trees dotted about and the odd cottage. I expect your friends live in a cottage, do they, Norman? I hope you've got some wellies, because you'll need your wellies if you're going to Suffolk; it can be ever so muddy in the country.'

'I expect I'll have to get some.' Norman wished they would change the subject. 'I haven't thought much about it yet, to tell the truth.'

'You'll have to get yourself one of those nice waxed jackets to keep the rain out as well,' Elsie advised. 'Everybody wears them in the country, and you'll need some thermal underwear and some good, thick socks and corduroy trousers for warmth; we can't have you catching pneumonia, can we? You'll need warm pyjamas and I'd take a hot-water bottle if I were you because it's several degrees colder in Suffolk due to being that much closer to Siberia: I read an article about it recently in one of my magazines. You could even be snowed up, and then what? We shall have to get you organised, Norman, I can see it coming. I bet you haven't even got a nice woollen pullover to your name!'

'I don't think I have,' admitted Norman. 'I doubt if I have ever really needed one.'

'Well, you need one now,' declared Elsie, 'so we shall have to take you shopping; we shall have to take you in hand. I've noticed a new shop open in the precinct called Country Cousins, we shall have to go there and fit you out. They're sure to have all the gear. We've got to send you off looking the part, Norman; we can't have you letting the side down!'

'It's a lovely shop,' Genevra offered. 'Although I've only ever looked in the window, I've never been inside.'

'I think I'd better come as well,' said Yvonne. 'That is, if you've no objection, Norman. You don't want to look too smart in the country; you don't want everything looking as if you've just walked out of a shop. You need to be careful what you buy; you need to look comfy and a bit lived-in, like, otherwise you'll just end up looking daft.'

'Now, just you watch it, young lady,' warned Elsie. 'There's no way we're going to send our Norman off looking daft. He'll look every inch the country gentleman by the time we've finished with him, won't you, Norman?'

Norman smiled weakly and bent back to his statements. Wellingtons. Thermal underwear. Thick socks. Christmas in the country with the Fletcher-Smyths. *Oh, what a tangled web we weave...*

Chapter Fifteen

'...and so we thought we could hold the carol service in our own little chapel,' Nicola said, adding (in a doomed attempt to forestall the inevitability of argument) 'Of course, I realise it looks a bit bleak.'

'Bleak!' Rupert looked around in disbelief. 'The place is bloody derelict!'

'Watch your language,' Anna warned. 'We are in a church.'

'We are not in a *church*; we are in a bloody ruin! You can't be serious about this! We can't have a service for our guests in *here*; it's madness to even suggest it. It just isn't *possible*.'

It was true that the prospect was not encouraging. The tiny Rushbroke chapel, almost hidden from view amongst a tangle of undergrowth behind the rose garden, was in a perilously dilapidated state. The sky was visible through the timbers of the roof, the pews had almost rotted away, the leaded windows were broken and bowed. Brambles flourished in the aisle, a few saplings had thrust up in the apse, ferns flattened themselves against the walls, fungus sprouted in the corners, commemorative shields had slipped down the crumbling walls, flagstones heaved. Two once imposing family tombs complete with effigies and weeping angels were suffocated by ivy.

'It would please my father more than anything to have one last service in this chapel,' Nicola said. 'I don't need to tell you that his health is failing. Is there no possibility that we could do it for his sake?'

Rupert sighed. Didn't they understand *anything*? He placed an elbow resignedly upon the corner of the solitary pew which remained in an upright position. It sank to the ground immediately with a splutter of protest accompanied by a puff of decay. He looked at Anna in mute appeal.

Anna looked away. Common sense told her that it was impossible to save the chapel but she was not ready to acknowledge it, not yet. With her foot she scraped leaves and debris from a memorial flagstone. *Rufus Algernon Lawrence Percival Rushbroke*, she read. HE DIED AS HE LIVED. She scraped a little further in the expectation of something more but HE DIED AS HE LIVED was all there was. She wondered how he had lived, this particular Rushbroke; how he had died. She wondered who had been responsible for choosing such an evasive epitaph; if they had realised that every word was imbued with disapproval; steeped in disappointment. She wondered if it was possible for anyone to live a life without accomplishing anything which might count in his favour at the end of it. Poor Rufus Algernon Lawrence Percival, thought Anna, surely if someone had cast around a little wider they could have come up with a better recommendation to accompany him into eternity.

'We do need to hold a service for our guests,' Nicola continued, 'and we can hardly take them to St. Saviour's, not when my father has been barred for interrupting the Reverend Beresford-Barnes.'

'If Vivian's fallen out with St. Saviour's then you either have to travel further afield or forget about the service altogether. Let the guests make their own arrangements. Not everyone goes to church at Christmas anyway.' The set of Rupert's jaw indicated that he was not to be swayed by emotional blackmail. 'Even with God in my team, I can't work a bloody miracle on this place, Nicola. I just can't do it. The place is falling down; you would have to be blind not to see it. I'm already working with a budget strained to bloody breaking point.' He shot a vengeful glance at Anna who responded with a tight little smile. 'Anna knows,' Rupert said heavily, 'that there are things we should do to the house that have had to be put on hold because we don't have the money to do them.'

Yes, Anna did know. Looking around now, she could actually feel the hopelessness of the chapel; the weakness of their case. Her eyes strayed to the roof as she drew in the breath of resignation, prepared at last to admit defeat. She saw that each miniature hammer beam ended in a pair of cherubs and that their arms were wrapped around each other. She noticed that the cherubs had no pupils to their eyes and appeared to be blind. 'What did you say about being blind?' she asked Rupert.

'I said the bloody place is falling down, you would be blind not to see it.'

Anna looked thoughtful. 'Rupert, is there absolutely no way we could patch up the chapel, just as a temporary measure?'

'No.'

'No way at all?'

'No.'

'And if I said that it had to be done?'

'I'd say that if you think I can patch this place up without money, materials and manpower, you are out of your sodding mind!'

Anna looked up. The cherubs looked down; their tiny mouths wide with anxiety. 'Nevertheless, I do say it has to be done,' Anna said decidedly. 'You will have to find a way.'

God, she was impossible. Why could she never take no for an answer? Rupert gritted his teeth. 'We are standing here looking up at the sky! There's no bloody roof! You wouldn't be allowed to bring people in here; the place is *unsafe.*'

'The roof timbers are still here. You could make it safe for one day. You could make it safe for one service. You wouldn't have to buy anything. You have the labour. It's so tiny, surely you can patch it up with materials salvaged from the house?'

'*Anna!*' Rupert turned to her furiously. He might have taken her by the shoulders to shake some sense into her had not Nicola moved quietly to her side and met his eyes with her own level gaze. He looked from one to the other, at their still faces, their blue-grey eyes and felt a curious feeling of unease, of disquiet. They were separate people but they stood before him as one. Somehow he knew there was no point in further argument. 'OK. Let's be realistic about this. Say I agreed to do what I could without spending any money. Say I sheeted the roof with a tarpaulin, put in a few props to support the beams. Say I put some plain glass in the windows and re-laid the floor. Say I patched up the walls and cleaned up the place. All you would have is a *shell!* There's no *light!* There's no *heat!* There are no *pews!* There's no bloody *vicar!*'

'There has never been light, other than candles,' Nicola said. 'The sconces are still here.'

'People can sit on chairs,' Anna said. 'Chairs are more comfortable than pews.'

'And there are two fireplaces,' Nicola pointed out. 'We can burn logs. People will be wearing outdoor clothing. Nobody expects to be warm in church.'

The lack of a vicar was not to be dwelt upon. The fact that the chapel had been deconsecrated decades ago was not even worthy of discussion. They looked at him expectantly.

Rupert closed his eyes. When he opened them again they were still looking at him. He stared back at them in exasperation. Had they any idea what a colossal amount of work there was to do; how impossibly tight the schedule was; how short of money they were going to be? Now, as if he hadn't already enough on his plate, he seemed to have this bloody wreck of a chapel to deal with as well. But Anna was the boss; it was her project; her money. Finally he said 'As long as you *realise* that *all* you are getting is the *shell*. The rest is down to you. You have to organise the *seating*, the *lighting*, the *heating*, the sodding *vicar* and everything else!'

He would have slammed the door as he left but it had fallen off its hinges years ago. Now it leaned heavily against the wall, barely leaving enough room for him to squeeze through the gap. Brambles snagged at his overalls. It was difficult to leave with dignity.

* * *

At the house, the chimneys had been repaired, repointed and rebuilt where necessary according to the original twisted Tudor design, supervised both by the council and English Heritage who had passed them as satisfactory and fit for purpose. The chimney sweep had departed leaving behind a respectable mountain range of soot and rubble and twigs and a line of rooks laid out in the courtyard arranged like biological specimens in strict order of decomposition from full-feathered to skeletal. Now Anna, Rupert, Len and Sadie stood inside the mighty armorial fireplace in the great hall and peered upwards at the tiny circle of blue sky far above them whilst, at their feet, emanating from a few smouldering twigs and charred twists of paper, swirled an indecisive fog of grey smoke.

Rupert picked up a smouldering twig and held it aloft. They watched as the smoke fanned out and curled around them. He said 'I can't understand why there isn't any draw. The smoke would rather go anywhere than up the chimney.'

'Maybe the brickwork is just too cold and damp,' suggested Anna. 'Maybe it needs to be warmed up gently.'

Vivian appeared from the garden. 'Trouble with the chimney?' he wheezed hopefully. 'Anything I can do?' He put his head inside the fireplace. *'Not till the fire is dying in the grate, look we for kinship with the stars,'* he intoned.

'You're beginning to sound like Mavis,' Anna said.

'A fine woman, Mavis. *Price beyond rubies.* I'm introducing her to the Old Testament. As a matter of fact, as I remember, there's another chimney up there. There are two of the blighters. Hang on. I've just the remedy.' He tottered off across the hall in order to rummage in a cupboard along the brick passage. He returned with a salmon fishing rod and manipulated it into the fireplace, pointing it upwards. 'See that shadow?'

They nodded.

'Well, it isn't a shadow at all, it's an elbow. It's another chimney.' So saying, Vivian gave the elbow a vigorous poke with the rod, as a result of which the whole chimney appeared to move. Only Sadie, reacting to some canine sixth sense and making for the front door like greased lightning, managed to escape. The soot fell with a soft, prolonged whooshing sound liberally coating them all and landing with a gentle thud about knee height, from whence it overflowed in a steady avalanche into the hall, flooding the flagstones.

'There you are!' spluttered Vivian in triumph. 'What did I tell you? Two chimneys!'

Chapter Sixteen

'We don't listen to music at the table, thank you.' Mary Pomeroy plucked the earphones from her son's head.

'Oh, Ma,' he complained, 'do you have to?'

'I do,' said Mary. 'Somehow I have to cling to the last vestiges of civilised behaviour otherwise I am lost.' She sat down at the table and began to serve fish pie.

'No fish for me,' said Emily. 'I don't eat fish.'

'Since *when?*' her mother demanded.

Emily shrugged. 'I just find the idea of eating anything with a face totally repugnant now, that's all. No fish. No meat. No animal derivatives.'

Mary sighed. She scraped off the fish and handed Emily a mound of potato crusted with cheese. 'Help yourself to vegetables. You are still eating vegetables, I suppose? They're not contaminated with pesticides? They're not radioactive?'

Tony Pomeroy came into the conservatory dressed in a track suit and trainers. His hair was wet, his skin was pink and his face shone. 'You started without me,' he said accusingly.

'Yes,' said Mary.

'Is there anything to drink?'

'Try the refrigerator.'

'Runner beans again,' commented Tom. 'I hope they're not stringy.'

'They are not stringy,' said his mother.

'The last lot were.'

'That was because Emily inadvertently picked the ones I was leaving on the plant to make seed.'

'I didn't know that,' protested Emily. 'How was I to know that? I'm not psychic. Is this vegetarian cheese?'

'You were not to know because I omitted to tell you. Yes it is.'

'I bet it isn't.'

'All right, it isn't.'

'I can't eat it then. Ordinary cheese is made with calves' intestine.'

'Anybody seen the bottle opener?' Tony enquired.

'I have seen it somewhere, now you come to mention it,' Mary said. 'It was in a very unusual place. I can't remember where I saw it, but I do distinctly remember wondering how it came to be there.'

'Well, that's a fat lot of help, isn't it? That's a *fat* lot of good!' Tony returned to the kitchen. A great deal of scrabbling and crashing and slamming of drawers ensued.

'I really can't eat this,' Emily said. 'The very thought of it makes me want to puke.'

'They *are* stringy.' Tom removed a chewed remnant of runner bean from his mouth and laid it on the side of his plate in reproach. 'I *knew* they would be.'

'Has anybody *any* idea where the bloody corkscrew is?' shouted Tony. 'Somebody must know. Who had it last?'

'You, for a guess,' shouted Tom. 'There's only one alcoholic in this house!'

'And what is that supposed to mean?' Tony's face appeared round the kitchen door. 'Exactly *what* is that supposed to mean!'

'All it means,' said Tom placidly, 'is that, all things considered, you were possibly the last person to use the corkscrew yourself. Probably,' he added, scraping a heap of beans to the side of his plate. 'More than likely.'

Emily, having already scraped to the side of her plate any of the potato which might possibly have been in contact with the fish sauce, now began to pick away at the cheese topping. She said in an aggrieved tone, 'This cheese has gone right through the potato. By the time I've got rid of it, there will be nothing left to eat.'

'Well, don't count on the beans being edible,' said Tom, 'unless you happen to like chewing razor blades.'

'*Jesus Christ!*' Mary exploded. '*Stop it! All of you!*' Everyone fell silent. Tom put down his fork. Emily stopped scraping away the cheese. Tony stood in the doorway, a bottle of Sancerre and the corkscrew in one hand, a clutch of stemmed wineglasses in the other.

Tom was the first to speak. 'Hey, Ma,' he said. 'No need to lose your cool. It's no big deal.' His tone was casual but his eyes, when they met Emily's across the table, held a warning.

'We weren't doing anything,' Emily said defensively. 'We were just eating.'

'Mealtimes in this house are like a battlefield,' said Mary. 'Sometimes I wonder why I bother. Sometimes I wonder why I don't leave you to fend for yourselves; why I don't just open the kitchen cupboards and let you eat what you like, when you like; why I don't leave you to graze like cattle. Sometimes I wonder why I struggle to get you to the table when you would obviously prefer to be somewhere else; why I bother to prepare food you would generally prefer not to eat.'

Nobody moved. Nobody spoke.

'Sometimes,' said Mary Pomeroy, 'I would like to walk out of this house and take myself off to live in an hotel. I would occupy a single room and sleep in a single bed made up with fresh white linen every day. My wardrobe would be full of clothes which, if not actually new and unworn, would be cleaned and pressed for me by someone else. My meals would be prepared especially for me and my table for one would have a crisply laundered cloth and a white napkin, stiffly starched and folded into a Bishop's mitre. That is what I would like my life to be. Just me. Nobody else. Everything pristine.'

The silence deepened. Everyone waited.

Mary Pomeroy looked up into the roof of the conservatory, to where the thick stems and strong, dark leaves of a Hoya had formed a lattice, starred here and there with bright crowns of wax-like pink flowers. (Not that she saw it; not that she thought it beautiful. Not, for that matter, that any of them had really looked at it and thought it beautiful.) Mary Pomeroy took a deep breath. 'Well now,' she said with a determined brightness. 'Lemon anyone? Parsley sauce?'

Relief was tangible. Everyone relaxed. Tom picked up his fork. Emily pushed the offending cheese to the edge of her plate. Tony made his way to the table and sat beside Tom. 'Get your bloody hair cut,' he said by way of a greeting. 'You look like a girl.'

'Fuck off,' returned Tom affably.

Mary Pomeroy winced. 'Language, Tom, *please*.'

'What's wrong with looking like a girl?' Emily wanted

to know. Not that she wanted to look like one. Not now. Not yet.

Tony poured himself a glass of wine and drained it in one draught. He offered the bottle around the table without response and poured himself a second glass. 'Whoever would have thought,' he said, 'that a man could find himself sitting down to lunch with a son who wears his hair in a ponytail, and a daughter sporting a short back and sides and Doc Martens. I haven't a clue what is happening in the world, but I have a gut feeling that something has gone terribly wrong somewhere.'

'It's probably something to do with steroid hormone implants in beef cattle and sheep,' Emily said gloomily. 'Either that, or fertilizer run-off from crops contaminating the water supply.'

Her father peered at her over the top of his wine glass. 'What the devil have you done to your eyebrows?'

Emily raised a hand and felt the vacant area where her eyebrows had once been as if to ascertain that they had not crept back into place whilst her attention had been elsewhere. 'Oh, those,' she said airily. 'I've shaved them off. I didn't really need them. Eyebrows are relatively superfluous in the human species these days. I decided I could get along just as well without them.'

'Good God!' Tony drained his second glass of wine.

'I thought *something* was different.' Tom stared at his sister. 'I was trying to work out what it was. You realise you'll have to shave forever now, Em? Every day? Because they'll keep growing back. Every morning you'll look in the mirror and see two lines of stubble.'

Mary Pomeroy closed her eyes. Just lately, when she was with her family, she experienced the discomforting sensation of having somehow strayed into an alien landscape, into a world where everything was surreal; where only the irrational could be considered the norm. She felt she was losing control. She lacked co-ordination. She felt that if she tried to walk, her feet might not touch the ground; that she would float. She felt lost and disorientated. She felt confused. She could not properly comprehend how she had acquired this family, how it had come about. These people, this husband, these children, were neither what she had desired, nor what she had expected. They were as unfamiliar to her as they were unfathomable. They were strangers.

Normally, Mary would have discussed the meaning of these sensations with her mother, but this was no longer possible. Mary Pomeroy's mother was not entirely absent (were not her ashes reposing still upon the rosewood bureau in the study, as yet unrelinquished, as yet unscattered)? but their customary thrice-weekly conversations were, understandably, not as comforting to Mary as once they had been. And Mary was currently most sorely in need of her mother's advice, of her sound, lets-have-no-nonsense-my-girl; there's-plenty-who'd-be-glad-to-change-places-with-you, sort of common sense.

When Mary looked at Tony she saw a man who, thrust too early into his father's shoes, had found himself not only ill-prepared and inexperienced, but also not nearly as able or astute as he had imagined himself to be. Since then, knowingly or unknowingly, he had applied himself to the task of proving his worth at something, at anything, not only in the workplace, but also as a husband and father, as well as in an endless succession of hobbies and sporting pastimes, every one of them entered into with the most enormous enthusiasm (not to mention expense) only to be abandoned the very moment it became clear that he was not destined to achieve the excellence he so desperately desired. For Tony Pomeroy was a driven man. Relentless in pursuit of some elusive inner satisfaction, never content and rarely relaxed, he was forever striving to demonstrate his ability, seeking not only to justify his position in life (for his father had left him a substantial fortune as well as a business with such well-schooled and practiced management that Tony had felt superfluous from the first day of his directorship) but also to vindicate himself for having fallen short of parental satisfaction. Mary had found this endearing at first but now she was, quite simply, exhausted. Mary's mother had taken the stout-hearted view that Mary could have done very much worse. 'He provides for you,' she had pointed out. 'You have a lovely home, a car, designer clothes, expensive holidays, private schooling for the children. You lack for nothing.' (There had been so many things lacking in her own married life that she was able to speak from a position of authority on this point.) 'And Tony obviously adores you. Be grateful for that.'

When Mary considered Tom, she saw a boy who had dropped out of university for no good reason that anyone had been able to establish, who had deliberately turned his back upon any kind of academic achievement or qualifications, who saw ambition as something to be pitied rather than admired, and who regarded conformity as a political plot perpetuated by the establishment in order to subjugate the individual. When Mary had despaired of Tom, her mother had told her not to worry. 'Tom will be all right. Tom's bright. He's just reacting to his father, that's all. He looks at Tony and he doesn't like what he sees. Should we blame him for that? Give him some space. Give him time. Tom's a sensible lad. He'll sort himself out.'

When Mary looked at Emily she shrank back in alarm.

She could not understand how her pretty, golden-haired daughter had turned overnight (or so it seemed) into this antagonistic, shaven creature stomping about the house in her hideous farm-labourer boots and her misshapen garments with their trailing hems and puckered seams; garments that looked as if they had been run up by an arthritic seamstress on a defective machine out of a pair of old curtains and a bedspread. When Mary recoiled from Emily, her mother had defended her. 'Don't interfere,' she had warned. 'Whatever you do, don't nag. Just accept her as she is. There's nothing wrong with Emily. She's just a normal teenager feeling her way in a dubious world. She's having an identity crisis. Emily's a clever girl. Look at her school reports. Look at her O-level results. She'll find her way eventually. Be patient.'

Now, Mary Pomeroy collected plates and conveyed them to the kitchen, returning with a bowl of fruit which she placed in the centre of the table. Her family looked at the fruit and then, as she resumed her position at the table, at Mary Pomeroy.

Tony spoke first. 'Is that it?' he enquired in a disappointed tone. 'We're not having a proper pudding then?'

'We are having fruit for pudding,' said Mary in a tense voice. 'If you care to cast your mind back to yesterday, when there was a proper pudding, you had to take off somewhere in a tearing hurry and were unable to partake of it. Tom was not hungry. Emily, for moralistic, ecological, or possibly even sociological reasons, declined. Today there is fruit.'

'Fine.' Tom selected a banana. 'Fruit's fine. What's wrong with fruit?'

Emily, with a show of reluctance helped herself to an apple.

'Don't ask me if they are organically grown,' her mother warned. 'Just don't say it.'

Emily, who had indeed been about to enquire into the provenance of her apple, contented herself by polishing it vigorously with her napkin to remove any surface contamination.

Tony poured himself another glass of wine. The bottle was almost empty. 'I'll stick with the grape, if you don't mind.'

'Why should I mind?' said Mary. 'Who cares whether I mind or not, anyway? What difference does it make?'

'You used to disapprove of more than one glass at lunchtime,' Tony reminded her. 'Somehow it used to make subsequent glasses taste that much better. Unrestricted drinking isn't half as much fun.'

And even that is my fault, I suppose, thought Mary. Even the taste of the third glass of wine is lacking because of something I have said or not said. Nothing I do or say is right for this family. Every word, every action only serves to earn me more reproach. Mary would have preferred to have felt anger but a great wave of misery washed over her instead, flooding her eyes with tears. 'I'll make some coffee.' She stumbled to her feet.

In the designer kitchen that her mother had so admired and coveted, Mary Pomeroy stood at the Butler sink, her hands gripping the cold porcelain. She closed her eyes against the grief and the despair but the scalding tears forced their way through her eyelids and dropped into the basin.

'Crikey, what are we supposed to have done now?' In Mary's absence Emily helped herself to the last inch and a half of wine. 'What was that about?'

Tony put a warning finger to his lips. 'I haven't the

faintest idea.' He looked with regret at the empty wine bottle. 'Quite honestly, I haven't a clue.'

'The happy pills don't seem to have done much good,' Tom said in a low voice. 'They were a dead loss. I think you should persuade Ma to go back to the quack.'

'You might care to suggest it yourself sometime,' said Tony wearily. 'The last time I mentioned it the balloon really went up. Anyone would have thought I'd suggested men in white coats and a test drive in a straitjacket.'

'Couldn't the quack do a home visit?' Emily wondered.

'Not unless the patient is unable to attend the surgery, apparently. When I last had words with the doctor, he said it was quite common to suffer a mild form of clinical depression following the death of a close relative. He seemed think it was premature to think in terms of prescribing long-term anti-depressant drugs or psychotherapy. He advised that we should just continue to be patient and understanding and see what happens.'

'What happens will be that we shall all end up needing psychotherapy,' Emily said glumly. 'That's what will happen.'

'Well, let's not dismiss it out of hand,' said Tom. 'We could go as a group. We could enrol for collective therapy. It might be more enjoyable than we think. It might be just the activity to fill our long winter evenings.'

'Don't be flippant,' warned Tony. 'Not about this, anyway.'

'I think it would help if we persuaded Ma to scatter Gran's ashes,' said Emily. 'I think it's really weird and unhealthy keeping them in the house. I think it's morbid. I don't think Gran would approve of it if she knew.'

'Where did Gran want to be scattered anyway?' Tom

wanted to know. 'Does anybody know? Did she leave any instructions?'

Tony shrugged. 'Not to my knowledge.'

'That's not like Gran, is it? She was always such an organised sort of bod; I'd have thought she'd have everything covered right down to the last knockings.'

'I think it would be a nice idea to scatter her over the vegetable patch,' Emily said. 'I think the ashes...'

'If you are about to say that Gran is biodegradable,' interposed Tony swiftly, 'I seriously warn you against it.'

'What I was about to say,' said Emily with dignity, 'is that the ashes would act as fertilizer and enrich the soil. Gran was particularly keen on recycling. She was always going on about waste, and I wasn't being disrespectful in the least.'

'Whilst that may very well be true,' said Tony, 'I doubt if your mother would be very receptive to such a suggestion at the moment, and I hope that nobody would be tactless enough to mention the disposal of Gran's ashes in the present circumstances.'

'We won't,' agreed Tom. 'No way. Positively not.'

'It was only a suggestion,' Emily said grumpily. 'Do you think we're going to get coffee, or not?'

'Remember what the good doctor said,' Tony reminded her. 'Be patient.'

'I don't suppose he specified exactly how long we had to be patient for?' Emily looked at her outsize black plastic Swatch. 'I've got to be in Bromley by three.'

Encouraging sounds came from the kitchen. China chinked. Coffee spoons rattled into saucers.

'Hold on,' said Tom. 'It's all about to happen.'

'Should I offer to help?' Emily looked questioningly at Tony.

Tony shook his head. 'Let's keep things normal, shall we? Just be here when it arrives, that's all.'

'Christmas is going to be a real barrel of laughs this year,' Tom commented morosely. 'We managed to ignore it last year, with Gran dying on Christmas Eve, but this year it's going to be pretty desperate. I don't know how we're going to get Ma through it.'

Tony said 'I've been thinking about that. I thought we might go away for Christmas this year, spend it somewhere different. It would mean we could avoid having to do all the usual things like putting up decorations and buying a tree; we could just pile into the car and take off. What do you think?'

Emily stared. 'Dad, I think you've just made a brilliant suggestion!'

'Well, there's no need to look so flabbergasted; I have been known to come up with a good idea now and again!'

'But where would we go?' Tom sounded doubtful. 'I can't imagine Ma enjoying a synthetic hotel Christmas with paper hats and party poppers. It could be pretty foul, you know. Maybe we should go abroad?'

'I don't think we should go abroad,' said Emily. 'Ma doesn't like flying, for a start, and we'd need to fly to get anywhere half decent, anywhere hot.'

Tom said 'Who wants to be hot at Christmas? Hey, maybe we should go to Scotland; we could go skiing.'

'Not skiing.' Tony had tried skiing without success.

'It would be good to go somewhere lively.' Emily had obviously taken to the idea. 'What about London? We could stay in the West End. The West End would be great.'

'Not London, and certainly not the West End. Roistering crowds and traffic jams and packed tubes are definitely not on the agenda. We need to find somewhere

149

peaceful. I was thinking along the lines of a really comfortable country house hotel with great food, squashy leather armchairs and huge log fires.' Already Tony had a vision of himself as a country gentleman; a good shot; a hard man to hounds. 'You know the sort of thing; kedgeree for breakfast, bracing walks, country pursuits...'

'...a great selection of malts, exceptional vintage port and a good wine cellar,' added Tom knowingly.

Further speculation was cut short by the appearance of Mary Pomeroy with a calm demeanour and a cafetière.

'Ah, here comes coffee,' Tony exclaimed warmly. 'Just what the doctor ordered. I don't suppose there are any mints?'

'You're not allowed mints at lunchtime,' Tom reminded him, 'only after dinner. Think of your waistline. Think of the hours you spend on the treadmill.'

'Thanks, Ma,' Emily said. 'It is de-caff, I suppose?'

'It is,' said Mary Pomeroy.

'I bet it isn't.'

'All right then, it isn't.'

'I'll drink it anyway,' said Emily graciously.

Chapter Seventeen

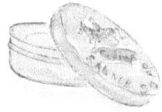

Christmas had come and gone almost unnoticed. January and February had, to Anna's eyes, been frittered away in endless form-filling, meetings with the council, and visits from various official bodies concerned with everything from the amount of effluent to be discharged into the septic tank to the exact amount of electricity required to power a commercial kitchen. English Heritage, as Rupert had predicted, had certainly "put their oar in", inspecting the plans and requesting amendments everywhere, specifying the type of bricks (handmade) and tiles (reclaimed), the specific ingredients of cement and plaster (unbelievable) and the size and origin of timbers to be used in the restoration.

The only work that had been completed so far was the new accommodation for Vivian and Lavinia, which had only required building regulations in order to proceed. The west wing apartment was now comfortably furnished and centrally heated and a source of continuous delight to its occupants. Now, as Anna carried a bacon sandwich and coffee to the stables (Nicola had missed breakfast because she was expecting an early visit from the vet) she could hear the piano tuner plinking and plonking his way up and down the keyboard of the grand piano. It had taken four men to move it into the apartment and when the legs and the pedals had been reattached, the only piano tuner within twenty miles had had looked at it in despair. He was a melancholy soul who sighed and shook his head a lot. Apparently a new string was needed, and replacement felt, plus a pedal refurbishment, which should have been good news for a person of his occupation, yet the prospect of actually tackling the job seemed only to increase his despondency. Anna had attempted to cheer him along with a mug of tea and a chocolate biscuit, reiterating that all necessary work should be carried out with the utmost speed and efficiency whilst Lady Lavinia had hovered nearby in an agony of anxiety. Peering at him through one of the windows, Anna wondered if this could actually be the same man who had been described to her as a genius with a stringed instrument.

Len had produced a hand-picked team of experienced, hard-working men, mostly Polish, who looked upon the job as a challenge and pitched in with a will. They had organised themselves cheerfully into a temporary Portakabin village in the kitchen garden and were enthusiastically grateful for the mammoth fried breakfasts and sandwich lunches which Anna prepared for them. In the evenings they repaired to the local hostelry. Previously known as The Rushbroke Arms, the half-timbered inn had been the subject of an extensive and extremely unpopular Dickensian refurbishment and subsequently rechristened the Cricket in the Hearth. Local youths had long ago removed the E, T, and H from the sign (spelled out in thick rounded lettering reminiscent of Cecil Aldin) which had been attached to the pink, pebble-dashed wall of the Pickwick Restaurant, and after several attempts to replace the lettering had been similarly thwarted, the brewery had given up. The sign now read The Crick in the Heart but the establishment was popularly known to the residents of Rushall St. Mary as The Crick in the Neck; a reference to its low, heavily beamed ceilings and its painfully perilous lintels; the latter being rather too easily disregarded after a few rounds of Adnams best. At The Crick in the Neck the workmen dined on burgers, steak pies, and scampi and chips, drank pints of Adnams and played darts and dominoes with the locals in Sam Weller's Bar.

It was now March and there was a welcome spell of good weather, although the men faced the perilous uncertainty of having half of the main roof stripped down to the bare timbers when a change in the weather could mean it could rain, or even snow, and catch them on the hop. Around the central part of the house there was a proliferation of impossibly tall, leaning stacks of tiles which looked in imminent danger of collapse. Great rolls of roofing felt were stacked up everywhere, mountains of battening lay under any available shelter. A mind-numbing hammering went on all day long. Chainsaws screeched and whined as great worm-eaten timbers were cut out. Transistor radios were turned up to full volume as an accompaniment to curses, constant banter and toneless singing punctuated by the occasional howl of anguish. The dust, dirt and debris, in fact everything that was part and parcel of life with a gang of workmen, was hard on the nerves, just as Rupert had predicted.

A vast new beam was now being hoisted aloft by a crane accompanied by shouted instructions and much vocal encouragement from above and below. The undertaking was being watched from a safe distance by Len, Sadie and Rupert plus a local artist who, armed with a sketchbook and quite a bit of creative imagination, was producing a series of charming thumbnail sketches with which to illustrate the advertising brochure.

Barry was standing on a scaffolding tower constructed for him by Len, who had quoted health and safety to Anna when seeing him perched on top of a wobbling ladder. Engaged in carving back the tops of the hedges with a pair of powerful electric clippers, Barry's beaming round face was shining with sweat and stuck all over with yew trimmings. Built like a bison with powerful arms and shoulders, already brown as a nut, garbed in shorts, luminous singlet and enormous trainers, Barry was a tremendous success, working like three men and eating like four. Mute he may have been but he was not stupid and listened intently to all that was said, looking to Mavis now and again for reassurance, ever ready to tackle even the most daunting task with an energetic enthusiasm that seemed to Anna nothing short of heroic.

Vivian sat on a seat a short distance away, deep in conversation with Mavis Sholto who was her customary spotless self in pink jeans, pearl-buttoned cardigan, short floral wellington boots and an outsize sun visor. Mavis may have looked anything but a gardener but along the rose walk a miracle had already been wrought. The standards had been pruned back, unsightly suckers had been removed, leaning standards had been staked and tied. Old, straggling bushes had been trimmed back to neatness, climbers and ramblers had been tied into arches and supports repaired by Barry, the metalwork welded by Len. The grass borders were trimmed and sharply edged, the gravel paths weeded and topped up, the beds turned and fed with manure from the stables.

Anna was cheered and immensely touched by the industry that had achieved such a transformation and Mavis, perceiving that by this feat alone she had earned her larger canvas, was triumphant.

'Although the lavender has had to go, Miss Gabriel, and more's the pity, but it was too far gone even for Dr. Hellyer; half dead already and nearly all bare wood, such hard, thick stems as you ever did see. But where there's life there's hope and I've taken hundreds of cuttings and I've got them rooting in one of the old cold frames Barry's fixed up for me, so we'll be able to replant next year at no expense to anybody. I can be quite an economist, Miss Gabriel, when I have to be, you can take my word for it. My Arnold used to say "Mavis, you could make a mountain out of a molehill" and I could, I really could.'

Anna needed an economist. Money was being spent at a terrifying rate. Already economies had been made wherever possible. Reduced budgets and targets had been prepared. Corners had been cut, plans compromised. It was already clear that very much more than eight hundred and fifty thousand pounds would be needed and that the appalling prospect of having to go, cap in hand, to Francis Sparrow to beg for a further loan was becoming a real possibility. Anna managed not to think about it too much during the day, but the nights were a different matter. The previous night, the Barclay's eagle had appeared to her in a dream, flying in through the window, casting a great shadow and alighting on her bed, rending the linen with its massive talons. In vain Anna had protested that it was the wrong bank, the wrong logo but, pinning her to her pillow by the intensity of its splendidly golden and hypnotic eyes, it had suddenly and unexpectedly thrown back its head in order to regurgitate, via its wickedly curved and sharpened beak, a single scrap of paper which, when it had departed (opening its huge and powerful wings, causing the bed to rock and sway like a small boat on a rough sea, and uttering a hoarse and terrible cry) proved to be a message from Francis Sparrow, inscribed in his own excessively neat and tiny hand. *Small businesses,* he had reminded her, a*ccount for more than* 80% *of personal insolvencies.*

The vet's car was in the stable yard although neither Nicola nor the vet were in evidence. Anna left the bacon sandwich in the tack room beside a pile of worming syringes, fly repellent sprays and gamgee, clearly recently delivered. Anna breathed in the smell of the tack room; a heady mix of saddle soap and leather. When she was earning her own living, riding had become a luxury she could no longer afford and she missed it. Perhaps one day, when Rushbroke Hall was up and running and successful, she would be able to have a horse of her own. Smiling at such an optimistic thought, and looking round the tack room she appreciated that the leatherwork and saddlery was, if not new, of good quality, soaped and supple and some of it recently repaired. Bits and stirrups were expensive stainless steel; piled up rugs were clean and had been professionally patched and mended. Likewise, out in the yard, greeting the little bay mare, the newly arrived chestnut and the grey gelding, Anna saw that their beds were thickly laid with generously banked up sides made of the best quality long straw, and that their nets were full of hay. Looking up, she noticed that the stable roofs had been repaired. Hinges had been replaced so the doors hung properly. Some professional maintenance had been done here.

Thoughtfully, Anna wandered into the barn where,

lifting the lids of a line of galvanized bins, she found them full of top quality rolled oats and bruised barley, dried sugar beet, bran, linseed, chaff, and on a shelf above, tubs of molasses and half a dozen proprietary feed supplements. How on earth did Nicola manage to pay for all this? Anna knew there was not much money to be made out of schooling horses, and there were no lessons given, and only one horse at livery, in this yard.

Where did the money come from? Did Nicola have a small private income? Anna doubted it. Yet barley of this quality, oats like these—Anna raised a handful to her nose and breathed in their sweet, floury scent—were expensive. These horses lived better than the humans at Rushbroke Hall.

Standing in the semi-darkness of the barn, some sound; some movement perhaps, caused her to look up. Through a dusty, cobweb draped window she looked out into a small covered rickyard. She saw the discarded clothes first, thrown carelessly over a bale. Then she saw Nicola (at least, she saw part of what was recognisably Nicola) the rest being partially obscured by the dark-haired, middle-aged man lying on top of her, who was presumably the vet. Anna froze. As the portly buttocks of the vet rose and fell with an energetic and mesmerising rhythm, she remembered the corn merchant's lorry in the yard when she had arrived with the drowned man, and how Nicola had emerged from the barn with the golden-haired youth. 'Oh, my God, Nicola,' she whispered to herself. '*Is this how you pay your bills?*'

Chapter Eighteen

'...and so I was thinking, Madam,' Harry Featherstone said, scooping up the youngest member of the family, who was something of a solitary individual and had been sitting in a corner of the bedroom staring fixedly at a particularly uninteresting section of skirting board, 'that we might take the family away for a holiday over the Christmas period. I was thinking it might be congenial, Madam, to have a bit of a change this year, seeing as Freddie... well, seeing as we won't have the pleasure of Freddie's company for the seasonal festivities, and him being so sadly missed. I was thinking it might be beneficial.'

Mrs Maitland-Dell patted her small Cupid's bow of a mouth with a peach-coloured napkin embroidered with a 'C' for Clarissa, and replaced it upon the tray which bore the remains of her breakfast: grapefruit segments (tinned) with strawberries (fresh), a lightly boiled egg (free-range, size o, four minutes exactly), with high-bran bread (one thick slice, toasted and cut into four uniform fingers with the crusts removed), spread with slightly salted butter (Danish), a small pot of tea (Ceylon) with semi-skimmed milk (no sugar), the whole served from bone china (Minton Marlow) on a matching peach linen tray cloth accompanied by solid silver cutlery (London, 1900, fiddle and shell pattern). 'Christmas in the country?' she exclaimed in surprise. 'What an extremely novel idea, Harry.'

'I thought it might be beneficial for you, Madam,' said Harry respectfully, 'and for the family too, of course.'

'Beneficial for me, and for the family.' Mrs Maitland-Dell considered this for a moment. Her pretty blue eyes twinkled. The corners of her mouth twitched. 'I don't suppose it would be at all beneficial for you, Harry? I don't suppose you would enjoy a Christmas holiday in the country one little bit?'

'Oh, I most likely would, Madam,' Harry admitted. 'In fact, I might enjoy it a lot and, if I might be so bold as to say so, it might be very congenial to have someone else take charge of the Christmas festivities just this once. That would be very congenial indeed, and I can't help thinking how extremely congenial it might be to experience a little seasonal cheer in different surroundings with, if I might be forgiven for saying so, a few fresh faces to add a bit of variety to the proceedings.' Here, Harry Featherstone's eyes shifted slightly to meet the unblinking, slightly thyroid gaze of the family who, according to their individual temperament, regarded him with affability, anticipation, disinterest or open hostility from amongst peach satin pillows arranged below the quilted headboard of the queen-sized bed against which Madam was propped, wearing a fluffy angora jacket over a delicate lace-trimmed nightdress with her hair encased in Harry's favourite slumber net with the little pink bow at the front, making her look so feminine and so nice. 'That's not intending any disrespect to anybody present,' added Harry hastily, 'not in any way, shape, or form whatsoever.'

'No, of course not, Harry, and no disrespect registered, I feel sure.' Mrs Maitland-Dell fell silent and thoughtful for quite a few minutes, one small, impeccably manicured hand toying with, and finally rejecting, the last finger of toast on the delicately fluted plate. 'Well, Harry,' she said at length, 'You have made a very interesting suggestion and I can see that we may very well benefit from a little holiday, especially at Christmas when memories of Freddie will be particularly poignant, and although I cannot make any firm promises, and I would like that to be completely *understood*, Harry, I do think it is a proposition worthy of our consideration.'

'You have my permission to investigate the possibility, with the *provision*,' and here Mrs Maitland-Dell held up a cautionary hand, 'with the *strict* provision that an entirely suitable establishment can be found, and if such is the case; if all of our requirements can be met, then I feel sure that a Christmas holiday will be both beneficial and congenial. I must confess that spending Christmas in the country has a certain appeal, and it will give you an extremely well-deserved break from routine. I feel sure that the family will enjoy a change of scenery, won't you, my darlings?'

The family, shifting slightly in agreement, (although their comprehension was, as usual, virtually nil) caused the holy golden and white Shih Tzu to slide off his rightfully elevated position to be replaced in an instant by the grey and white Shih Tzu who, as well as being the most athletic member of the family, was also something of an opportunist; although the gold star for opportunism would have to go the most diminutive member who, taking advantage of this minor disturbance, neatly removed the last finger of toast from the fluted plate and disappeared beneath the eiderdown.

'There will, of course, be certain requirements to be fulfilled in the way of accommodation and facilities,' said Mrs Maitland-Dell a trifle grandly, 'before I can commit myself to any reservation.'

'And what would those requirements be, Madam?' Harry placed the youngest member of the family on the eiderdown and stood to attention on the peach-coloured Wilton, ready to receive instructions. The youngest Shih Tzu who, as well as being the most solitary individual, was also the most intuitive member of the family, instinctively sat up to attention with its ears pricked (as much as a Shih Tzu is capable of pricking its ears) and its rounded, shining eyes fixed upon Harry's face with all the eager devotion of a promising recruit.

'Any hotel will have to be situated in the very heart of the countryside. There are to be positively no dangerous main roads and no audible traffic in the vicinity. The country,' said Mrs Maitland-Dell firmly, 'is the country, after all.'

'Quite,' agreed Harry Featherstone. 'No traffic and no main roads. Situated in the heart of the countryside. That should be no problem at all, Madam. That's quite understood.'

'We shall not be requiring any organised entertainment,' said Mrs Maitland-Dell. 'We shall not be requiring anything in the way of fireworks, dance bands, discotheques or anything of a similar nature. We shall require absolute peace and quiet.'

'Absolute peace and quiet,' repeated Harry dutifully. 'No entertainment of any description.' His face betrayed only the slightest hint of disappointment.

'Although I have specified that the hotel should be situated in the country,' said Mrs Maitland-Dell, 'I should like you to make absolutely sure that there are no potentially dangerous beasts at large in the grounds. No safari parks and no herds of deer. Nor would the family wish to be confronted with farmyard livestock whilst taking the air, and although I have to insist upon free-range eggs and fresh garden produce from the kitchens, I would not tolerate free-range poultry on the premises. There must not be any wandering chickens. The family might be inclined to give chase and I would not wish any restrictions to be placed upon them. The family must be allowed complete freedom. This is to be their holiday just as much as it is ours.'

'Quite so, Madam, quite so,' agreed Harry. 'Absolute freedom for the family. No farm livestock. Free-range eggs. No wandering chickens.'

'I would also like to be assured that there will be no disagreeable aromas of an agricultural nature, Harry. Silage, farmyard manure, chemical sprays, chicken and pig farms all smell extremely unpleasant. The air must be clean and fresh. I do insist upon it.'

'No smells,' said Harry. 'Definitely.'

'And no large dogs. Large dogs can be boisterous as well as unfriendly.'

'That's very true, Madam. No large dogs. I'll make sure of it.'

'I am sure I don't have to tell you, Harry, that the standard of cooking must be excellent. We do not require extravagant meals, just fresh country produce beautifully prepared and presented. I cannot abide establishments where every single dish is served positive drowning in an excessively rich sauce. My digestion will not stand up to it.'

'Plain food,' said Harry. 'No sauces.' By this time the youngest Shih Tzu had fallen asleep at its post.

'We shall require a suite of rooms with all the usual conveniences. En-suite with bath *and* shower. A bidet would be a welcome addition.'

'All mod cons, Madam, I shall see to that,' said Harry stoutly.

'Colour television. Radio. Direct dial telephone.' (Mrs Maitland-Dell hardly ever made telephone calls, nor had she ever been known to listen to the radio.) 'Good linen, Harry, is an absolute priority. Egyptian cotton is an absolute must. I cannot be expected to sleep on artificial fibres. My skin is extremely sensitive.'

'Colour television. Radio. Telephone. Good linen,' repeated Harry.

'I shall take my own pillows, of course.'

'Duly noted, Madam.'

'Open fires would be very cheerful and welcoming,' continued Mrs Maitland-Dell. 'Not gas logs, Harry. I do mean real fires burning genuine wood cut from trees. I do not believe the family have ever experienced the warmth of a traditional, old-fashioned fire.'

'I don't believe they have, Madam,' said Harry. 'A proper open fire would be most congenial.'

'A small establishment, Harry, don't you agree? We would not feel at home in a large impersonal establishment operated by some faceless international conglomerate. An owner-manager would be ideal; someone who could attend personally to all our needs. We must have room service. There must always be someone available to provide all our usual little home comforts.'

'I shall see what can be arranged, Madam' said Harry manfully.

'I feel sure you will, Harry,' said Mrs Maitland-Dell warmly. 'I must confess that I am looking forward to our little holiday already. I am so glad you suggested it. You may take the tray now.'

As Harry approached the headboard and bent deferentially in order to remove the breakfast tray, the most senior member of the family stiffened. Her eyes bulged threateningly. From her throat issued forth a sound not unlike that of a vacuum cleaner or a small lawn mower. The rest of the family regarded her with interest.

'And Harry, there is just one final thing,' Mrs Maitland-Dell reached out for her dainty reading glasses with pearlised frames and her neatly folded copy of the *Daily Mail*. 'Not too many other guests, if that can possibly be arranged. Just a few carefully selected people.'

Harry carried the breakfast tray down the wide staircase carpeted edge-to-edge in pale green Axminster with a decorative border and brass stair-rods. At a discreet distance, the youngest Shih Tzu followed, hugging the skirting board, keeping low to the ground as if on a secret mission. Even with their widely differing levels of intelligence, both human and canine realised that Christmas in the country promised to be a tough assignment.

Chapter Nineteen

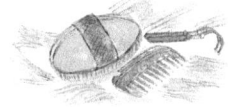

Anna was away for three days on one of her unexplained absences. These always served to make Rupert feel aggrieved. Where did she go? Who did she see? Why wouldn't she even talk about it? After a supper (cooked by Mavis, who seemed to be able to turn her hand to anything) Rupert strolled down to the stables. He found Nicola in one of the loose boxes attending to a small chestnut mare with a coat like a flame and the distinctive dished face of an Arabian.

'You didn't come in for supper. Mavis says I'm to tell you yours is keeping warm in the bottom oven. She's put foil on it so it won't dry out. She wasn't sure how long you would be.'

'I wasn't sure what would happen about supper with Anna being away.' Nicola looked up from the neat, dark hoof she was picking out into a bucket. 'I'm almost done, anyway.' The stable floor had been swept clear of bedding, revealing a floor of blue bricks; the clean straw, forked into a pile in one corner, resting against glazed tiles of a deep, sea green. These were old stables, a hundred years old at least, but of a quality the modern horse owner could only dream about.

Rupert leaned on the half door. 'We've started on the chapel. The men have sort of adopted it as an off-duty project. They're using the slates from the old outhouses for the roof. Len's left them to their own devices. They've already re-laid the floor. They've even found the bell. Vivian's in his element.'

'I can imagine.' Nicola released the mare's foot and moved herself and the bucket round to her other side. The mare lifted the appropriate foot in an obliging manner. 'I'm really grateful. To be honest, Rupert, it wasn't just the Christmas service I was thinking about; Vivian has always wanted to be buried in the chapel. He *is* the last baronet, after all, and the other Rushbrokes are all buried there. The title and the Rushbroke name will die with him. It's rather sad, actually.'

'It is. I hadn't thought of that.'

'Why would you? There should have been an heir but it never happened. There were miscarriages, I believe. I was the only surviving child. It must have been a great disappointment.'

'I can't believe you were a disappointment to anybody. Lavinia looks much younger than your father though.'

'Twenty years younger. Vivian plucked her from the tail-end of a career as a singer. She was quite well known in her day, apparently. Her family had practically disowned her; it wasn't considered quite the thing that girls from her background did. It's hard to believe now. She was always somewhat distrait, I gather; it was probably part of her charm. But after the miscarriages she retreated into her own cosy little world. Now, she has completely lost touch with reality and has been officially diagnosed as having dementia; well, you can see how things are.'

'Yes, it's a shame. It's been hard on you, I can see that.'

'It's been hard on everyone. In retrospect, Vivian made a bad decision when he married Lavinia. He should have married money. He should have married a strong woman, someone who could have helped him run the estate. Someone who could cope.'

'You don't choose who you fall in love with.'

'That may be true. But all the same, there are practicalities to be considered when you own an estate like Rushbroke.'

Rupert rested his arms along the stable door. The atmosphere of the stable was restful. He watched as Nicola moved around the mare's hind legs, appreciating that her handling of the horse was sure, and kind, and confident in a way that he himself (who was unused to large animals and horses in particular) both envied and admired. He said, wonderingly, 'Nicola, what do you *really* think of all this?'

'All this?' Nicola raised a questioning face from a hind hoof.

'Well, you have to admit that it's a bit of a sea change, isn't it? I mean, one minute you're riding down the lane minding your own business then suddenly Anna appears out of nowhere, plucks your father out of the mere and sets about turning your home into a hotel. It's a bloody traumatic and unusual event, whichever way you look at it.'

'Rushbroke ceased to be anything like a home a long time ago; that's one way of looking at it.'

'It can't have been very comfortable, I grant you, but at least you had your privacy; at least the place was your own.'

'Ah, but for how long?' Nicola's upturned face regarded him from beneath the mare's shining flank. 'The estate was in hock to the bank. We were living on borrowed money and our debt was growing larger with every breath we took. Time was running out for us.' Setting down the mare's foot, she straightened up, moving the bucket out of range with the toe of her boot. 'I would have thought that was rather obvious.'

'Well, yes, I suppose it was...' Rupert watched as Nicola removed the mare's checked cotton sheet, moving with her habitual steady calmness. He wondered what it had been like for her, growing up on this crumbling wreck of an estate with her deranged mother and her eccentric father, as first the comforts and then the necessities of life had dwindled away. He wondered if she had ever felt that fate had been unkind; if she had ever given way to anger and frustration; if she had wept. '...But the point I'm making is that you seem to have taken it all so remarkably calmly. If I was in your position I'd find it bloody hard to swallow. I'd feel sidelined, I feel sure. I'd certainly feel some resentment.'

'Yes,' Nicola considered him thoughtfully. 'I believe you would. But then you are not me, are you?' As she leaned over a wooden box of grooming equipment she lifted a hand to hook back a stray wing of hair in a gesture at once familiar and unsettling. 'What *I* feel,' she said as she selected a metal implement with several rows of sharp teeth, 'is that this was meant to happen. Anna is our salvation. We have been given another chance and Anna is the instrument of that. At the moment I don't care who she is, or where she has come from. All I know is that she is here and I'm glad. I don't feel sidelined, Rupert. I don't feel resentful. I feel gratitude. I feel saved. That's what I feel.'

Rupert watched as she picked out of the box an oval

leather-backed brush with short, soft bristles. She began to brush the mare's fiery coat with firm, sweeping strokes, running the brush across the teeth of the curry comb after each alternate stroke, every now and again pausing to knock the comb out on the stable floor, releasing a small shower of grey dust. Rupert found the scene relaxing and curiously evocative. There was a comfortingly timelessness about the horse and the stable which, though unfamiliar to him in reality, was at the same time familiar through countless half-experienced paintings and story book illustrations and was thus rendered recognisable in all its homely detail; in the way the headcollar rope dangled from the mare's lowered head; in the wisp of hay suspended from her soft mouth; in the folds of the check sheet thrown across the wooden manger in the shadowy corner. After all the trauma of the last six months he was soothed into a feeling of rare quiescence.

'So what about you, Rupert,' Nicola said eventually. 'Where do you stand in all this? Why are you here?'

The question was not altogether welcome. 'Why do you think I'm here? I'm an employee. I'm here because of my professional expertise. I'm a bloody hotel manager. I'm here to do a job.'

'No need to be so touchy.' Across the mare's gleaming neck, Nicola regarded him with amusement. 'Nothing to do with being hopelessly in love with Anna, then?'

There was a short but tense silence, after which Rupert capitulated with a groan of despair.

'Bloody hell, Nicola, is it so transparently obvious?'

Nicola took the mare's tail in one hand and began to brush it out, a few hairs at a time. The mare flipped one ear backwards in a half-hearted way but was otherwise unper-turbed. 'I'm afraid so. Is it totally unrequited?'

'Absolutely and soddingly totally.'

His voice was so vengefully despondent that she burst into laughter. They both laughed, but 'It must be very difficult.' Nicola said. 'For you, it is no laughing matter.'

'It hasn't been, until now,' he agreed.

'Is there a reason? Could there be someone else, do you think?'

'I don't know. Sometimes I think there must be. Where has she gone today, for example? She often goes away for days at a time. She never talks about it. It's a touchy subject.' He watched as the mare's tail was brushed into a gleaming fall of auburn silk and understood for the first time why young women with long, straight hair and sleek legs were described as having thoroughbred looks; there was certainly a comparison to be made with the hard, bony elegance of the horse's lower limbs and the shining, silken glory of the tail hair.

Nicola moved round to give her attention to the horse's mane. 'Perhaps I should do some gentle probing on your behalf. See what I can find out.'

'I doubt you'll be successful. Anna's a dark horse—no pun intended.' He was grateful though, for her offer of assistance; for her empathy. After Anna, tense and tetchy (and frightened, but Rupert was not to know that) Nicola's presence and obvious kindness were like a soothing balm. After the hell of the house with its swarming carpenters, plasterers, electricians and plumbers, the stable was an oasis of tranquillity. It was dusk now and the light was fading. All he could hear, as he leaned over the stable door, was the gentle chomp of the chestnut's jaw as she pulled hay from the net and the occasional snort and scrape of a shod hoof on brick from the stable next door; companionable sounds; timeless and calming. (Ah, the gentle seductiveness of the stable; the female has always recognised it; the male succumbs less often.) 'What about you, Nicola?' he said eventually. 'Have you ever been in love?'

'Goodness, do you always ask such searchingly personal questions?'

'I've told you about my love life, or the lack of it, now it's your turn.'

'Is it indeed?' Nicola looked at him thoughtfully over the horse's neck. 'I can see I might have to get used to shared confidences.' She considered the question carefully as she replaced the horse's rug. 'Well, this may not be the answer you are expecting, but if you are talking about *love*, as opposed to physical relationships, I think I have been in love from the moment I saw my first horse. Sometimes,' she stretched out a hand and touched the underside of the mare's jaw where the skin was loose and warm and softer than velvet, 'I look at one of these beautiful creatures and I only have to catch a certain tilt of a head or the curve of an ear and I honestly could weep for love. And although I know they are not capable of returning my love it doesn't matter; if anything, it just intensifies it. I *think* that is love,' she said, turning to him. 'I think it *must* be love, and, if I am right, then the answer to your question is yes, most definitely I have been, I *am* in love... don't you think?'

Rupert was melted by this honest and touching declaration of a love untainted by lust or pride, possessiveness, or even expectation. He forgot his fear of horses, unbolted the lower door and went into the stable. He put an arm around Nicola's waist and pulled her close. Because he had been lonely and miserable, because he was in need of comfort and desperate to be loved, he kissed her open mouth and her startled grey eyes and smoothed her hair away from her face. His hands were on the warm softness of her breasts almost before he realised it, and he drew back at once, ready to apologise, to beg forgiveness, except that she took his hand and led him to the pile of straw in the corner of the stable, and unbuttoned her blouse, and after that everything else was forgotten.

Chapter Twenty

The department, discreetly labelled *MILITARY AND SPORTING* was on the second floor and furnished like a gentleman's club with mahogany panelling, heavy drapes, leather chairs and pleated lampshades on brass stands. A lone sales assistant, white-haired and stooped like an aged manservant, was peering into a ledger on a leather-topped desk as Tony Pomeroy arrived, treading silently on well-felted navy blue carpet.

Tony cleared his throat in order to indicate his arrival. 'Good morning,' he said. 'I would like to purchase a hunting outfit.'

The sales assistant raised his head and his expression was pained. 'Oh, good gracious me, Sir, not a hunting outfit; never in a million years. What you require are hunting *clothes.*'

'In that case,' said Tony obligingly, 'I would like to purchase a set of hunting clothes.'

'You would like to purchase *hunting clothes.*' The assistant looked at him in reproof. 'Not an outfit, not a kit, and most certainly not a set.'

'Hunting clothes,' agreed Tony, and seeing that this could be a long drawn out affair, he sat down on one of the leather chairs.

'May I enquire for which pack?'

'Sorry?'

'I was enquiring, Sir, as to which pack of hounds you will be hunting with?'

'Oh, I see. Well... to be honest, I don't actually know. Does it matter?'

'It would be advisable to know, Sir, whether you will be hunting with foxhounds, staghounds, harriers, beagles or draghounds.'

Tony had no idea that packs of hounds came in such a bewildering variety. 'Surely all hunts are more or less the same?'

'In many ways they are much the same, Sir, but as I am sure you are aware, foxhounds hunt fox, staghounds hunt deer, harriers hunt hare, draghounds hunt an artificial line, and beagles are followed on foot.'

'I shall not be following on foot,' said Tony with confidence. 'I shall be on a horse. Most definitely.'

'Then perhaps we should begin by establishing which country you will be hunting in.'

Tony thought the question absurd. 'Why, here, of course, in England. As I'm a total novice at this I would hardly be venturing abroad.'

The sales assistant found it necessary to inspect a pincushion which resembled a wine coaster, having a base of turned mahogany and a green baize hillock in the centre liberally stuck with pins. 'Have you any idea which *county* you will be hunting over, Sir,' he enquired in a careful voice.

'Suffolk. Around Framlingham, I imagine. The place

I'm staying is in a village called Rushall St. Mary, and the Boxing Day meet is local.'

'Foxhounds or Harriers then, Sir, I think we may safely assume. All the same, it would be advisable to consult Baily.'

'Baily's your resident hunting expert, is he?'

'You could say that, Sir, yes, you could certainly say that.' With some considerable difficulty, the aged assistant creaked across the sales floor and pulled out one of a row of uniform red volumes from a shelf above a restrained display consisting of a dun waistcoat, one spur and a bowler hat. '*Baily's Hunting Directory*. Published annually since 1897, and a veritable mine of information. Our resident expert. So to speak.' There followed a goodly interval during which the sales assistant shuffled back to his desk and began to leaf back and forth through many pages of dense print interrupted, but not very often, by black and white photographs of hounds, horses and hunt servants, until finally the required entry was located. 'Now we have it, Sir. Yes, I think we may safely presume your country to be that of the Easton Harriers. If I may quote Baily on the subject:

'The country covers an area of about 25 miles square in East Suffolk.

Centres: Framlingham, Wickham Market and Woodbridge.

Meet: Thursday, Saturday and some Mondays.

Hunt Uniform: Green.

Distinctive Collar: Fawn.'

.   .   .

175

He closed the book with some resignation and returned it to the shelf. 'Not exactly the Quorn, Sir, one has to say. But we can certainly assist you with the selection of appropriate clothing for the conditions. Ditch country, as I am sure you appreciate. Dykes and ditches. No hedges. No upright fences and very little grass. Plough and clay. Rather exposed. An ever-prevailing wind. Not the most comfortable country in the British Isles in which to hunt, Sir, not by any means. Not like the shires. Oh no, nothing like the shires. Not at all.'

'Did I hear you say the hunt uniform was *green*?' The exceedingly pessimistic description of the Eastern Harriers country had, mercifully, been wasted on Tony. 'Because I rather fancied a red jacket, actually, not a green one.'

'Scarlet is the correct terminology, if I may say so, Sir,' the assistant said in a deeply censorious tone. 'And we would say coat in preference to jacket. A hunt *coat*. One might own a riding *jacket*, but for hunting one would wear a *coat*. Harriers, Sir, wear green coats by tradition.'

'That's a shame.' Tony was disappointed. He had pictured himself mounted upon a gleaming hunter, resplendent in a top hat and scarlet coat (as opposed to a red jacket), totally unrecognised by his wife and children as he rode past them as part of the glorious pageantry of the hunt. He had visualised their utter amazement when he made himself known to them and their absolute astonishment and admiration of his prowess as he sailed, in impeccable style, over hedges and five-bar gates as if born to the saddle. Of course, Tony was gifted with a fine and creative imagination and this flight of fancy was totally divorced from the harsh reality of hunting in East Anglia, as he was yet to discover, but at this particular moment, the loss of the scarlet coat was a grievous blow. Another was soon to follow.

'You may not be aware, Sir,' the sales assistant said, 'that the invitation to wear scarlet, green, or even blue, as the case may be, is still the prerogative of the Master. Tradition and etiquette are very strict where dress is concerned and I would not care to see you fall foul of it. The wearing of the hunt colours, or even the hunt button, is not an automatic right, not even to members who pay the full subscription.'

Tony looked at him in resignation. 'Then you had better tell me what I can wear. I had no idea that it was going to be so complicated. What does Baily say about it?'

'I am afraid that Baily will not be of much help to you in this matter, Sir. Baily does assume a certain degree of cognisance in its readership. It does not discuss matters of dress or etiquette.' No doubt observing the depth of his client's disappointment, the assistant added, in a benevolent tone, 'Would you allow me to make a suggestion, Sir?'

'I would,' said Tony, with feeling. 'I'm completely out of my depth with all this tradition and etiquette business. I haven't a clue. Feel free to make any suggestion you like.'

'You would be wanting the full hunt coat?'

'I certainly wouldn't be wanting half of one.'

'Then I would suggest a good black melton, Sir, with perhaps a Tattersall check lining and a waterproof skirt.'

'And that would be allowed, would it? A good black melton wouldn't offend the cognoscenti? Baily would approve of that, would he?'

'Bailey would certainly approve the black melton, Sir. It would be entirely appropriate. Eminently suitable.'

'I'll settle for one of those then.' Tony stood up at last, prepared to be measured. 'How long will it take you to make it?'

'Best to allow six months.'

177

'Six months!' Tony was appalled. 'I can't wait six months! I need it for Boxing Day!'

'Boxing Day is out of the question, Sir, for a bespoke garment. The full hunt coat requires at least two fittings. We insist upon it. However,' the assistant laid a hand, the back of which was speckled with grave spots, on Tony's arm in a soothing manner. 'If you could care to follow me, we could perhaps peruse our selection of ready-to-wear hunt coats and hope we may be able to adapt one to fit in time for Boxing Day.'

With a sigh, Tony allowed himself to be led (at the speed of an arthritic tortoise) to a rail of garments built into a recess and hidden by a curtain. After a certain amount of deliberation, the assistant selected a black hunt coat and held it up for Tony to try.

'Good grief! It weighs a ton!'

'The full hunt coat is a substantial garment, Sir. Highly suitable for the country, if I may say so. You will have cause to be grateful for the weight and the waterproof quality of the melton cloth, Sir, when hunting in East Anglia. You will appreciate the insulating properties of the woollen lining, as well as the moisture-proof skirt panels when you are following the Eastern Harriers. Oh yes, Sir, our melton full hunt coat can be worn with confidence in any country. It would earn you the unqualified approval of Baily, there is no doubt about it.' After some prolonged fumbling with stout bone buttons and stiff buttonholes, he stood back and surveyed Tony's upper half with pride. 'Remarkable. A remarkably good fit, Sir. A most miraculous fit indeed, as I am sure you will agree. I can see no necessity for alterations whatsoever. None at all.'

Mollified, Tony stared at his reflection in a heavily carved mahogany cheval mirror. He was delighted with what he saw. The Melton Full Hunt Coat was magnificent in every way, with high cut lapels, a well-defined and elegant waist, the skirt below made important by its water-proof lining. Bespoke or not, the cut was superb; the quality most blatantly obvious. 'I think this will do very well,' he said decisively. 'As a matter of interest, have we discussed the price?'

'We have not, Sir.' The sales assistant stooped again to the buttons, adding, without the least trace of embarrass-ment, 'The price of the Melton Full Hunt Coat is nine hundred and seventy five pounds.'

Even Tony, who was not short of money by any means and accustomed to buying expensive clothes, winced. 'And if I had one made to measure?'

'You would be looking at a price of up to one thousand five hundred pounds. And to be perfectly honest, Sir, to the layman, the fit would not have been appreciatively different.'

'In that case, I've just saved myself over five hundred pounds.' Having justified the purchase of the Melton Full Hunt Coat, Tony was ready to turn his attention to the next item. 'Now for the boots,' he said with relish.

'I rather think the breeches first, Sir, the boots later.' He pronounced them *britches*.

'Britches it is then. White, I think. White britches would be appropriate, don't you think?'

'White britches would not be at all appropriate, Sir, unless you are thinking of show jumping at Wembley Stadium. For the Eastern Harriers, I would suggest a medium fawn, drab or stone colour. One would not wish to recommend anything too light in colour for hunting in East Anglia, due to the nature of the country. I'm thinking in particular of the plough, the mud and the clay. The going can be somewhat... deep.'

'Only when it rains, surely.' Tony was not easily deterred. 'How about sorting me out a selection to try?'

Half an hour later, after struggling in and out of several pairs of drab, stone or fawn britches, Tony, pink and perspiring, leaned against the burgundy flock wallpaper in his king size changing room complete with its own wing-backed leather chair and carved mahogany cheval mirror, and mopped his brow. He had now been in the department for almost two hours and had so far only made one purchase. He put his head round the curtain in order to summon the assistant and saw that he appeared to have dropped off to sleep whilst standing up like an old horse. He awoke with a start to Tony's explanation of how all the britches were both too tight and too long, 'and all these little buttons are the very devil to do up, even with the hook thing. I couldn't even sit down in most of them; I'd have no chance of getting up on a horse.' Remembering Emily's pony-mad stage, he added 'I don't suppose you have any stretch joddie things?'

'Stretch joddie things we don't do, Sir,' the assistant said solemnly. 'The traditional cavalry twill britches do need to be broken in, of course, and as to the length and width, you are a little short of leg, Sir, if you will forgive me for saying so, and a trifle thick around the calf. However, if you have no objection to a certain percentage of man-made fibre in the cloth, I think I can find you some britches in a blended material which is designed to allow a certain amount of two-way stretch, and the Velcro fastenings may be more convenient for you to manage.'

The two-way stretch britches with Velcro fastenings, albeit proffered with an air of reluctance which implied that they were not perhaps in the best of taste and might not pass the scrutiny of Baily, were nevertheless pronounced a good enough fit to try with a boot.

'I don't suppose you could *make* me a pair of boots?' Tony wondered, worried now about being a little short of leg and a trifle thick around the calf.

The assistant shook his head. 'Not in time for Boxing Day. Waxed calf twelve months. Box calf nine months.'

'Then I shall have to settle for waxed calf ready-mades.'

'Regretfully, ready-made boots come in box calf only, Sir.'

Another hour later, surrounded by abandoned boots; too narrow, too wide, too small, too large, too long and too short, a pair was finally deemed satisfactory although Tony walked around the sales floor like a toy soldier, quite unable to flex his ankles or his knees.

'The length will drop slightly around the ankles in wear, Sir, have no fear,' the assistant assured him. 'You will find them extremely comfortable when you are mounted and they will give excellent protection against brambles, blackthorn and gateposts. Boots such as the Belvoir Supreme are not intended for walking.'

The selection of a handsome waistcoat in Tattersall check to match the lining of the Melton Full Hunt Coat was followed by a hunting shirt of a surprising length made out of soft, fine wool and without a collar in order to accommodate the stock. The stock, an unnerving item made of folded white linen and several feet in length, was catastrophic. Despite much patient tuition, Tony's inept and impatient fingers were quite unable to master the intricate technique required to transform the length of linen into even a passable imitation of the elegant neckwear which graced the neck of those photographed for *Baily's Hunting Directory*. In Tony's hands, the stock resembled a bandage applied to some imaginary injury by a child in a nurse's uniform, managing to be both tight and loose and lopsided into the bargain. At length, even the patience and perseverance of the aged assistant failed and he fell back, exhausted. Excusing himself for quite a few minutes, he returned with a stock of the ready tied variety, no doubt discreetly tucked out of sight in the stock room for such an emergency as this. It was, he informed Tony, something akin to wearing a made up bow tie for the opera, but in the circumstances...

Tony was now prepared to take a lively interest in what form the stock pin might take, but the one displayed for his inspection upon a small pad of maroon velvet was disappointingly plain, resembling nothing more than a giant safety pin in nine carat gold. 'Pins with fox head or horseshoe decorations we do not stock sir. The decorated pin is definitely not to be recommended. They are not worn, even in East Anglia in the country of the Easton Harriers.'

String and felted woollen gloves were selected. Two pairs. One (apparently) to be tucked under the saddle flap to be exchanged when the first pair became wet with rain or sweat from the horse's neck and began to slip on the reins. The gloves were followed by the most thrilling purchase of the day, which was the hunting whip. This exceedingly fine object, the leather covered shaft of which bore two solid silver mounts, had at one end a curved bone handle, and at the other a plaited thong several feet in length with a lash at the tip like the flickering red tongue of a serpent. Tony was enchanted. Luckily for the aged assistant, no tuition was called for as the whip came complete with a small manual of instructions designed to enable the novice to master the etiquette and technique of whipmanship in the privacy of his or her own home (or in Tony's case, the office).

Spurs were offered and declined with regret and the

final item of expenditure discussed at length. Tony was dismayed to hear that the top hat he had pictured himself wearing when part of the glorious pageantry of the hunt, was an absolute impossibility.

'Not a silk hat, not with the black melton, Sir, oh, no, not correct at all, I'm afraid. As for the bowler hat, that is only permissible with ratcatcher which, as I am sure you are aware, consists of a tweed coat and brown boots, traditionally worn for cub hunting. The velvet cap is, of course, the prerogative of hunt servants and lady members, which leaves just the skull cap, Sir, with the harness attached, the whole made relatively bearable by the addition of a silk cover with a peak as worn by the Prince of Wales.'

There was little Tony could do other than agree. And so, with the mental picture of himself slightly adjusted to allow for the Melton Full Hunt Coat instead of the scarlet, and the elegance of the Top Hat replaced by the skull cap with a black silk cover as worn by the Prince of Wales, he finally handed over his debit card. He tried not to notice the astonishing total.

Some three hours and thirty minutes after his arrival, Tony bade an affectionate farewell to the aged assistant, who thanked him for his custom and wished him good hunting. 'Best make the most of it while you can, Sir,' he advised. 'They'll ban it, you know; the antis. Eventually they'll get their way and they'll put a stop to it and there'll be no more hunting. We can't even put hunting clothes in the window now without getting a brick thrown through it. There are more of them than there are of us, Sir, and that's the long and short of it.'

'Grief,' said Tony, thinking of the cheque he had just signed. 'Then what?'

'You'll be drag hunting, Sir. That's what. You'll be

following bloodhounds. They'll be following a smelly sausage along a pre-arranged route. A good gallop over some nicely maintained fences and home in time for tea. No skill attached to it. All the science and the knowledge, the long history and the wonderful unpredictability and the thrill of the chase lost forever. Baily will turn in his grave.' The aged assistant turned back to his ledger.

Encumbered with many large carrier bags, Tony made his way carefully down the brass railed staircase and hailed a taxi. He had missed his planned lunch at the Institute of Directors and would have to head back to the office and send one of the girls out to Pret a Manger for a smoked salmon and cream cheese sandwich and a double shot latte. Whilst the taxi stalled in the inevitable snarl of traffic in Regent Street, and with absolutely no sense of having put the cart before the horse, Tony occupied his mind with his next objective; that of organising a crash course of riding lessons.

Chapter Twenty-One

Anna couldn't stop thinking about Nicola. Could she have been mistaken? Was this just a relationship with the vet and nothing more? Was her imagination making two and two into five? She had to find out. On the morning the blacksmith was due she made two mugs of coffee, added a bowl of sugar and some biscuits, and made her way down to the stables.

The blacksmith's van with its portable forge was parked in the yard. Anna listened for the sound of rasping or hammering but all was silent. She left the coffee in the tack room and walked over to the barn, approaching the window into the rickyard cautiously; silently; with all the stealth of an accomplished voyeur.

The first thing she noticed was that the blacksmith was not plump, like the vet; he was wiry and grey-haired and, considering his age, remarkably energetic. His arms and his hands, where he held onto the hay bale which supported Nicola, were knotted with veins, and even from where Anna stood she could see that his fingernails were black. As she watched, his scrawny buttocks abruptly ceased pumping. At first he fell forward and afterwards (unfortunately for Anna) rolled over and revealed, in a nest of wet, grey hair, intimate parts that should have remained private, and would henceforth feature (together with the Barclay's eagle) in her worst nightmares.

How could she! How *could* she! Anna was still shaking as she cut through the rose garden towards the sanctuary of her newly fitted stainless steel kitchen—a chef's dream with its gas hobs, Rational steam ovens, eye-level grills, fryers, bain-maries and a servery complete with plate warming cupboards and halogen lights to keep food hot. Her progress was arrested by Mavis, waving a large piece of plasterboard like a flag.

'I wonder if you could spare a moment to look at this, Miss Gabriel? I'm in creative mode at the present. I'm unstoppable. You can't argue with the stars when they're in the ascendant; you just have to go with the flow. You can't change your destiny. I put it down to being a Sagittarian, born with an active mind and a burning desire to achieve. The best hearts are the bravest, and so say all of us.'

Anna, already traumatised by the episode in the rick-yard, collapsed onto one of the beautiful, new wooden seats set in the four arbours surrounding the central rose bed and gazed in despair at a meticulously detailed plan of the Rush-broke crest depicted in a truly ghastly raised cushion of nicotiana, salvias, dwarf French marigolds and begonias, doubtless designed to enliven the main courtyard, but more suited to a municipal seaside pleasure garden.

From beneath a straw hat with a floppy brim and a pink spotted ribbon, Mavis regarded her with consternation. 'If you don't mind my saying so, you don't look quite yourself, Miss Gabriel, you don't look well at all. You're working too hard and you've probably overdone it, that's what it is,' she decided. 'My Arnold was a great one for putting the brake on; "If you don't stop now, Mavis", he used to say, "you'll knock yourself up, and then where shall we be?" I can see you've got a lot on your plate here and nobody to share the burden with, although we're all behind you, I can tell you that; we're all with you, willing you to succeed. Of course, it's easier for me, being guided by the stars, my course is set; but you shouldn't have to shoulder all this responsibility on your own. You can believe me though, Miss Gabriel, when I say that the planetary aspects are beginning to reform around you even as we sit; I can feel it in my bones. So don't you fret because here comes the Good Lord, and it wouldn't do for him to see you looking glum, not with his health the way it is, and that's a certain fact.'

Startled, Anna looked up, hoping to see God coming to her rescue at the head of the heavenly host, but all she saw was Vivian hurrying along the rose walk. 'I bring you good tidings,' he wheezed, 'in the form of paying customers making reservations by telephone!'

'There now,' Mavis stood up, dusted off her trousers, replaced her hat and picked up her piece of plasterboard. 'What did I tell you? Things are looking up already.'

'What've you got there, Mavis?' Vivian peered at the plasterboard plan. 'Christ alive, not bedding rubbish! Best steer clear of that! The crest was always succulents; last for years as long as you keep the dammed slugs at bay. Sedums, saxifrage, house leeks, and all that sort of thing. They like the dry courtyard. Happy as Larry in a bit of gravel.' Vivian flopped onto the seat beside Anna. 'Tell you what, Mavis, take yourself off to Beth Chatto. Used to come and lay it out for us in the old days. Daresay she's still got the plans. She'll put you right.' He waved an arm expansively. 'Put everything on my account. I think I'm up to date.'

'Better still,' Anna interposed hastily, 'ask Rupert for a cheque. He's in the office. And take Barry with you to help.'

Mavis, initially crestfallen, was now inclined to be philosophical. 'You're quite right, Sir Vivian, of course you are. There's no point in jumping the gun with bedding plants because they'll be over before your first guests arrive. I tend to be a bit previous, that's my trouble. It's all due to my line of fate reaching the mount of Saturn. I tend to try to exceed my own powers at times. My Arnold used to say, "You don't stop to think, Mavis, you've got to learn to look before you leap", and he was right, he really was.'

'Excellent woman.' Vivian watched her departure. '*Pearl of great price.*'

Anna, grateful for the solution to at least one problem, put a hand on his arm. It felt skeletal, fleshless. Despite all the good food she was careful to provide, Vivian didn't seem to be putting on weight. She made a mental note to have a word with Dr. McLoughlin. 'Reservations, did you say? Bookings for the Christmas House Party?' This had been Rupert's idea: a four-day Christmas break with guests arriving on Christmas Eve and leaving the day after Boxing Day. The dining room would also be open to non-residents during this time. Advertisements had been placed. A website had been set up. They were committed. Now all they had to do was fill the guest rooms; rooms where the plaster had not even had time to dry; rooms for which the custom-made window frames had still not arrived; rooms where half the floorboards were missing and those that remained were stacked with copper piping, radiators and electricity cables. Anna closed her eyes. Some things, she reflected, just didn't bear thinking about.

'One suite and two singles and a horse for people called Pommery, or something very similar, Rupert did tell me.

Then there was a call I answered from a chap who asked the very devil of a lot of questions. Harry Feather-some-thing-or-other. Asked if we'd any objection to small, well-behaved dogs. Could be two of the little beggars so I hope that's all right. He's booked a suite and another single. He's confirming by letter. All happened within the space of half an hour. Came straight out to tell you. Thought you'd be pleased.'

Rupert had agreed that they would accommodate the occasional small, well-behaved dog, but 'A horse?' Anna opened her eyes, surprised. 'Do they want livery for it?'

'He just wants to hire one. Wants us to mount him for the Boxing Day meet. It's all do-able. I'll speak to Nicola.'

So will I, Anna said to herself. *I have to talk to her. I can't allow this... awfulness to continue.* Aloud she said doubtfully, 'Have we got a horse in the stable suitable for a man to hunt?'

Vivian lifted his bony shoulders. 'She might be able to use the grey thing.'

'The grey thing isn't insured and it doesn't belong to Nicola. It's also unreliable in traffic.'

Vivian chose to disregard the first two points in favour of the third. 'Not much traffic at the Boxing Day meet. Have to make sure it stays in the middle of the field. Have to keep it sandwiched in between the others.'

'All the same,' Anna was concerned for the safety of her customer, 'the grey gelding isn't a suitable mount for a novice. Is this man an experienced rider?'

Vivian had not thought to enquire but thought it a fore-gone conclusion. 'Got to be experienced if he wants a horse to hunt. Give the man *some* credit. Can't be a complete fool.'

'For everyone's sake,' Anna said in a heartfelt voice, 'I hope you are right.'

* * *

'One of the workers has done a runner.' Len sat down on a stone mushroom. 'Left without even giving his notice.' Sadie had flopped down beside him. Her eyes had closed even before she hit the ground. She was finding the new job hard work.

'*Left?* Just like that? Deadlines too tight for him? Feeling the strain, was he?' Rupert was not inclined to be sympathetic. 'Did he give a reason?'

'I can't work it out, really. I didn't even get a chance to talk to him; he was gone before I knew it. As far as I can tell, it was nothing to do with the work. It's all a bit of a rum do really; I can't work it out. Apparently, they were coming home from the pub last night and he nipped into a field along the drive to take a leak. According to the rest of the team, the next minute he came barrelling out, practically jumped over the gate, white as a sheet and gibbering like an idiot. All they could get out of him was that he saw something in the dark, coming towards him across the field. I don't know what it was, but the foreman said it scared him shitless.'

'*Saw something in the dark?*' Rupert was incredulous. 'What is he, a man or a bloody mouse?'

'I know it sounds ridiculous, but I can only tell you what I know. The foreman said he described it as a huge creature with burning eyes and great yellow fangs. I know, I *know!*' Len held up a hand against Rupert's disbelief. I know it sounds ridiculous! I know it's nonsense! The thing is, I wouldn't have taken Maciej for a chap with an over-active imagination; he seemed a steady enough type to me. I've managed a lot of teams in my time and I'm usually a pretty good judge of character. I know it's hard to believe, but he certainly believed it.'

'Burning eyes? Great yellow fangs?' Rupert laughed out loud. 'Now you're sounding as if you almost believe it yourself! Don't be so bloody daft, Dad. This is *Suffolk*, not some Polish forest in the back of beyond. There are no monsters in Suffolk, not to my knowledge anyway. It must have been a bloody *cow*. He'd just downed too many pints of Adnams, that's what I think.'

'That's what the men said. He wouldn't have it. Sat up all night, wrapped in a duvet, shaking like a leaf. Caught the first bus to Colchester this morning. Didn't even wait for his wages. The gang said he was terrified out of his mind. Spooked them all, to be honest.'

'So we're a man short now.'

'Yes, and I'm sorry about that. He was a good worker.'

'Well, one less wage to pay. It'll help the finances,' Rupert said grimly. 'And that's going to be our next problem —getting Anna to go back to the bank.'

'And if they say no?'

'Don't go there, Dad. Just don't bloody well go there.'

The old King James family bible was open on the stone eagle lectern. Something had been marked, circled in bold black felt tipped pen.

It were better for him that a millstone were hanged about his neck, and he cast into the sea than that he should offend one of these little ones.

Anna looked up at the freshly plastered and emulsioned

roof, where once there had been sky; at the hammerbeams, waxed and glowing, where there had once been dust and ivy; at the cherubs, lovingly burnished now, with shining curls and polished cheeks. It might have been coincidence but somehow she knew it was not. It might not have been intended as a message for her, yet only she would have understood its significance. She knew that this was her message.

So Vivian knew. Perhaps he had always known.

Chapter Twenty-Two

'Well, Norman you're all set now!' Yvonne gestured towards the array of green plastic carrier bags which almost filled the claustrophobic area behind the shop, which served as restroom, cloakroom and stockroom. The shelves were heaped with commemorative memorabilia from at least three royal weddings, a silver jubilee, and VE day, where faded Valentine cards and dysfunctional musical and pop-up cards were stacked alongside awkwardly shaped cards awaiting a similarly shaped envelope, and irregularly shaped envelopes awaiting a similarly shaped card, every-thing gathering dust and facing an increasingly uncertain future.

'You're all equipped for the country now, Norman,' said Yvonne, whose hair was today swept up at the back and secured on top of her head with a contraption equipped with upstanding filaments of electric blue and shocking pink, not unlike the plume in the headpiece of a circus pony's bridle. 'You're all ready to step out in style with the... what did you say the name of your friends was? I've gone and forgotten.'

'The Fletcher-Smyths,' said Norman in an exhausted voice. He sank down on a banked row of photocopy paper boxes and looked at the carrier bags in despair. He had been unable to extricate himself from the shopping expedition to Country Cousins with the result that he had never spent so much money in so short a period of time in his entire life, and for what? Why was he so weak-willed? What had happened to his spirit? At what point had he become the sort of person he was now? Reclusive. Feeble. Emasculated.

'Oh yes, spelled with a "y", I remember now.' Yvonne looked at Norman in a speculative manner, her head on one side, her dramatically fringed eyes wide, her decorative filaments oscillating gently. 'Elsie and Genevra had a lovely time, didn't they? Choosing all your kit; dressing you up in this and that. I've never seen them so animated.'

'Yes,' said Norman wearily. 'They did seem to enjoy it.' If he didn't pull himself together and get his life organised he could see himself ending up like Mr Allison with his drooping clothes and moustache, his pathetic hair and general air of hopelessness. But what to do? How to do it?

'For all the talking they've done about it, you'd think it might be them going to spend Christmas in the country, Norman, not you, don't you think?'

'Yes,' agreed Norman listlessly. 'Yes, you would think so. I do believe you would.'

What would become of him? Norman could see the future and didn't like what he saw one little bit.

'Except that you're not going away for Christmas, are you, Norman? You're not going to Suffolk at all; and these friends of yours, these Fletcher-Smyths with a hyphen and spelled with a "y", they don't exist, do they, Norman? You made them up, didn't you?'

Norman raised his eyes to Yvonne, his expression anguished.

'Well, I guessed you *had*, didn't I? I had my suspicions all along, but I only knew for sure when we was in the shop; there was just this one terrible moment when you was in them moleskin trousers and pulling on them green wellies, and you had the Barbour jacket on and looked all hot and bothered, then Elsie found you that hat like a little waxed flower pot and put it on your head and you panicked, you really did. You went all white and funny and I said to myself, Norman's either going to pass out or he's going to make a bolt for it. I knew then for sure that you wasn't going to Suffolk for Christmas, I knew you was doing no such thing. Well, I can see how it *happened*, Norman, you don't have to explain it to me; it started out as an excuse not to have to do the expected thing, and suddenly Elsie's got the bit between her teeth and there's no stopping her; she's off like a blooming rocket and before you can say Bob's your uncle, you're up to your neck in thermal vests and waxed cotton.'

Despairingly, Norman dropped his head into his hands. Not only had he been exposed as weak-willed but a coward and a liar to boot. 'Do you think Elsie and Genevra know I'm not going anywhere? Do you think they know I was just making excuses?'

'They haven't a clue.' Yvonne was comfortingly emphatic. 'I don't think it would have entered their heads to doubt you, not for a minute.'

'Well, that's one good thing, I suppose.'

'I suppose it is.' Yvonne sat down beside him on the photocopier boxes. They looked at one another and smiled, Yvonne in a sympathetic manner, Norman ruefully. 'Yvonne, what am I going to do?'

Yvonne toyed absently with the shower of blue plastic beads suspended from one of her ears whilst she considered his predicament. 'Well,' she said eventually, 'we could try taking the things back to the shop and asking for a refund. You could say your friends had cancelled, say they'd decided to go abroad for Christmas instead, or say somebody's died in the family, or cook up some other excuse.'

Norman looked hopeful. 'Do you think it would work? Would they give me my money back?'

'Not if they've got any sense, they won't,' Yvonne admitted. 'They're not obliged to, you know, not if you just change your mind. They're only a little shop, remember; it's not as if it's Marks and Sparks. They'll probably offer you a credit note to spend on something else. It's a bit different if you want to just change something for a different size, or if a garment's faulty. They've got to give you a refund if you've got a genuine complaint.'

'I've got a genuine complaint all right,' said Norman. 'I've got a mental complaint. I think I must be losing my mind to get involved in all this.' Was that it? Was he losing his faculties? Was he in the early stages of dementia? Alzheimer's?

'If you ask me, just being here, in this place, working with Elsie and Genevra all them years is enough to drive anybody round the bend. I don't know how you've stood it, Norman, I really don't. I'd be round the twist by now, if it was me.'

'It's a job, Yvonne. One has to live.'

'Call this living?'

Norman looked at her; at the soft, downy skin of her cheeks, at her splendidly elongated eyelashes, at the shimmering, trembling filaments on the top of her head. He smiled. 'Not really,' he said.

Yvonne looked momentarily thoughtful. 'Norman, this might sound daft, but do you really fancy spending Christmas in the country? In Suffolk? I mean *really?*'

Norman looked startled. You would have thought that such a prospect had never even occurred to him; as if it was a completely new idea. 'I don't know... I mean... I hadn't really thought about it... I hadn't actually considered...'

'Well, perhaps you should start actually considering now.' Yvonne put a hand on his arm, the fingers laden with silver rings of assorted ethnic design. 'Because I told you, didn't I, that my mum lives in Suffolk?'

'You did, but I wouldn't want to... I couldn't...'

'No, I'm not going to suggest you stay with us because there's no spare room, being just a bungalow, and anyway, my mum would drive you even further round the bend than Elsie and Genevra. She'd be reading your palm before you got in the front door.'

'But where would I... How could I...'

'Well, my mum's got herself a job as a gardener at this hotel, it's a new place, just been refurbished and it's opening for Christmas and it's only just down the road from our village. They're only letting out a few rooms to start with and as there's not much gardening doing in winter, my mum and myself, we're helping out with a bit of waitressing and such over the holiday. We thought it would help to pass the time and it's nice to help people to enjoy themselves, it being the festive season and all that, Christmas can be a bit glum otherwise.'

'But do you think I'd... I've never actually...'

'I'm not suggesting you *work*, Norman, I was just thinking that it's a lovely old place, a bit like a stately home, really, not that I've ever been inside, but if we booked you in, if you were to stay there over Christmas, give yourself a treat, for a change, I could keep my eye on you and we could go for walks and things.'

'Oh, I don't know... I'm not sure I...'

'Well it's high time you were sure, Norman,' Yvonne said decisively. 'It's not being sure that's got you in this mess, and at least you'd get to wear this little lot,' she gestured at the green carrier bags, 'at least you'd get your money's worth.'

She was right. Norman knew she was right. He had drifted for long enough. 'All right,' he said with resolve. 'Let's do it!' Just saying it made him feel better. Just making the decision made him feel that he had turned a corner, that somehow his life had suddenly taken a turn for the better. 'Suffolk, here I come! Who knows, I might even get to wear my green wellies.'

'And your big woolly and your Barbour jacket. Not the flower pot hat though,' Yvonne said sniffily. 'I shan't go walking with you if you wear that hat.'

'And whilst we were on our walks, we could make up some tales to entertain Elsie and Genevra when we come back.'

Yvonne thought it the wrong moment to mention that she had no intention of coming back. 'You could bring your violin and play for my mum one evening, she'd love that, she really would. Genevra says you play it lovely.'

'Well, I *was* a professional once.' Norman imagined coming into the warmth of a beautiful country house after a walk with Yvonne. There would be a roaring log fire and a squashy armchair and a whisky and dry ginger with ice in a chunky glass. There would be a Christmas tree and swags of ivy and holly and mistletoe and his bed would be plump with pillows and a goose down duvet.

'That's you sorted then. I'll ring my mum tonight and

get her to book you in.' Yvonne stood up and pulled down her microscopic skirt. 'Best get back to work then, Norman, don't you think? We don't want Elsie getting any funny ideas about what we might be up to in the stock room, do we?'

Chapter Twenty-Three

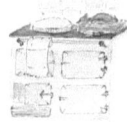

Anna had resolved to talk to Nicola, to offer her money to help keep the horses, anything to prevent her from doing what she was doing. Anna had not wanted to believe it but now she knew it to be true. She didn't understand how Nicola could bear to do it. The mere idea of it made her feel physically sick. The memory of the encounters she had witnessed filled her with revulsion, shame too. The whole thing was shameful. Anna herself was shamed that she had witnessed them, as if by seeing them, by watching, somehow it had made her complicit. There was nobody she could talk to about it. Nor did she feel like telling anyone. She wondered if the tradesmen talked to one another after a few beers in the Crick; if there was ribald laughter; if there were lewd comparisons. She wondered if there was talk in the village. Villages being what they were; hotbeds of gossip; she surmised that there probably was. It had to be stopped. Well, she must somehow put a stop to it. But how to do it? What to say? Whatever was said she must not allow herself to condemn or moralise; there must be no hint of reproach, no recriminations. However Anna felt about it,

Nicola had done what she did in order to survive and, just as Anna had taken charge of her own life, this was Nicola's way of taking charge of her own.

After dinner, in the cool of the evening, she walked down to the stables. The stables were empty. Anna remembered the scorched paddock. Nicola now turned her horses out to graze with David Williamson's cattle at night, bringing them back to the yard in the early morning before anyone was about.

She walked through the barn glancing, almost out of habit, through the window into the rickyard. This one was young. His body was like marble; pale and perfect. At first Anna supposed it to be one of the young Polish workmen. But there was an urgency, almost a ferocity in his movements, a hopeless, familiar anger in his climax, and afterwards, as he collapsed against her in despair, Nicola ran her fingers consolingly through hair that Anna knew only too well. Cold, silky, black hair.

Rupert.

* * *

Len had called a meeting. Whatever it was about it was urgent and required everyone to be present apart from Vivian and Lavinia.

They met in the back kitchen. Away from the stainless steel extravaganza that was the commercial kitchen, this one was homely. The range had been taken to bits and reassembled and now, converted to oil and servicing two radiators it made the room a comfortable place. The plank table had been removed from the main kitchen (hygiene regulations did not permit the use of wooden tables) and its chairs and two armchairs plus the old iron chandelier had also found a home here. Vivian had unearthed some old hunting prints to hang on the walls and it was all very cosy. The workmen ate here and now had adjourned to the Crick. Rupert was the first to arrive. His overalls were splattered with plaster from handing up the moulded Tudor roses for the hall ceiling to the artisan specialist who was perched on a plank suspended between two stepladders. Anna could not look at him.

She took herself away to make frothy coffee for everyone in the shiny new coffee machine in the main kitchen, putting beans into the coffee grinder, measuring the coffee, tamping it down, filling stainless steel jugs with milk, fiddling with warmed cups, thermometers and steam nozzles; glad there was nobody to see how her hands trembled. This was going to be a difficult meeting. Even worse than the financial matters that were sure to be the subject of it, there was Rupert, and there was Nicola. Anna was not sure how she felt about Nicola, but was beginning to know how she felt about Rupert. When they had first met she had imagined that she could put the past behind her, that she could make a fresh start in a new relationship; that she might love him. She remembered (although she would have preferred to forget) how his mouth had opened against hers, how his body had moved against hers, of how it had been when she had rejected him, how angry he had been, how desperate. She asked herself why, if she hadn't wanted him then, she should feel the loss of him now. And she *did* feel the loss; a great hollow emptiness inside, a permanent ache in her stomach, an actual pain in the vicinity of her heart. Yet was this truly love and loss or could it be jealousy that she felt? Would the feelings have been different if Rupert's relationship had been with someone other than Nicola? Was Nicola actually the problem? All Anna knew was that to see them together had caused her pain. Knowing about it hurt; God, how it hurt. Now she understood why Rupert had no longer been able to look her in the eye recently; why, whenever they spoke, he stood, not close, as would have been usual, but away from her, out of reach; no longer needing to be near, no longer wanting to touch her.

She took the tray of coffee into the back kitchen. Rupert looked up. He had a two-day stubble, dark smudges under his eyes, and splashes of plaster on his face. He looked wretched. He looked ill. And yet, 'Are you OK?' he asked. 'You look pale.'

The nerve of him, when he, Rupert, looked to be at death's door. It was on the tip of her tongue to make a childish retort: *What's it to you? Why would you care?* But mercifully, Len and Sadie arrived, followed by Nicola, and then they were sitting at the plank table, spooning froth, talking about the progress of the work, the decorating, the imminent arrival of carpets, the furnishings, the problems of storage until Len called them to attention.

'Thanks for coming.' Len looked around the table. 'There's something I want to talk about and it's something that concerns everybody, all of us, but Anna and Nicola in particular.'

'Money. I realise this will be about money,' said Anna. 'I know it's running low. I know I'll have to go back to the bank. I just wonder if we have enough equity. They're going to want their surveyor to come round to re-evaluate. I'm just so desperately worried that...'

'Hold on, girl, you haven't heard me out yet.' Len unzipped a bag at his feet and produced a large pad, which he slapped on the table. Sadie, flat out on the flagstones opened one eye and closed it again. Already, this was a slimmer, fitter Sadie. The new job was suiting her. 'There's something I want to run past you. I'm not exactly unaccustomed to clients running out of money; it happens more often than you might think. I've looked at the finances, and I've looked at what the bank might or might not do. As things stand it's not a lot. So I've been looking round and I've been doing some thinking. I've got a proposal.'

Rupert sat back. *They weren't going to like this.* He was glad it was Len who was dealing with it. Rupert rather felt he had sold his soul to the devil already. Now they would both think he had betrayed them. *Bloody hell, Len,* he thought. *Bloody fucking hell.* Suddenly his nerve failed him. 'Are you sure we're not being a bit premature,' he said, 'shouldn't we talk it through a bit more first?'

'I'm not much of a talker.' This was true; Len was more of a doer, 'and neither are you, these days.' The truth was that Rupert was always too busy to talk, either that or he was absent. Rupert now had unexplained absences of his own and Len had a jolly good idea what he was doing during these absences and he didn't approve of it one little bit. But that was a subject for another day. Today they had to think about finances. Today he had a proposition.

'OK. Go on then,' Rupert said reluctantly. 'Let's hear it.'

'Just one thing before I start.' Len held up a warning finger to Anna and Nicola. 'You have to promise you won't shout me down before I'm finished. You have to give me time to explain what I think we should do and *then* we can have the conversation. *Afterwards.* When you know the *facts.*' Len flipped open the pad, revealing drawings, plans. 'We need money to finish this job. A lot of it. And we don't want borrowed money; at least, we do initially, but we need to be able to pay it back quickly. You can't start a business like this under-capitalised. Bank loan interest is a killer. We need a way to generate money and

I have a suggestion.' Having gained their attention, Len sat back in his chair before delivering what he knew would be a bombshell. 'My thinking is that we should convert the stable block into apartments. Potentially, it's a great site. It's a natural for a courtyard development, something really upmarket; we could get six or seven apartments out of it. Then there are the barns. The potential is enormous.'

There was a silence, then 'Not the stables,' Anna said in a stricken voice. 'No. We can't.'

'The development could make a lot of money,' Len held up a warning hand. 'Well over two million, by my reckoning.'

Nicola stared. 'Two *million*? Are you serious?'

'Deadly serious. I've done the sums.'

'I *said*, not the stables,' Anna said again. 'We *can't.*'

'And I *said*, just hear me out.' Len placed a hand on Anna's arm. One felt he had travelled this road before.

'Would the council allow it?' Nicola wanted to know. 'Surely we would never get planning permission?'

'I've already spoken to the council. The last thing they want is for places like this to become crumbling ruins. They want to see Rushbroke restored and paying its way; paying rates in particular. But we need to get the detailed plans in as soon as possible. I'm talking now, within the next week or so. We need to catch the planning meeting after this one. We need to move quickly if we want to get the bank on board; we need something to show them, and the sooner the better. We can't wait until we run out of money; until we can't pay the wages.'

Rupert knew the plans were drawn. In truth, the plans were already in, signed off by Len. Apparently you needn't be the owner of a property in order to apply for outline planning permission. God only knew what Anna would think of that. Rupert was not about to mention it.

'And we'll need to get a scale model made, showing exactly how the development will look, so we can sell off-plan; we need to get a few apartments sold before we start to build.' Len looked around the table. 'Well, now you have it. My proposal. Two million. Enough to fund the rest of the restoration. Enough equity and potential to satisfy the bank. What do you think?'

Anna put her head in her hands. She had promised Vivian that Nicola would keep the stables. 'We can't do it,' Anna said. 'I know you mean well, Len, but we can't... *I can't*, do it.'

Nicola looked at Rupert. 'You knew about this and you didn't say a word?'

Rupert lifted his hands in supplication. 'What could I say? There was never a suitable moment.'

'There was always a suitable moment. Nicola was *promised* the stables.' Anna lifted her head. 'I promised Vivian. It was part of the deal. I can't let it happen, after the promises I have made. After the sacrifices Nicola has made.' *After the corn merchant*, Anna thought, *after the vet, the blacksmith*. She preferred not to think about Rupert. 'I can't do it. I can't. The horses are Nicola's life.'

'And this place is *your* bloody life,' Rupert said heatedly. 'Your money is vanishing into it like a brick in a swamp. Soon there will be nothing left, and then what? Anna, you can't *afford* to keep your promise about the stables. We're talking about keeping the job afloat here. We're talking about survival, for fuck's sake!'

'*There has to be another way.*'

'There isn't another way. If you don't agree to this we're going to run out of money. And you're going to have to go back to the bank on your bloody hands and knees. You're not going to want to do that either.'

Len pushed a colour brochure across the table to Nicola. 'We could build you a nice little timber stable yard on the paddock. You could have a perfectly decent range of timber buildings to accommodate the horses. We're not asking you to give them up. We wouldn't do that. We know how important they are to you.'

'A purpose built block would be a lot more convenient. You would have electricity, for a start,' Rupert added. 'A washroom. All mod cons.'

'I don't think that will be necessary.' Nicola got up from the table. She didn't even glance at the brochure.

'Please don't go.' Anna grabbed her by the arm. 'We won't do it. I won't allow it to happen.'

'Anna, you have no choice.' Nicola detached herself, gently, firmly. 'Two million is too much to pay for a promise. I knew something like this was going to happen sooner or later, I am not a fool. I could see it coming.'

Anna knew that if she had been in Nicola's position she would have ranted and raved; she would have screamed. She would have felt betrayed—well, she knew what that felt like. But Len and Rupert were right. Nicola was right. She couldn't refuse. If they were to survive, the development had to go ahead. She closed her eyes in despair. Len had just presented her with the solution to her biggest problem, a way to banish her worst nightmares, and she had never felt so miserable in her life.

Rupert got up from the table. 'Nicola... wait.'

Nicola smiled at him; her habitual, calm, self-contained smile. She put a finger to her lips. To look at her you would not imagine that her life had just been swept away, that something she had struggled and sacrificed to preserve against all the odds just had been brushed aside, taken from her as if it was of no importance; as if it counted for nothing. 'Rupert. I'm fine with it. You don't need to apologise. Time for Plan B,' was all she said.

* * *

Anna stood on the stone which marked the resting place of *Rufus Algernon Lawrence Percival Rushbroke, HE DIED AS HE LIVED*. She felt that things were slipping out of her grasp, that she was losing control. She hadn't managed to talk to Nicola. And now, because of Rupert, because of Nicola *and* Rupert, how could she? And now her longing, her need for Rupert had surfaced (from *where*? Had it been there all the time? Dormant? Unacknowledged?) She was hurt, she was wounded, and it was her own fault. She couldn't even ask herself why Rupert had done this. She knew why; Rupert had been stressed and overworked and he had needed her and she had not been there for him, not even with the promised friendship she had been at pains to describe when she had needed him to be on her team. Somehow there had been no time. Somehow everything else had got in the way. No, Anna did not have to ask herself why. And Nicola, well, Nicola had just done what Nicola did, and now she was to lose the stables and Anna would have broken her promise to Vivian, and Vivian was fading. There was to be money, but everywhere else her life had descended into chaos and misery. Anna's eyes smarted. Grew hot. Tears forced their way through her tightly closed eyelids. She opened them and saw the King James Bible with a passage circled in black.

...but if any provide not for his own, and specially for

those of his own house, he hath denied the faith, and is worse than an infidel.

Vivian. Vivian's guilt. Yet none of the current situation was his doing. None of it was his fault. Anna felt she was to blame for all of it. And perhaps the answer to it all was in her own hands. There is something I should have done before now, she told herself, a decision I should have made earlier, for all of their sakes. I have been prevaricating, postponing, but now that the future of the business is assured, now that I know how I feel about Rupert, the time has come to put my cards on the table. Win or lose.

Crossing the re-laid flagstones, flat and sealed and shiny, to the door, which now swung sweetly on its reworked hinges, Anna went to make a telephone call.

Chapter Twenty-Four

'*Darling, I am growing old,*
Silver threads amongst the gold
Shine upon my brow today,
Life is slipping fast away...'

'Lavinia, I was wondering if you would like to play for our guests?'

'I should *adore* to play for our guests. At what time are they due to arrive?' Lavinia was dressed in a long, slender gown of discoloured grey crêpe de Chine, which had an old dry-cleaning ticket pinned to one sleeve. Her beautiful hair was secured with its usual melee of pins and combs and a haphazard application of rouge to her cheeks gave her a hectic air.

Anna bent to remove the ticket from her sleeve, blinking hard. There must not be tears. There could never be tears. As always, looking at Lavinia, being with her, seeing how she was, caught at her heart, snagged it. She told herself that it was self pity. That all that mattered was that Lavinia herself was perfectly happy in her own little world. It didn't make her feel any better. She supposed that there were some things, some lost things, some things that could never be recovered, that would always be regretted; mourned; grieved over. The reluctant safety pin released itself at last, leaving a small rust stain on the material. On the pedals of the piano, she could see thick brown socks that were clearly Vivian's and, on top, a pair of narrow, pearlised pink ankle strap shoes that might once have been just the thing for *Thé Dansant* at the Savoy. 'I don't mean today. Nobody is coming today. I mean when our guests arrive for the Christmas house party. I wondered if you might like to play in the dining room whilst they are having dinner? Only if you would like to, of course. Only if you would enjoy it.'

'But, my dear, I simply *love* the idea! I shall be *delighted* to play for them whilst they are having dinner. Would evening dress be appropriate? I shall go and change at once. Perhaps you could assist me to select a suitable gown? At what time did you say they were expected?'

* * *

Anna, mounted on the chestnut livery, with Nicola on the grey gelding, rode out of the drive and into the lane leading to the bridleway. It had been Nicola's idea and Anna had been pleased to get away from the house and its workmen, and Rupert in particular.

Summer had come and gone and the banks were dry and scorched. The last of the wild roses in the hedgerows were turning to hips, elderberry branches were heavy with fruit and blackberries were ripening everywhere. Riding along the lane with the regular clop of hooves in her ears, becoming accustomed to feeling the length of her legs against the horse's sides, the weight of her feet in the stirrups, the soft, steady feel of the horse's mouth on the end of the reins, Anna realised how much she had missed the physical pleasure and intimacy with a horse that, once experienced, is never forgotten. But this ride had a serious purpose. It was her opportunity to talk to Nicola. Alone. The perfect opportunity. She had planned to lead into the subject gently.

'Nicola,' she began as they rode, stirrup to stirrup, along the lane. 'We need to talk about the stables.'

'Let's not talk about the stables,' Nicola said.

'Well then, perhaps we should talk about the horses; about keeping them; about how you manage to keep them.'

'Let's not talk about the horses,' Nicola said.

Anna had not anticipated that it takes two to make meaningful conversation. 'But there are things I need to say to you. We have to talk about it.'

'We have to talk about some things,' Nicola allowed. 'But not the stables and not the horses. Not today. Not now.'

That then, appeared to be the end of that. They rode along in silence for a while.

'When you first came to Rushbroke, I thought you and Rupert were an item,' Nicola said. 'I was surprised to find you weren't. Presumably there is a relationship elsewhere.'

Anna, who had set out to talk to Nicola, now found the tables turned. Well, perhaps she had to share a few confidences in order to get something in return. 'Yes. It started a long time ago. I was a student at catering college. He was one of the tutors.'

'Isn't that against the rules?'

'It is. I thought that was why we had to be discreet.'

'And it wasn't?'

'One day I was sitting in the park reading a book and I saw him with his wife and two small children, a perfectly happy little family, laughing together and feeding the ducks.'

'That must have been awful for you. I suppose that was the end of it.'

'It could have been. Perhaps it should have been.' Anna could not bring herself to say she wished it had been. She didn't want to dwell on the pain, the hurt, the feeling of betrayal. Nor the fact that, in many ways, there would never be an end to it; never could be. 'No, it was by no means the end of it.'

Nicola looked thoughtful. 'Shouldn't you have told him? Rupert, I mean. Rather than leave him hanging on? Wouldn't it have been fairer?'

'I couldn't tell him. I wasn't ready. There was another issue. It's complicated.'

'Everything's complicated if you allow it to be. You seem to have mastered the art of leaving people guessing. Of making excuses. Of keeping secrets. It isn't good, Anna. It isn't fair.'

'You are probably right.' Anna fell silent, listening to the sound of the chestnut gelding's hooves on the lane: one, two, three, four. One, two, three, four. A perfectly regular gait. Four beats to the bar. She had learned about gaits. It was all coming back to her now. She knew she was prevaricating. 'Not just probably,' she admitted. 'You are right. I know you are.'

'There are things we need to talk about,' Nicola said, 'and I don't mean the stables or the horses, I mean about us, about family. It's all very well, pressing on without saying anything, assuming we don't know who you are, but it needs to be out in the open. It needs to be discussed. Surely we can talk about it.'

The gait of the horse was regular but Anna was wrong-footed. This was not the moment. She was not prepared. Everything needed to be in place, and it wasn't quite, not yet. 'It isn't that I don't want to talk about it. It's... It's just that...' She hesitated, knowing that she had to say some-thing, and being unprepared, was not sure what it might be. 'Nicola, you have to *know*; I have to be *sure* that you *know*; that the reason I came here wasn't... what I'm trying to say is that I haven't come here to claim *anything*. I don't *want*, I don't *expect* anything. If I'm to gain anything at all out of it, it has to be because I have earned it; not because I think I'm entitled, but because I've done something to help; because I've contributed. So in a way, what I'm doing is nothing to do with what you already know; nothing to do with who I am and what I haven't said because I didn't come here to take away anything that is yours, and now we are taking away the stables,' Anna's voice petered out on a miserable note, 'and that wasn't part of the plan.'

'We are not talking about the stables,' Nicola said firmly, and then: 'He tried to find you, you know. Vivian. Afterwards.'

Anna kept her eyes on the chestnut livery's silken mane. She didn't want to hear this. She wasn't ready for it.

'He always felt it; the guilt. But when he married her he didn't know. He had no idea. And neither did she. But Vivian made her do it. He couldn't bear the thought of not being the father. He wanted an heir. He didn't get one. That was his punishment. It was very Old Testament.'

'He leaves me clues,' Anna said miserably. 'Passages marked in the St. James Bible.'

'He's very fond of the Old Testament. He's very Old School. It's partly why he's banned from St. Saviour's. He can't stand the new prayer book. He can't abide modern hymns. The man with the guitar was the last straw.'

'He tried to find me? *Really?*'

'He did. And he succeeded. But by then he... *we...* had nothing to offer you. By then we had lost everything, and Lavinia was... well, you have seen for yourself how Lavinia is.'

'Yes.' Of course Anna knew how Lavinia was. It had been the worst thing.

'I know you haven't come to claim anything,' Nicola said. 'Not that there is anything to claim anyway, and I am glad that you are here—glad, glad, glad. But Vivian is not good. He isn't going to last. You need to talk to him. He needs to know that he is forgiven.'

'How could there be anything to forgive? It was all a very long time ago. And. after all, I had no idea that I was not their child until after my adoptive parents had died. They had instructed their solicitor to tell me. To give me what little information they had. To enable me to do what I thought was best.' Anna remembered the last time she had returned to her parent's home to find bulldozers already at work in the garden, grubbing up lawns and flattening flower beds, their great wheels smashing the rose bushes, crushing everything into the earth. It had been a shock. It had really hit her then. They had never been a close family unit. Her childhood, though well provided for and lacking for nothing in practical terms, had been short on love and affection. Her parents were not demonstrative, tactile people. They had a narrow social life. Visitors were few and those who came were regarded as an intrusion, an inconvenience; their presence something to be endured rather than celebrated. They were so wrapped up in themselves; their garden maintenance; their household routines, that Anna had often felt, especially once she left home for college, that she didn't really belong; that she was no more welcome than the visitors they greeted with such false conviviality. Anna had missed them of course. She had been alone afterwards and vulnerable: she had been fair game...

'There really is nothing to forgive and I will talk to Vivian. I do plan to. But there is another issue to deal with first, and for that I shall need your help.'

Nicola's look was speculative. 'What sort of issue?'

'Something you need to know about; something you don't know about me. And you do need to know, Vivian needs to know, Rupert needs to know. At least,' Anna corrected herself, remembering, 'I *thought* he did, before... you know, before you and he...'

Nicola said pensively 'So you know about Rupert.' It wasn't a question.

'I know about Rupert.'

'Then you should know that he only comes to me because he's lonely and miserable and he can't come to you. You should know that it's you he wants. He comes to me and he doesn't know why. He really hasn't a clue about all this. I would have thought it obvious but he hasn't realised. He only comes to me, Anna, because I remind him of you.' Nicola knew when it was time to move on. 'We will deal with your issue, Anna, whatever it is. I'll do whatever you need me to do. But that's enough for now, I think.'

The horses went into trot. It *was* enough. Anna needed time to absorb what had been said. Now was not the time to deal with it. She packed it away carefully in her mind for later perusal. For contemplation. For meticulous examination. Later, in the privacy of her room she would unpack it and examine every detail and ponder its significance. Now, she concentrated on the chestnut livery's hooves as they hit the lane. One, two. One, two. One, two. A perfectly correct and rhythmic gait. Two beats to the bar. By tacit agreement the subject was closed.

The perfectly correct and rhythmic gait was shortly interrupted by the grey gelding who, perceiving that a car had appeared behind them and was about to overtake, began to lift up his feet like a hackney and sidle towards the bank, his eyes rolling in alarm. The chestnut livery, sensing impending trouble, shot forward, taking Anna by surprise, leaving the grey horse exposed to the car as it inched past. The woman driver, with an anxious smile and the very best of intentions, attempted to minimise the disturbance by slowing down even more, causing the grey gelding, wild-eyed, to try to escape crabwise up the bank. He was only just prevented from diving through the hedge by some vigorous hauling at his head and the smart application of a whip, with the result that he slithered back onto the lane as the driver of the car accelerated away in relief. Anna brought the chestnut livery, now distinctly skittish, back alongside Nicola, who rode on as if nothing untoward had occurred. Anna could only applaud her calmness in the saddle. In comparison, the grey horse was a nervous wreck. His neck was streaked with sweat. He let out a long, shuddering sigh, dropped his head in exhaustion and closed his eyes. He looked if he had just been an unwilling participant in the Grand National.

'He doesn't seem to be getting any better. I'm a bit worried about the Boxing Day meet.'

'It's going to take some time, I'm afraid. It's a shame because otherwise he's a really good horse; he jumps and events, but he's murder to box and if I can't cure him, he's for the glue factory. I thought I might ask David Williamson if I could put him in that little strip of field that runs alongside the lane for a few hours every day, just to get him used to a bit of traffic going past. He only uses it as a cattle trap when they are ready for market. As for Boxing Day, I might lead him to the Crick and Mr Pomeroy can mount up at the meet. That way there won't be any traffic problems at the start of the day, at least.'

It seemed a reasonable plan. They turned onto the bridleway; the horse's hooves sounding hollow on the bone dry ground. Together they cantered along a wide, grassy ride which took them around the edge of the village, past a new development of houses which, despite vociferous opposition from almost all the inhabitants of Rushall St. Mary, were already rising from their foundations, past The Crick in the Neck, until they reached the top of a narrow road from which they could rejoin the drive to Rushbroke Hall. It was at this point that David Williamson unexpectedly appeared round a bend, in his Land Rover.

The shock of suddenly being confronted with Nicola and two of her unspeakable equines caused him to brake violently and noisily in front of them. Horrified, the grey gelding flung himself to one side in a half rear, as a result of which he slid backwards into the ditch, pitching Nicola onto his neck. The chestnut livery, having absorbed traffic hysteria from the grey gelding like an infection, ran backwards away from the scene despite the energetic application of Anna's heels, and only a thwack from her stick arrested her progress. As the Land Rover stalled and swerved to a standstill, David Williamson fell forward onto the steering wheel and inadvertently set off the horn, occasioning further upset. There was a goodly interval of chaos before a relative calm was restored.

After several abortive attempts, Nicola, seizing the moment, managed to persuade the grey gelding to approach the Land Rover, which it did with a great show of reluctance, lifting its feet up in an exaggeratedly high, slow motion, as if it had springs attached to its hooves, the performance accompanied by a lot of indignant snorting, its neck held unnaturally high, crested and wrinkled with effort, and as solid as a plank.

Anna, too far away to hear what was being said, could nevertheless see a nervous tic working furiously in David Williamson's cheek and his hands set fast upon the wheel.

She urged the chestnut livery nearer.

'You don't really mean no,' Nicola was saying, despite the antics of the grey horse, who was now furiously digging a hole in the drive with one of his front hooves. 'I'm sure you mean yes, really. And I'll pay you. I'll pay you any way you like. Perhaps you would like to think about it?' She smiled down at David Williamson (who looked almost as wild-eyed as the grey gelding) in what could only be described as a provocative manner, 'About how you would like to be rewarded? About how I could possibly repay you?'

David Williamson didn't even stop to think about it. The Land Rover suddenly roared into life as if it the flag had gone down at Brand's Hatch. It bucketed off down the lane at a furious rate, scattering gravel. Wheels squealed in protest as it turned onto the drive leading to the Home Farm.

'Good,' Nicola said with satisfaction. She turned the by now completely demented grey gelding into the wrought iron entrance gates, restored to their former glory by Len and his welding equipment, against which Rupert had propped a sign:

RUSHBROKE HALL COUNTRY HOUSE.
LUXURY ACCOMMODATION AND
RESTAURANT.
OPENING SHORTLY.

'*That* seems to be settled then.'

Chapter Twenty-Five

The library was finished, the carpet laid, books purchased by the metre supplied by the second hand book shop in Hadleigh filled the shelves. Squashy leather chairs and small tables with lamps were set into companionable groups. Len had set up the scale model of the stable development on a library table in one corner. It sat on a board; a miniature miracle; the apartments set around a courtyard with a central fountain, the whole complete with realistic little people, sponge rubber trees and shrubbery.

'It looks great,' Rupert said approvingly. 'If things had turned out differently, I could even imagine living there myself.'

'Dream on, my boy. You'd never afford it anyway. This is a top of the range development. The council wouldn't agree to anything else.'

'Not an affordable housing scheme then?'

'Hardly. You need a car to live here,' Len pointed out. 'And it is a tad isolated. But then that's what will attract our buyers; hopefully the sort of people who will use the hotel as a facility. Rupert, sit down a minute. I need to tell you something.'

'What sort of something? Not another workman done a runner?'

'No, not that.' Len sat down in a wing back chair and looked around appreciatively. 'Nice, this room. Comfortable. Not too new looking.'

'Yes, Anna has a knack of putting things together. Everything works. The bedrooms are beautiful.'

'It's about Anna I wanted to talk.'

'Oh.' Rupert looked uncomfortable. Sadie put her head on his knee. Although she could not have known what was coming, it was as though she sensed it might not be good news.

'Look, Dad, Nicola has...'

'I'm not going to lecture you. You've done what you've done for your own reasons. It's none of my business.'

'Thanks.' Rupert looked marginally relieved. 'But Nicola...'

'Me first. You can tell me your news later, if it's still appropriate. What I want to tell you is that I went to see Anna to ask about the gardener's cottage. It's a ruin and it's small, but, done up, it would have been ideal for Sadie and me.'

'But what about your own house; yours and mum's? What about The Close?' Whatever Rupert had expected, it hadn't been this.

'Too many memories. And I've grown to love this place, I've got attached to it, and to Anna too; she's a great, courageous girl and she's done a brilliant job so far. I've been proud to help and I've got you to thank for that because this job has given me my life back. I just thought it would be good to live on the premises, you know, do up the cottage at my own expense, stay on to look after the building, only...'

'Only she said no.'

'She said yes.'

'So what's the problem?' Rupert was still trying to get his head around the fact that Len would actually consider leaving The Close, his conservatory, and his wife's beloved garden; that he was ready to move on.

'There's something you need to know.'

'And that is?' Rupert's tone implied that already he suspected that this would not end well.

'Anna asked me if I would renovate the gatehouse. She wants to live there.'

'Makes sense, I suppose. At least she can get away from the kitchen. She will need her own space.'

'Ah, that's the point. The space isn't just for Anna. She's bringing someone to live with her. I'm sorry Rupert; I had to tell you.'

'I already know. Nicola told me.' Rupert stroked Sadie's soft head, feeling the hard bone of her skull beneath his fingers. If he lived to be a hundred he would never understand why Anna had chosen not to tell him there was someone else. True to her word, Nicola had told him what she had found out. That Anna had a relationship and that it was not over. And it bloody well hurt. God, how it hurt. Why hadn't she told him? Surely he had a right to know? And now he had burned his boats with Nicola, and he was angry with Anna, angry with himself, angry with the world. But sorry for Len; for spoiling his plans.

'I've already written out my notice,' he said. 'I'll stay until after Christmas; until she finds another manager. I won't leave her in the lurch. But I'm really sorry, Dad. I'm sorry that it should end like this after all the work, all our plans, all *your* plans. I can't stay though. I don't want to be a part of it any more, not... not if...' He put his head in his hands. It took all the self control he could muster not to give way to the grief he felt. 'I'm sorry Dad. I'm so bloody fucking well sorry.'

'I'm sorry too. But it isn't your fault. Anna should have told you. You shouldn't have had to hear it from other people. I'm surprised at her; disappointed. What about Nicola?'

'Nicola isn't...' Rupert couldn't bring himself to say important because it would not have been fair and it was not what he meant. 'It was never going to be serious between Nicola and me.'

In Len's day, people didn't sleep together if it wasn't serious. Well, perhaps this was for the best. Rupert's affair, if affair was what it was, had not made the situation any easier; nor had it made his son happy. Rupert looked strained and wretched. He had lost weight. To get away, to start afresh, was the best thing he could do in the circumstances.

'There's no reason for you to change your plans, Dad. You still have the apartments to build. And you could still do up the gardener's cottage, if you wanted to.'

'Without you here? Seeing Anna with somebody else when it should have been you?' Len looked at his son wearily. 'I'd not have the heart for it.'

Chapter Twenty-Six

Due to the paucity of top class equitation establishments within reasonable motoring distance of home, Tony had been obliged to patronise a distinctly unsmart local riding school staffed by young women in anoraks and sweat-encrusted rubber boots who, if presented with a hunting stock, would probably imagine it was something to be applied to the top of a horse's tail in the manner of a bandage.

It was clear from the moment he walked into the scruffy, straw-strewn yard, resplendent in the Full Melton Hunt Coat, the shiny box calf boots, and the skullcap with the black silk cover as worn by Prince Charles, that they were not accustomed to dealing with the hunting fraternity.

Instead of the smooth-running thoroughbred he was expecting, his mount (when they had managed to drag it out of its stable) had been black and white like a cow with a corrugated pink nose and a wall eye. It regarded him with suspicion but to its credit, had remained stationary until Tony had mounted, which had been no easy matter due, as he had explained to the pink-faced girl holding the horse by the bridle, to the fact that his boots had yet to be broken in around the ankles. The piebald creature (surely the most unprepossessing animal ever presented to someone whose apparel had been almost personally selected by Baily) was both small and wide. Nevertheless, having gained the saddle, Tony felt perilously high off the ground and most unexpectedly insecure.

Tony had purchased from Amazon a book optimistically entitled *Learn to Ride in a Weekend*, and thus considered himself well acquainted with the theory of horsemanship, but when he squeezed the animal with his legs and eased the reins in the manner prescribed by the author to encourage his mount to move off at a walk, the brute merely lifted its tail and farted. The pink-faced girl, whose hair was a dried blonde haystack showing black at the roots, was obliged to take the pony by the rein and lead him into the scruffy manège as if Tony had been an absolute beginner or a child. Tony could not fail to notice that although her features had been composed into an expression of serious intent, her shoulders were shaking uncontrollably.

It was not at all how he had imagined it. Booking a course of lessons over the telephone without a preliminary inspection of the premises had obviously been a terrible mistake. Tony began to feel a rising panic. He wondered how he could make his escape. He wouldn't learn anything about the art of horsemanship here. He felt horribly out of place and uncomfortably aware that he was grotesquely overdressed for such a low grade establishment. As the pony moved off, he grabbed the front arch of the saddle, feeling he was about to fall off at any moment. He felt ridiculous; humiliated.

The manège contained several rusty oil drums, a few

scuffed show jumps and his instructress; an overweight girl whose stretch joddie things were so impossibly tight that her legs looked as though they had been inflated with a bicycle pump. Her grubby sweat shirt was topped with a quilted waistcoat so lacerated that it looked as if she had been attacked by a wild beast. She was eating cold baked beans straight from the tin. 'Sorry,' she said, waving a spoon in the manner of a greeting. 'No time for lunch and missed breakfast this morning.' She crammed a couple more large spoonfuls into her mouth before abandoning the tin on one of the posts surrounding the manège.

Tony opened his mouth to plead an unexpected engagement, but before she had even swallowed the last of the beans, she had addressed herself to correcting his position in the saddle, arranging his person without the least reticence regarding the handling of his bottom and his thighs, moving them around with a firmness and authority which was both surprising and alarming. When his body was rearranged to her satisfaction, she clipped a lungeing rein to the pony's cumbersome noseband and produced a whip of frightening length and suppleness.

Tony realised he had left it too late to escape. He told himself that if he could survive the first lesson, he could cancel the rest of the course. He would just have to make the best of it. It was only an hour, after all. Afterwards, he would find a better class of establishment; one where he would be treated with respect.

Unsportingly, they had shaved off the pony's mane (Baily would not have approved of *that*) replacing it with an insubstantial neckstrap. Even more unsportingly, his pneumatic instructress removed Tony's boots from the stirrups (where he had positioned his feet with care; toes up, heels down as shown in the diagram in the opening chapter of

Learn to Ride in a Weekend) and crossed both stirrups and leathers in front of the saddle, leaving his legs completely unsupported. This was an unexpected and frightening development. Tony clutched at the reins and the neckstrap in dismay feeling himself horribly unstable and very much at a disadvantage.

Pointing the whip at the piebald's shoulder, his instructress encouraged the pony to walk in a large circle around her. Tony hated every rolling, gyratory moment of it. It was worse than being on a yacht in a rough sea (Tony had tried yachting and had been catastrophically seasick). He had assumed that riding a horse was largely a matter of balance, and as he had (at one time or another) become nearly proficient at skiing, windsurfing and roller blading (to name just a few of the activities which he had only just failed to master), he had expectations of having a fairly easy ride. But even at a walk, Tony found that the ride was not easy. In fact, a few minutes in the saddle were sufficient to demonstrate to Tony that learning to ride was not only horribly uncomfortable but also most horribly difficult, even more horribly difficult that he had been led to believe by *Learn to Ride in a Weekend* which, to be fair, had not actually promised that learning to ride in a weekend was either easy or actually possible.

'Now, Mr Pommey, let go of your reins and fold your arms.'

'Pomeroy. The name's Pomeroy. I can't let go of the reins. I'll fall off.' Was the woman mad? Tony gripped the reins tighter. He felt horribly unsafe. To think he had imagined himself galloping after the hunt, flying over five-bar gates. The idea was ludicrous.

'Of course you won't fall off. The reins aren't there to

hold onto. You use the reins to communicate with the horse. The reins won't keep you in the saddle.'

'Well, I won't stay on without them. I can't let go. I don't feel safe.' Tony wished she would put down the whip. Was she going to poke him with it? Was the woman a dominatrix?

'Try. Just try, Mr Pommey. Try. You're all tensed up. Try to relax into the saddle. Let your body absorb the movement. Let the horse do the work. All you have to do is sit there. That's better. Now, take just one hand off the reins.'

All you have to do is sit there. Tony thought the idea absurd. At least on the yacht he had been fitted with a lifeline. And novice trapeze artists always had a safety net. (It had not occurred to Tony to try walking the high wire, possibly because he suffered from vertigo.) All he could see beneath his boots was the ground which, being cinders, did not promise a cushioned landing. Tony averted his gaze and looked between the pony's ears as recommended by *Learn to Ride in a Weekend*. Unwillingly, he took one hand off the reins. It did not make an appreciable difference to his stability. He removed the other, letting the reins fall on the cow-like animal's shaved neck. Miraculously, he found that he could indeed fold his arms and, to his surprise, he did not fall off.

'Well done. Now relax your legs, Mr Pommey, and don't let your knees creep up the saddle. Keep your legs long and relaxed. Look straight ahead. Let your seat and your waist absorb the movement. Think about the rhythm of the gait. The walk is four-time. Count with me. One, two, three, four. One, two, three, four. Feel the rhythm. Relax into it.'

After a few minutes the instructions began to speed up. 'Now put your hands on top of your head, Mr Pommey.

Now fold your arms behind your back. Now lean down and touch your left toe with your right hand. Now the right toe with the left hand.'

'Are these gymnastics really necessary?' Tony was feeling very hot and bothered in the Full Melton Hunt Coat. It was still very stiff and it was difficult to move his arms. 'I'm only going hunting, you know. I'm not going to join a circus.'

'If it wasn't necessary I wouldn't be asking. You need to develop an independent seat. You have to get your balance. Shall we try a trot?'

'I don't know. Can I have my reins and stirrups back?'

'Not yet. Hold onto the neckstrap and relax your whole body. It'll be a bit bumpy.'

Bumpy wasn't the word for it. Rib-rattling was more like it. Tony grabbed the front arch of the saddle and hung on for grim death. Almost at once he felt himself slipping to one side in a terrifyingly perilous manner.

'Let your legs hang long and loose. Your knees are tightening up again. Relax. Relax. *Legs long and loose*, Mr Pommey! Don't let your knees creep up the flaps! Relax down into the saddle! Straighten those knees!'

'I can't! I'm falling off!' Tony had slipped further to one side and reached the point of no return. He hit the ground with a resounding thump and lay on the cinders, shocked and winded. He wondered if he had broken something. Tentatively he moved his arms and legs, relieved to find that his limbs seemed to work normally. The piebald pony, schooled to revolve at a steady gait whatever the eventuality, had continued on the circle and now found its path obstructed. Tony, thinking he was about to be trampled, let out a yelp of alarm, but the animal stopped dead with its face inches from his person. It regarded him with its wall eye, looking rather surprised, as if it had no idea how he had got there. His instructress appeared at his side and helped him up in a casually unconcerned manner. Ineffectually, she dusted down the Full Hunt Coat. 'Are you OK, Mr Pommey?'

'Yes, I think so.' Tony had rarely felt so ridiculously undignified. 'And the name's Pomeroy. Look here, I don't think I'm going to be very good at this. I don't think I want to carry on. I think I'll call it a day.' Tony could no longer picture himself as a hunting man, galloping after hounds, flying over five-bar gates. Faced with the reality he realised it had been nothing more than an unrealistic pipe dream. Yet another folly in the wake of numerous other follies. He was never going to master the art of horsemanship. He was going to have to cancel everything; the lessons; the hire of the horse for the Boxing Day meet. There was no doubt about it. So what if he would be letting down not only the hallowed institution of Baily but also the venerable sales assistant of Bespoke? (He tried not to think of the astronomical price he had paid for his hunting clothes.) All for a pipe dream. All for a folly. 'Throwing in the towel already?' His instructress's eyes widened. 'Don't be daft, Mr Pommey, you were doing really well.'

'I doubt it,' Tony said. 'A minute ago you had to pick me up off the ground.'

'So what does a fall matter? Look, Mr Pommey, if you want to learn to ride well enough not to disgrace yourself at the hunt, we can do it, honestly we can. I wouldn't say we could if we couldn't. But you really have to *want* to do it—I mean *really want to*.'

Tony looked at her. Was she serious? Did this unprepossessing girl working in this unbelievably down-at-heel establishment, eating a lunch of baked beans out of a tin, really think she could make a rider out of such unpromising material? Perhaps she did. And anyway, what did he have to lose? 'I don't know,' he said. 'To be honest, I didn't think riding would be so difficult. But I suppose I do want to—if you think I can do it.'

'Then let's go for it, shall we? Look, shall we take that heavy coat off? I think you'd do a lot better without it.'

They removed the coat and hung it on the post and rail next to the tin of beans.

'That's better. Now let's get you back in the saddle.' She grabbed hold of his ankle and gave him an energetic leg up. 'We'll work on the walk for a bit and do a few more exercises until you get your confidence back.'

So off they went again. 'Remember to relax, Mr Pommey. Let your legs hang loose.'

'Tony. My name's Tony.'

'And mine's Janine. And he's The Pied Piper; Piper for short. He's not much to look at but he's steady and he's kind. He'll teach you the basics. I can't promise we'll get you riding over fences in just ten lessons, but we'll have a jolly good shot at the rest. Fox hunt is it?'

'Harriers.'

'That's a stroke of luck. Harriers just chase round in circles don't they? Not much jumping with harriers.'

Even Baily had not thought to mention that. Tony patted the piebald's neck. 'Hello Piper.' One furry ear flipped backwards in acknowledgement. Suddenly everything felt better.

'Are you ready to have another bash at trot, Tony?'

'I'll give it a go.'

'Good man. Lean into it then. Ready? Tr-ot Piper!'

Piper lurched forward.

'Now don't hang onto the front of the saddle as if your

life depends on it because it doesn't. You don't need to do it. I want you to get used to the gait and slowly let go of the saddle. The trot's two-time. Count with me: one, two. One, two. That's better but you're still trying too hard, Tony. Relax. The horse is doing the work. Just go with it. Watch those knees, they're rising up again. Now loosen your grip. Do it gradually. Let go a finger at a time. Go on Tony, you can do it!'

Bumpity, bumpity bump. It was agonising. But, amazingly, after a few more revolutions, he was down to one finger on the front of the saddle. One loose finger.

'Now you're forgetting the knees again. They're starting to creep up. If you let your knees stiffen and creep up the saddle you'll fall off again. Relax your legs and keep them long. Pretend you have weights attached to your feet.'

'That's better! Well, done, Tony! Well done! Walk, Piper, walk now boy. Stand. Good boy. We'll have a breather, then we'll have another go on the other rein; that just means going the other way round, so you and the horse don't get one-sided. After that we'll give you some stirrups and reins back and we'll try a few stops and starts.'

After another half hour they made their way back to the yard, Tony riding Piper off the rein with a confidence he would have considered impossible an hour ago.

'Next time we'll try to get you posting at the trot,' Janine promised. 'Once you can post you'll be a lot more comfortable. It does get easier, I promise. We had a rocky start but you've done well today, Tony.'

You've done well today, Tony. Tony grinned as he drove out of the car park. He had done well, Janine had said so, and he believed her. Despite his initial discomfort and scepticism he had done well, and in the end he had enjoyed it. He felt a wave of affection for the piebald pony; for Piper.

After all, he was the perfect learning vehicle and one would hardly learn to drive in a Ferrari, would one? And nobody would ever see him in beginner mode; not the family (from whom all of this was a closely guarded secret); and certainly not anyone from Baily. He went back to the office, changed back into his pinstripes and shiny shoes, and threw himself into his afternoon schedule of appointments and paperwork with a gusto born of anticipated success.

The next day Tony could hardly walk. He lurched round the office in agony, quite unable to sit at his desk. He sent his secretary out to buy him a soft cushion. It didn't make any difference. His thighs and posterior took a full week to recover.

He had to invent a gym membership to explain it away to Mary.

For his lesson the following week he wore an old anorak instead of the Melton Full Hunt Coat.

The week after that he took the velvet cover off the skull cap.

Chapter Twenty-Seven

'Are you ready for this?' Nicola asked.

The solemn little person with pigtails standing beside Anna nodded. Anna hoped she was doing the right thing, springing it on everyone like this. But Nicola had thought it the best thing to do. Get it over with. Kill two birds with one stone. Well, the first stone would be easier to cast than the second.

Nicola opened the door.

In what was now the residents' lounge, with its well-upholstered sofas and coffee tables, sat several people: Vivian and Lavinia, Nicola and Rupert, Len and Sadie. Without any hesitation the small person with pigtails went in first; positively dived in. The lounge might have been a swimming pool on the hottest of days. She had been waiting for this moment. Living for it. Counting the days. She was wearing her favourite white fleece top and the leopard print tights she considered her best, her *very* best and most suited to the occasion, together with her new patent leather ankle boots. She seemed to have taken charge. She looked around at the gathering. Assessing. Deciding. She was six years old.

'This is Grace,' Anna said. 'My daughter. She's been in foster care until I could provide a home for her. I thought it was time, well, more than time perhaps, that you met.' It sounded far too matter of fact for such a momentous introduction.

Eyes widened. Grace beamed. Rupert stood up, opened his mouth, then closed it and sat down again. His face was ashen. Even Sadie, who had got to her feet in welcome, didn't know what to make of it. She sat down abruptly and looked at Len for reassurance.

Everyone appeared to have been struck dumb. 'Perhaps we had better introduce ourselves,' Nicola suggested.

'But I already know who everybody *is*,' Grace protested. 'I could tell you, if you like. It could be a sort of a game, couldn't it? A guessing game?'

'We talked about you all the time,' Anna explained. 'We spoke all the time about Rushbroke... about family.'

'Why don't you do that, Grace.' Len was the first to find his voice. 'Welcome to Rushbroke.' He looked at his son's anguished face. *Unexplained absences*, he thought. *Oh My God.*

Grace pointed to Nicola. 'I already know my Aunt Nicola and she trains horses. I'm having riding lessons and when I don't fall off so much, we are going riding together, but I won't be riding the horse that runs through hedges.'

'Absolutely not,' Nicola said. 'We shall find you a nice quiet pony.'

Remembering that it was rude to point, Grace went over to where Vivian was sitting and touched his knee. 'You are a baronet, which is very special, and you are my grandfather, and if you are not quite that, then I would really, really like you to be.'

Vivian tried to smile but found his mouth wouldn't move. He nodded.

Tears were pouring down Lavinia's cheeks. She looked at Vivian in wonder. She said 'Vivian, you *found* her, you darling man, you absolute darling, *darling* man.' She held out her arms to Grace. 'Come here, come to me my dearest, *dearest* child; my own dearest lost child, come home to me at last.'

Grace looked at Anna. Anna nodded. Quite desperately she wanted to say to Lavinia, *no! I am your lost child!* Yet what good would it do? And if Grace could open a window in Lavinia's mind, however briefly, however skewed the view, what did it matter if the homecoming, the welcome, skipped a generation?

Grace kissed Lavinia dutifully on the cheek. From the pocket of her fleece she produced a tissue and dabbed gently at her Grandmother's cheeks. 'I've been having piano lessons for ages,' she said. 'We could play duet, if you like.' Lavinia put her arms around the child and held her tightly; too tightly. Anna could not move. It was Nicola who detached Grace from Lavinia's grip. 'Let her finish the guessing game and then you can have her back,' she promised. Lavinia took Vivian's hands and raised them to her cheek. 'You, dear, *dear*, man. Thank you. *Thank You.*' Vivian, bewildered, looked to Anna for guidance.

'It's fine,' she told him. 'Whatever she believes is fine.'

Grace, in the meantime, was eyeing Len; considering him, her head on one side. 'You must be my Uncle Len, because this is Sadie, and Sadie will be my friend because Sadie is friends with everybody.' Grace knelt down and put her arms around Sadie who gave her a large slobbering lick.

Grace moved onto the last person in the room. 'And you

are Rupert.' She looked round the room just to be sure. 'You must be Rupert because there's nobody else left.'

'I'm Rupert,' he agreed in a strained voice. 'Although at this particular moment I would much prefer to be someone else.' He looked across at Anna, not vengefully as might have been expected, but in devastation. He looked absolutely destroyed; totally heartbroken. 'To be perfectly honest, Grace, I would prefer to be anyone else in the whole world, rather than me.'

Anna bit her lip. Two birds with one stone and this was the final one. Was it too late? Was Nicola's confidence misplaced? She had no idea what Rupert's reaction was going to be.

Grace looked at Rupert in concern. 'Can't you just be Rupert for a minute? Because I can't ask my question if you are going to be someone else.' She looked anxiously at Anna, who nodded encouragement. 'You see if you really *are* Rupert, Mummy wants me to ask if you might like to be my Daddy. Because I don't actually have one. And most people do.'

Having said this and waited for an answer that failed to materialise, Grace looked round the room in consternation and then at Anna with accusation; her face puckered with disappointment; with the injustice of promises previously made and suddenly revealed to be false. 'You *said* they'd be *pleased!*'

'They *are* pleased!' After the first stunned moment of incredulity, Rupert had shot to his feet. '*We are pleased!* We are all *incredibly* pleased! We are so bloody pleased we are bloody speechless!'

'Then why is everybody *crying?*'

Chapter Twenty-Eight

It was evening. They sat alone at the plank table holding hands across it. Grace, cock-a-hoop about her new family, had been returned to her foster home to tell her somewhat bemused foster parents all about her day. They would be devastated to lose her but had known it was going to happen and were prepared for it. They would not lose touch; there would be visits back and forth, hopefully for a lifetime.

'I know I should have told you earlier, but I didn't know how I felt about you, not really; not until Nicola...'

'I have a lot to thank Nicola for,' Rupert said ruefully. 'I'm sorry. I was lonely and unhappy and Nicola has a knack; she made it better, at least for a while. I could almost believe she was you. Now I know why.'

Anna wondered if Nicola had also made it better for the corn merchant, the vet and the blacksmith, but would not tell Rupert about this until much later. 'I don't blame you. I was at fault. I should have explained the situation. I should have been more open but there was a lot going on.'

'There were a lot of secrets. Too many. I had no idea. Looking back, knowing what I know now, I should have seen it; I should have realised there was a bloody good reason for you to do what you did. I must have been blind.'

'You thought I was out of my mind.'

'Whatever I thought, and sometimes it wasn't good, I never stopped loving you, Anna. Not for a moment.'

'I'm very lucky. I know it now.'

'I'm the lucky one. I have you, and you, Anna, are all I have ever wanted. I even have a family, and we will have a house. I can hardly believe it.'

'We are all a family.' And they were. It had been Anna's dream, this family. And now the dream had become a reality. Lavinia, Vivian, Nicola, Anna, Grace, Rupert, Len, even Sadie. They *were* a family. 'And this is a family business.'

'And we have to make it work. We will make it work. We won't fail, Anna, I promise you.'

'The only thing that still worries me is Nicola and the stable development. I know we have to do it. She knows we have to do it. But she won't talk about it. It's so hard on her. Everyone else has gained, but Nicola has lost even what she had. It isn't fair. I broke my promise.'

'I'll talk to her. See if I can persuade her to let us build her a new stable block. Nicola is a bit like you though, in that respect; she's deep. Nicola is not easy to read; it's hard to get under the surface. Anyway, leave it to me. I need to talk to her anyway to make sure things are OK between us. I want to thank her. I probably owe her an apology too—an explanation anyway.'

'I doubt it. Nicola knew what she was doing. She knows how it was. Bringing Grace here today, introducing her like that; getting her to ask the question; it was all Nicola's idea.'

'Grace is wonderful. Grace is brilliant. She is going to be so happy here. Spoiled rotten probably.'

'And you really don't mind that...'

'That I'm not her biological father? No. Grace is part of you; Grace is part of our story; yours and mine. She comes as part of the package. Dad is besotted. I've never seen him as happy in years. He's absolutely made up.'

'Did he tell you he's going to do up the gardener's cottage?'

'He did. I've pulled rank and told him he's got to do the lodge first. He'll keep the team working on the cottages until we get the final detailed plans through for the development. It's all worked out brilliantly.'

'So now there's just Nicola.'

'Yes. There's just Nicola.'

* * *

David Williamson was on his way to the plucking shed with the wages when he heard the unmistakable whine of a chainsaw coming from the direction of his Christmas tree plantation. Having already steeled himself to enter the plucking shed (the stench of entrails and hot wax never failed to turn his stomach) he was rather anxious to get it over with, but the sound of the chainsaw stopped him in his tracks.

It was a late December afternoon and dusk, but there was light enough for him to look down across the lane into the plantation in time to observe a magnificent specimen of Norwegian spruce (left standing because it was considered too large for the domestic market) begin first to vibrate, then to rock violently from side to side, before falling to the ground with an audible crash very near the spot where Sir Vivian Rushbroke of Rushbroke was standing alongside his ancient Rover, to which was attached a flatbed trailer previous utilised by Nicola to hawk stable manure around the local gardening community.

This was not the first outrage of the day. Earlier, David Williamson had watched through his binoculars as the woman with the intense gaze and the frightening make-up who told fortunes at the annual church fete, assisted by the village mute, cut great boughs of berried holly from his trees, and dragged away severed branches of ivy from their trunks. The ivy was perhaps not entirely to be regretted, being parasitic, invasive and actively damaging to its host, but it was *his* ivy nevertheless, as was the berried holly *his* holly, and the Norwegian spruce currently being manhandled on to the trailer by the village mute assisted by a grey-haired man with a black Labrador at his heels, *his* tree. There was no doubt about this at all in David Williamson's mind. Right was on his side. The law of the land was on his side. In theory it should have been a simple matter to obtain justice but in practice the local constabulary were unhelpful, to say the very least, and when it came to tackling the Rushbrokes face to face he knew himself to be totally inadequate. A confrontation with even one Rushbroke, Nicola for example, caused him to become intensely overwrought, rendered him almost completely inarticulate, and inevitably left him feeling deeply distressed. As a result, all he could do was stand back and watch as his property was openly plundered and violated. It was an impossible situation, but when it came to taking direct action against the Rushbrokes, David Williamson was helpless.

Of course, David Williamson seethed. David Williamson twitched, trembled and positively shook with anger. Of course, his instinct was to jump into his Land Rover, race down the drive, burst into the plantation and challenge the thieving scoundrels on the spot; his instinct was to make a fight of it. But his physical health and mental state were delicately balanced. He dare not risk it. After all, he knew from previous experience that such a confrontation would be to no avail. He knew in advance what their argument would be, how they would protest that although he, David Williamson, now *owned* the land, the holly trees had been *purchased* and *planted* by a previous generation of Rushbrokes, and as for the Christmas tree plantation, why the infant trees had been planted by Sir Vivian's *own hand* within the last decade, so how could they, the Rushbrokes of Rushbroke, custodians of the land for *centuries*, possibly be begrudged what was practically theirs by divine right?

David Williamson watched as the tree was secured on the trailer. He watched the old car draw away accompanied by some energetic acceleration and a plume of black smoke from the exhaust. David Williamson watched as his magnificent Norwegian spruce made stately progress along the Rushbroke drive. He could see, quite clearly, the pale wound of the trunk where the tree had been amputated several feet from the ground, leaving only a circlet of branches still attached to the root in the plantation.

Rushbroke Hall looked enchanting. Every window in the place appeared to be lit and the warm, golden lights were reflected in the moat which surrounded it. The house looked too good to be true, like a magical stage set or a beautiful illustration in a children's story book. The Rushbrokes were prospering. What was even more disturbing was that their supporters were multiplying. Furthermore, in a matter of days, when Rushbroke Hall opened as a hotel, there would be guests guaranteed to cause further aggravation; blocking the lanes with their expensive cars, trespassing on his land, trampling his crops, quite possibly accompanied by undisciplined children and dogs who would be allowed to harass his livestock. The situation could only get worse. Whichever way he looked at his situation, David Williamson felt that unquantifiable forces were ranged against him.

Just thinking about it made him feel ill. He walked unsteadily back across the farmyard and pushed open the back door of the house. In the kitchen he sat down at the Formica-topped table which still bore the remains of his lunch; half a sliced white loaf and a lump of corned beef on a saucer. There was a big fly on the corned beef and when he waved an arm at it, it rose languorously into the air and lurched around the room making a loud buzzing sound; an out-of-season fly, dazed and disorientated. Eventually it landed in the sink amidst a pile of unwashed plates and saucepans. Somehow the fly was symbolic of the disgust David Williamson felt when he looked around the kitchen. Of course, he was equally disgusted by the state of every room in the house and one day he would do something about it, but not now, not on a day when his energies were quite depleted; not when he was, physically and mentally, so exceedingly plagued and exercised by the Rushbrokes.

Wearily, he dropped his head onto the table, his face colliding with the wage packets. He had forgotten about the wages and the realisation that he must steel himself anew to face the plucking shed caused him to groan out loud. He wondered, not for the first time, why he had allowed himself to become a farmer when it was obvious that he was totally unsuited to the life. The truth was that it was the only life he knew. The Williamsons had always been farmers and he had grown up with the expectation that he would be a farmer too. Throughout his schooldays he had worked alongside his father not only during the holidays, but also in the early mornings before school began, and in the evenings after it had closed its doors. Small wonder that he had little aptitude for lessons; he had precious little energy left for school work.

Five years ago, when his father had died, he continued to manage the farm almost by default. His mother had died when he was twelve years old. Never robust, she had sickened gradually and almost imperceptibly, so that by the time anyone realised there was something seriously wrong it was already too late. When he had last visited her in hospital she had been blanched and sunken, sucked dry by the cancer. Encouraged by his father, he had held her hand and been terrified by its lightness, by its insubstantiality, by the way the skin had become fragile and transparent like that of a dragonfly, as if it could barely manage contain the veins and the bones within. His mother had seemed to him to be little more than a husk after threshing; recognisable only in the way that a flower pressed for years between the pages of a book is still a fragile approximation of its living counterpart.

There had been few women in his life since. One or two adolescent friendships which had amounted to very little. A short-lived relationship with the bad-tempered daughter of a neighbouring farmer. Another with the daughter of the garage proprietor in Rushall St. Mary which had seemed promising until she had proclaimed herself tired of village life and taken herself off to a job in London and a bedsit above an Indian restaurant in Crouch End Broadway. Now and again there had been overtures but he had never followed them up. Last year one of the girls in the plucking shed had taken a shine to him and given him a Christmas present of a festive table decoration she had made herself. She had been shy and embarrassed when she had given it to him, and he had been touched. He had placed it on the mantleshelf above the defunct kitchen range and it was still there. Time had reduced it to three twigs and a scrap of dusty ribbon sticking out of a discoloured cube of crumbling oasis. She hadn't come back this year.

In the plucking shed the workers toiled at trestle tables set end to end in an approximation of a production line. They were a robust crowd, and needed to be, with no pretensions as to sensitivity. Most were regulars, familiar faces who turned up year after year, glad of the extra cash in hand to help with the expense of Christmas. That each took a turkey home, albeit a damaged one, was an added bonus.

The freshly killed birds were set above a bleeding trough at one end of the production line, then pushed along an overhead rail to the rough pluckers. Once plucked, they moved on to the hot wax dip, after which they were stripped clean before drawing. A weathered old boy who had sat in the same place doing the same job for as long as anyone could remember, hooked out the tough leg tendons by means of a bent nail, with surprising speed and dexterity. Two girls were in charge of the giblets, and when they and the neck had been inserted, the birds moved on to be trussed and finished before being carted off to the cold store to await delivery or collection.

The shed was heated by several Calor gas burners and the workers were entertained by a ghetto blaster turned to full volume. When David Williamson walked into the shed with the wages, the heat, the smell, and the solid wall of sound, knocked him back. Hell, he thought, might prove to be marginally more congenial than this. Averting his eyes from the wheeled bins of entrails, heads and claws, he made his way to where the woman who organised the workers on his behalf was tying together the legs of the still warm birds and hooking them onto the rail. 'You wanted me to give you the final count, David,' she yelled at him above the hubbub. 'I've the last bird coming through now and that makes five hundred and ninety six altogether. How many did you think you were short?'

Throughout the rearing season fatalities were inevitable. Losses in the early weeks were sometimes heavy, turkey poults being notoriously prone to mass hysteria which could easily result in trampling and suffocation. But by twenty-five weeks the birds were full grown, strong, and flappingly aggressive. They were by no means an easy catch and, moving in a large flock, were intimidating to potential predators, man or beast. Housed in the barn by nightfall, losses at this stage were unusual; nevertheless David Williamson had been resigned to the loss of one or two birds as in previous years, but when he had carried out his customary live head count a few days prior to killing, he had calculated that he was four short this year. Now he knew that it was six. *Six of his birds hanging in the Rushbroke larder. Six!* It was intolerable! It was time for action!

David Williamson walked out of the plucking shed. He went back to the farmhouse and climbed the stairs. In what had been his parent's bedroom, he pulled open the door of an old-fashioned wardrobe and took from within a ghastly, evil-smelling suit constructed of fur. He removed his outer garments and stepped into it. From the top of the wardrobe he took down the box containing *American Werewolf de Luxe in Latex*. Carefully, he removed it from its tissue wrapping and, inserting his hands inside the mask in the prescribed manner, pulled it down over his head.

The door of the old wardrobe incorporated a long mirror, flecked with age. David Williamson looked at his reflection. A diabolical creature stared back at him; a terrifyingly inhuman being, hideous and unspeakable; an unimaginable horror.

Nicola had gone too far this time. As soon as the turkey shed fell silent, as soon as the lights were extinguished and the last of the cars had departed, he would be ready. The minute Nicola set foot on his land to turn loose her cursed equines, she was going to have an encounter she would never, ever, forget.

Work on the house had intensified. After a day filled with final touches and Christmas decorations Rupert and Len had set out to inspect the gatehouse lodge. They had found it not as bad as they had feared. Although it was covered with a jungle of ivy and surrounded by dense undergrowth, when they had pushed their way through they found that the brickwork was still fairly good and the roof was intact. Even the chimneys were in reasonable order. The windows had gone, the floorboards had rotted, but it was by no means beyond restoration. The lodge was small. Upstairs there were just two bedrooms and space for a bathroom. Downstairs there was a tiny kitchen which needed extending and a surprisingly spacious sitting room with a magnificent and blessedly unrestored brick and bressumer beamed open fireplace. There was another tiny room, not much bigger than a cupboard really, but Rupert thought would make an office, and the kitchen had a pantry, which would please Anna. Already Len had plans for a conservatory.

They sat on the step, discussing their change in fortunes, the work schedule, the gatehouse lodge, the gardener's cottage, the proposed sale of The Close, the plans for the stable conversion, whilst Sadie snuffled about in the undergrowth in and around the tumbledown outside lavatory on the trail of goodness knew what. Dusk had fallen. Len looked at his watch and realised he was almost due at the Crick where he had arranged to have supper with the workmen.

'You take the torch,' Rupert said. 'I've got a beam on my key ring if I need it. There's a good moon tonight and it's not as if I don't know the way back.'

Len set off down the lane with Sadie at his heels. Sadie liked the Crick, and as soon as she got through the door would wander off to claim her habitual sleeping place on the flagstones by the fire. Rupert had declined to accompany them because he wanted to catch Nicola at evening stables. He walked back towards the house still marvelling at how much his life had changed during the last month. He could still hardly believe it. The gatehouse was to be his home. Anna loved him. They had a business. Len was part of it. *Suddenly everything is bloody marvellous*, he thought. *Bloody fucking sodding marvellous.*

He would never know what made him stop and lean over the gate into the pasture where Nicola's horses were illicitly turned out with David Williamson's cattle. In the moonlight he thought he could just distinguish the shape of the horses grazing amongst the cattle. But all he remembered afterwards was the horrific shambling creature he saw coming towards him along the hedgerow. He saw it stop and look at him. In the moonlight he saw the terrible bestial face of it; the yellow fangs; the red rimmed eyes, the black, verminous pelt of it. After the first disbelieving, terrible, frozen moment, Rupert ran. He had never run so fast in his life. He ran as if the devil himself was on his tail. Up the drive and through the gates and into the back door of the kitchen he ran, and slammed the door.

He sank down at the plank table. Gasping. Terrified. *Too many pints of Adnams*, he had said to Len. *Don't be daft, there are no monsters in Suffolk. It must have been a bloody cow.* Well, it hadn't been a cow. So what the hell was it? *What the fucking hell was it!*

Staggering to his feet he opened the cupboard and found a bottle of cooking brandy. With shaking hands he poured an uncommonly generous measure into a teacup. His hands trembled so violently that the liquid barely survived the journey to his mouth. *What the fuck had he seen? What the hell was it?* More to the point, what was he going to do about it? If there really was a monster out there, what the bloody fucking hell was he going to do now?

* * *

Early winter sunshine made it pleasant to be outdoors. The following day, Rupert found the foreman and his gang sitting on the bridge over the moat eating Anna's lunchtime sandwiches.

Now and again they threw a crust into the moat. Instantly the surface of the water became a boiling, threshing mass of shining, powerful bodies. As the result of being the daily beneficiaries of kitchen scraps, the carp were now enormous. Rupert looked down at their wide, round mouths, their rolled, pink lips and their little horn-like feelers. They were solid fish, much bigger and heavier, much broader and deeper, than they appeared in the water when viewed from above.

The Rushbrokes had dined on the carp for centuries. When Anna had enquired what they were like to eat Nicola had grimaced and replied that they had a muddy taste and required plenty of seasoning. Carp had not hitherto been a part of Anna's repertoire but, knowing them to be part of the Rushbroke tradition, she had felt them worthy of a little experimentation. In her battered copy of *Larousse* she had discovered three different recipes from France. Vivian had promptly spiked his fishing hooks with bacon and returned after a very short interval with three fine specimens.

Anna found that the flesh was firm and meaty yet flaked easily. Of the recipes, the one which called for prolonged marination and a short cooking time followed by a twenty-four hour chilling period, was proclaimed the most successful, closely followed by the baked version stuffed with herbs, lemon, roe and breadcrumbs. The third recipe, that for carp steaks in red wine with garlic was not universally liked by the workmen, who had appointed themselves Anna's panel of experts. They had proved to be willing and enthusiastic guinea pigs, avid to participate in any culinary experiment and ever ready to contribute advice and suggestions as to how a particular dish might be improved. Thus cold marinated carp and baked stuffed carp were definitely set to feature as Christmas fare in the dining room and would continue to be offered thereafter as a Rushbroke speciality. As the fish came free, the percentage profit they represented was considered by Rupert to be a great benefit.

Now Rupert sat down on the wall next to the foreman who, since the end of the summer, had become a frequent visitor to the kitchen, bearing rabbits, pigeons and the odd illicit pheasant or partridge for Anna's table.

'Can I ask a favour, Leon?'

'You ask favour any time you like, Rupert. If I can do favour for you, then I do it with pleasure.'

'You know the gun you shoot rabbits with?'

'Yes, I know it.'

'Can I borrow it?'

'You want for to shoot rabbits?'

'Not exactly, no.'

Leon threw his crusts into the moat. Two mallards sped across the water but they were no match for the carp. 'I think I know why you borrow it,' he said. 'I think you see something, Rupert. I think you see something terrible. I think you see what Maciej saw.'

Rupert said nothing. What could he say? He was not about to spread panic in the ranks.

'I tell Len when it happen. Is *truth* in this. I tell him I *know* Maciej. Is my friend for many years, and if Maciej say he see something, he not make up. Is out there; this thing; this monster. You want I come with you?'

'No thanks, I'll do this on my own.'

Chapter Twenty-Nine

It was the following evening. The workmen had gone off to the Crick. Len had gone back to The Close. After delivering game pie, sweet potato and spinach to Vivian and Lavinia, Anna was waiting for Rupert and Nicola to join her in the family kitchen. Rupert came in first having been supervising the electricians who had been installing light fittings in the bedrooms. He looked exhausted. He had said nothing to anyone and the previous night he had hardly slept at all.

Together they waited for Nicola. When it came to eight o'clock, Anna began to worry. She transferred their game pie and sweet potato wedges to the holding oven. 'I think we should go down to the stables,' she said. 'She's never this late and all she had to do was to turn out the horses. She's been gone since six. She's never late for supper; never has been. Something has happened. I know it.' Anna imagined that one of the horses might have escaped.

Rupert's imaginings were of a far darker nature. 'I'll go.' He got up from the table. He said firmly, 'Stay here, Anna.

Wait here until I get back. I need to talk to Nicola anyway.'
He took a powerful torch from the shelf.

Anna sensed that something was not quite right.
Through the kitchen window she watched Rupert cross the
yard. She saw him go into the building that was now the
laundry. He came out with a shotgun. *What? What was
this? What was happening?* Anna had no idea what was
going on but she was not prepared to stay behind and
remain in ignorance. Did Rupert know about the corn
merchant, the vet and the blacksmith? Was he about to see
them off with a shotgun? Surely not. So what did he
imagine was out there in the darkness? Rabbits? Foxes?
Suddenly she remembered Maciej and the wild stories of a
creature, a fiend; a beast so terrifying that Maciej had left
without even waiting for his wages.

'*Rupert, wait!*' Anna ran after him. 'Rupert! *Wait
for me!*'

Already Rupert was in the stable yard. The stables were
empty. He looked in the barn, the rickyard. There was no
sign of Nicola. He looked in the tack room. The headcollars
were gone. She had taken the horses up to the pasture. He
groaned.

He was moving quickly along the drive towards the
pasture by the time Anna managed to catch up with him.

'Rupert, why have you got a gun?'

'I told you to stay in the house. Do you never do as you
are told?'

'Not often, no.'

It was too late for prevarication. 'Last night, coming
back from the lodge, I saw something in the pasture.'

'*Something?* You mean like Maciej? A creature? *Rupert,
you saw a creature in the field?*'

'Yes.'

'But why didn't you say? Why didn't you tell me? What was it? What did it look like? Where has it come from?'

Too many questions. 'I don't know. But now you know why I wanted you to stay behind.' Rupert put his hand on her arm; pleaded with her. 'Anna, go back. *Please.*'

Even in the dark he could see that her eyes were wide with fright. Nevertheless, 'I can't leave you on your own, Rupert! No. *No! I can't* go back! *We need to find Nicola!*'

He motioned her to be silent. He said in a low voice 'The gate's open! Why would the bloody gate be open? Let's see if the horses are in the field.'

They were. 'But their headcollar ropes haven't been unclipped,' Anna whispered. This was evident; the ropes trailed after the horses as they grazed. '*Oh my God, Rupert, you don't think...?*'

'I don't know what to think.'

By the gatepost into the lane there was a scrap of something dark. Anna shone the torch onto it. 'It looks like hair or black fur, and what's this?' she knelt beside a dark stain on the ground. 'Rupert,' she said faintly, 'this looks like blood.'

Rupert put his fingers into it. It was red. Sticky. Fresh.

'There's more, look, there's a trail, and more of the hair. Oh my God, *Nicola!*'

They ran, following the trail; the dark splashes on the drive; the clumps of hair. They stopped at the drive to the home farm, casting around like bloodhounds following a line. 'Here, Rupert, here! Leading up to the farmhouse! Look, here's a big chunk of fur and more blood! Rupert, you don't think... you don't think Nicola....'

'*I don't know what I bloody well think but I'm going to fucking well find out!*' Rupert pounded furiously up to the farmhouse door with Anna at his heels. The door was open.

Lights were burning. On the kitchen table was a bowl of blood. What appeared to be the flayed skin of some massive, hairy animal lay across the floor. Anna screamed. Rupert flew around opening doors, and finding nothing, no one, set off up the stairs. Anna followed, terrified; filled with dread; expecting any moment to find Nicola disembowelled, decapitated, butchered; quite possibly hacked into several pieces. Instead, when they opened the door to one of the bedrooms they found David Williamson with a great bloody bandage around his head and Nicola on top of him, both completely naked and indulging in some mutually enjoyable and energetic activity.

At the sight of Rupert and the shotgun, David Williamson let out a yelp of fright. 'Don't shoot!' he yelled. 'For God's sake, don't shoot!' Nicola rolled to one side, looked round at them in surprise then covered their nakedness with a sheet. 'Sorry,' she said in a calm tone. 'Obviously, we were not expecting visitors.'

'*Bloody hell, Nicola,*' Rupert collapsed against the door. 'We thought you were dead. We saw the blood. And the hair. We really thought the creature had got you.'

'It was the other way round, actually; I got him,' she indicated the bandage around David Williamson's head. 'I picked up a branch and socked him with it. Well, heavens above, whatever did he imagine he was doing, trying to frighten people like that?'

'I wasn't trying to frighten *people*,' David Williamson said heatedly. 'I was trying to frighten *you*. I went to a lot of trouble with that costume; the mask alone cost me an arm and a leg. You were stealing from me, Nicola; my grazing, my turkeys, my logs, my holly, even my best Christmas tree.'

'I saw the basin of blood,' Anna said. 'I thought he had killed you.'

'Killed me? David? Why would he do that? He loves me. He watches my every movement through his binoculars. I have driven him almost insane. He has always loved me. He's mad about me. He just didn't know it,' Nicola said.

David Williamson looked at her. Was it true? Rather reluctantly he supposed it might possibly be nearly the truth.

'But we've sorted it out now,' Nicola said calmly. 'Now that we have agreed to get married.'

'Have we?' He looked at her in astonishment. 'Did I actually say that?'

'Well, I'm not moving in here to look after you unless it's going to be a permanent arrangement,' Nicola said. 'And you certainly need someone to look after you; you are not eating properly.' She looked at David Williamson critically, as if he was a newly arrived equine delinquent to be studied and assessed before being prescribed a less heating diet with boiled barley twice a week and linseed on Fridays. She made a slight adjustment to his bandage, which had slipped down over one eye. 'You must admit that the house is a disgrace. You really should be ashamed of yourself. Your mother would turn in her grave if she saw how you have neglected it. I think our arrangement will work very well. I will move my horses into your farm buildings and start a proper livery and riding stable, and you can do as much or as little farming as you wish. You know you hate farming, David. You have always hated it.'

'Should that wound on your head be looked at?' Anna wanted to know. 'Does it need stitches?'

'It's fairly superficial,' Nicola said. 'Head wounds tend to bleed a lot; they always look worse than they really are. I'm sorry we gave you such a shock.' To David Williamson she added, 'Of course, if you do marry me, you will have to change your name to Rushbroke. You do realise that? We can't let the family name disappear.'

'*Change my name?*' Outrage flared momentarily. Here was Nicola, in his bed, without any clothes on, having almost knocked his head off; possibly causing permanent damage to his brain, making him a proposal which would not only fill his buildings with delinquent equines and give her family access to all of his land, but also, in a crowning act of dispossession, she was suggesting that he should actually become a Rushbroke himself. It was so monstrous, it was laughable.

'*Oh my God, David!* If you can't beat them, you may as well join them!' Laughter suddenly welled up in Rupert like a fountain, bursting out of him as a result of the depth of his relief and the sheer hysterical absurdness of the situation. 'At least we'll be family! At least we shall all be on the same side!'

Nicola and David Williamson, thought Anna in wonder. *Plan B. Who would have thought it?* But really, wasn't it the perfect solution?

'Well, David, what do you think?' Nicola asked.

'I shall need time to think about it,' he said, but actually, he didn't need any time at all. He could see at once that if he became a Rushbroke, he would no longer be on the outside looking in, watching them through his binoculars; he would be part of the family. He knew that Nicola would look after him, and the house, and even if his farmyard was filled with delinquent equines, wouldn't that be a relatively small price to pay? For peace of mind? For being married to this wonderfully desirable, calm, courageous and unshakeable girl? A girl who, confronted with a fiend in the darkness, had, instead of taking to her heels as the men had done, had promptly picked up a branch and walloped him with it. He thought of his parents. How delighted they would have been. How proud. But he could not abandon his own family name for their sake. It would have to be incorporated. His name would have to become Williamson Rushbroke. *David Williamson Rushbroke.* He repeated it aloud a few times whilst Nicola smiled at him with approval. *David Williamson Rushbroke.* It was unthinkable! It was unbelievable! And actually, the more he said it, the more he grew to like the sound of it. *David Williamson Rushbroke.* It was marvellous! What a day! Quite suddenly he was overcome by fatigue. He could take no more. It had all been too much. David Williamson Rushbroke slumped back against the pillows and went out like a light.

RUSHBROKE HALL COUNTRY HOUSE HOTEL
CHRISTMAS HOUSE PARTY
Christmas Eve, Wednesday 24th December

16.30hrs

On arrival, our delicious Afternoon Tea will be
served in the Library or the Residents' Lounge.

19.30hrs

A pre-dinner drink of your choice with chef's
freshly baked nibbles will be served in the Library,
the Residents' Lounge or, if you prefer,
by Room Service

From 20.00hrs

Dinner will be served in the Yellow Dining Room.
There will be musical entertainment

23.30hrs

Transport will be provided for those wishing to attend
Midnight Mass at St. Saviour's, Rushbroke St. Mary
Hot drinks and snacks will be served on your return

Chapter Thirty

As the Rolls Royce turned into the narrow lane, the holy golden and white Shih Tzu fell off the rear window-ledge and, tumbling down the cream hide upholstery, bounced off the seat onto the caramel Wilton from whence, as soon as he had regained his composure, he regarded the rest of the family (who had observed his descent with acute interest untouched by any possibility of concern) with eyes positively white-rimmed with accusation.

'I do hope that this is not a bad omen, Harry,' commented Mrs Maitland-Dell who, having allowed herself the luxury of a comfortable little doze, had been awakened by the startled yelp of alarm which had accompanied the golden and white Shih Tzu's fall.

'No bad omens in the heart of the countryside,' replied Harry Featherstone stoutly as the car approached the turning into the Rushbroke drive. 'No omens, no potentially dangerous beasts, no wandering chickens, Madam. Everything according to instructions.' Harry was feeling distinctly cheerful and optimistic, having already sampled the congeniality of The Crick in the Neck on the pretext of obtaining directions (there being no satellite navigation devices prior to the millennium). Entering Sam Weller's Bar, Harry had been vastly encouraged to find a log fire blazing merrily in an inglenook, a welcoming face behind the bar and (possibly even more agreeable) a dartboard. A swift half pint and a packet of polo mints later, he had returned to Madam and the family most enormously cheered to have discovered a bolt-holt that would undoubtedly prove to be exceedingly congenial. Now, all that remained was for Harry to ensure that the holiday was universally enjoyed by making absolutely certain that all of Madam's little requirements were met. To this end it seemed advisable to draw attention to certain points during their slow and stately progress.

'No main roads, Madam. No discernible traffic in the vicinity and,' Harry placed a gloved finger upon the button which activated Madam's wonderfully silent, electronically operated window in order to demonstrate the veracity of his final statement, 'no disagreeable aromas of an agricultural nature.'

'Thank you, Harry,' said Mrs Maitland-Dell graciously. 'The air is indeed quite fresh and pure. Please be good enough to raise the window now as the family are feeling the draught.' The family, who had been rather invigorated by the breeze and had risen in anticipation at the lowering of the window, straining their short necks towards the plough, sniffing and snuffling the fresh, pure air through their button-hole nostrils, settled down again with a collective air of mild disappointment.

As they turned into the Rushbroke drive, Mrs Maitland-Dell regarded the family motto above the gates with a small frown. 'Prudence Before Valour. A not altogether chivalrous motto, Harry, one feels. Not a motto with which to lead one wholeheartedly into battle, one has to say. A somewhat dubious motto, in my opinion.'

'Most definitely so, Madam. Not a chivalrous motto at all; in fact a motto with a smack of cowardice about it, if you were to ask me what I thought, but just take a look at *that*, Madam,' said Harry Featherstone in appreciation, 'because that's a very rare beauty of a house, that is. That's a very fine house indeed. That's a chivalrous house, if ever there was one. My word, Madam, that's a house and a half by anybody's standards.'

'The house is indeed lovely, Harry,' agreed Mrs Maitland-Dell, as their regal progress took them between domes of yew clipped to within an inch of their lives. 'Although I am less happy to see the moat, it has to be said. The family are so terribly drawn to water, as well you know. They have a penchant for it. A particular fascination for water is a well-documented peccadillo of the breed.'

'I shall make sure the family steer clear of the water, don't you fear, Madam,' promised Harry, who had not the faintest idea what a peccadillo was but very much liked the sound of the word and hoped to include it in his own vocabulary once he had mastered the meaning of it. 'I shan't let them out of my sight for a minute. You can depend on me.'

'Of course I can, and well I know it,' said Mrs Maitland-Dell warmly. 'How well I remember the day you so bravely rescued my darling Freddie when the current was carrying him away towards the weir. How could I ever forget it? And now, Harry, I do believe there is someone ready and willing to assist you with the luggage. How extremely opportune and considerate.'

'How very extremely opportune and considerate,' repeated Harry, who would have preferred an arrival marked by rather less consideration and opportunism for reasons unknown to his employer. 'How exceedingly considerate indeed.' He drew the Rolls Royce onto the carriage sweep with a slight feeling of unease. He had planned to enter the hotel in advance of Madam in order to have a tactful and apologetic word with the management about the size of the family, the problem being that Harry had not been altogether forthcoming and absolutely truthful when he had made the reservation; the problem being that had Harry been absolutely truthful and altogether forthcoming when he had made the reservation then no reservation would have been made because it was an indisputable fact confirmed by over fifty telephone calls to hotels the length and breadth of England, that no establishment in the country was prepared to allow eight dogs to share a suite with one of their prospective guests, however impeccable their pedigree. Finally, having been turned down even by The Crown Hotel in Framlingham (who had, however, helpfully informed him of the imminent opening of Rushbroke Hall), Harry had resorted to subterfuge by enquiring in a general manner, if the management had any objection to accommodating small, remarkably well-behaved dogs and, having received an encouraging response, had made the reservation on the somewhat optimistic and unrealistic grounds that if the management had no objection to small dogs in the plural, they would quite possibly have no objection to the accommodation of eight.

It was therefore not surprising that Harry felt obliged to provide some prior explanation to the handsome, dark-haired young man who walked towards the car as the tyres settled into the gravel and the engine purred away into silence, but Madam was indicating that Harry should assist her to alight and there was nothing for it but to oblige, and before Harry could utter even a word or two to smooth the arrival, Madam was out of the car with the family all around her feet in a melee of floating hair and eyes popping in anticipation, and the young man, after only an initial blench, had recovered his composure like a true professional, and welcomed Madam with a warm greeting and, taking four gilt and leather leads in each hand, conducted the family and Madam (wearing Harry's favourite coat of pale, silky mink) across the courtyard and up the steps into the hotel, as if eight Shih Tzus arrived in a Rolls Royce every day of the week; as if there was nothing even remotely unusual about it.

But when the young man returned after a short interval in order to assist Harry with Madam's substantial pile of luggage, he looked at Harry in a somewhat tight-lipped and quizzical manner. 'Eight dogs?' He raised a sceptical eyebrow. 'Was the fact that there were *eight* dogs actually mentioned when you made the reservation?'

'I'm glad you mentioned the reservation.' Harry picked out two hat boxes, a vanity case and a matching holdall from Madam's luggage, every piece so lovely and elegant in buttermilk leather and embossed with a C for Clarissa. 'Because I was intending to mention it to you myself. I was intending to make you an apology because I tried everywhere and nobody would take the dogs and I so wanted to find somewhere congenial for Madam's little holiday. I was desperate. To tell the truth, I got myself into something of a peccadillo about it...'

* * *

The Pomeroys had not had a happy journey. The new Range Rover had consumed petrol with the voracity of a ravening beast and Tony, having failed to peruse the manufacturer's handbook and therefore unaware that smooth progress depended upon certain refinements of driving technique, had driven in his habitual competitive manner, swerving from lane to lane, diving to a standstill at traffic lights and accelerating away at speed, racing around bends and roundabouts, with the result that Emily, seated in the back on a well-upholstered but slippery leather seat, had felt extremely queasy for most of the journey, whilst Mary Pomeroy, who would have much preferred to stay at home orchestrating a low key Christmas and was as a consequence positively rigid with nervous tension and reluctance, had felt perilously high and most cruelly exposed upon the passenger seat after the discreetly tinted and relatively low-slung comfort of the Jaguar.

Tony and Tom had attempted to keep a conversation flowing with dogged tenacity but had flagged at last in the face of a wall of silence from the rest of the party, and communication had gradually petered out on the odd remark until it finally ceased altogether so that by the time the Range Rover turned into the gates of Rushbroke Hall, the silence was so unequivocal, so balefully absolute, that it seemed the Pomeroys might never again utter another word. It was not a promising start.

During the journey Tony had begun to wonder why he had suggested this holiday; why he had ever thought it was a good idea. It was hard to believe he had thought that his family, *this* family, would enjoy being cooped up for three whole days in some claustrophobic country house miles from civilization, closeted with complete strangers they would probably loathe on sight, lodged in accommodation practically guaranteed to be not nearly as comfortable as that they had left behind in West Wickham. *If I ever believed that this would be a success,* Tony thought, *I must have been out of my bloody mind.* Could the heady prospect of riding to hounds have influenced his judgement? Surely the hunting had been an afterthought. Tony reminded himself that this holiday had been arranged for the benefit of Mary. Its specific purpose had been to remove his sad and emotional wife from the earthly reminders (and the mortal remains) of her mother. Yet had not her physician told him only a few days ago that, in his considered opinion, the only person who could help Mary Pomeroy now, was Mary Pomeroy? Family and friends did what they could for the bereaved, medication might delay the suffering, but in the end the fact of the death was there to be faced, the grief must be endured and the farewell acknowledged before the recovery could begin. 'When Mary is ready to let go,' her physician had said to Tony, 'she will do it. When the time is right, it will happen.' But *when?* thought Tony in despair, *when?*

Tony had wondered how long he would have to tiptoe around this changed and unstable Mary. He wondered if life would ever return to anything resembling normality. Because now, when even a simple conversational overture was a minefield in which a misplaced word might invoke a flood of unstoppable tears; when a simple request could precipitate a burst of hysterical fury, he didn't know what to do.

Looking across at Mary Pomeroy, scrutinizing her, observing the set of her jaw, the unyielding rigidity of her body, the way she stared fixedly ahead, Tony wondered if things would ever be quite the same again between them. He knew that events changed people. Time changed people. People did not, in general, go back to what they had been; they went on to what they would become. As people grew older they became more true to themselves in that they were less inclined to adapt to what others perceived or desired them to be. Life itself changed people. In that moment Tony had realised that he had probably lost the old Mary for good, and the new Mary, the Mary who looked at Tony, and at Tom and Emily, in a way that was an objective reappraisal, would come back to them on her own terms. If she came back at all.

Emily had not wanted to come to the country. Despite her green principles, her vegetarian diet, her holistic leanings and her fervent desire to save the world from ecological disaster, Emily was a town girl at heart, happiest with pavement under her boots, preferably pavement lined with dubiously lit, bazaar-type shops, pulsating with weird music, selling ethnic jewellery and the sort of ragbag clothing appreciated by Emily and her like-minded friends.

Ever since the reservation had been confirmed, the family had been subjected to a passionate tirade against the evils of the countryside in which farmers were seen as ecological vandals hell bent on the destruction of the countryside who, when they were not tearing up trees, grubbing out hedges and ploughing over footpaths in headlong pursuit of surpluses that even the EEC could not find a use for, were busily loosing into the atmosphere fungicides, pesticides, weed killers and highly toxic artificial fertilizers which, as well as poisoning the land, seeped into rivers and went on to pollute the oceans of the world. Farmers were, according to Emily, personally responsible for all types of cancer, the increased incidence of asthma, and for every other possible allergy and complaint known to man. Single-handedly, they were changing the traditional landscape of the country, planting alien crops, causing the very soil to be eroded and destroying the habitat of countless flora and fauna, resulting in the near extinction of the brown hare, the dormouse, the stone curlew, the brown fritillary, the large blue butterfly, the lady's slipper orchid and the common cowslip, whilst seriously threatening the continued existence of the song thrush, the natterjack toad and the greater horseshoe bat. Farms themselves were nothing less than animal concentration camps where chickens were imprisoned in battery cages and where every cow that didn't actually have TB or bovine spongiform encephalopathy was forced to permanently produce milk that the EEC poured down the drain, whilst their calves were either butchered at birth or shipped on the hoof to live out their pitifully short lives in veal crates. No, Emily had not wanted to spend Christmas in the country, and only the fact that she was feeling unwell prevented her from letting them all know just how much she was going to loathe every single moment.

There had been no reaction from Tom. Tom had just smiled his rather wry smile and shrugged his shoulders to signify... what? Why did Tom so rarely offer an opinion on anything? Why did he never have a point of view? Why didn't he find a job? Tony did not consider Tom's current occupation a proper job. Driving a florist's delivery van was not a suitable job for a boy with a decent brain and a university education (or to be perfectly accurate, half a university education). Tony had hopes of Tom taking his place in the family business, but he was not interested. Tony suspected that the trouble with Tom was that he was not interested in anything. Other lads of his age had hobbies. They played soccer, did weight-training, got into mountain biking, photography or cricket. They were into stock cars, they surfed the internet, they went out with girls, they went on pub crawls but what did Tom do? Tom did nothing. But at least, thought Tony in resignation, Tom did not particularly care where his Christmas was spent, and in that he was the least problematical member of the family.

My God, thought Tony as the Range Rover traversed the drive to Rushbroke Hall, *how did I imagine that a few days of festive cheer would transform this severely dysfunctional family unit into a happy and harmonious one?* He was within a whisper of turning round and heading back to West Wickham when Rushbroke Hall came into view; a perfect jewel of a house with twin turrets and stepped gables, its rosy brick warmed by a late afternoon sun that turned its windows to flame and the moat which surrounded it to molten lava.

'How my mother would have loved this,' Mary said softly.

'Hey, Dad, this is a *fantastic* place!' Tom had never sounded so enthusiastic and, as the Range Rover turned onto the carriage sweep in the front courtyard and a young man, darkly handsome, came down the entrance steps to meet them, Emily opened her mouth for the first time in almost three hours. 'I think I might grow to like the country,' she said. 'The view gets better all the time.'

'I say, how very convenient! That's well met, eh? Give me a hand with these boxes, would you, there's a good chap? There're not particularly heavy, just a dashed inconvenient size. I want to get them inside without being spotted by the other ranks. Just take a hold of that one, then, if I put this one on the top you can follow on like a good 'un. *Wide is the gate and broad is the way*, and all that, eh?'

Norman, having abandoned on the steps his own luggage (painstakingly selected as appropriate for the country by Yvonne and comprising a matching set of three canvas holdalls in a colour that could most kindly be described as mud green, bound with tan leather-look plastic) followed the stooped and elderly figure across the courtyard towards the east wing apartment, his progress and his vision much hampered by two enormously long and cumbersome cardboard boxes. It had not been the welcome he had envisaged but, on the other hand, he was flattered to be of use and also curious as to what the boxes might contain because the fact was that they were so light it was hard to imagine they might contain anything at all.

'Feathers.' Vivian, grappling with two large, square and only slightly less cumbersome boxes, might have read his mind. 'Wings, to be entirely accurate. That's why the boxes are such a devilish shape. Had to drive all the way to Norwich to pick them up. Damned long trip. I'd forgotten how far it was, to tell the truth. Wasn't sure the old bus would make it. Still, we got back in the end. Mission accomplished, as they say. Lavinia! Lavinia, are you in there?' He banged on a door with his elbow. 'You can bet your bottom dollar she isn't, you know. They've moved the piano again, that's the rub. They've this wild idea she'll play in the dining room for the punters. Well, she may or she may not. Difficult to say, actually. Never can tell with Lavinia. Might have to help out myself if the going gets sticky. Rather a fine baritone voice once. Might still have it, for all I know. Never tried it recently. Still, at least we'll be able to let rip at the carol service. Looking forward to it. Organising the whole thing myself. Given a free rein. *Make a joyful noise unto God*, and all that. *Open thou my lips and my mouth shall show forth thy praise.* Lavinia! Lavinia! Damn and blast the woman. Tell you what, old chap, got a key in my pocket somewhere. Don't suppose you could have a rummage? Got a spare hand, have you?'

Norman had not, and freeing one involved a complicated adjustment of the boxes with due regard to the possible fragility of their truly astonishing contents. *Feathers?* thought Norman with incredulity. *Wings?* In due course the key was located in the inside pocket of Vivian's ancient Barbour jacket (Norman was able to recognise the genuine article having tried one himself in Country Cousins before noticing the price and opting for a cheaper alternative) and the door was opened and the boxes manipulated through a small kitchen into a sitting room where they were deposited on the carpet with much relief and some agonised arm stretching to restore lost circulation.

Norman was anxious to reclaim his luggage but Vivian was not inclined to let him escape without a reward in the form of a glass of whisky. 'Can't let you go off without a stiffener, old chap. Don't know what I would have done without you. Not really supposed to have any spirits, actually. Have to resort to subterfuge. Have to nip down the cellar when nobody's looking. Staying long, are you? Jolly nice jacket you've got; just the job for the country. Don't suppose you fancy a spot of rough shooting whilst you're here? Not everybody's cup of tea these days, I know, but I daresay we could raise something for the pot. Might just be able to put my hand on a few cartridges my daughter doesn't know about. Hides them from me, you know. Nose like a Labrador. Doesn't trust me with a gun these days. Thinks I might shoot myself in the foot.' Without any warning at all, the whisky glass fell from his hand. His face turned red, then white, and his breathing became laboured and ragged. 'No cause for alarm,' he gasped. 'Happens all the time. Got a thingamajig somewhere. Blasted inhaler whatsit.' He patted his pockets ineffectually whilst he struggled for breath. His face had turned purple. 'Perhaps better raise the alarm, eh, old chap? Just in case. *Lord, make me to know mine end, and the measure of my days...*'

Norman, who had helped him to a chair, captured the rolling glass and dried the carpet with his handkerchief, now found himself directed through a door which led, via a passageway, into a library devoid of any living soul. A door on the opposite wall opened into an equally unpopulated anteroom furnished with armchairs and a writing desk. Hastening onward he entered a great hall with a vast log burning in the fireplace. A dark-haired young man was coming down an impressively carved staircase. When Norman explained what had happened he ran towards the apartment. Norman was about to follow but something stopped him in his tracks.

Norman heard music. He heard someone playing the piano. He heard someone singing. Not only that, but he had heard it before, that unmistakably light touch on the keyboard, that same sweet, clear voice, singing that same evocative song.

> '*I remember you, of course I do*
> *Not just when church bells chime*
> *Dear, I miss you all the time*
> *I remember you.*'

The sound of it transported him back forty years; hit him like a physical blow. Norman forgot his errand of mercy. He forgot he was sixty-nine years of age because, for a moment, he was twenty-three again; he was third violin, playing his heart out for a vocalist who hardly knew he existed. He opened the door of the dining room and he looked at the woman seated at the piano. She looked up at him and smiled.

> *'I remember you, of course I do*
> *Not just when skies are blue above*
> *Or when someone speaks of love*
> *I remember you*
> *Of course I do.'*

He saw perhaps, exactly what he wanted to see. He did not notice that the beautiful hair was frosted with grey, nor that the fine skin was no longer smooth and unlined, nor even that the clear, slate-blue eyes he remembered so well were perhaps a little empty now. Why would he? How could he? The memory of her had been lodged like a splinter in his heart for what seemed like an eternity.

'Lilly,' he said softly. 'Lilly Lamont. Why, you haven't changed a bit. I would have known you anywhere.'

* * *

'*Left*, Henry,' said Penelope Lamb. 'I said *left* at the junction, and you have turned right. You have taken the wrong road. You will have to go back.'

'No, my dearest, it is a right turn at the junction,' said Henry Lamb benevolently. 'I expect you are reading the map upside down. Right is the correct route to take without a shadow of a doubt. Trust me, my darling. Have faith. Leave the navigation in my capable hands.'

'Oh, of course,' Penelope said dryly. 'Henry the Navigator. How could I possibly overlook your unerring sense of direction, your inherent powers of observation, and your world famous map reading ability.'

'Nevertheless, I think we are on the right track now,' said Henry peaceably. 'I think this is the right road.'

'We may be on the *right* road; the point I am making is that we should be on the *left* road.' Penelope adjusted her spectacles, looped their safety cord behind her ears and peered down at the map of East Anglia spread across her solid knees. 'I am perfectly capable of reading a map correctly, Henry, *perfectly*, but this edition was a very poor choice, if I may say so; the print is so ridiculously small that I need a magnifying glass in order to decipher it. I really can't be expected to strain my eyes like this now that it is beginning to get dark, and particularly so, Henry, *particularly* so, when you purposely choose to ignore my instructions. I am afraid we shall have to abandon the map. We shall have to find someone who can furnish us with instructions.'

'Someone to provide us with directions would be very handy,' Henry agreed. 'Some passer-by with local knowledge would be a most welcome sight. A house, in fact, would be singularly welcome, or even a farm. It is remarkably unpopulated in this area, is it not, my beloved, my precious sweetheart?'

'The countryside is supposed to be unpopulated,' Penelope said in a scathing tone. 'The countryside consists of fields and trees and hedges, Henry. That is why people like it.'

'Fields and trees and hedges can be very atmospheric,' said Henry Lamb. 'I find them very atmospheric indeed, especially in the fading light. Do you find fields and trees and hedges atmospheric, my dearest one?'

'All I want to find at this particular moment,' said Penelope sharply, 'is the hotel.'

'A certain atmosphere,' said Henry Lamb thoughtfully,

'and a sense of isolation. The sense of isolation is almost tangible, don't you think, my treasure?'

'I think we should turn back,' said Penelope. 'I think you should reverse into the very next gateway and drive back to the junction where you turned right instead of left. *Do it*, Henry, *turn round.*'

'A most tangible sense of isolation,' continued Henry Lamb, 'and the slightest hint of menace in the air. Do you sense it, my darling? Do you feel the slightest hint of menace in the air, my own true love?'

'If you would really like to know what I feel, Henry,' Penelope said in exasperation, 'it is lost. We are *lost*, Henry. You must turn back at once. You must do it immediately. You must *turn back!*'

'I was just thinking, Penelope,' said Henry Lamb, 'what a perfectly appropriate setting this would be for a heinous crime; this terribly isolated spot amongst all these atmospheric hedges and trees would be most conducive to the very darkest of deeds, would it not? When one can almost sense malevolent forces at large; when one can so easily imagine that evil stalks abroad in such surroundings? Can you sense malevolent forces at large, Penelope, my love? Can you imagine that evil stalks abroad, my precious darling?'

'Henry,' said Penelope in a strong voice with only the very slightest trace of a falter. 'You are behaving very oddly. I want you to stop it. I want you to turn into the next gateway and reverse the car. I want you to turn back.'

'Oh, it is too late to turn back,' said Henry Lamb. 'I want to describe to you a murder, my sweet. I want to share with you a most particularly blood-curling and gruesome murder, Penelope. Is not your curiosity aroused? Are you not avid to hear more?'

'No,' said Penelope stoutly. 'Most certainly not. I don't know what has got into you, Henry. I don't like it,' and as something pale and huge flapped momentarily alongside her window, 'Oh, my goodness gracious! Whatever was that? Henry, *what was that?*'

'Just an owl, my dear,' said Henry Lamb soothingly. 'Just an old barn owl looking for his supper, looking for some small, furry, defenceless animal to pick up in his talons; to tear apart with his wickedly sharp beak. Just an owl about to commit a very tiny murder, my own sweet darling; a very insignificant murder in the scale of such things, Penelope, my love, nothing at all like the murder I, myself, have been contemplating, my dearest heart, nothing like it at all,' and, as the car negotiated a sharp bend and began to descend a hill, 'Ah, now this looks promising,' said Henry Lamb with satisfaction. 'This looks very promising indeed.'

It looked, to Penelope's immense relief, like a village. A painted sign announced its identity as Polstead.

'There now.' Henry Lamb, beaming, engaged a lower gear as they coasted along the dark and deserted village street. 'Here we are at last. The very place where Maria Marten was murdered in the Red Barn. One of the most famous murders of all time, wouldn't you say, my love, my own sweet darling? I planned this little detour to bring you to the very spot where the poor victim's decomposed body was unearthed, shot, stabbed and strangled; in a crime so exceptionally foul and sensational that the executioner's rope was sold for a guinea an inch, and the records of the trial were bound in the murderer's skin. No!' Henry lifted an admonitory hand. 'Don't try to thank me! This is my little treat. This is my surprise. Sit back, Penelope, my precious one, my treasure. Sit back and enjoy!'

Chapter Thirty-One

To the muted strains of Bach's *Christmas Oratorio*, the family came down the great staircase in a cascade, each member adorned with a golden ribbon.

'Good evening, Madam.' Rupert stepped out from behind the Christmas tree. 'May I presume that our furry friends will not be accompanying you into the dining room?'

'You may presume no such thing, Mr Truscott,' said Mrs Maitland-Dell. 'Most certainly they will accompany me and they will be impeccably behaved, having dined themselves already. I did take the precaution of bringing with me today's menu, but tomorrow at four I should like two boiled hens, a cup of steamed rice and one chopped carrot. Also, a little mild pâté without garlic and eight slices of wholemeal toast. It is, after all,' Madam looked down at the family with an indulgent smile, 'Christmas.'

'It is indeed,' agreed Harry Featherstone. 'And most congenial it is too, if I may say so.'

Rupert favoured Harry with a steely look.

'Room service, of course, Mr Truscott,' said Mrs Maitland-Dell.

'Room service, of course.' With professional courtesy Rupert moved aside in order to open a door for Mavis who, in black satin leggings and perilously high heels, was bound for the library with a tray of drinks. 'Room service, naturally.'

'And Mr Truscott,' Mrs Maitland-Dell placed a small but implacable hand on his arm. 'Be so kind as to remove the crusts from the toast.'

* * *

'Have you *seen* this?' Entering Tom's bedroom without even a cursory knock, Emily threw herself down on the bed, displacing the plaid throw on the luxuriously quilted duvet. In her hand she held a card.

'Have I seen what?' Tom tossed a pair of trainers into the bottom of the commodiously fitted wardrobe. 'What is it?'

'It's a programme of events for the Christmas break. It was in my room so you must have one somewhere. Did you know there's going to be a hunt on Boxing Day? Do you realise they're actually expecting us to go to a *hunt?*'

'So what?' Tom shrugged. 'We're in the country now. Hunting, shooting and fishing are country pursuits. What did you expect? A visit to the opera?'

'But I can't go to a *hunt!* I *can't!* It's against my principles! It's a blood sport!'

'If you quote Oscar Wilde again, just once, I might brain you,' Tom warned. 'Anyway, you don't have to go, I'm sure it isn't compulsory. Stay behind. Read a book; collect sticks for the fire; sew a fine seam, or whatever else people do in the country when they're not actively engaged in the slaughter of innocent creatures.'

'Don't be flippant.' Emily lay back sulkily. 'This is serious.'

'I don't doubt it.' Tom stared at Emily's right ear. 'You've had another hole punched! Five studs in one ear is grotesque, Em! What'll you have done next; your nose or your nipple?'

'I'd thought my navel, actually.'

'Jesus! Wait until Dad notices! Is that a new tattoo on the back of your neck as well? God, he'll go ape shit!'

'He won't notice if you don't draw attention to it. Anyway, Dad's far too taken up with mum's problems to worry about me.'

'Not necessarily true; he just has to prioritise; so,' Tom pitched his holdall neatly onto the top shelf, 'what shall we do instead of going to the hunt then, any ideas?'

Emily swung her legs, clad in black cobweb tights ending in black pointed shoes with death's head buckles, off the bed. For the holiday, she had opted for the Goth look. 'I haven't decided, *definitely*, not to go yet.'

'I wouldn't advise going, Em; you'll only wind yourself up. Better stay cool. Stage a silent protest. Stay away.'

'I'm not sure that I *should* stay away.' Emily fingered the heavy linked chain around her neck that supported a giant crucifix of hammered metal. 'I think I might stage a protest, actually. I think I might demonstrate.'

'Now that really is a *prat* of an idea!' Tom looked at his sister in exasperation. 'What difference do you think one protester is going to make? Unless you're planning to do something completely over the top like hurling yourself in front of fifty galloping horses like Emily Davison, you haven't a hope of achieving anything! Think of Ma, Em. Say you got hurt! Say you were injured! Think what a great end to the holiday *that* would be! Forget the hunt. Think peace and goodwill. Stay away.'

Emily got up from the bed and began to walk about the room, pulling at her dress of crushed black velvet which trailed on the floor behind her and was cut into jagged points at the bodice, each point ending in a red plastic droplet like a drop of blood. 'I wasn't thinking of anything as dramatic as that,' she said crossly. 'Nothing *dangerous*. I was just thinking I might put the hounds off the scent somehow; foil the line or whatever it is the antis do; lay a false trail or something.'

'Lay a false trail of *what?*' demanded Tom. 'Emily, you don't know the first thing about hunting or hounds. For Christ's sake, *knock it off!* You have to know what you're doing to be a hunt saboteur.'

'I might not know anything about *hunting!*' Emily's voice rose in agitation. 'But I know what my *principles* are! I know that killing animals for sport is *gross!* I know that it is *murder!*'

Tom put his hands over his ears. 'Hey, keep the volume down, will you; the people in the room next door will be calling the manager.'

'Let them call the manager! *Tom,*' Emily gripped his arm in entreaty, '*say I did it*. Say I got something from the kitchen; spices, pepper, things like that; you wouldn't tell, would you? You wouldn't squeal?'

Tom sighed. 'And what if Ma sees you, Em? How's she going to react? What about Dad? He'll go ballistic.'

'They won't see me. Nobody will see me because I'll be in disguise. Did you bring your balaclava?'

'I think this is a really prattish idea, Em; I want you to know that.'

'*Tom, did you bring your balaclava?*'

Tom crossed to the chest of drawers in resignation. 'Just don't expect any support from me, little sister. You're on your own in this. I'm having nothing to do with it.'

'Just give me the balaclava, Tom.'

'You are going to end up in deep shit if you go ahead with this, Em. You are going to be in shit right up to your bloody neck.'

'I am not going to end up in shit! I am going to end up saving a life! I am going to foil the pursuit of the unspeak—' Emily was abruptly silenced by a black balaclava received full in the face.

'I *told* you,' said Tom unfeelingly, '*no Oscar Wilde.*'

'The very minute I saw that obelisk at the side of the road for the second time, I knew you were lost, Henry,' said Penelope Lamb. 'You always were a hopeless navigator, simply hopeless; I thought we should *never* get here.'

'Well, here we are now, my darling.' Henry, laden with suitcases, followed his wife into the great hall. 'Here we are now, my dearest.'

'And very welcome you are too.' Yvonne, comfortably installed behind the reception desk and revelling in the responsibility of making the late arrivals feel instantly at home, consulted the reservation list. 'And you must be Mr and Mrs Lamb because everybody else is ticked off. Not that you're late,' she hastened to assure them, 'there's still an hour to go before dinner and plenty of time for baths and a nice strong drink of whatever you fancy. Let me just get you signed in then I'll ring Rupert to help with the bags and we'll get you nice and settled in your room. We'll soon have you all warm and cosy, Mr and Mrs Lamb, don't you worry, because it's turned quite cold again, don't you think? Still, we don't want it mild at Christmas, do we? We want a bit of a nip in the air; the forecast said there could be snow in the north except this isn't the north, is it? This is the east,' Yvonne gave a little trill of laughter. 'Oh, Mr and Mrs Lamb you're going to have such a lovely time; honestly you are; I just know it.'

Penelope looked at Yvonne, her gaze taking in the skin-tight dress, the racehorse legs, the plunging neckline, the sprig of real mistletoe in the bird's nest hairstyle. Penelope pursed her lips. After which Penelope Lamb looked at Henry.

Henry Lamb smiled winningly.

From the window of a bedroom above the courtyard Tony Pomeroy had watched the arrival of a solid looking woman followed by a smaller man with curly hair carrying a lot of luggage. Earlier he had watched a man exercising a pack of small, long-haired, comical looking dogs. It was quite an establishment that was prepared to accept such eccentricity, he thought admiringly, and his heart warmed towards it. Tony's heart was already feeling quite warm, its warmth greatly assisted by a large Famous Grouse with a chunk of ice, which had been delivered promptly to the door by room service in the shape of a leggy young thing in a skimpy black dress and a frilly apron whose hair was skewered to the top of her head with a clump of mistletoe.

The suite, tastefully decorated in and around its elabo-rately carved beams in old rose, apple green and cream, had waxed floors and stripped oak furnishings, with satisfyingly fat pillows and plump duvets on a bed set in a beamed alcove. A crooked little stairway led to a private bathroom which, despite its period features, managed to contain every modern convenience. In the stone fireplace, what at first glance had appeared to be a log burning fire had turned out to be electric; nevertheless, its pretend blaze waving merrily behind a brass guard in front of a glowing Persian rug upon which were set two comfortable armchairs and a polished oak coffee table, made the room feel like a home.

Mary Pomeroy was humming a nostalgic tune, which someone had been playing on a piano when they had arrived, as she unpacked the suitcases. Tony thought this a very good sign. Despite his earlier misgivings he saw it as cast iron proof that it had been the right decision to remove his wife from the reminders and the remains of his late mother-in-Law. Tony began to feel optimistic that, separated at last from the *memento mori*, Mary might actually begin to recover from her depression. After another mouthful of Famous Grouse Tony began to anticipate the astonishment of his family when he appeared at the Boxing Day meet splendidly mounted and attired in the Melton Full Hunt Coat. He couldn't wait. Mounted on a smooth-running thoroughbred (instead of the miniature carthorse that had been his learning vehicle) he was confident that his newly (and painfully) acquired riding skills would invoke gasps of amazement from his nearest and dearest. After all, he could now post to the trot and had mastered the canter. Piper didn't do a gallop, but Janine had assured him that it was the same as a canter, only faster. 'Just sit low and lean forward,' she had told him. As long as there were no jumps, he would be home and dry. The thought of his hunting clothes hidden away in the boot of the Range Rover, together with the last dregs of Famous Grouse, gave him an extra warm glow which lasted until he saw his wife take from the bottom of her suitcase the casket containing her mother's ashes and set it in pride of place on the dressing table.

* * *

'*Eight of the little buggers!*' Rupert said in a savage tone. He had entered the kitchen through two sets of swing doors on a tide of irritation. 'I'd like to get my hands on the person who took *that* little reservation!'

'I think it was Vivian. He probably didn't understand what he was being asked. I think the question was did we have any objection to small, well-behaved dogs. I believe that was how Mr Featherstone phrased it.' Anna was dressed in traditional kitchen whites with a long apron smoothing her hips. She rolled up, by means of a strip of baking parchment, a delicate mushroom roulade for the vegetarian guest and transferred it with infinite care onto a baking tray.

'But eight of them, *eight!* They are all over the bloody place and the woman is impossible to deal with; she insists on having them with her all the time and there will be God only knows what all over the carpets and dog hairs all over the bloody upholstery.' Rupert, having renounced the responsibility for anything to do with soft furnishings and left it all to Anna, was now inclined to be zealously protective.

'They seem to be very clean, well-groomed little dogs, actually,' Nicola observed. 'I think they are rather sweet.' She regarded him solemnly from behind a line of miniature trifles topped with fat swirls of cream onto which she was arranging plump glacé cherries and jewel-like strips of angelica.

'Perhaps we should regard them as decorative conversation pieces,' suggested Anna. 'They do add to the atmosphere, and animals certainly help to break the ice amongst strangers. Mavis is already totally smitten.'

'*Mavis* has not just taken an order for two boiled hens, a cup of steamed rice, a chopped carrot, a little mild pâté and eight slices of wholemeal toast without crusts! All to be delivered by room service at four o'clock tomorrow afternoon!'

Anna kept her eyes on the spinach moulds she was turning out into a serving dish. 'Somebody will have to tell David about the hens.'

'I'll tell him when I take him some supper.' Nicola had not yet moved into Home Farm. Anna had persuaded her to get in a firm of cleaners and decorators first. Len was organizing the installation of a modern bathroom and sorting out some units for the kitchen. The kitchen range had already been dismantled and rebuilt.

Anna had expressed concern about Plan B. 'Nicola, you can't go to Home Farm if there is even the slightest doubt in your mind,' she had said. 'Rushbroke Hall is *your* home after all. You must promise you won't do it unless you are absolutely sure what you are getting into, unless you are absolutely certain it is going to work out.'

'How can I possibly be absolutely certain it is going to work out?' Nicola had replied. 'How do any of us know if any relationship is going to work? Surely such knowledge can only be retrospective? All I can say is that David needs someone to care for him and I need a home and a place for my horses. I believe I have the best of the bargain. And I know enough about David to know that he is a good man, and kind. I may not have learned much in my life but I do know that we can survive most things if we are brave, and if we are kind. I may not be wise, I cannot promise that I will always be good,' Nicola had said, 'but I hope that I shall always be kind, and I am not afraid.'

With which Anna had to be content.

Rupert, having vented his ire, began to roam around the kitchen, inspecting crisp and fragrant onion tarts, tasting the carrot and coriander soup, peering at the creamy salmon mousse and the sweetly perfumed melons awaiting their port sorbet, opening the warming oven to view the ribs of beef left to settle in their juices prior to carving, checking the pierced gastro trays of vegetables ready for steaming in the combi oven. He peered into the bain-marie, at the hand-made custard and the hollandaise sauce, poked at the butter pats floating amidst the ice cubes in their water tub, checked (for the umpteenth time) the condition of the stilton shrouded in its snowy cloth, straightened the lines of freshly baked rolls cooling on their wire racks, breathing in all the time the varied and wonderful aromas overlaid with the particularly pungent, aromatic and spicy smell of the apple and cinnamon plait which was the hot pudding alternative to the cold delights of the vanilla bavarois with sharp red cherries in liqueur, and the trifles. The smell, the sight, the richness and abundance, after all they had endured, after all they had been through, threatened, quite suddenly to over-whelm him with emotion. He took Anna's hands in his own and looked at them. Short fingernails, a little chapped, the wrists striped with burns, spotted with scalds. The hands of a cook. 'Well, this seems to be it,' he said. 'This is what it has all been about. We have got this far. Now it is sink or swim time. Make or break.'

Mavis skittered into the kitchen on her heels like a star-tled pony. Her hair was a burning bush, her apron worn over a black angora tunic suitably decorated with silver crescent moons and stars. 'Sorry to disturb, Mr Truscott, Miss Gabriel, only I need some more cheese straws and olives and I've been asked for a Campari by that nice washed-out Mrs Pomeroy, and I'm not sure if I should be using the spirit measure or the sherry.'

* * *

'You mean you actually knew her, Norman, you *knew* Lady Lav?' Yvonne said incredulously.

'I knew her well,' said Norman. 'We were very close at one time. Of course, she wasn't Lady Lavinia Rushbroke then, she was just plain Lilly Lamont, although plain wouldn't have been the word to describe her then; she was beautiful, absolutely lovely, and she had a lot of fans, many admirers; older men, in particular, were mad about her.'

'Well, she still is lovely,' Yvonne allowed. 'She's got good bones, smashing hair, and ever such nice eyes; you've only got to look at her to know she was a beauty in her day.'

'She was.' Norman stared into the fanned flames of the fire, a faraway look on his face. 'Oh, she certainly was.'

'Was you one of the men who was mad about her, Norman?' Yvonne had knocked at Norman's bedroom door with a sherry and some cheese straws on a tray, wanting to keep an eye on him in case he was feeling lonely and awkward and a bit shy about coming down to dinner. Norman, who loathed sherry, especially the sweet variety, and only ever drank it to please Elsie, would have vastly preferred a bottle of beer or a scotch and dry but, seated in his handsome fireside chair beside the fire in his exceedingly comfortable room, he sipped it gamely. 'I was mad about her, Yvonne. But I was just a young and inexperienced third violin. I was beneath her notice. After the war, when I was first violin and we were playing duets together, we had an affair. I was passionately in love with her, besotted, but it was hard to tell if she felt the same—she was—how can I put it; always so light-minded, detached. At the time I was not very well off. I didn't know if I could support a wife. I suppose I would have asked her to marry me eventually but then I was sent off on loan to another band for a few weeks, just to help them out, and when I came back she had gone. Gone off to get married, they told me. I was devastated.'

'That must have been a blow for you, Norman. But you must know that she is proper doolally now. She doesn't even know what day it is. All she seems to do is sit at the piano. Most of the time she's away with the fairies.'

'She was a bit absent-minded even then, as I recall. It didn't matter to me. I loved her.'

He had realised almost at once, of course he had. She had greeted him with all the long-remembered charm, patted a chair beside her, but there had been no recognition in her eyes. When he had asked her if she was indeed Lilly Lamont she had laughed delightedly, fluttered a hand in a painfully familiar gesture. 'Used to be, my dear, used to be Lilly Lamont.' When he had said 'I'm Norman. Norman Simkins. I used to play first violin with Sidney Fenton. We worked together. We used to be friends,' she had been effusive, but it was clear that she had forgotten. She did not know him. And after all the years cherishing the memory of her, polishing it, it had been an almost unbearable blow to find her again like this. So he had said, 'Play for me, please' and she had played *Someday I'll find You* and *Moonlight Becomes You*, and the tears had run down his face in streams.

'Sidney Fenton's music always suited her. She had the

right voice for it. We were strong on nostalgia; our sort of music appealed to an earlier generation; I suppose that's why the older men worshipped her.'

'Well I think it's ever so romantic, Norman, even though it's sad as well. But you could tell Sir Viv, couldn't you; not about being in love if you don't want, but the rest of it; how you worked together and all that? It would give you something to talk about because he's especially asked me to see if you'd sit with him and Len at dinner. He seems to have taken quite a shine to you after his little upset and he does love a bit of company. Lady Lav's supposed to be playing the piano, but as you never quite know if the penny's dropped or not, it's a bit touch and go, if you know what I mean. Still, there's always the CD player to fall back on.'

'Or the violinist,' said Norman, vacating his fireside chair in order to change for dinner with some reluctance, 'if the worst comes to the worst.'

RUSHBROKE HALL COUNTRY HOUSE HOTEL

CHRISTMAS HOUSE PARTY

Christmas Day, Thursday 25th December

From 8 am

Breakfast will be served in the Yellow Dining Room

12.30pm

You are invited to attend a

Champagne reception in the Great Hall.

13.30hrs

Christmas Lunch will be served in the Yellow

Dining Room with musical entertainment

17.00hrs

Afternoon Tea will be served in the Residents' Lounge

19.00hrs

You are invited to attend a carol service in the Rushbroke Chapel

20.30hrs

A Buffet supper will be available

in the Yellow Dining Room

Chapter Thirty-Two

'Well, Mother, what do you think of this? I expect you are in your element here. This is the perfect place, isn't it?' Mary Pomeroy set the casket of ashes down beside her on the stone seat. 'I wouldn't be at all surprised if this was all your own idea, infiltrated into my dear husband's subconscious in the still of the night. Well, if it was, it was inspirational. The whole place is inspirational.' Mary Pomeroy pulled the hooded collar of her Aquascutum camel coat up around her ears in order to more comfortably drink in the beauty of the house; its warm brick and fine windows, its romantic pepper-pot turrets and majestic chimneys. The air of tranquillity that surrounded it, accentuated by the wide moat with its crumbling brick bridges, its ancient yew and the gnarled, old rose bushes and standards in the rose garden where she now sat, was like a balm to Mary. Peace seeped out of the very stones beneath her feet like a blessing.

The previous night, after their wonderful meal, she had climbed into the unfamiliar bed and slept soundly until she had awoken to astonishment and morning tea at eight. This, for Mary Pomeroy, accustomed to waking four, five or six times during the night, restless and overheated, to rearrange the bedding, to make tea, to roam the house in despair and distraction, was like a miracle. It *was* a miracle.

Was there, as Mary's mother had always maintained, a tangible atmosphere, a stillness about old houses that was entirely absent in their modern counterparts? And if it existed, as Mary thought it might, of what was it composed? Of continuity perhaps, of acceptance certainly, of the sense of the ongoing, unstoppable rhythm of life, the endless pattern of births and marriages and deaths, of joys, of celebrations, of grief and heartache experienced through many generations. *I should like to live in a house like this*, thought Mary, *so that I can feel its quiet centre; so that I can steady myself against the stillness of its antiquity.*

You see, Mother, how I am coming round to your way of thinking, said Mary silently. *You can see that I am getting there in the end.* For her mother had not liked (apart from her admiration of the kitchen) Mary's spacious, modern house with its large bland rooms, its picture windows, its open staircase and flush hardwood doors. She had also not approved of the way Mary had allowed herself to be totally absorbed by her family, by the way she had allowed them to mop up all of her days like a sponge so that not a drip of time remained for herself. It was true that Mary had gradually dropped, due to the demands of her children, her husband and her home, not only her part-time job as a speech therapist and her water-colour painting, but also her friends and the fringe interests that made her a person in her own right instead of just an adjunct to somebody else; somebody's mother, somebody's wife. And yet Mary had made these decisions, they had been hers alone; she had been free to choose. Nobody had forced the issue.

Down by one of the bridges across the moat Mary could

see Tom talking to the pretty waitress. As she watched they sank, by mutual consent, down onto the wall, clearly happy to be in each other's company. Emily was on her knees at the water's edge, apparently feeding fish from her fingers. There was laughter. Tony had gone for what he described vaguely as a ramble. (In actual fact he gone to the stables to make the acquaintance of the horse he was to ride the following day, but Mary was not to know that.)

'I shall probably go back to work,' Mary told her mother. 'I know that will please you. I shall have to take a retraining course but I know that I have to do something constructive with the rest of my life. The children are no longer dependent and next year Emily will go to university. It will do Tom good to have to look after himself. I may even get my painting brushes out again, but first of all a change of house. Oh yes, most *definitely* a change of house.'

Mary's conversation was suddenly terminated by a veritable tide of exuberant Shih Tzus as the family came racing into the rose garden through the archway in the yew hedge with Harry Featherstone puffing along behind taking seriously his promise not to allow them anywhere near the waters of the moat. Spotting Mary, the most affectionate and sociable member, together with the most athletic grey and white Shih Tzu, flew along the gravel path to greet her, the grey and white Shih Tzu landing with a flying leap on the seat beside her, upsetting the casket and causing the top to become detached and a gritty, greyish, lumpy substance to pour onto the ground.

'My mother,' explained Mary to Harry, scooping her up and throwing her over the roses. 'She loved gardening and roses in particular, and was a life-long supporter of the National Trust. She adored romantic old houses and never got to live in one. She would have so loved this place and I know this was exactly what she would have wanted.' Mary Pomeroy lobbed a particularly knobbly, grey chunk cheerfully into the centre of the rose bed. 'And now I have the perfect excuse to come back as often as I wish.' And with a final caress for the most affectionate member of the family, Mary walked away towards her children.

* * *

'My, now that is a truly magnificent knife.' Henry Lamb watched with admiration as Rupert sliced rapidly through a turkey breast. 'It must be extremely sharp to cut through the breast so cleanly.'

'It certainly is.' Rupert slid two slices of fragrantly steaming turkey breast onto a warmed plate to which he added a moist cake of stuffing, two chipolatas and a bacon roll. He looked enquiringly at Penelope. 'Will that be enough for you, Mrs Lamb, or can I give you a little more?'

'Oh, good heavens, I couldn't possibly manage any more than that, Mr Truscott. I have a very small appetite.' Penelope patted her solid midriff. 'My stomach is rather delicate. I am a martyr to it.'

'I expect you have a fine collection of knives in your kitchen,' said Henry Lamb pleasantly. 'A knife for every occasion? A knife for every purpose, no doubt?'

'We have indeed.' Rupert lifted Henry Lamb's portion of turkey aloft on the blade. 'A good set of professional knives is the first essential in any kitchen, commercial or otherwise.'

'Knives for gutting and boning, I suppose?' enquired Henry Lamb. 'Heavy duty knives for butchery? Cleavers?'

'We have all of those, Mr Lamb, and more besides. Would you care for bread sauce for your turkey? Cranberry?' Side dishes of Brussels sprouts with fried bread-crumbs, pancetta and chestnuts; roast potatoes and parsnips as well as a dish of creamy mashed potato with a well of melted butter on top were set upon the snowy cloth together with a miniature tureen of piping hot gravy. 'I do hope you will enjoy your meal, Mr and Mrs Lamb.'

'Henry,' said Penelope when Rupert and his trolley had moved along to the Maitland-Dell table, 'Henry, may I please have the benefit of your attention?'

Henry, who had been watching Rupert's knife slide through Mrs Maitland-Dell's portion of turkey breast with a faraway expression on his face, looked back at his wife with benevolence. 'But of course you shall have my attention, my dearest; what is it you wish to say?'

Penelope looked solemn. She picked up her knife and fork and put it down again. She straightened the napkin protecting her substantial thighs. She said, 'I have some-thing very important to tell you, Henry. It is difficult to know where to begin.'

Henry Lamb took a sip of his wine. He smiled sweetly at his wife. 'Begin at the beginning, my treasure,' he suggested. 'It is as good a place as any to start.'

Penelope's gaze sharpened. 'Sarcasm is not helpful at moments like this, Henry. I was hoping for a sympathetic ear.'

'And you shall have one,' promised Henry comfortably. 'You shall have two sympathetic ears. What is it, my darling? What have you to tell me?'

'It's about Ensleigh Gardens,' said Penelope. 'I want to talk to you about Ensleigh Gardens.'

'Ensleigh Gardens, my sweet? What is it about Ensleigh Gardens?'

'Before we left home, Henry, I rang the agent and told him we were no longer interested.'

'No longer interested, my beloved, but I thought you were very interested, I thought it was all settled.'

'It is not settled, Henry, that is what I am trying to tell you; that is what I am trying to say. We are not going to retire to Ensleigh Gardens. I have decided against it.'

'Decided against Ensleigh Gardens, Penelope? Not going to Ensleigh Gardens after all? But where will we be going, my love, if we don't go to Ensleigh Gardens?'

'*We* will not be going anywhere, Henry,' said Penelope. '*We* are not going anywhere at all.'

'Not going anywhere?' Henry looked at his wife in astonishment. 'Whatever can you mean, my love, not going anywhere at all?'

'What I mean, Henry, is exactly what I said; *we* are not going anywhere,' said Penelope firmly. 'I am not going anywhere with you. *I* am going to live in a very nice one-bedroom flat quite near to my sister in Tunbridge Wells.'

'A one-bedroom flat in Tunbridge Wells?' Henry repeated in amazement. 'But, Penelope...'

'No buts,' said Penelope. 'I am going to live on my own, Henry. I would like you to know that I have considered my options most carefully and my decision must be regarded as absolutely final. The matter is not open to negotiation. All of my arrangements are made.'

'But Penelope, my sweetheart, I thought...'

'I know what you thought, Henry, and I realise that this will be a great shock to you and I am very sorry, but I have to be honest and say that the thought of spending the rest of my life with you hanging around the house, messing around with your dusty old books, fiddling about with string and cardboard boxes, is more than my flesh and blood can stand.

I just can't put up with it, Henry, it simply isn't on. The truth of the matter is that I just can't put up with *you.*'

'But, Penelope, beloved, we have always been...'

'*We* have not *always been* anything,' said Penelope sharply. 'I have always found you extremely irritating. You have always got on my nerves. It isn't just your books, it is everything about you. I don't like your ingratiating manner. I don't like your simpering voice. Your ridiculous endearments set my teeth on edge. I don't like your silly smile and I can't stand your hair. I have never liked you very much at all,' said Penelope with feeling, 'I can't think why I married you in the first place. Probably because I doubted that anyone else would ever ask me.' Penelope picked up her knife and fork.

Henry Lamb looked at his wife in a speculative manner for a few moments before picking up his own knife and fork. There was a silence for some minutes as the Lambs applied themselves to their turkey which, by this time, was not as hot as it might have been. After a goodly interval Henry Lamb said, in a conversational tone, 'It's a funny thing that you should be going to Tunbridge Wells, Penelope, it is a very odd thing altogether that you should have made alternative arrangements, because I have made some alternative arrangements of my own.'

Penelope stopped eating. She stared.

'I am going to live in Suffolk,' said Henry.

'*You?*' Penelope was incredulous. 'In *Suffolk?*'

'Oh, I have always been extremely fond of Suffolk, Penelope, I have always had a very soft spot for Suffolk, and I have a few regular customers here, as well you know, my darling. I have taken the lease of a small retail outlet with a one-bedroom flat above at Snape Maltings. What do you think of that, my dearest? What do you make of that for alternative arrangements?'

Penelope's jaw dropped in disbelief. 'You mean you... you've already... I don't believe it! Why Henry, you little worm...'

'Well, I could hardly spend the rest of my life being henpecked by you, my darling, could I? Being nagged and browbeaten by you, Penelope? Being bullied and tidied up and vacuumed around by you, my dearest, I couldn't face it; it would be more than my own flesh and blood could stand.'

'Well, of all the... and when were you going to inform me of these alternative arrangements of yours?' Penelope demanded.

'Oh, I wasn't intending to *inform* you about anything,' said Henry Lamb in an unruffled tone. 'I wasn't going to say a word.'

'You mean you were just going to sneak off?' Penelope was incensed. 'You were just going to move out without any explanation!'

'If I had carried out my plan, my precious one, no explanation would have been necessary.'

'What *plan*? Why not?'

'Because I was going to murder you,' said Henry Lamb.

Penelope gave a bark of laughter. 'Murder *me*? *You*! Don't be ridiculous, Henry. You haven't the nerve for murder. You couldn't kill a fly.'

'Well, of course I couldn't.' Henry Lamb smiled affectionately across the table at his wife. 'It was just a fantasy. It was just a pipedream. It was just silly old Henry indulging in a little make-believe.'

'*Murder?*' Penelope raised her napkin to her mouth to stifle her mirth. '*You*? Why, last Christmas you had to leave the kitchen when I opened the bag of turkey giblets!'

'That was a personal phobia, Penelope,' said Henry in a wounded voice, 'and it is a little unkind of you to mention it, if I may say so. I just could not bear to look at the neck. It looked rather like... it reminded me of my... well, whatever it reminded me of, I didn't like it. It was a most distressing experience.'

Penelope wiped her eyes with her napkin. 'Oh, Henry, you are *priceless*, absolutely *priceless*.'

'Am I, my darling? Am I really priceless?' Henry Lamb smiled sweetly at Penelope. 'Silly old Henry,' he said. 'Ridiculous old Henry. What a silly old, ridiculous old, priceless old Henry I am.'

* * *

Mrs Maitland-Dell had invited Harry to join her at the table for Christmas lunch. It was really rather pleasant. The family, having already dined, were lying under the table with paws outstretched front and back (this being another well-documented peccadillo of the breed). The dining room was lovely, the panels between the ornamental plasterwork of the ceiling had been picked out in pale yellow and great garlands of holly and ivy and old man's beard had been hung on the pale yellow plaster above the polished panelling. The stone frieze over the fireplace (wherein burned a genuine log fire) bore the Rushbroke coat of arms and festive arrangements of spruce and ivy and gilded fir cones twinkled in the light of dozens of creamy wax candles.

The previous evening Mrs Maitland-Dell had experienced a moment of discomfiture. It had been nothing to do with the ambience, the food or the service, but it had a lot to do with Harry. Mrs Maitland-Dell had taken a chair by the library fire after dinner with the family around her. Harry had dined with Sir Vivian, Len, and Norman and very jolly they had appeared too. Alone at her table Mrs Maitland-Dell had felt quite left out. When Harry had returned to enquire if there was anything she required, Mrs Maitland-Dell had graciously suggested he return to his new-found friends until it was time for the family to take the air before bedtime.

Harry on holiday was a rather different Harry to the one she knew. They had agreed that he should wear his own clothes and they suited him. Relaxed and companionable, he mixed easily. He was quite good looking in a rugged sort of way and in good shape for his age. It had occurred to Mrs Maitland-Dell that Harry would soon be of an age to retire. She wondered what would happen then. The thought of having to share her home with someone else, of having a stranger in the house, was quite intolerable. As if anyone else would look after her, would love and care for the family as Harry had done. She could not imagine it. And as the family members dwindled, as had begun with poor dear Freddie, she would not be in a position to take on new members, to cope with puppyhood, she would be too old herself. Thinking about it, looking across at Harry, so debonair in his tweeds, so manly and friendly, so popular and companionable, she had come to a decision. Rupert had just delivered a tray of drinks to the gentlemen's table. Mrs Maitland-Dell had raised a dainty hand in his direction. 'Mr Truscott, a moment of your time, if you would be so kind...'

Now she said to Harry, 'I have something to say to you, Harry, and it may come as a surprise, perhaps even a shock.'

Harry's first thought was that he was going to be made redundant. *Whatever would he do?* His heart clenched. Life without madam and the family was not to be imagined.

'This little holiday, Harry, was a very good idea, and the hotel is an absolute find. I must congratulate you.'

That was it then. Madam was going to stay here, live at the hotel with the family, his services dispensed with. A chill crept into Harry Featherstone's heart.

'I like it so much that I have arranged to purchase one of the apartments they are going to build in the stable block. I am assured that it will be a very high class development. Obviously the family will benefit by having their own home whenever we come to stay.'

Harry's world collapsed round him. He put down his knife and fork.

'I shall keep the house on, of course, but I shall spend quite a lot of time here, all this healthy air, this lovely old house, the beautiful grounds, the wonderful food, the service, the company, all here for us to enjoy.'

Harry closed his eyes. He felt devastated.

Mrs Maitland-Dell placed a small hand on his arm, the fingernails coloured a delicate shade of peach. 'Harry, I am tired of being a widow,' she said.

A claw of jealousy clutched at Harry's heart. So she had managed to find a prospective husband. Not that he should be surprised. There was no doubt that Madam was still a very attractive woman. *But how? Where?*

'I wondered if you would agree to marry me, Harry,' enquired Mrs Maitland-Dell.

Harry was so startled he almost fell off his chair. In regaining his balance he trod on the most venerable Shih Tzu who promptly nipped him on the ankle. 'Me... but Madam, I'm not... I couldn't possibly presume... I'm not... I mean...' Harry said with forceful chagrin, '*My Dad was a London cabbie!*'

'I know how you must feel Harry, but now I shall tell

you something you don't know about me. It is not something the late Mr Maitland-Dell liked to dwell upon.' Madam's eyes twinkled at Harry mischievously. 'My father was a fishmonger in Commercial Road. We lived above the shop.'

Harry stared.

'He started out as a porter at Billingsgate. After which he opened a shop, and after that another shop. When he had six shops we moved to Highgate. When he went into the food hall at Harrods we moved to Blackheath.'

'A porter at *Billingsgate? Really?*' Harry gave a shout of delighted laughter causing a disturbance beneath the tablecloth.

'So what do you say, Harry?'

'Oh. I accept, Madam, gratefully, most gratefully and delightfully.' Relief washed through Harry, leaving him quite limp. 'My own dear Madam, I can't think of anything that would be more congenial.'

'Then I think you should start calling me Clarissa,' said Mrs Maitland-Dell. 'And do eat your turkey, Harry, before it gets cold.'

* * *

Yvonne was delivering desserts to the Pomeroy table. 'I expect you'll be going to the hunt tomorrow, Tom, will you?' she asked him.

Tom grinned up at her. 'I expect I will.'

'I'll see you there, then.' She went off to help Mavis with a family table from the village.

'I think you've made a conquest there,' said Tony admiringly. 'Nice little number.'

'You had better watch out for her mother,' said Mary. 'She's the one with the flashing hair slides.'

'Really?' Tony looked round at the village table where Yvonne and Mavis were collecting up cracker debris. 'She's not bad, either. Not sure about the red hair though.'

'Stop letching at the staff,' Emily ordered. 'Tom's got something to tell you.'

'Tom?' Over her dish of trifle Mary looked at him enquiringly.

'Well, I wasn't going to say anything yet, not until I've firmed up the details, but since Emily has mentioned it...' he grimaced in her direction. 'Funny how some people want you to keep their secrets yet don't give you the same consideration...'

Emily tried to kick him under the table but missed.

'Ow!' exclaimed Tony, 'what was that for?' He was not about to make a fuss. The lunch had been delicious. And Tony was in love with the grey gelding. Never before in his life had he seen such a beautiful, noble animal and, what was more, it had seemed to take to him straight away. It had greeted him with a nicker of welcome, had nuzzled his pockets and had allowed him to stroke its neck and fondle its ears. Even Nicola, the girl who had introduced them had said, 'He really likes you. He never does that for me.' Tony was thrilled. He had elected to ride to the meet, declining Nicola's offer to meet him there. Tomorrow morning could not come soon enough. 'So what's your news, Tom? Getting engaged to that pretty waitress?'

'Hold on a bit; we've only just met.'

'I proposed to your mother in the first week.'

'Weren't you always the impulsive one! Come on then Tom, you may as well tell them,' Emily urged.

'It's just that I've been offered a job.'

'How? Where?' Mary and Tony looked at him in surprise.

'Here. I've been helping out a bit. I helped Len and Barry; he's mute, Mum, you might try a bit of therapy on him; anyway, I helped them get the logs in this morning, then I arranged the flowers for the hall table because Mavis got into a muddle, then I was helping Yvonne, she's the waitress, and Rupert, that's Mr Truscott, to lay up the tables, or rather he was showing me how it should be done because there's more to it than you might think, and he said "You're quite a useful chap, do you want a job?" I thought he was joking but he was serious. Apparently he's looking for an assistant manager to start at Easter. There won't be any accommodation available until then.'

'Assistant Manager, you? But you don't know the first thing about hotel work.' Tony could hardly believe it.

'I can learn on the job. I have to be prepared to help out everywhere but I don't mind that. And I have to do day release at a local catering college. I like the idea of hotel management. Imagine managing a place like this. It would be ace. I'd really like it.'

Mary and Tony looked at Tom in astonishment. Here was their son, not interested in anything, waxing lyrical about hotel management. It was a miracle.

It's this place, thought Mary. *The magic is spreading to all of my family. Thank you, Mother.*

'So you definitely won't be coming into the family business,' said Tony in resignation. 'I can count you out.'

'But I will,' said Emily. 'You can count me in.'

'You?' Tony frowned. 'A precision engineer?'

'Maybe not exactly that, but I'm doing business studies at Uni, and accountancy, and I could probably look into engineering, perhaps even law. Law is always useful,' said Emily.

'My God.'

'I know you haven't considered me, it's been Tom you wanted, but perhaps you should look at me as a prospective employee? Perhaps I could help out in the office in the holidays? Get a feel for it? Unless it's a gender issue.' Emily looked at her father in a combative manner.

'There's no gender issue,' Tony said hastily. 'I just thought... well, to be honest, I'd never even thought of you in the context of the business.'

'Well, think about me now. Because I'm interested. It's the family firm; it's Gramps's firm. And I don't want to spend three years at Uni without a job at the end of it. Not when you need me.' Emily grinned. 'You needn't worry. I can be pinstriped.'

'At least my stripes will be from Dad's tailor,' said Tom. 'Emily's will probably be tattooed on.'

'We are not mentioning tattoos,' snapped Emily.

'Or piercings,' added Tom pointedly.

'You may wish to know,' said Mary Pomeroy, 'that I scattered Mother on the rose garden today,' and was rewarded by the abrupt cessation of all vocal and culinary activity around the table.

When the desserts had been cleared away, Norman got out his violin and went over to join Lavinia at the piano. They played the old tunes, the Sidney Fenton songs and it sounded wonderful. Everyone in the dining room was entranced.

As Vivian watched, his eyes grew damp. As Lavinia played the years seemed to drop away and she became again the woman he had married; beautiful; enchanting. He looked at Norman. God, he could play that violin! He could make the instrument speak. He saw the way they looked at one another as they played; the glances they exchanged. They played as if they had always played together; as if they had never been apart. They played with ease and empathy and, he thought, with love. It was magical. It was bewitching. Vivian remembered that there had been talk, at the time, of a violinist. Was he? Could he be? Suddenly, like the combination of the safe Rupert had installed in the office, the tumblers all fell into place. Vivian got up from the table. He stumbled across the hall where the Yule log burned and a continuous line of insects were evacuating across the carpet from the hearth. He tottered down the brick passage and pushed through the swing doors into the kitchen where the coffee and petit fours were being laid out on trays ready for service.

He said to Anna, 'Better go and look at this violinist chap. Might be your father.'

Chapter Thirty-Three

The bell was tolling, calling the guests to the carol service. There had been sunshine during the day but along the overhung, woody path to the chapel it was crisp underfoot and the bare branches were white with rime. Guests were surprised to be welcomed at the chapel door by a splendid figure, his purple and golden garments crusted with a great deal of ecclesiastical embroidery, wearing a bishop's mitre and holding a staff.

The Bishop, smiling and nodding but in all other respects mute, threw open the heavy door revealing a scene so amazingly theatrical, so bizarre, that people imagined they might have been unexpectedly thrust onto the stage in the middle of some absurdly fantastic, extravagantly designed, wildly over the top musical in the West End.

The chapel, which was very small, was lit by a great many candles, spluttering and leaping against the draught, giving off a shifting, golden light. Great swathes of greenery sprayed with gold paint and artificial snow filled the window sills, niches and corners. A smiling angel with flowing pre-Raphaelite curls, having the most beautiful folded white feathered wings and a long robe of red and gold handed out printed sheets as a second, more energetic angel, took up a shovel in order to hurl pine cones at a roaring, crackling fire. Positioned in an alcove, Lady Lavinia, wearing a cloak of biblical blue with a cowl hood, was playing Corelli's Christmas Concerto on an electronic keyboard with a pipe-organ facility, accompanied by Norman Simkins on his violin. The mesmeric quality of the music, the fluctuating movement of the light, the ancient walls of the chapel with their memorial plaques and shadowy tombs looking like a carefully painted backdrop gave the guests such a sense of unreality, of surrealism, that many staggered a little as they took their seats (which they found rather small, as they had been borrowed from the Rushbroke St. Mary primary school especially for the occasion).

The family were wearing their Christmas reindeer antlers. They were accustomed to these as they wore them every year for at least a part of the festivities. They sat on a chair each and were unaware of the grotesque shadows their antlers cast on the chapel walls. Despite the efforts of the pre-Raphaelite angel, continually stoking two cavernous fireplaces, an icy chill emanated from the stone-flagged floor, the striking intensity of which caused Clarissa to hope that there would be no obligation to kneel for prayers as there was not a hassock in sight.

In such an atmosphere, nobody appeared to be unduly disturbed when a fur-covered fiend with fangs and bloodshot eyes bounded up the aisle, setting the Shih Tzu members of the congregation erect with outrage on their seats. Having reached the front row, the monster patted the black Labrador with a hairy paw and sat down next to Nicola. Then, as Lady Lavinia, prompted by Norman

Simkins, went into *In Dulci Jubilo*, the mute Bishop threw open the door and in walked Father Christmas.

'*Come unto me all ye that labour and are heavily laden and I will give you rest*,' thundered Father Christmas as he made his ponderous progress up the aisle. '*The kingdom of heaven is like unto a net, that was cast into the sea, and gathered every kind. My soul thirsteth for thee, my flesh longeth for thee in a dry and thirsty land. He only is my rock and salvation; he is my defence; I shall not be moved.*'

They stood and sang *It Came Upon a Midnight Clear* and the most vocal member of the Shih Tzu family lifted its head and joined in, being rewarded by the close attention of the rest of the family, some of whom were obliged to turn round on their seats in order to view the vocalist through the back frame of their chairs. Tears of emotion ran down Father Christmas's cheeks at the sound of a congregation in the Rushbroke chapel after almost a lifetime of neglect and decay, and Nicola was similarly hard-pressed to read the first lesson without losing control over her voice.

Other lessons, carols, and inexplicable exhortations followed, during which red wine infused with spices and fortified with brandy spluttered and spat as red hot pokers were thrust into earthenware jugs, and steaming beakers were handed round by the baroque angels in a welcome attempt to prevent the rising chill from paralyzing the congregation's most vital parts. The Bishop handed round a platter of warmed mince pies.

'*Are not two sparrows sold for a farthing?*' demanded Father Christmas as the angel at his side nibbled a mince pie. '*I returned, and saw under the sun, that the race was not to the swift, nor the battle to the strong, neither yet bread to the wise, nor yet riches to men of understanding. A living dog is better than a dead lion.*'

The Bishop moved from chair to chair, shaking the human congregation by the hand, smiling and nodding, stroking the canine members and patting their heads, provoking a show of indignation from the most elderly Shih Tzu, and a prolonged fit of sneezing in another. A catastrophe was narrowly averted when a baroque angel, standing perilously close to a candle flame, caught alight and a sheet of flame shooting up through the pre-Raphaelite hair had to be smothered with the altar cloth. The smell of burned synthetics wafted around the chapel like incense. As the finale, Norman's unaccompanied recital of Massinet's *Meditation* rendered everyone near to tears and the little congregation left the left the chapel wrung with emotion, each and every one to be clasped in an unexpectedly warm parting embrace by the Bishop whose affectionate nature had expanded with every warming beaker he had imbibed.

None thought to question if God had been present because His presence had never been in doubt. As to what He made of it all, only God himself knew the answer to that.

RUSHBROKE HALL COUNTRY HOUSE HOTEL

CHRISTMAS HOUSE PARTY

Boxing Day, Thursday 26th December

From 8 am

Breakfast in the Yellow Dining Room

10.30am

You are invited to attend the traditional Boxing Day
Meet of the Easton Harriers at The Cricket in the
Hearth, Rushall St. Mary. A traditional stirrup cup
will be provided in the Sam Weller Bar.

From 13.30hrs

A Buffet Lunch will be available
in the Yellow Dining Room all afternoon

Afternoon Tea, as and when required,
will be served in the Residents' Lounge

From 20.00hrs

Dinner will be served
in the Yellow Dining Room
There will be musical entertainment

Friday 27th December

Brunch will be served in the Yellow Dining Room

from 8am to 11 am prior to your departure

Chapter Thirty-Four

'Baroque *angels?* Mince *pies?*'

Falling into conversation with a thin-faced individual wearing a quilted anorak and a clerical collar in the Sam Weller Bar, Mary Pomeroy, left on her own, (Tom preferring the company of Yvonne, Emily saying she would follow with Tony, who was sleeping off a hangover, or so he had said) had, in all innocence, described the most delightful and unusual service she had attended the previous evening to the Reverend Nicholas Beresford-Barnes.

Faced with his righteous wrath out in the car park, Vivian regarded a passing hound with as much attention as a judge at Peterborough. 'I am still officially a church warden,' he said with dignity, 'and have the right to take the service if the incumbent is indisposed.'

'The *incumbent* was not *asked!*'

'Since the incumbent would have refused point blank, the point is hardly worth making, I should say.' Vivian squinted down the hill to where two riders were approaching his field of vision, one of them his daughter.

The Pomeroy fellow, with his loose reins and flapping legs, did not appear to be much of a rider.

'Father *Christmas?*' The Reverend Nicholas Beresford-Barnes' lanky frame quivered with scandalised indignation. 'Alcoholic refreshment on *God's premises!*'

'No worse than communion wine, I'd have thought. Nor would God have wanted his congregation to freeze to death,' Vivian said with restraint, his eyes on the approaching riders.

'God would not have been present, I assure you!'

This, to Vivian, was a step too far. 'Rubbish! *Rubbish, I tell you!*' He turned on the cleric. His face had flushed a dull red. His voice shook. 'My chapel is still a viable place of worship in *His* eyes, even if it has failed to gain your own personal seal of approval! *Where two or three people are gathered together in my name there I am in the midst of them!*' Vivian poked the Reverend Nicholas Beresford-Barnes in the chest with a bony finger that trembled with anger. 'His words, not mine! Put that in your pipe and smoke it, Vicar!'

The Reverend was not about to take this lying down. 'Believe me, Sir Vivian, this is not the end of the matter. This is not the last you will hear if it. You have overstepped the mark this time; this time there will be retribution! *You will live to regret this,*' he promised in a voice cold with repressed fury. '*There will be retribution!*'

'Retribution over my dead body,' shouted Vivian. 'Retribution over my sodding *arse!*'

He staggered off towards the oncoming horses.

At the other end of the Sam Weller Bar, the rest of the Rushbroke party was warming up nicely. Madam (Harry was finding it difficult to think of her as Clarissa) having been persuaded to leave the family in the car for reasons of safety, (the current generation of Easton hounds having something of a reputation for gobbling up curs in the absence of legitimate prey) had, once the complimentary stirrup cup had been consumed, insisted on paying for several more rounds in celebration of the engagement and the party, which included Mary, Tom and Yvonne, Norman, Len, Mavis, Barry, the Lambs and Harry Featherstone, were (Barry excepted) engaged in noisy conversation.

Tom and Yvonne moved to the window and stood looking out at the meet through fake leaded lights studded with bottle end glass. Bar staff, dodging hooves and swishing tails, proffered salvers of sausage rolls and goblets of port to hunt servants in their green livery and mounted followers. Horses and ponies snorted and fidgeted and scraped at the tarmac in their impatience to be off. Foot followers conversed in groups, their breath turning to steam in the frosty air. Hounds wandered away from the pack whenever the opportunity arose, happy to be petted and fed sausage rolls until rated and returned to the pack by a whipper-in.

'Oh, goody, here comes Nicola at last,' Yvonne pointed out two horses just about to enter the car park. 'And, look, there's Sir Viv going to meet her. Don't know who's riding the grey horse though. Never seen him before.'

'No, neither have I.' But then Tom, after a more searching appraisal, found that he had seen the rider of the grey horse before and, in fact, knew him very well. '*Oh my God!* I don't believe it! I just don't *believe* it! Hey, Ma! Come over here! Just come and get a look at *this!*'

* * *

Tony did not feel at all safe on the grey gelding. His confidently held theory that a good quality thoroughbred horse would give him a smoother, easier ride had not held up in practice. Legged up into the saddle by Nicola (who had understandably assumed more competency on his part than was actually the case) Tony had felt very high off the ground indeed. This taller, altogether narrower, racier animal, however beautiful, however friendly, did nothing for his sense of security, or his painfully acquired balance. Instead of the short, shaved, and blessedly solid neck of the little piebald to whom he had become accustomed, the grey gelding possessed a neck of alarming length and slenderness ending in two exceedingly sharp and mobile ears which flipped backwards and forwards, both together and independently, with every movement Tony made.

Nicola had led the way at a walk along the length of the drive, giving Tony time to accustom himself to the swinging movement of the grey gelding. He noticed that there was not a neckstrap, but there was a mane, which might be useful to hold onto in an emergency. It was not a long mane, more of a fringe really, but it was something.

Out in the lane the horses went into trot. Tony bumped up and down trying to master the rhythm of the grey gelding's raking stride, so different to Piper's short, choppy one. Nicola regarded his progress with consternation, fearing not only for his safety, but also for that of the grey gelding, despite his uncertain future. As a car approached she sandwiched the grey between the chestnut livery and the hedge, but thankfully the grey appeared not to notice it, seemingly far more concerned with the fumblings and lurching of his rider.

'We don't actually have to follow hounds, if you don't feel comfortable about it,' Nicola offered. 'We can just turn up for the meet, if you prefer, then cut away home. The going will be like iron today, anyway.'

Tony was grateful to have in reserve this tactfully phrased way to save face, especially as when they rode into the forecourt of the Cricket in the Hearth and the grey gelding spotted hounds, he began to prance and sidle. Prancing and sidling had not been a feature of The Pied Piper's repertoire, nor had it featured in *Learn to Ride in a Weekend*, and as Tony's hands, made clumsy by the felted woollen gloves and the silver mounted whip, took a tighter grip on the reins, the grey horse began to swish his tail and perform a piaffe.

'Let go of his head,' Nicola advised. 'Let him settle.'

Sir Vivian wandered up to them, stirrup cup in hand. 'You going to be all right, old chap?' he enquired. 'Might get a bit hairy, you know, once this lot get the wind under their tails.' In an aside to Nicola, he muttered, 'I'd get him back home first opportunity. Fellow will break his neck otherwise. Not fit to ride a bicycle, in my opinion.'

With the reins lying loose on the horse's neck, Tony managed to down a couple of glasses of port and felt rather better. The Hunt Secretary rode up to them with a felt bag on the end of a stick. 'Cap for the British Field Sports Society and the Hunt Servant's Benefit Fund, if you would be so kind.'

Tony had purchased a slim but informative book entitled *Riding to Hounds* from Foyles, and was prepared for this, stuffing into the bag what seemed to Nicola an excessive amount of notes. The Hunt Secretary bypassed Nicola with a rueful smile, knowing rather better than to attempt to extract hard cash from a Rushbroke.

As they rode around the edge of the gathering in order to calm the grey gelding's nerves, Tony caught a glimpse of himself in the windows of the Pickwick Restaurant. He was enchanted by what he saw. The grey gelding was a dashing mount indeed with a noble head carriage and a high-stepping walk. As for Tony himself, why, with the possible exception of the hunt staff, (who had the undoubted advantage of the green livery) he was certainly the best turned out rider at the meet. Leaning down in the saddle, he helped himself to a further goblet of port from a passing tray. Nicola relieved him of the empty glass in dismay and suggested they might go home. Waving cheerily to Tom and Mary, who were watching with faces quite stiff with amazement from the window of the Sam Weller Bar, Tony clapped the grey gelding confidently on its neck. 'No fear,' he said. 'I'm not giving up now. I'm only just getting into the swing of it. I wouldn't miss this for anything.'

A burst on the horn signalled that it was time to move off. Goblets were hastily replaced on trays. Flasks were returned to pockets. Gloves were pulled on. Chinstraps were tightened. Reins were gathered up. As hounds and hunt staff swept across the forecourt the grey horse shot backwards and nearly pitched Tony over his shoulder.

Excitement was intense. The Field Master followed on after hounds and the followers fell in behind, the horses skittering and plunging and flinging their heads in an agony of impatience to be out in the open and away. Tony was carried away in the throng, overcome with the thrill of it, all care and caution gone to the wind, stirrup to stirrup with complete strangers, the grey gelding's face in another horse's tail, mopped along with the crash and clatter of hooves in his ears, his reins loose, and one hand gripping the horse's mane. Nicola, a few horses back, could only pray that he would manage, somehow, to live to tell the tale.

As the horses vanished down the lane towards the first draw, the car followers ran for their vehicles. Tom, Mavis,

Yvonne, Norman and Mary scrambled into Vivian's ancient Rover.

'What on earth does he think he's *doing*,' groaned Mary in anguish. 'He can't even *ride!*'

'Damn fool's likely to get himself killed.' Vivian engaged the ignition and pulled out the choke which resulted in a loud explosion accompanied by a cloud of black smoke from the exhaust. The car leapt forward. The story of this Christmas, thought Norman, would keep Elsie and Genevra spellbound for months.

In the flurry of the departure, as Harry helped Madam into the Rolls Royce, with the family jumping about and sneezing and yelping, eyes popping and positively beside themselves with excitement, nobody noticed that the youngest Shih Tzu was not amongst them.

* * *

Held up by the Master at the edge of a stubblefield, the field fumed and fretted up and down alongside a deep and overgrown ditch. Tony, having survived the ride along the lane which had been, for him, every bit as thrilling as anything he had experienced in his life before, managed, in between some disconcerting leaps by the grey horse, to remove the stopper from his flask and pour into his throat a good quantity of Hine brandy. Nicola, who had given up suggesting they should go home, sat on the chestnut livery resignedly, conveniently placed to offer assistance and first aid, hoping with all her heart that hounds would not put up a hare, but after no time at all there was a sharp burst on the horn and the Master was off at a gallop.

The field, taken by surprise, plunged and bucketed after him. The grey horse had leapt in the air and galloped off with the best of them before Nicola could even gather her wits.

Flask and stopper were lost as Tony, flung half out of the saddle, flattened himself along the horse's neck and, clinging to its mane, inched his way desperately back into the saddle as the horse fled across the stubble. The ground rushed past at a terrifying rate, the wind stung his eyes and a powerful thudding of hooves surrounded him. As Tony regained the saddle a wide ditch yawned ahead. He closed his eyes in terror as the horse gathered itself for the jump.

Galloping along behind with her heart in her mouth, the chestnut livery being no match for the grey gelding's raking stride, Nicola saw the grey steady himself, lengthen into the approach to the ditch and fly over it in copybook style. Tony appeared to take the obstacle quite separately, there being several feet of daylight between himself and the horse, but saddle and man were miraculously reunited on the landing and the grey horse galloped relentlessly on.

The hare ran in a large circle and hounds were almost back alongside the Cricket in the Hearth when they checked at a ditch and began to cast about in an uncertain manner, running up and down distractedly with their noses to the ground, trying to find the line. The field, thundering up behind, took heed of the Master's raised hand, but Tony could not. The Master yelled at him to '*Hold hard, there! Hold bloody hard!*' But how could he? Indeed, it was a miracle that he was still in the saddle. Tony knew that he could not hold on for much longer, but when he looked down and saw the ground rushing past and the grey's great iron-shod hooves flying, his grip on the pommel tightened and his toes were thrust even more desperately down in the stirrups.

Having received no discernible instructions from his

rider, the grey gelding had done another complete lap of the headland by the time a particularly enterprising hound had picked up a fresh and interesting scent and began to speak. As one man, the rest of the pack gathered on the line and raced away in pursuit of what would later be described by onlookers in the lane as a small, unidentifiable, long-haired creature, round-headed, apparently earless, with a plumed tail, very short in the leg, with no turn of speed to speak of; a creature, in fact, so unlike a hare that even a blind man could spot the difference.

'Keep back! *Keep bloody back, Sir!*' roared the Master as the grey gelding thundered up to him for the second time.

'*Riot! 'ware cur!*' yelled the Huntsman to the Whipper-In as he caught sight of the quarry. '*Riot! They've picked up a bloody cur!*' Both men simultaneously clapped their heels to their horse's sides and set off after hounds at a flat out, flying gallop.

Emily had found the walk from Rushbroke Hall to the Cricket in the Hearth longer than expected. She had waited out of sight behind a yew hedge until everyone had left for the meet. Only Rupert and Anna had remained behind to prepare the buffet lunch which must be made ready for the return of their guests.

She had emptied all her purloined canisters and packets into a plastic bag and mixed them all together. The smell had been potent and made her eyes sting. Stumbling over frozen plough, she wondered if it had been a bad idea to take the cross-country route rather than sticking to the lanes. Below her was a long stretch of stubble and beyond it, more plough. Beyond that, she hoped, was the Cricket in the Hearth.

Where was the hunt, for heaven's sake? The countryside all around seemed as still and silent as the grave. It was also unbearably cold. Behind her, the twisted brick chimneys of Rushbroke Hall smoked gently, promising crackling log fires, warmth and comfort. But as she adjusted her balaclava, and began seriously to contemplate calling it a day, Emily heard the rattle of hooves on the lane. Soon afterwards she heard an approaching sound like a discordant chiming of bells and realised, with a shiver of apprehension, that what she was hearing was a pack of hounds in full cry.

Emily saw the hare first, covering the plough with enormous leaps, moving incredibly fast, well ahead of hounds who were racing along so close together that a tablecloth would have covered them. Down the plough they came and onto the stubble only to falter, then check completely, fanning out in confusion on the far side of a ditch which divided the field. They had lost the scent.

Emily had just lifted her fists into the air as a victory salute for the hare when she saw a movement on the near side of the ditch and something began to run in her direction, something far too small to be a hare, something far too hairy to be a rabbit, something with white-rimmed eyes starting out of its head with terror. At the very same moment, hounds picked up its scent and with a frightening unearthly clamour, raced after it.

Screaming like a banshee, Emily ran towards them.

The onlookers in the lane were now treated to the spectacle of several things happening at once. First, the grey gelding, with Tony Pomeroy still clinging to the saddle, galloped through the pack, scattering them in all directions. Secondly, a black figure wearing a balaclava hurled itself in to the melee causing the grey horse to swerve violently and precipitate its rider headlong in amongst the startled and disorientated pack. As the black figure grabbed up the quarry, something exploded, sending a reddish dust into the air. Hounds, having been inexplicably and abruptly deprived of their illegitimate prey, and no doubt mindful of the furious abuse advancing upon them in the shape of the hunt servants, began to run around distractedly, waving their sterns and sneezing uncontrollably.

As Tony lurched to his feet, the black figure in the balaclava stared at him and said in a tone of the very greatest astonishment and incredulity, '*Dad?*'

As the grey gelding, having lapped the stubble field with reins and stirrups flapping, returned to stand nearby with froth dripping from his flanks and mouth, and his sides pumping like a bellows, Tony looked at the black figure in the balaclava and said in absolute amazement, '*Emily?*'

And as the hunt staff rode up to the scene with their faces scarlet with temper and exertion, and their horse's necks plastered with sweat, Emily, with the youngest member of the Shih Tzu family clutched protectively to her chest, turned on the Huntsman. 'I hope you realise,' she said severely, 'that if your hounds had killed this valuable dog today, you would most certainly have been prosecuted.'

'And I hope you realise,' returned the Huntsman in an extremely sour voice, 'that thanks to you two, if my hounds had managed to kill *anything* today, it would have been a bloody miracle!'

Chapter Thirty-Five

'...and then this *darling* girl appeared out of nowhere, and I do mean out of absolutely nowhere, and simply *hurled* herself in front of the slavering pack...' Clarissa Maitland-Dell was relating to Rupert the excitements of the chase. 'I just cannot bear to *imagine* what would have become of my precious little dog had she not intervened when she did, and as for her father, as for Tony Pomeroy, why, he just spurred his horse right into the middle of the pack and threw himself off at a gallop. It was the most enthralling and heroic act I have ever witnessed and I shall be beholden to the Pomeroy family until my dying day.'

If this was not an entirely accurate account of what had occurred, nobody was about to say so. Emily held the smallest Shih Tzu in her arms, the little dome of his head warm under her chin.

'Of course, he can't stay with the family now, not possibly. He is far too adventurous and independent and such a little escape artist. Emily has asked if she can keep him and I have agreed. It is the perfect solution. It has all ended in a most satisfactory manner. I will have a sliver of smoked salmon, if you please, Mr Truscott, and some egg mayonnaise. I wonder if I could trouble you for a little brown bread and butter?'

'Not try it again?' Tony looked at his wife in astonishment as they picked up their plates for the buffet. '*Not try it again?* Mary, you may not realise it but today was the most thrilling experience of my life! What a ride! What a horse! What a sport!' Tony stuck a serving spoon into a bowl of creamy Dauphinoise potatoes with enthusiasm. 'I have spent half a lifetime looking for something like this and not only have I every intention of trying it again, but I have decided to buy the grey gelding. Apparently the owners are willing to sell him for a very reasonable price. I can keep it at livery with Nicola, and I need to talk to you about buying one of the stable apartments. Then we can all come here whenever we need a break. Don't you think it's a brilliant idea? You could visit your mother, I could ride my horse. Come to think of it, Tom could live in the apartment if he wanted to. Well, Mary, what do you think?'

'Carp? You mean carp out of the *moat?*' Emily gave a groan of disgust. 'I don't know how you can stand there and serve that, Yvonne. We were only feeding them this morning!'

'Well, we wasn't feeding this one because he's been in the chiller since yesterday.' Yvonne placed a meaty chunk on Tony's plate. 'And it's not as if they're pets exactly, is it? They do need thinning out a bit and the Rushbrokes have eaten them for hundreds of years, so it's traditional. Sir Viv fishes them out with a rod and a bit of bacon rind and he does chuck the little ones back in, so it's quite fair really. Watch out for bones, Mr Pomeroy. There might be a few left in.'

'Oh, it's quite *fair*,' Emily said darkly. 'It might not seem so fair if you'd got a metal hook through your own throat.'

'Emily,' Mary Pomeroy said warningly. 'Let's not ride hobby horses at dinner, please.'

* * *

'Well, Norman, I hope you've enjoyed your Christmas in the country, did you like it?' Yvonne beamed at him over a tray bearing his morning tea and a plate of Chef's biscuits.

'Did I like it?' Norman, in plaid thermal pyjamas courtesy of Country Cousins, sat up in his high half tester bed, propped with fat pillows, an open copy of *Country Living* at his side. 'It has been the most amazing experience of my life from start to finish. Suddenly I have a family and they want to give me a home. I can't quite get to grips with it yet; it hasn't quite sunk in.'

'So you won't be an accountant any more then, and you'll be saying cheery-bye to Elsie and Genevra?' Yvonne settled the tray on the bedside table and perched on the bed. Today her hair was backcombed into an astonishing beehive with two yellow and black furry bees clipped onto it to emphasise the point.

'Well, yes and no to that. I'll still be an accountant because I've offered to look after the book- keeping side of things for the hotel. That, and the violin playing, should earn my keep, I think. But I will be saying goodbye to Elsie and Genevra. I shall go back to work my notice and sell my house. My, how things have changed, Yvonne! I can hardly believe it.'

'I know. It's amazing, Norman, it really is. And to think you never knew you had a daughter, and now you have a grand-daughter as well. It's a good job you decided to come and stay here, instead of with those friends of yours, you know, the Fletcher-Smyths, the hyphenated ones, spelled with a "y".'

'Isn't it just.' They laughed. Norman looked at Yvonne affectionately. 'And you? Will you go back to Elsie and Genevra?'

'No fear! I'll be giving in my notice as well because Rupert's offered me a permanent job here; I'll be part housemaid, part waitress and part receptionist. I'm ever so pleased Norman, because I shall be able to live with my mum, and Tom is starting as assistant manager at Easter, and his dad is buying one of the stable apartments so he'll move in there eventually, I expect. It's all so exciting and I'm ever so pleased about it. Oh, Norman, isn't it all just *brilliant!*'

Mavis tapped on the door and went into Vivian's bedroom. She placed the tray with his morning tea carefully on his bedside table and opened the curtains with a flourish. That this provoked no reaction was hardly surprising because Vivian was quite dead and had been for some hours.

Mavis, her sixth sense on high alert, went to the bedside and looked at the occupant. Sir Vivian stared glassily upwards from a face that could have been carved out of marble. Mavis thought he looked very peaceful and that his nose, in particular, looked very fine. She straightened the collar of his pyjamas, smoothed the sheets, tweaked the pillows and replaced the eiderdown on the bed. When everything was tidy she said a little prayer for Vivian's departed spirit and poured herself a cup of tea. After which she picked up the tray and went back to the kitchen to break the news.

Dr. McLoughlin, summoned to the bedside, pronounced the cause of death to be a massive heart attack. 'Quite sudden, there's nay a doubt; he wouldna have known anything about it. I'll do a wee certificate so you can register the death. He was a great man, Sir Vivian. Aye, he was a fine upstanding gentleman and we shall miss him sorely.'

The undertakers in Rushall St. Mary were helpful and genuinely sympathetic. Nicola sat at the plank table, white-faced. Stunned. 'Somebody should tell Mother,' she said.

'I'll tell her,' Anna took off her apron. Nobody was due down for breakfast for at least an hour. 'Let me do it.'

Lavinia was sitting up in bed looking expectant. Her face fell when she saw that Anna was not carrying a tray.

'I am afraid I have some bad news,' Anna said gently.

'Oh, I do hope not,' Lavinia said. She fumbled beneath her pillow and produced a paper tissue, making ready for tears. 'I do so hate to receive bad news before I have had my morning tea.'

'Vivian has gone,' said Anna.

'I see.' Lavinia appeared relieved to hear this. 'When will he be coming back?'

'He won't be coming back,' Anna said. 'He passed away in the night. He had a heart attack. Vivian is dead.'

'What a shame.' Lavinia looked down at the paper tissue as if she was unsure where it had come from and what should be done with it. 'Have you any good news?'

'Well, Nicola and David Williamson are to be married. Grace is coming to live with us in the summer. Norman is staying on for a few days and then he will come back here to live.'

Lavinia frowned. She looked at Anna in annoyance. 'I

don't know why you are telling me about these people. I don't know any of them. And I don't think I have yet had my morning tea. When did you say Vivian will be back?'

Mavis was waiting for Anna outside the door. Her mascara and powdered lids were no longer the glory they had been when she arrived for her breakfast shift. Anna closed the door and leaned against it. 'I can't get through to her at all. It's as if she doesn't want to know.'

'Not doesn't want to, Miss Gabriel, if you'll forgive me for saying so. She can't. Her brain won't process the information; it won't retain anything at all. You mustn't worry about things you can't change. We'll do the grieving for her. We'll all grieve for Sir Vivian. We all loved him; he was a wonderful man. He was the last of a dying breed and he was a true gentleman, he absolutely was.'

'You know what we should do, Mavis, don't you? You are familiar with the procedures? After your experience with Arnold,' Anna said. 'You will be able to advise us?'

Mavis looked nonplussed. 'After my Arnold? Oh, God bless you, Miss Gabriel, my Arnold isn't *dead*! My Arnold left of his own volition. It was probably pre-ordained but I couldn't see it. "Mavis," he said, "It's no good, I just can't live with you any longer. I've tried, God knows I've tried, but this is the end of the road and I'm off." Oh yes, he went off, Miss Gabriel, and he didn't go off alone, I might tell you; he went off with Glenda Franklin from the Happy Baker in Stradishall High Street. Not what you might call an oil painting, in my opinion, and a bit overweight, I have to say it, but a very nice sort of person in her way, very jolly, always a smile for everybody, the sort you could warm to, although it hurts to admit it, it really does.' Mavis blotted her eyes, took Anna by the arm and steered her back to the kitchen. 'Now, Miss Gabriel, we have brunch to prepare and guests departing, and the grieving and the procedures can wait. Sir Vivian isn't in a hurry to go anywhere and the least said the better for the moment. Let's put a brave face on it and get everybody looked after and leaving in a happy frame of mind. "Smile in public, weep in private," that's what my Arnold used to say, and he was right about that, he really was.'

Chapter Thirty-Six

'Henry, I am speaking to you!' As they drove out of the Rushbroke gates, Penelope looked across at her husband in annoyance. 'Are you with me, Henry, or are you already in Snape?'

Henry, who had indeed been thinking of Snape; of an unencumbered future spent arranging books on shelves, patted Penelope's knee in a friendly manner. 'No, I am not in Snape, my love, I am listening to every word to have to say. Speak up, Penelope. Fire away.'

'I was just saying that it would be nice to keep in touch,' said Penelope. 'I should like to keep in touch with you, Henry. I shall want to know how you are. I would not want you to think that because I am going to Tunbridge Wells I no longer care what happens to you. I would like there to be a line of communication open between us. I want to keep in touch.'

'Of course you do, my darling,' said Henry agreeably. 'Of course you want to stay in touch, and so do I. Just because I was planning to murder you, just because I had arranged to escape to a new Penelope-free life in Snape, doesn't mean that my feelings have changed, does it? Of course it doesn't! We must certainly stay in touch, my dearest, what had you in mind? A quarterly letter? A twice-yearly telephone call?'

'As a matter of fact, Henry, as this Christmas treat of yours was such a good idea, and has been so very enjoyable, I thought it would be rather nice if we agreed to meet up here again next Christmas. If it proved successful, we might make it an annual event. It would provide us with an enjoyable opportunity to catch up. Something to look forward to. Christmas might be rather dreary otherwise.'

Henry Lamb beamed at his wife in delight. 'Now that really is a commendable idea, Penelope, an absolute brainwave! Oh, clever, clever, Penelope, what a diamond you are! We shall make the reservation the minute we get home!'

'Separate *rooms*, of course,' said Penelope.

'Separate *rooms*, of course,' Henry chuckled. 'Separate rooms, Penelope, my precious jewel, *definitely*.'

* * *

'Dad, are you really serious about buying the grey horse?' Emily wanted to know. 'When I talked to Nicola about it, she said it was suicidal in traffic.'

'Not any more it isn't.' This was the truth. Many horse boxes and vehicles had passed them as they had made their way back from the hunt and the grey gelding had not turned a hair. Tony, with his loose reins and insecure seat had seemingly worked a miracle. Nicola had been astonished enough to dig a little further into his background and had discovered that the horse had always had male owners until his latest owner; a girl who had herself been already traumatised by a traffic shy horse. A sensitive beast, it had not taken the grey gelding long to pick up the fact that, to his rider, a vehicle was a threat. So his traffic problems had become a gender issue. The grey gelding liked to be ridden and handled by men. Nicola remembered how he had tried to follow Rupert up the lane, when they had first met. How he had immediately taken to Tony. Wisely, she did not communicate her findings to the owner, who had agreed to sell the horse for a fraction of his worth. It was a marriage made in heaven. 'I have already agreed a price and Nicola tells me it's a fraction of his true worth. She's going to livery him here at the Rushbroke Home Farm.'

'And what will you do with him when the anti's persuade the government to ban hunting?' Emily cuddled the youngest Shih Tzu protectively. 'Because they will, Dad. It's only a matter of time. It really is a gross sport; it's totally barbaric.'

'I'll show jump him, probably. Nicola says he also has potential as an eventer.'

'Goodness,' said Mary, thinking of the unlimited potential for future disasters that this represented.

'It's great that you're buying one of the stable apartments,' Tom said with enthusiasm. 'I think that's an ace idea.'

'Especially as you are going to get to live in it,' said Emily sourly.

'You will have to keep it clean and tidy,' said Mary. 'I shall expect the kitchen and the bathroom to be spotless. We shall be visiting regularly to check.'

'No parties. No fags. No orgies,' said Tony.

'As if I *would*.'

'You'll be kept too busy for any of that anyway,' Tony said, 'if I know Rupert.'

'Actually, I wanted to talk to you all about houses,' said

Mary. 'Because now Tom is leaving home, and as Emily goes to Uni next year, I think we should start looking for a smaller property.'

'Move?' Tony was astonished. 'Move from The Glebe? I thought you liked the house.'

'I have never really liked The Glebe,' admitted Mary, 'and I should very much like to live in an old house; a house with a bit of history to it; something with character.'

'But what about us?' Emily protested. 'We shall need to come home in the holidays. We won't be away *all* the time.'

'I realise that. I thought we could find a place with an annex. Somewhere separate for you and Tom, so you can have a bit of independence,'

'Sounds great to me,' said Tom.

'Sounds OK, I suppose,' Emily agreed grudgingly.

'Well, this holiday has certainly brought some changes,' Tony marvelled. 'Tom's got himself a job, Emily's got herself a dog, I've got myself a horse; we've paid a holding deposit on the largest apartment in the stable block, and now your mother's going to find us a new house.'

'And Gran's in the rose bed,' added Emily.

'Where she will be very, very happy,' said Mary confidently.

'I should like you to arrange a return visit at Easter, Harry.' Clarissa was sitting on the front seat for the first time, and enjoying the experience. Harry, although he was wearing his dark suit, had dispensed with his chauffeurs cap.

'Mr Truscott senior...'

'Len,' interposed Harry.

'Len,' agreed Clarissa, 'Len tells me that the detailed

plans for the apartment will be ready for inspection by then. We shall need to advise him of any small alterations and adjustments we would like him to make. We shall need to keep a close eye on the project, Harry; we shall need to ensure that all our requirements will be met.'

'We certainly will,' said Harry. 'We shall need to keep a very close eye on the project indeed.'

'And I thought we might be married at the same time,' Clarissa said. 'Mr Truscott...'

'Rupert,' interposed Harry. Married. He felt a little tug of joy at the word. *Married to Madam! Harry Featherstone married to Clarissa Maitland-Dell!*

'Rupert,' agreed Clarissa, 'says they will have a licence for civil ceremonies by then. Perhaps you and he could liaise regarding the details. We shall require just a simple ceremony, Harry, nothing too extravagant. Just some extremely tasteful flower arrangements for the ceremony room, followed by a delicious meal in the private dining room would be ideal, don't you think?'

'You can leave the arrangements in my capable hands, Clarissa,' said Harry warmly. 'Perhaps I could ask Len if he would be my best man.'

'You could indeed,' agreed Clarissa.

'Were you thinking of inviting the Pomeroy family?'

'Most certainly,' Clarissa said comfortably. 'They are such a wonderful family, and it will be the perfect opportunity to be reunited with dear little Oscar. I have become very fond of Emily, despite her odd appearance, and I know he will be very happy with her. She did save his life, after all.' She glanced at the family through the window. They were already fast asleep on the back seat, totally exhausted by their first experience of a holiday; snuffling and snoring in their Shih Tzu dreams. 'They have had such an enjoyable time,' she said fondly. 'They are all quite worn out.'

'We have all had an enjoyable time,' said Harry. 'It has been extremely congenial. A most wonderful holiday indeed.' The holiday had indeed turned out to be a resounding success. And now he was to be married to Clarissa at Easter. An Easter wedding! Who would have thought it! Who would ever have believed it! He patted Clarissa's hands, so small and delicate and clad in Harry's favourite eau-de-nil leather gloves, so soft and elegant and nice. He would have to buy her an engagement ring. He would enjoy that. They would choose it together.

'On our next visit, Harry, I am thinking of asking Mrs Sholto...'

'Mavis,' interposed Harry.

'I am thinking of asking Mavis...' agreed Clarissa.

'If she would be a witness?' supplied Harry.

Clarissa gave a mischievous little smile and put a daintily gloved hand on Harry's knee. 'What a very good idea, Harry, but actually I was thinking of asking her if it would be possible to have astrological charts drawn up for all the family.'

In the chapel, Anna lit the altar candles. She sat on one of the little chairs. She had felt the need for solitude. She needed time to think.

So much had happened it was difficult to get her thoughts in order. Vivian had made provision for Nicola with a hefty insurance policy payable on his death. Whatever else he had not paid, he had kept up the payments on this. Anna thought back to the millstone and the mere and wondered if they would have paid out on a suicide? She doubted if Vivian had ever perused the small print. And what now for Lavinia? She was not safe to leave alone in the apartment. She wondered if Norman would move in with her. She thought he probably would. He would certainly look after her. He loved her. She may not remember him but it did not worry him. 'I remember her,' he said, 'I have remembered her for almost forty years, every day of every week, of every month, of every year. And that is enough. After all, she has the rest of her life to get to know me again.' Well, Anna thought, thank heavens for Norman.

To discover that Norman Simkins was almost certainly her father had been a shock and a surprise and she was still coming to terms with it. Vivian had been extraordinarily pleased, as had Rupert. They still had to introduce Norman to Grace, who was coming to stay at Rushbroke for a week before she returned to school. They planned to close Rushbroke Hall for two weeks after New Year to rest and plan the work schedule for the following year. Grace would move to Rushbroke as soon as the gatehouse lodge was ready for occupation. She couldn't wait. She may have lost one grandfather but she had gained another; one who would help her with her violin and piano studies. The musical talent had skipped a generation, Anna thought ruefully, yet she had her own creative talent, her cooking and kitchen organizational skills and they had certainly been tried and tested during the Christmas break. She had not been found wanting, and she was happy about that.

They had known that Vivian was fading, of course they had. Nevertheless, his death had been a shock. But really, if he had to die, Anna supposed he could not have picked a better time. Perhaps he had chosen to give up the struggle, to let go, now that everything was in place; the business up and running and likely to be a success; Nicola moving into Home Farm with David Williamson; Norman reunited with Lavinia, Rupert and Anna restoring the gatehouse lodge to make a home for themselves and Grace. The chapel restored and ready to receive him. She could imagine him rubbing his bony, spotted hands together. 'All done,' he might have said. 'All sorted. Best not to hang around.' She smiled at the thought.

Sitting in the little chapel with the flickering candles casting their uncertain light on the memorial plaques and the tombs of long departed Rushbrokes, Anna felt a rush of gratitude toward her adoptive parents, without whose legacy none of this would have been possible. With her eyes tightly closed and her hands clasped together (as if God might actually be listening; as if he might even be capable of passing on her message) she sent them silent but heartfelt love and thanks. After that, as a paralysing chill seeped into her bones, peace seeped into her soul at last.

The King James Bible was open on the lectern. Her message, her final message, was ringed in black. *Many daughters have done virtuously, but thou excelleth them all.*

* * *

'No!' Nicola faced the Reverend Nicholas Beresford-Barnes in steadfast and determined defence of the doorstep. 'You are not coming into this house with your talk of retribution and damnation! You are not welcome here! *Go away!*'

She would have closed the door but the Reverend had been a replacement window salesman before taking holy orders and was skilled at preventative measures. 'If you can bear to hear me out,' he said, regarding her with gravity, having inserted himself neatly between the door and the frame, 'I have come to ask if I might be allowed to conduct the funeral service at St. Saviour's.'

As Nicola made no move, he said, 'The Rushbrokes have maintained the church for centuries, it is their church, just as much as it is ours. It will not be possible to hold the service in your own little chapel because the whole village will wish to attend. He has been their baronet, as well as yours, and they will wish to pay their respects. Already they have insisted that the new development be renamed in his honour: Rushbroke Avenue, Vivian Drive, Valentyne Close. We even have plans for a memorial plaque in the chancel.'

And as Nicola still made no move to admit him, he said, 'I promise that I have come here in *peace*. I have come in a spirit of *humility*. I have come to make *amends*. I have come to apologise. I... *we*, need Sir Vivian to come back to St. Saviour's. He needs to know that he is welcome, that it is *his* church. He needs to know that he is forgiven.' The Reverend Beresford-Barnes added in a softer tone, 'and so do I.'

'In that case,' said Nicola, 'you had better come in.'

One week after a packed service at St. Saviour's Church, Rushall St. Mary, conducted by the Reverend Nicholas Beresford-Barnes, Sir Vivian's ashes were interred in the Rushbroke chapel during a simple ceremony with appropriate readings from the Old Testament.

The engraving on the slab, lifted with the most enormous difficulty and slotted into place by Len, Barry, Norman and Rupert, read as follows:

Caroline Akrill

**SIR VIVIAN VALENTYNE RUFUS PERCIVAL
ALGERNON RUSHBROKE Bt.
1902 - 1986
THE LAST BARONET
HE DIED AS HE LIVED
IN GLORY**

According to Anna, God was most certainly present at the ceremony.

About the Author

Caroline Akrill began her career writing for *Pony Magazine*, spilling the beans on the showing world and proving to be one of their most successful columnists. It was while she was writing for *Pony* that she started her first novel, *Caroline Canters Home,* based on her own experiences in the show ring. She soon struck out from showing, and her books are based in the worlds of dressage, eventing, and film work. Her eventing series is one of the most successful horse series of all time. As well as writing, Caroline has run a riding school, bred show ponies, run a country pub, and been an antiquarian horse book dealer, as well as working for J A Allen, the horse book publisher, for over 20 years. She and her husband, James, ran a hotel in North Wales until they retired. She has now moved back to Suffolk, where she edits and prints the local community magazine and observes the horse world from a safe distance.

You can find Caroline on Facebook.

Acknowledgments

For faith and encouragement I would like to thank Christine Lunness, Lesley Gowers, Gill Jackson, Chris Stafford and, most especially, Jane Badger. For unflagging support when things got tough I send blessings to my late and beloved husband, James, and also to the Lehain family. To Emma James, who produced the lovely artwork for the cover, thanks for your care and patience in interpreting what was never a clear brief and for coming up with exactly what was required. Finally, my very special thanks to my sadly missed friend, Karen Bush, without whose unstinting help and advice *Christmas with the Rushbrokes* would still be in a dusty cardboard box marked Caroline's Unfinished Novel.

Other books by Caroline Akrill

Jane Badger Books

Jane Badger Books is dedicated to bringing back classic pony fiction, some of which has been out of print for over 50 years. Authors available so far include:

Caroline Akrill

Gillian Baxter

Joanna Cannan

Victoria Eveleigh

Ruby Ferguson

Patricia Leitch

Patience McElwee

Marjorie Mary Oliver & Eva Ducat

Hazel M Peel

Christine Pullein-Thompson

Diana Pullein-Thompson

Josephine Pullein-Thompson

Siân Shipley

* * *

www.janebadgerbooks.co.uk

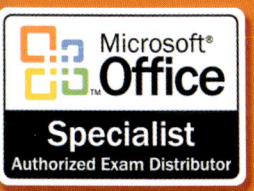

Windows XP
Home Edition

Copyright - Editions ENI - January 2002
ISBN: 2-7460- 1586-2
Original edition: ISBN: 2-7460-1569-2

Editions ENI

BP 32125
44021 NANTES Cedex 1

Tél. 02.51.80.15.15
Fax 02.51.80.15.16

e-mail : editions@ediENI.COM
http://www.editions-eni.com

WAY IN collection directed by Corinne Hervo
English edition by Andrew BLACKBURN

Foreword

This book has been written for beginners who want to know how to get the most from a computer operating system. It describes only the essential features of Windows XP that are required to organise your working environment efficiently.

The different parts of this book can be consulted separately but they are designed to be taken in order. This way, you first discover the Windows environment and the features that all common to all Windows applications. Next, you will see how to manage files and use multimedia applications such as Windows Movie Maker, the Windows Media Player and Windows Messenger. The third part deals with organising the contents of your computer's hard disk, especially using the My Documents window. The last part will complement what you already know by showing you how to customize your working environment (by defining several user accounts, changing your desktop and installing a printer, for example).

This is not just a book for reading; it can also be put into practice. Sit down at your computer and try out the actions described by following the examples. Keep this book close to your computer and you will find it a useful reference for finding a function or term that you may have forgotten.

You will not just find information about Windows XP features; you will also find tips on what not to do and what not to forget as well as shortcuts to help you save time. It is often possible to carry out the same action using the mouse, the keyboard or the menus. These symbols will help you differentiate between each type of method: for a keyboard method,  for a method that uses the mouse and ▤ for the method using the menus. You may also come across the following symbols:

 indicates a comment with extra information about the current topic.

 indicates a useful tip.

The only way to learn about your system is to use it: settle down in front of your computer, prop this book up next to the keyboard... and you will soon see that Windows XP is not as complicated as you might think.

Table
of **Contents**

Table
of **Contents**

Table
of **Contents**

Table

of **Contents**

Table
of **Contents**

Changing the environment   4th Part

Managing users   Chapter 4.1

Table of **Contents**

Customizing the desktop   Chapter 4.2

Table
of **Contents**

Installing

Appendix

1st

This part introduces you to the Windows environment. It describes the main items you can see on your screen and explains how to manage different windows.

Part

Discovering the XP environment

Getting started with Windows XP

Windows is the name of the operating system on your Personal Computer. Your computer could not run without this basic software, as it would not be able to start. PCs (Personal Computers) run the Windows system, while Macintosh computers run a different operating system.

Windows XP is a multi-user system. This means that you can create several user accounts on it. In this way, several users can work on the same computer and each user can customise his/her workspace, without affecting the workspaces of the other users. Each user has his/her own **My Documents** folder in which he/she can save the documents that he/she creates. The user can decide to allow, or not allow other users to access this folder.

STARTING WINDOWS XP

▓ When you start your computer, by default, the users of your computer appear in the Windows XP Welcome screen.

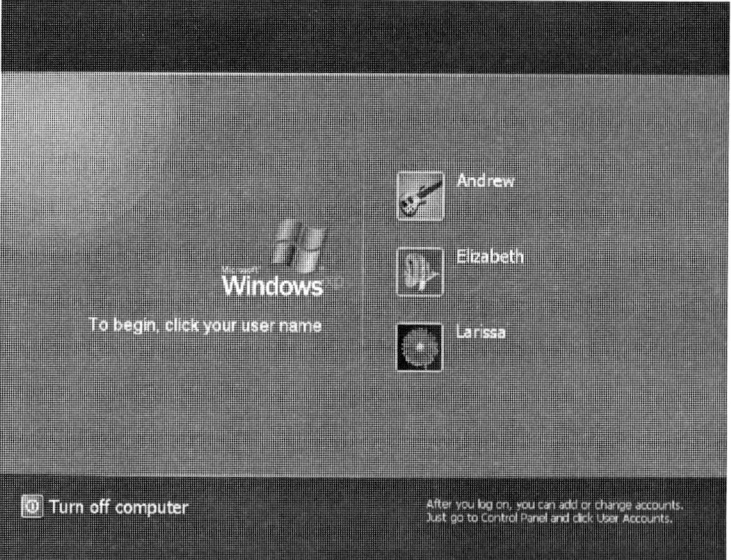

In the above example, 3 users have been created.

If you are the only user of the computer (if you have just bought your computer or if you have not yet created other user profiles, for example) then this screen will not appear: Windows XP will open your working session automatically and you will go straight into the Windows desktop. In this case, you can skip the rest of this section and go straight on to the next section, **Discovering the Windows XP desktop**.

If several users have been created and you do not see the Windows XP Welcome screen, it means that this screen has been deactivated. In this case, to log on to the computer, you must enter your user name and any password you may have, in the **Log On to Windows** dialog box.

Otherwise, to log on, click your user name on the Welcome screen, as it prompts you to, then enter any password you may have. If you have forgotten your password, click the ? button to view any text you entered as a password hint when you defined it: this text should help you to remember your password (cf. Managing users - Associating a password with a user).

When you enter your password, it appears as a set of dots.

When you have finished entering your password, click the ➡ button or press the ↵ key to validate it.

Your workspace or desktop appears on the screen.

Getting started with Windows XP

When you have logged on to your computer, the Windows desktop appears on the screen. This desktop provides access to the different items on your computer (it allows you to start Word or Excel for example, or to access the files on your hard disk, etc.). The example below shows the desktop by default. However, as you can customize it, your desktop may appear differently.

DISCOVERING THE WINDOWS XP DESKTOP

- However, your desktop will always show the following items:
  - the **taskbar** (a) provides a button to access each open application (in the above example, no applications have yet been opened). You can set the taskbar to hide itself when you are not using it or to show the Quick Launch bar, etc. (cf. Managing the taskbar).
  - The **start** button (b) provides access to the main Windows menu.
  - The **notification area** (c) displays the system time along with a number of notification icons. For example, it may show an icon to let you know that you have received e-mail.
  - The **Recycle Bin** (d) is there to receive the files you delete. By default, when you delete a file, the system transfers it to the **Recycle Bin**. This approach allows you to retrieve any files you deleted by mistake.

The desktop may also show other icons (objects) such as shortcuts, which provide quick access to applications or files.

You can generally access the different items on your computer in a number of different ways. For example, you may be able to start an application (such as Word or Excel) directly from your desktop, if it shows the corresponding icon. Otherwise, you can always start applications from the start menu.

START MENU

▒ To display the Windows XP **start** menu, click the **start** button. Alternatively, you can press the ⊞ key or press ⌷Ctrl⌷⌷Esc⌷ on your keyboard.

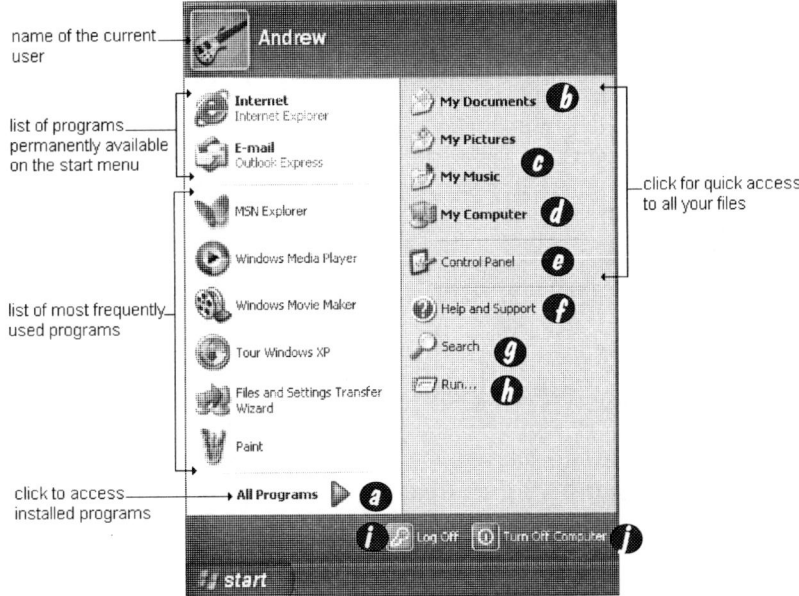

name of the current user

list of programs permanently available on the start menu

list of most frequently used programs

click to access installed programs

click for quick access to all your files

▒ By default, the top level of the Windows XP **start** menu contains the following items:

- The **All Programs** menu (a) lists all the applications installed on the computer.

Discovering the XP environment

- The **My Documents** option (b) opens a window of the same name that contains two folders, by default: **My Music** and **My Pictures**. It is recommended that each user of the computer saves his/her documents in this **My Documents** folder.
- The **My Music** and **My Pictures** options (c) provide direct access to the corresponding folders.
- The **My Computer** option (d) provides access to all the components of your computer. These components are divided into different categories that depend on how your computer is set up.
- The **Control Panel** option (e) opens a window of the same name that allows you to modify your working environment (by setting up your network connections, managing the user accounts, configuring your devices, adding or removing programs and so forth).
- The **Help and Support** option (f) provides access to the Windows XP **Help and Support Center** application.
- The **Search** option (g) provides access to a number of options that allow you to find files, folders, people (in an address book) and computers on the network. As its name suggests, you can use the **Search the Internet** option in the **Search Companion** bar to carry out a search on the Internet.
- The **Run** option (h) allows you to run a program by specifying the corresponding executable file.
- The **Log Off** option (i) closes the current session and allows another user to log on.
- The **Turn Off Computer** option (j) opens the **Turn off computer** dialog box. This dialog box allows you to turn off your computer, to restart it or to put it into hibernation (Windows XP saves your desktop environment onto your hard disk before turning off your computer, so it can restore your desktop as you left it when you restart your computer).
  - If you open the **start** menu by mistake, you can close it again by clicking anywhere on the desktop or by pressing Esc.

 This book does not describe all the menus and options that the **start** menu provides. It concentrates on essential features such as the Windows XP Help (Section 1.1), certain **Applications** (Part 2), the **My Documents** window (Part 3) and **Modifying the environment** (Part 4).

Windows supplies an online help application that provides information on all the features it offers. Windows presents this information under different topics. It groups these topics under different themes and it groups these themes under different categories. Do not hesitate to use this help facility should you need to.

SEARCHING FOR HELP INFORMATION USING KEYWORDS OR THE INDEX

▨ **start - Help and Support** or ⬚F1⬚

▨ To look for help using keywords, click in the **Search** box in the top left of the screen, enter the keywords that you want to use for your search then click the

⬚ button or press the ⬚ key.

The **Stop** button stops the current search.
If you do not stop the search, Windows displays the results after a few seconds.

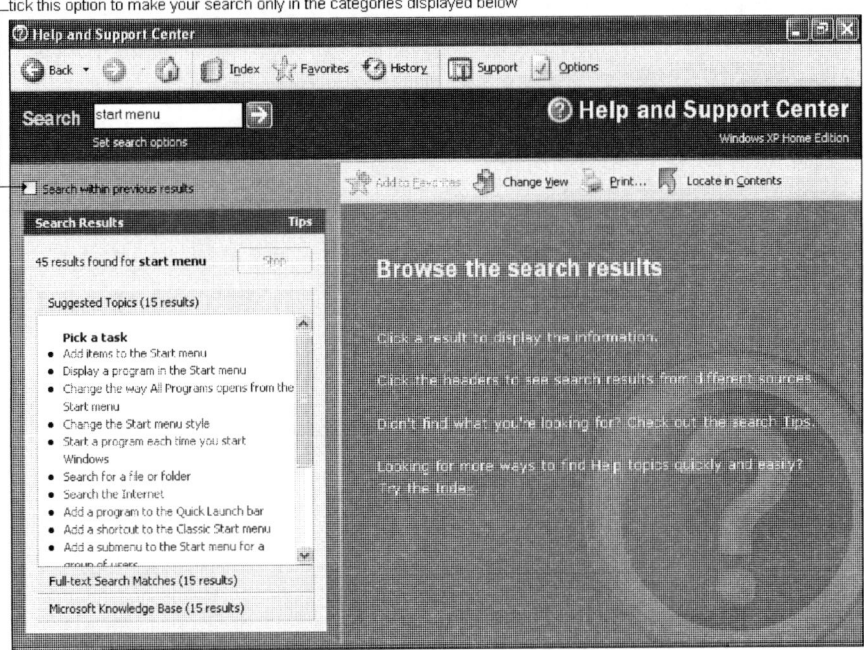

The **Search Results** appear in the left-hand frame of the window. Three sets of results appear, found according to three different search methods:

Suggested Topics list the results that are likely to be the most relevant: to produce this list, Windows compares the words you entered with the keywords associated with its help documents.

Full-text Search Matches list documents that contain the text you entered, but not necessarily as their keywords. Full-text matches are listed only when there are no keyword-based (**Suggested Topics**) results.

If your computer has an Internet connection, Windows searches the **Microsoft Knowledge Base** and lists the results under this heading. This knowledge base contains technical support information and other tools aimed at Microsoft products.

▓ If necessary, click the button corresponding to the type of results you want to browse then click the link to the help item you require.

▓ To search the help index, click the **Index** ⬚ tool button.

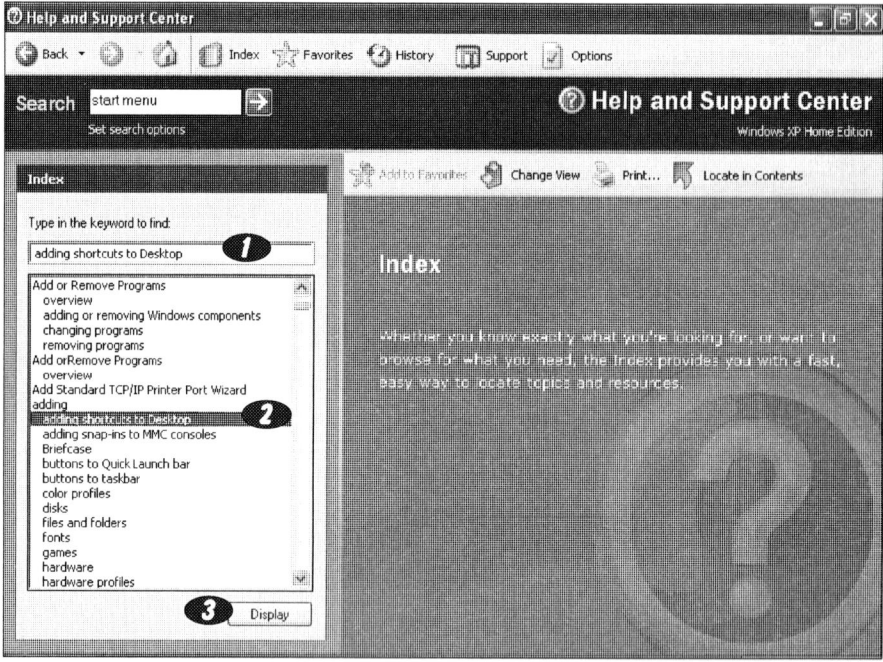

1. To go quickly to the index entries for the help items you want to view, type the first few characters of **the keyword to find**, as Windows suggests.

2. In the **Index** list, select the help topic you want to view.

3. Click the **Display** button (or double-click the help topic concerned).

For some topics, instead of showing the corresponding help information immediately, Windows displays the **Topics Found** dialog box. In this case, double-click the title whose help information you want to view.

▓ Click the ☒ button to close the **Help and Support Center** window, when you have found the help you need.

You can also get help using the hyperlinks the **Help and Support Center** window provides.

Click the **Print** 🖨 button to print the selected help topic.

Click the **Add to Favorites** ✦ button to add the selected topic to your list of favorites. Click the **Favorites** ✦ button to view this list and access your favorites rapidly.

Windows XP opens a session for each user who logs on. When the user logs off, he/she closes his/her session along with all the files and applications that he/she opened. It is recommended to close all open sessions before switching the computer off.

CLOSING A WINDOWS XP SESSION (LOGGING OFF)

▓ If necessary, save any modifications you have made to any open files.

▓ Click the **start** button followed by the **Log Off** 🔑 button.

▓ In the **Log Off Windows** dialog box that appears, click the **Log Off** button.

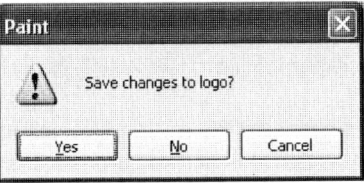

If you have left a file open without saving modifications you have made to it, this type of message appears.

▓ If you see this type of message and you want to save your changes, click the **Yes** button. Otherwise, click the **No** button.

Windows saves your settings then displays the Welcome screen (or the **Log On to Windows** dialog box) to allow you to log on again.

*To switch on your computer, you need only press its **Power** button. If you want to switch off your computer, you must inform Windows of your intention before you press this button. Windows can then warn you if your intended action could cause problems, such as the loss of the data on which you are working.*

SWITCHING OFF YOUR COMPUTER

- Close all current sessions (cf. Closing a Windows XP session (logging off)).

- Click the **Start** button followed by the **Turn Off Computer** button.
  The **Turn off computer** dialog box appears.

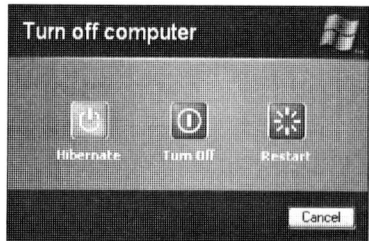

The **Cancel** button of this dialog box cancels this action.

The **Restart** button () shuts down Windows and re-opens it immediately afterwards, while the **Hibernate** button () shuts down Windows after saving your desktop environment onto your hard disk (for example, it saves to your hard disk, the layout of the windows on the screen and the state of any open applications so that it can open them in the same state the next time you restart your computer).

- Click the **Turn Off** button () to close Windows so that you can switch off your computer.

- According to the type of computer, your computer will switch itself off automatically or Windows will advise you that it is safe for you to switch off your computer. In the latter case, press the **Power** button on the main unit of your computer (you may need to keep this button pressed in for several seconds before the computer switches off).

 If any other users are still logged on when you attempt to shut down Windows, this message will appear:

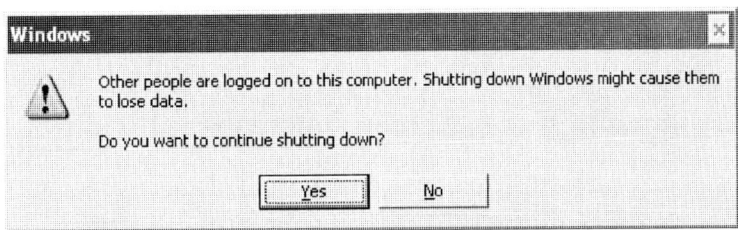

If you click **Yes** you might lose data, if you click **No** you will cancel your action.

Managing windows

Once you have started your computer, you will not be content just to sit and admire your desktop! To start using your computer and set up your documents, you must open an application (or program). For example, if you want to write a letter, you may want to use a word processor such as Word, or if you want to make calculations, you may want to use a spreadsheet application such as Excel. To access an application you must be able to see it on the screen: you can then "start" or "run" the application.

STARTING AN APPLICATION FROM THE START MENU

▓ Click the **start** button to open the main menu of Windows XP.

▓ If necessary, point to the **All Programs** option.

▓ If necessary, move the mouse pointer, to open the appropriate menu or submenu.

▓ Click the name of the application you want to run.

The application window opens and the application's button appears on the taskbar:

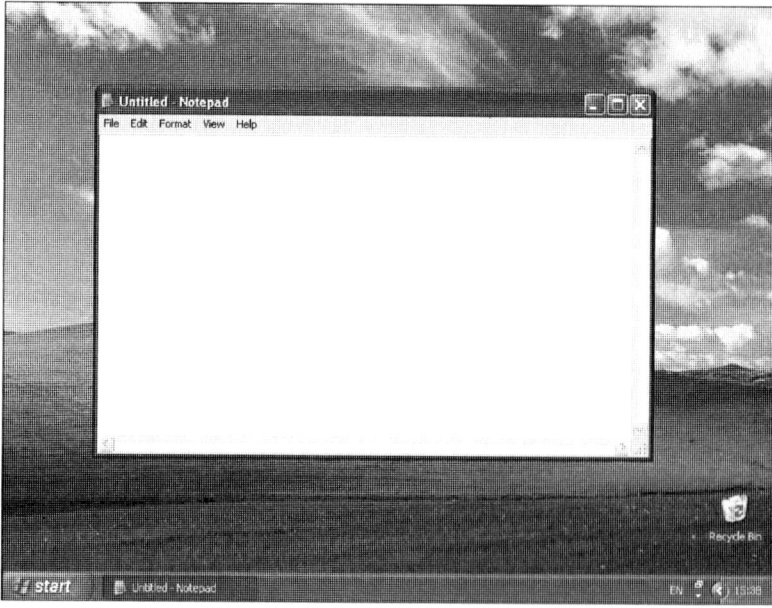

For example, to start the **Notepad** application, click the **start** button,
point to the **All Programs** option then to the **Accessories** menu
and click the **Notepad** option.

The **Notepad** application is installed automatically when you install Windows: it allows you to write text with very simple formatting.

Programs that you have used recently may appear directly in the **start** menu. To run one of these programs, just open the **start** menu and click the name of the application.

Every application appears in its own window. The window is the basic element of the Windows system (hence its name). All windows have a number of common items, with which you must be familiar.

GENERAL WINDOW ITEMS

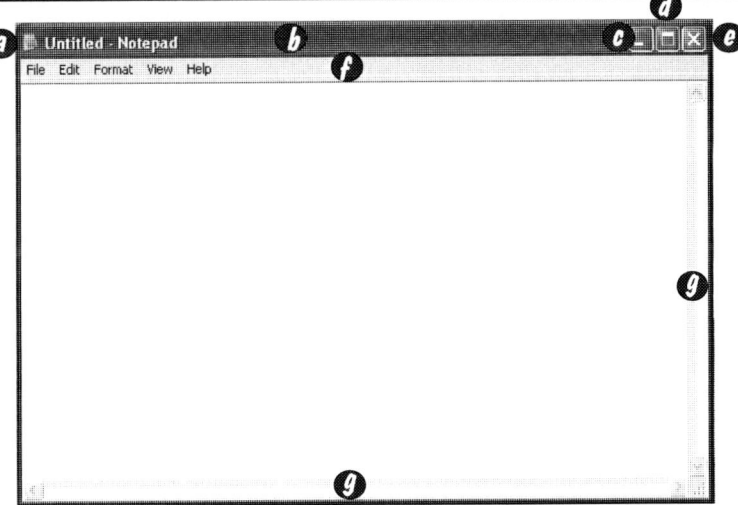

The scroll bars (g) appear greyed-out because the window is empty.

Every window has the following items:

- **Control** menu (a): allows you to manage the window (by moving it or changing its size); in practice, this menu is hardly ever used, as you can carry out the actions it offers in more direct ways.
- **Title bar** (b): displays the name of the active document (in the above example, this "title" is **Untitled**, as this new document has not yet been saved to disk), followed by the name of the application (Notepad in this example).
- **Minimize** (c) and **Maximize** (d) buttons: these collapse the window into its scroll bar button and enlarge the window to the full screen size, respectively.
- **Close** button (e): closes the window and the application.
- **Menu bar** (f): contains the different menus of the application; these menus are closed in this example.
- **Scroll bars** and **scroll cursors** (g): allow you to scroll through the contents of the window (the **scroll cursors** or **scroll boxes** do not appear in this example because the window is empty).

 When you open a document, such as a letter you have already prepared, it appears in a document window within the application window.

When you start a program, the application window may fill the screen (in this case it is said to be in "full-screen" mode). When an application window does not fill the screen, you can see the desktop in the background. If a window is in your way, you can resize it to make it smaller or move it to a more convenient position.

MOVING AND RESIZING A WINDOW

To move a window, point to its title bar (b) then hold down the mouse button, drag to the required position and release the mouse button.

To minimize the window (into its taskbar button) leaving the application active, click the ▬ button (c).

Here, the **Notepad** application window has been minimized.

To restore one of your active windows, click its button on the taskbar.

▓ To enlarge the window so that it fills the screen, click the **Maximize** button (▢) on the window's title bar.

The window now covers the whole screen: only the taskbar remains visible (and you can hide this if you wish). The ▢ button is replaced by the Restore Down button (▢).

▓ To restore the window to its previous size, click the ▢ button.

▓ To change the height or width of a window that is not in full-screen mode, point to one of the edges of the window: to change the height <u>and</u> the width of the window, point to one of the corners of the window.

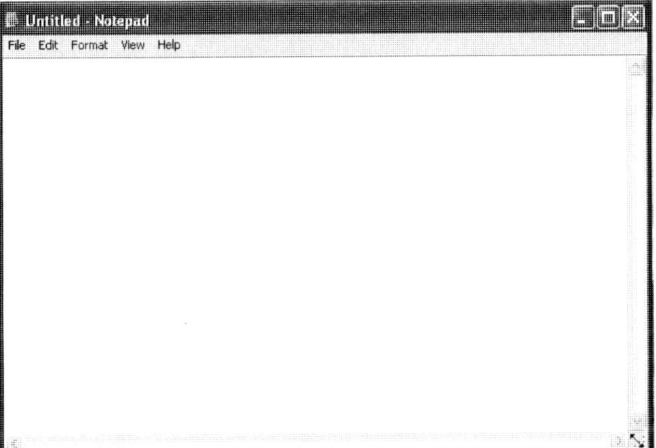

The mouse pointer appears as a dou-ble-headed arrow.

Hold down the mouse button and drag the mouse to resize the window as required, then release the mouse button.

Managing windows

As you can run several applications at once, you can have several open windows that overlap each other. From time to time, you may need to "tidy your desktop".

MANAGING SEVERAL WINDOWS

When several windows overlap, you can recognise the active window by the colour of its title bar. By default, the title bar of the active window is blue (while the title bars of inactive windows are light blue) and the taskbar button of the active application appears pressed-in.

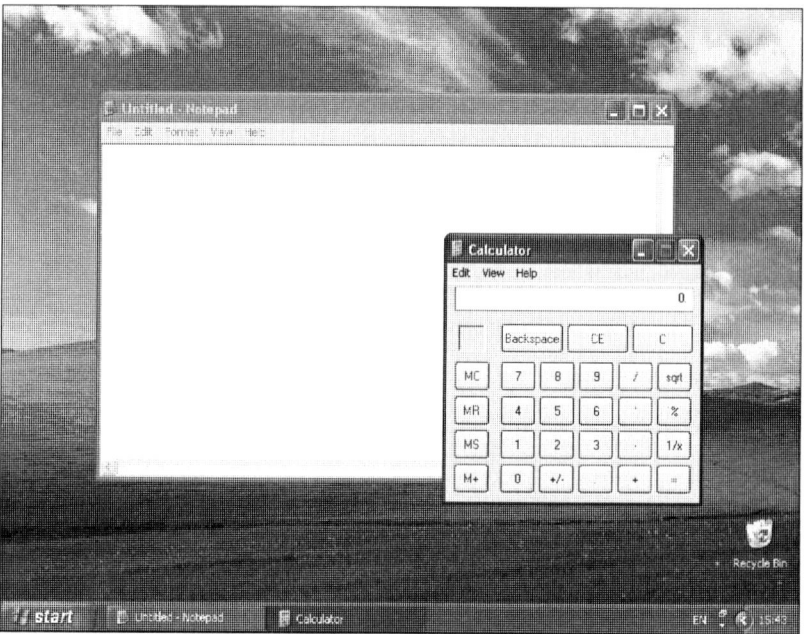

*For example, after you have started **Notepad**, run the **Calculator** application by clicking the **start** button, pointing to the **All Programs** option then to the **Accessories** menu and clicking **Calculator**.*

To access a window and activate the corresponding application, click in the window if it is visible, or click its button on the taskbar, or hold down the ⌊Alt⌋ key and press the ⌊↹⌋ key once or more until you select the icon corresponding to the window concerned.

The active window appears in the foreground.

To modify the window layout, right-click an empty space on the taskbar to view the menu that is associated with it.

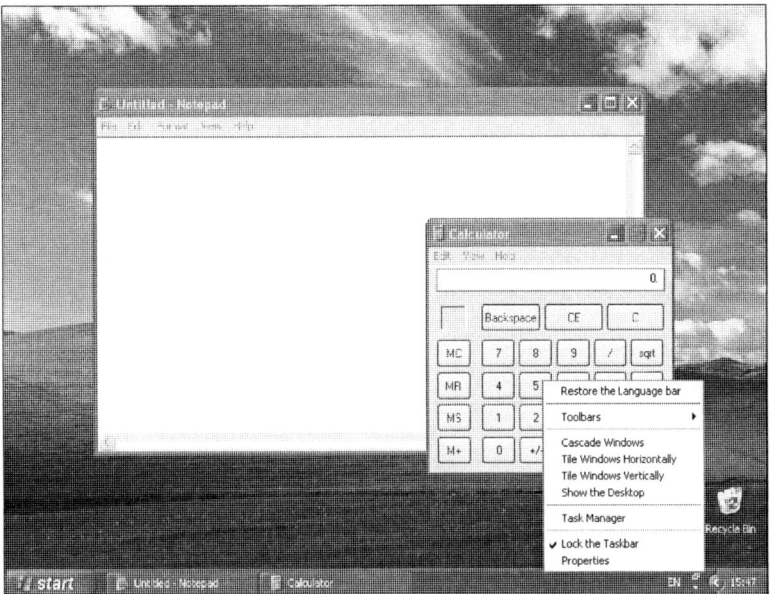

The menu associated with the taskbar is called the taskbar's shortcut menu.

Choose one of the following options:

Cascade Windows   to arrange the windows so that they overlap each other.

Tile Windows Horizontally   to arrange the windows so that they appear one underneath the other.

Tile Windows Vertically   to arrange the windows so that they appear side by side.

To minimize all the windows into their taskbar buttons, right-click an empty space on the taskbar and click the **Show the Desktop** option.

To restore all the windows you minimized when you chose the **Show the Desktop** option, display the taskbar shortcut menu and click the **Show Open Windows** option.

This action will restore your previous window layout.

Managing windows

You have started your application and perhaps maximized the application window to have as much space as possible: you are now ready to start working. According to the application you are using, you may start entering text or making calculations or doing a drawing. Whatever the application you are using, sooner or later you will need to use the menus that appear under the window's title bar. When you start the application, these menus are closed. To use one of these menus, you must start by opening it.

MANAGING AN APPLICATION'S MENUS AND OPTIONS

To open a menu, click its name on the menu bar.

The menu's options appear.

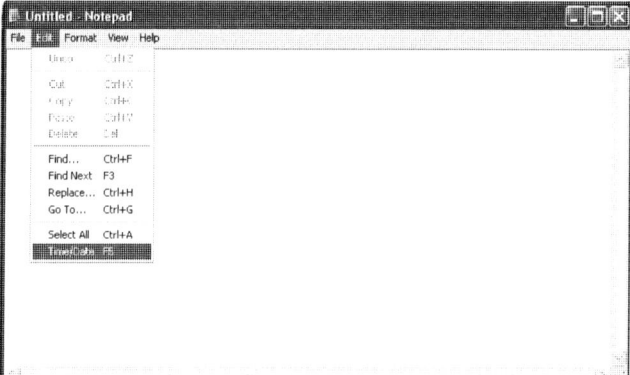

*For example, to open Notepad's **Edit** menu, click **Edit**.*

You cannot use the greyed-out options, as they are unavailable at the present time.

An ellipsis (...) to the right of an option indicates that you will see a dialog box when you choose the option.

A key or key combination to the right of an option indicates a shortcut key. It shows how you can activate the option quickly, by using the keyboard instead of selecting the option in the menu.

- To open an adjacent menu, point to its name.
- To activate a menu option, slide the mouse up or down (without clicking) until you are pointing to the option, then click.
- To close a menu without activating one of its options, click elsewhere in the window.

Discovering the XP environment

▓ To access the menu bar from the keyboard, press the ⬚Alt key or the ⬚F10 key.

This action selects the first menu on the menu bar, without opening it. One letter in each menu name appears underlined.

▓ To select an adjacent menu, press the ⬚→ key or the ⬚← key. To open a menu that you have selected, press the ⬚↵ key or the ⬚↓ key.

▓ To open a menu directly, hold down the ⬚Alt key and press the underlined (mnemonic) letter for the menu concerned.

For example, in Notepad, the ⬚Alt E key combination opens the Edit menu.

▓ To activate a menu option, use the ⬚→, ⬚←, ⬚↑ and/or ⬚↓ keys to select the option then press the ⬚↵ key. Alternatively you can simply press the underlined letter for the option concerned (after having opened the menu concerned using one of the techniques described above).

For example, in Notepad, use the ⬚Alt E key combination to open the Edit menu then press D to activate the Time/Date option.

 **Here are a few commonly-used terms and expressions: a menu is made up of options. To run (or use) a command means to open the appropriate menu and activate the option concerned: for example, to run the File - Page Setup command means to open the File menu and click the Page Setup option.**

 A shortcut key (key combination) shown to the right of some menu options allows you to run the option concerned without opening the menu. For example, in **Notepad**, the ⬚F5 function key allows you to insert the time and date into your document without having to open the **Edit** menu and click the **Time/Date** option.

Managing windows

*With some menu options a small new window may appear on your screen. With these menu options, an ellipsis (...) appears to the right of the option name indicating that the application needs further information before it can complete the action you require. For example, with the **File - Page Setup** command, you must indicate the paper format and orientation with which you want to print. These small windows are called dialog boxes. When a dialog box opens you must close it before you can return to your document and continue working on it.*

FILLING IN DIALOG BOXES

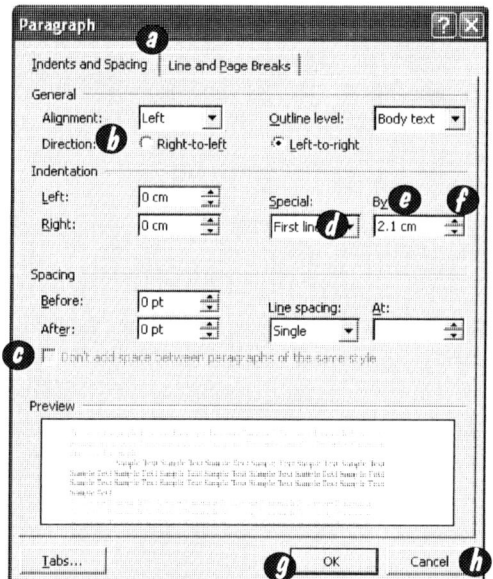

This dialog box offers more features than the **FIle - Page Setup** dialog box in **Notepad**.

▨ A dialog box can contain the following items:

- Tabs (a): provide access to the different pages in the dialog box.
- Option buttons (b): allow you to choose between different exclusive options; a black dot indicates the active option; only one option can be active at the same time in the same group (such as the **Direction** group in the example).
- Check boxes (c): a tick in the check box indicates that the option is active; to activate or deactivate the option, click the check box.

- List boxes (d): allow you to choose from a list (the example shows a drop-down list box). Click the ▾ button to open the list box and choose a list item; click this button again to close the list box. An ordinary list box sometimes provides a scroll bar and arrows that you can use to scroll through the list contents (as in a window).

- Text boxes (e): allow you to enter information; if the text box accepts numbers it may contain increment buttons (f) which you can click to increase or decrease the displayed value.

- **OK** button (g): closes the dialog box, keeping any changes you have made to the different options.

- **Cancel** button (h): closes the dialog box, cancelling any changes you have made to the different options (clicking this button has the same effect as clicking the ✕ button).

- **Apply** button: sometimes appears in dialog boxes; it allows you to view the effects of your changes without closing the dialog box.

- ? button: allows you to view specific help information on the different items in the dialog box (see below).

▨ If your mouse breaks down, you can change the options in a dialog box using the keyboard: to access the different options you can use the ⇆ and Shift ⇆ keys; alternatively you can hold down the Alt key and press the letter that appears underlined for the option concerned.

▨ To move between the different options in a group or in a list, use the →, ←, ↑ and/or ↓ keys.
To activate or deactivate a check box, press the space bar.

Managing windows

The previous chapter described how you can use the Windows online help feature to find useful help information. You can also view specific help information on the different items on the screen, such as the items in a dialog box, for example.

VIEWING HELP ON DIALOG BOX ITEMS

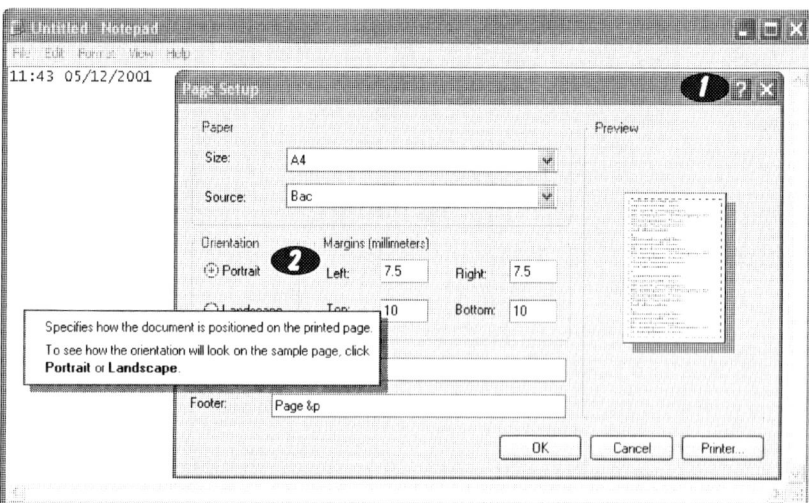

1. Click the  button: a question mark appears next to the mouse pointer.

2. Click the option on which you want help information: the help text appears in a box with a pale yellow background. This box is called a **ScreenTip**.

You can also get help on a dialog box item by right-clicking the item then clicking the **What's This?** option that appears.

When you start an application, it appears in its own window. The easiest way to close an application is to close its window.

LEAVING AN APPLICATION (CLOSING A WINDOW)

▨ To close an application, click the 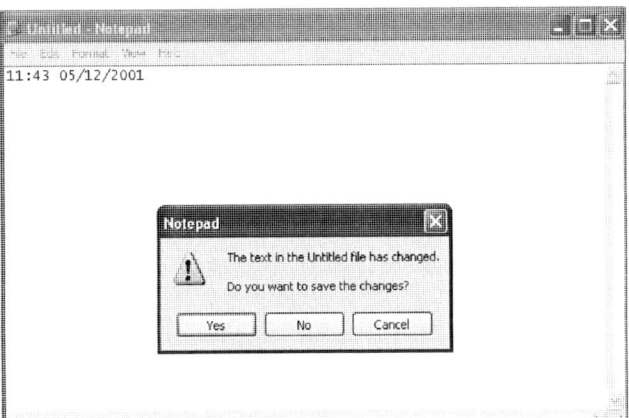 button in the top right-hand corner of the application window or press the `Alt` `F4` keys. Alternatively you can run the **File - Exit** command.

If the application window is minimized (if it appears only as a button on the taskbar) right-click its taskbar button and click the **Close** option.

If you try to close an application, without saving all the changes you have made to your document, Windows asks you if you want to save your changes before closing the window.

▨ Click **Yes** to save your document, click **No** to close the application without saving your changes or click **Cancel** to cancel your action (in this case your document will stay open).

The next chapter explains how to save your documents.

 In general, documents open in document windows (within the application window). To close a document window, click the 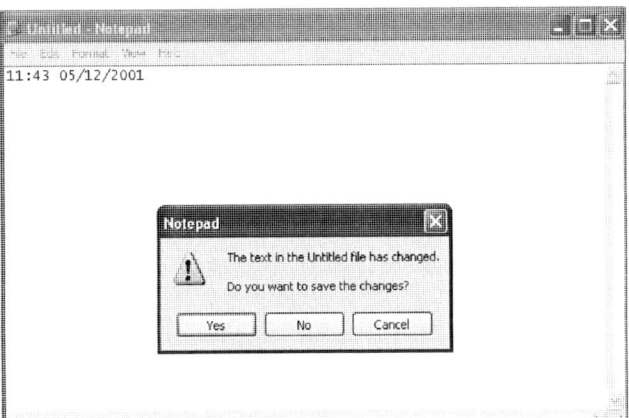 button in the top right-hand corner of the document window or press `Ctrl` `F4` (and not `Alt` `F4`) or run the **File - Close** command (and not the **File - Exit** command).

2nd

Now you are ready to manage your files and to use the applications that were installed with Windows. You may not need to use all of these applications but it is still interesting to know that they exist and what you can do with them.

Part

Applications & multimedia

Managing files

You run an application to work on a document (such as a letter, a table or a drawing etc.): you can either start working on a new file or you can continue working on a file that already exists. When you start a new file, you will use your keyboard to enter data into the file's window. When you enter this data, which may be in the form of text or numerical information, Windows stores it in the central memory of your computer. In other words, your data is in the electronic circuits of your computer and if you switch off the power, your data will disappear. To keep your data, you must save it on the hard disk of your computer. When you do this, you write your data onto the magnetic surface of your disk and they will stay there even if you switch the power off. The computer file refers to the complete set of data that makes up your document. When you save your document for the first time, you must specify the name of this file.

SAVING A NEW FILE

▨ **File - Save** or [💾] or [Ctrl] **S**

Not all applications offer the [💾] tool button or use the [Ctrl] **S** shortcut key.

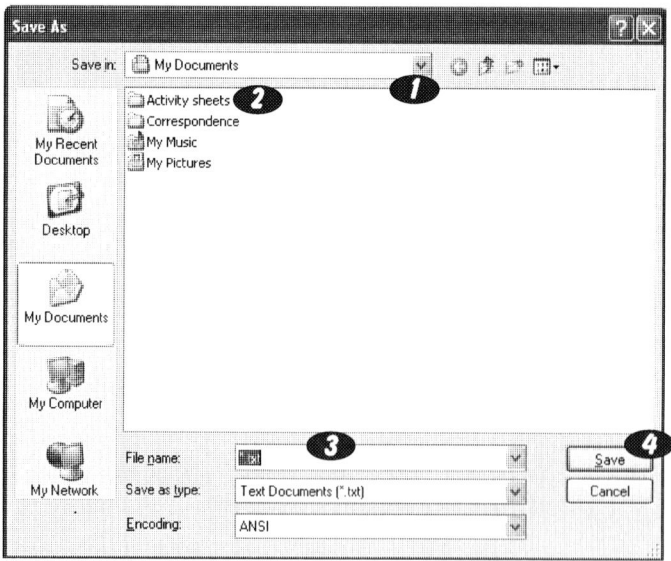

For example: open the Notepad application, enter a few words and run the File - Save command. The Save As dialog box appears. By default, Notepad suggests that you save your file in the My Documents folder.

1. If you do not want to save your file in the folder that the **Save in** list proposes by default, open this list then select where you want to save your file: either to a drive (for example, the **C:** icon, which represents your hard disk) or to a folder, such as the personal folder of another user of your computer (for example, **Elizabeth's Documents**) or the **Shared Documents** folder (which all users of the computer can access).

2. If necessary, access the folder or subfolder in which you want to save your file by double-clicking the folder icon: the name of this folder now appears in the **Save in** box.

3. Click in this box then enter the name you want to give to your file (your name can be up to 255 characters long, including spaces; however, you cannot insert the following characters: \ / ? : * " < > or |.

4. Save your file.

The file name appears in the title bar, possibly with the file name extension.

 The **File - Save As** command saves the active file under another name.

Managing files

As you work, you will change and add data to your file. You make these changes in central memory (in the electronic circuits of your computer). You update the computer file on your hard disk each time you save your file. When you open your file, it is always in the state it was when it was last saved. This means that if a power cut occurs, you will lose any changes you made since your file was last saved.

SAVING AN EXISTING FILE

File - Save or 🖫 or ⎣Ctrl⎦ **S**

Windows saves the file directly, without asking for confirmation.

A file name extension contains three characters. It indicates the file's format type. For example, text files often have a **txt** name extension, Excel workbooks have an **xls** name extension and Word documents have a **doc** name extension.

If you try to leave an application or ask Windows to turn off the computer without saving your latest changes to open files, Windows will offer to save your changes for you.

When you want to continue working on a file, on which you were working the day before, you must open it to view it on your screen.

OPENING A FILE

File - Open or 📂 or ⎣Ctrl⎦ **O**

Not all applications offer the 📂 tool button or use the ⎣Ctrl⎦ **O** shortcut key.

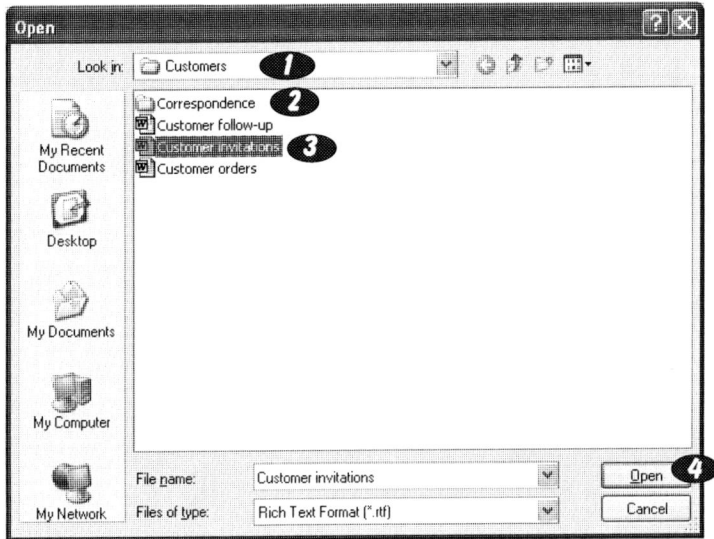

1. If the file you want to open is not in the folder that the **Look in** list proposes by default, open this list then select the location of your file: either a drive (for example, the **C:** icon, which represents your hard disk) or a folder, such as the personal folder of another user of your computer (for example, **Elizabeth's Documents**) or the **Shared Documents** folder (which all users of the computer can access).

2. If necessary, access the folder or subfolder that contains your file by double-clicking the (yellow) folder icon: the name of this folder then appears in the **Look in** box.

3. Select the file you want to open by clicking its icon or its name.

4. To open your file, click this button or double click the file name.

Managing files

Some applications do not allow you to open two files at the same time. In this case Windows will replace the file that is in the application window by the new file that you open. If you did not save your latest changes to the previous file, Windows asks you if you want to do so before replacing it with the new file.

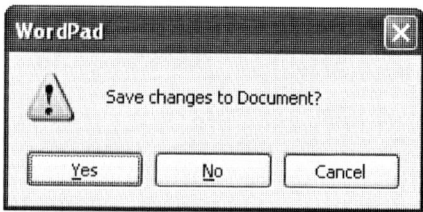

■ Click **Yes** to save the changes you made to the active file and to open the new file, click **No** not to save the changes you made to the active file and to open the new file, or click **Cancel** not to save the changes you made to the active file and not to open the new file.

 To close a document, close the window that contains it (cf. Section 1.2).

 With some applications, the four last files you used appear at the bottom of the **File** menu. To open one of these files, open this menu and click the name of the file you want to open.

Applications & multimedia

When you start an application, it provides an empty document in which you can start entering your data (text, or numerical information, for example). On the other hand, if you are working on an existing document and you want to start a new document, you must create a new file.

CREATING A NEW FILE

▨ **File - New** or  or `Ctrl` **N**

Not all applications offer the ⬜ tool button or support the `Ctrl` **N** shortcut key.

An empty document appears in the application window (with the **Notepad** application, for example, this new document is called **Untitled** by default).

Some applications (such as **Word** and **Excel** for example) allow you to open several files at the same time (each file appears in its own document window). If the application cannot manage several files at once, it replaces the current file by the new file. In this case, if you have made any unsaved changes to the file you want to close, Windows asks you if you want to save your changes.

Windows Movie Maker

Windows Movie Maker is a multimedia application that organises sound and/or video data into movies. You can view these movies from the hard disk of your computer or from the Internet, if they are stored on a Web server.

*First, you must arrange **clips** and **still pictures** into **collections**. Next you organise these sound and/or video items into a **project**. When you have set up and tested your project, you can record it as a **movie**.*

WINDOWS MOVIE MAKER WINDOW

▨ To start the **Windows Movie Maker** application, click the **start** button on the taskbar, point to the **All Programs** option followed by the **Accessories** option then click the **Windows Movie Maker** option.

The **Windows Movie Maker** window opens:

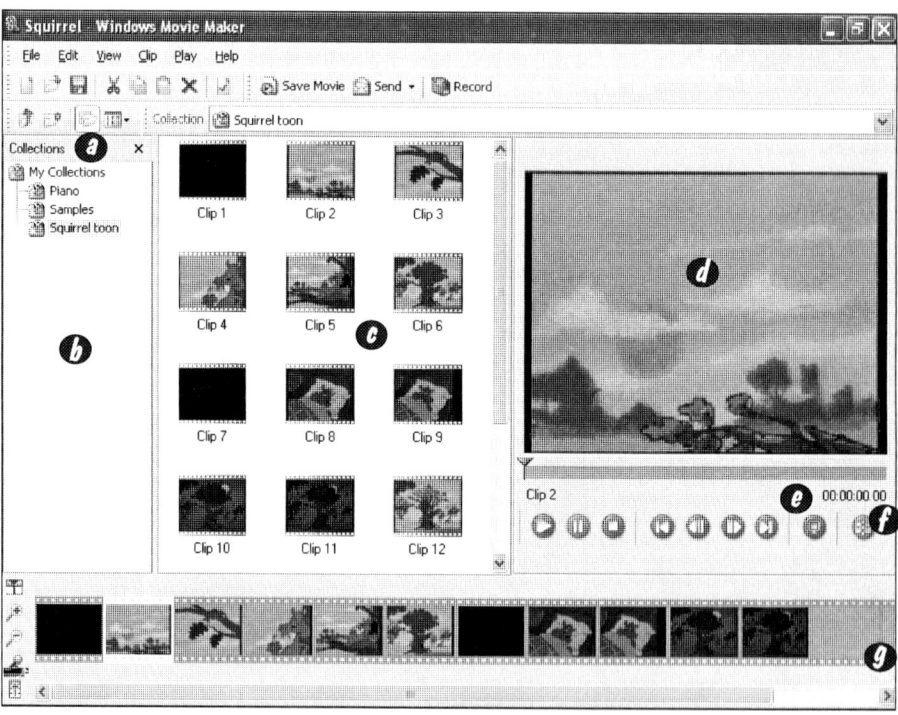

*In this example, the **Squirrel** project is open: it contains 11 video clips.*

Applications & multimedia

░ This window contains the elements you will find in all Windows applications: the **Minimize, Maximize** or **Restore**, and **Close** buttons, a title bar, a menu bar and (by default) four toolbars. In addition, it contains:

- The **collections area** (a), where you can arrange the sound, video or still picture files that you create or import. A list of your collections appears in the pane on the left (b) and the clips belonging to the current collection are listed in the pane on the right (c). To display or hide the pane on the left, click the [ ] button on the **Collections** toolbar or use the **View - Collections** command.

- The **monitor** (d), where you can view a particular clip or an entire project. It contains a **seek bar** (e) which changes position when you play a sound or video file or view a still picture. There is also a set of buttons (f) for moving around in the clip or project (**Play, Pause, Stop, Full Screen** etc.).

- The **workspace** (g), where you create and edit your projects before saving them as a movie. By clicking the appropriate option in the **View** menu, you can display this area in **Storyboard** view or in **Timeline** view. When the **Timeline** is active, two bars appear in the workspace: the first is where the video clips and fixed pictures are displayed and the second (the **audio bar**) is for sound clips. **Timeline** view also includes [ ] and [ ] buttons for viewing the clips in the project at different magnifications.

Before you set up your movie, you must save sound and/or video material in Windows Movie Maker, by converting it to Windows Media digital format. Once this is done, the source material appears as clips which can be included in one or more in several projects. You can record source material with a capture device such as a digital (or analogue) video camera, a Web cam or a microphone.

RECORDING SOURCE MATERIAL

Recording sound or video material

░ **File - Record** or [Record] or [Ctrl] **R**

Windows Movie Maker

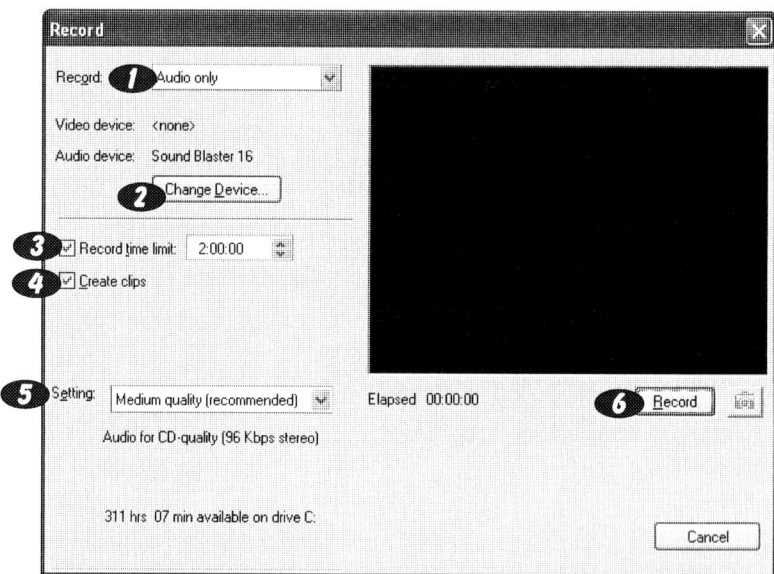

1. Open the **Record** list and click the option corresponding to the type of material you want to record.

2. You can use the **Change Device** button to select another capture device, if you have other devices installed on your computer.

3. If you want to record for a set time then stop automatically, make sure that the **Record time limit** check box is ticked then either type the time into the text box to the right of the option or use the increment buttons.

4. Tick the **Create clips** check box if you want Movie Maker to split up the sequence into clips, for ease of handling.

5. Open the **Setting** list and choose the quality you want to use for your recording. It is recommended that you choose the highest quality setting your device supports, since the quality of the final movie will depend on the quality of your source material. However, bear in mind that the higher the quality level you choose, the bigger your files will be.

6. Use the commands on your video recorder or your analogue video camera to locate the source material you want to record then click the **Record** button.

Applications & multimedia

The word **Recording** flashes to let you know that recording is in progress.

⬚ Use the controls of your video recorder or analogue video camera to play the source material you want to record: you can see the video materiel on the preview screen.

⬚ If you chose to record for a set time, recording will stop automatically once the time limit has been reached; to interrupt the recording manually click the **Stop** button.

The **Save Windows Media File** window opens unless you activated the **Auto generate file** option in the **Options** dialog box (using the **View - Options** command) and the **Record time limit** option in the **Record** dialog box. In this case, at the end of the time limit, Windows will automatically save the new file at the location you specified in the **Options** dialog box under a generic name: for example, Tape 1.wmv, Tape 2.wmv for video recordings and Tape 1.wma, Tape 2.wma for sound (audio) recordings.

⬚ In the **Save Windows Media File** window, select the drive or folder where you want to store the new file then specify its name in the **File name** box.

⬚ Click the **Save** button.

A new collection containing the material you have recorded appears in the collection area's left pane. The clips created from this material appear in the right pane.

⬚ Use the controls of your video recorder or your analogue video camera to stop the cassette.

Recording material with a digital video device connected to an IEEE 1394 (FireWire) card

This feature will be available only if your computer has a processor speed of at least 600 MHz and is equipped with an IEEE 1394 card.

⬚ Check that your video camera or your digital video recorder is properly connected, with the recorded video installed then set your device to read mode.

Important note: some cameras go into stand-by mode automatically when you insert a cassette and you can no longer record. In this case, restart your video camera then set it to read mode.

⬚ **File - Record** or ▣ Record or Ctrl **R**

Movie Maker may display the **Record** dialog box as soon as you connect your video device: in this case you do not need to select the **File - Record** command.

⬚ Use the controls on your digital video device to position the tape just before the place where you want to start recording.

Windows Movie Maker

- In the **Digital video camera controls** frame, click the 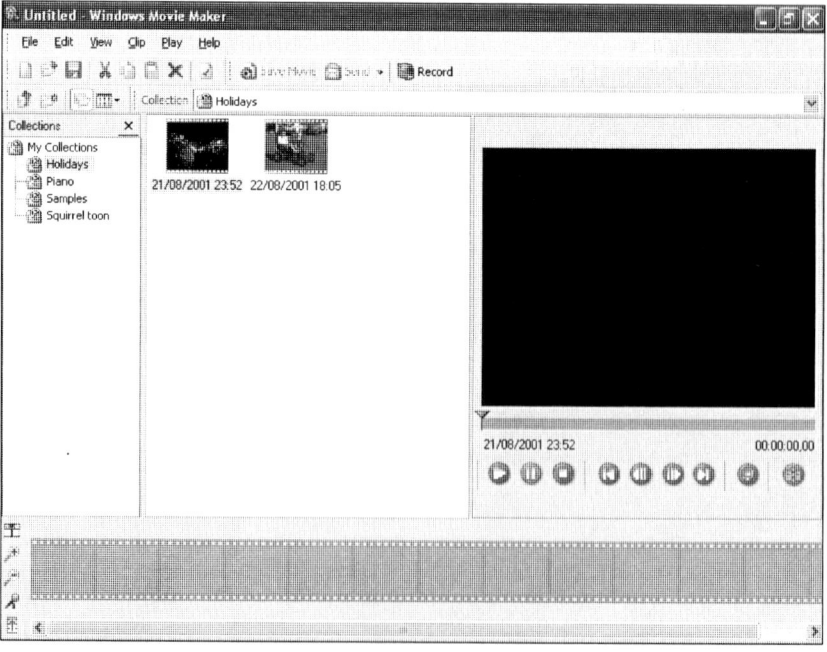 button.

  You can use the **Digital video camera controls** instead of those on your digital video device: having a single screen, with all the commands of Movie Maker and of your digital video device, is a very handy feature.

- Click the **Record** button to start recording the contents of the cassette from your digital video device.

  The word **Recording** flashes in the dialog box to let you know that recording is in progress and the **Record** button changes into a **Stop** button.

- Click the **Stop** button when you want to stop recording.

- In the **Save Windows Media File** window, select the drive or folder where you want to store the new file then specify its name in the **Filename** box.

  Windows will save the file in .wmv format.

- Click the **Save** button.

  The video appears as a sequence of clips if you activated the **Create clips** option in the **Record** dialog box.

- To view the clips, use the buttons under the preview frame in the right-hand pane.

As you filmed a video of your holidays last summer in Bognor, you can add a commentary by recording a suitable narration.

RECORDING A NARRATION

▓ Activate the **Timeline** view of the workspace, if you need to, by using the **View - Timeline** command or by clicking the ▣ button in the workspace.

▓ Use **File - Open Project** or ⌨ Ctrl **O** to open the project for which you want to add a narration.

▓ Run the **File - Record Narration** command or click the ▣ button in the workspace.

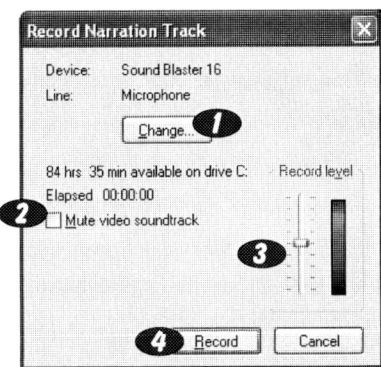

1. If the capture **Device** or the **Line** that appears at the top of the dialog box is not the right one, click the **Change** button, choose the correct settings then click **OK** to confirm your settings.

If you want to use a microphone, choose the **Mic Volume** option from the **Input line** list in the **Configure Audio** dialog box.

2. If your project contains a video clip that includes sound and you do not want to hear this soundtrack, activate the **Mute video sound-track** option in the **Record Narration Track** dialog box.

3. Use the slider in the **Record level** frame to increase or decrease the volume of your narration.

4. When you are ready to record the narration, click the **Record** button.

As you record your narration, the project runs in the monitor (preview frame).

▓ When you have finished, click the **Stop** button.

The **Save Narration Track Sound File** dialog box appears on the screen.

▓ In the **Save in** list, select the drive and the folder where you want to store the sound file then specify its name in the **File name** box.

▓ Click the **Save** button.

The narration is saved as a .wav sound file. It is automatically inserted as a sound clip at the beginning of the project's audio bar. You can see this bar in the workspace and in the current collection.

▓ If you need to, you can move the sound clip. For this purpose, click the name of the clip in the audio bar in the workspace (a) then drag it to the required position: for example, you could move it underneath the video clips and/or still pictures to which the commentary refers.

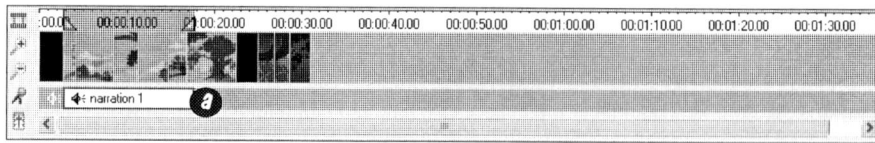

You can import sound files (.mp3, .asf, .wma etc.), video files (.wmv, .asf, .avi, .mpg etc.) or still pictures (.jpg, .gif etc.) into Windows Movie Maker. As with a source video sequence that you have just recorded, an imported file appears as a series of clips, which you can include in one or more projects.

IMPORTING A FILE

▓ Click the collection into which you want to import the file.

▓ **File - Import** or Ctrl I

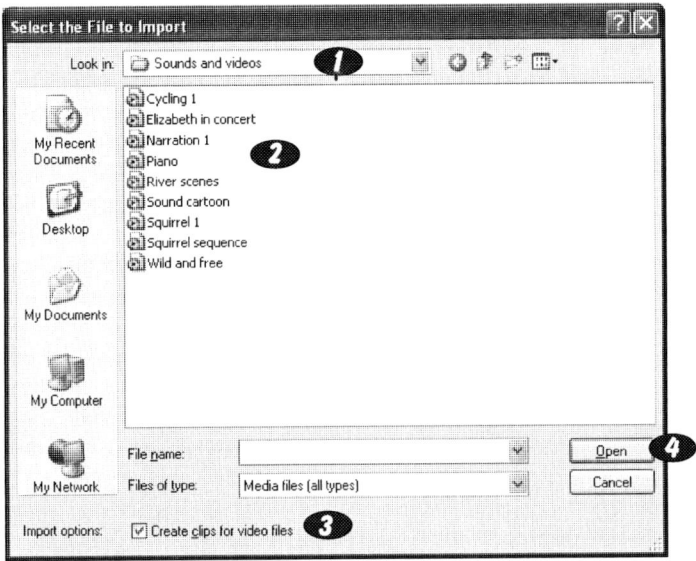

1. Select the drive and the folder where the file is located.

2. Select the file you want to import: to import several files, $\boxed{\text{Shift}}$-click to select them if they appear consecutively in the list or $\boxed{\text{Ctrl}}$-click to select them if they do not appear consecutively.

3. Activate the **Create clips for video files** option if you want Movie Maker to generate a clip for each frame, or deactivate this option if you want Movie Maker to generate a single clip for the whole file.

4. Click the **Open** button.

If you import a sound file or a still image file, the new clips are inserted into the current collection. If you import a video file, Windows Movie Maker puts the clips in a new collection, located in the **My Collections** folder. By default, this collection takes the name of the original imported file.

The source files used in Windows Movie Maker remain in their original locations. The clips in the collections area do not physically exist there, but appear by means of a formula that creates a link to the source file. If you try to work with clips whose source file has been deleted, moved or renamed, Windows Movie Maker prompts you to search for it. Click the **Yes** button only if the source file has been moved: the **Find** dialog box cannot be used to retrieve a deleted file or to identify one that has been renamed.

Windows Movie Maker

*By default, you save your sound and video clips in the **My Collections** folder. However, you can create other folders, to make it easier to manage your clips.*

CREATING A COLLECTION

▦ In the left pane of the collections area, click the name of the collection in which you want to create the new collection.

▦ **File - New - Collection** or [⚙]

▦ Type the name of the new collection and press [↵].

You can move and/or rename individual clips or complete collections and you can list them in different ways.

MANAGING CLIPS/COLLECTIONS

▦ To change the view of your clip lists, select one of the following options from the **View** menu or by clicking the [▦▾] button on the **Collections** toolbar:

Thumbnails displays each clip as a bitmap image with a title.

List displays a list of the names of all the clips.

Details displays a list containing the names and properties of all the clips.

The view you select applies to the clips in all the collections.

▦ To move a collection, select the collection you want to move by clicking its name. When the target collection appears highlighted, drag the collection to its new location and release the mouse button.

▦ To copy or move clips, select the clip(s) you want to copy or move: to select clips that appear consecutively in the list, click the first one, hold down the [Shift] key then click the last one; to select clips which are not listed consecutively, click the first one then hold down [Ctrl] and click each of the others. If you select a clip by mistake, [Ctrl]-click it to remove it from the selection.

You can also select a set of consecutive clips by dragging a rectangle around them with the mouse.

The names of selected clips appear on coloured backgrounds.

Point to one of the selected clips. If you want to make a copy, hold down the Ctrl key as you drag the selected clips into the left pane of the collection area and onto the name of the collection into which you want to insert them. If you are moving the clips, just drag them into the appropriate collection in the left pane of the window.

If you are moving clips, a rectangle appears next to the mouse pointer as you drag. If you are copying, a plus sign appears in the rectangle.

You can also use these methods to move or copy clips in a project.

To rename a collection or a clip, select the collection or the clip concerned by clicking its name.

Click the name of the collection or clip again or use the **Edit - Rename** command or press the F2 key.

Type the new name then press the ⏎ key to validate your entry.

You can rename only the clips that appear in the collections area; you cannot rename the ones displayed in the workspace. If you add a clip to the workspace and then rename it in the collections area, the clip in the workspace will keep the old name.

▒ To delete clips or a collection, go to the collections area, click the name of the collection you want to delete or select all the clips you want to delete.

You can delete several clips at once, but to delete several collections you must delete them one at a time.

Edit - Delete or ☒ or ⌐Del⌐

A message appears to warn you that the deletion of the clips or the collection will be final.

Click the **Yes** button to confirm the deletion.

 You can also use the **Edit - Delete** command or ☒ or ⌐Del⌐ to delete clips from the workspace.

As with any other application, you must save the work you do in Movie Maker. In the case of Movie Maker, you save the project: you must do this before you create your movie.

SAVING A NEW PROJECT

▒ After you have created a new project (using **File - New - Project** or ⌐Ctrl⌐ **N** or ⌐ ⌐) and after you have included in the workspace, video clips, audio clips and/or still pictures from your collections, use the command:

▒ **File - Save Project** or ⌐ ⌐ or ⌐Ctrl⌐ **S**

This command is not available if your workspace is empty.

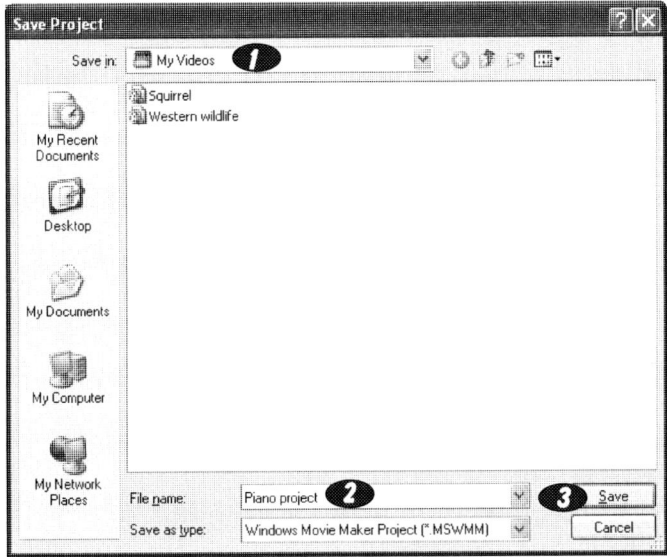

1. Select the drive and the folder where you want to store the project.

2. Enter a name for the project.

3. Click the **Save** button.

Project files have the extension MSWMM. You can use these files only in Windows Movie Maker.

 If you make any changes to this project, you must use the same command to save them.

To continue work on the project you saved yesterday, you must open it first.

OPENING A PROJECT

▪ **File - Open Project** or [icon] or `Ctrl` **O**

▪ In the **Look in** list, select the drive and the folder where the project is located.

By default, Movie Maker will look in the **My Videos** folder.

⬚ Select the project you want to open.

⬚ Click the **Open** button or double-click the project's name.

The project appears in the workspace.

To set up a movie you must add video clips, sound clips and still pictures into a project. In practical terms, you must choose clips from collections and insert them in the workspace.

ADDING A CLIP TO A PROJECT

⬚ If necessary, display the **Timeline** view of the workspace using the **View - Timeline** command or by clicking the 🖽 button in the workspace.

⬚ To make the timeline easier to read, you can zoom in on it using the 🔍 button.

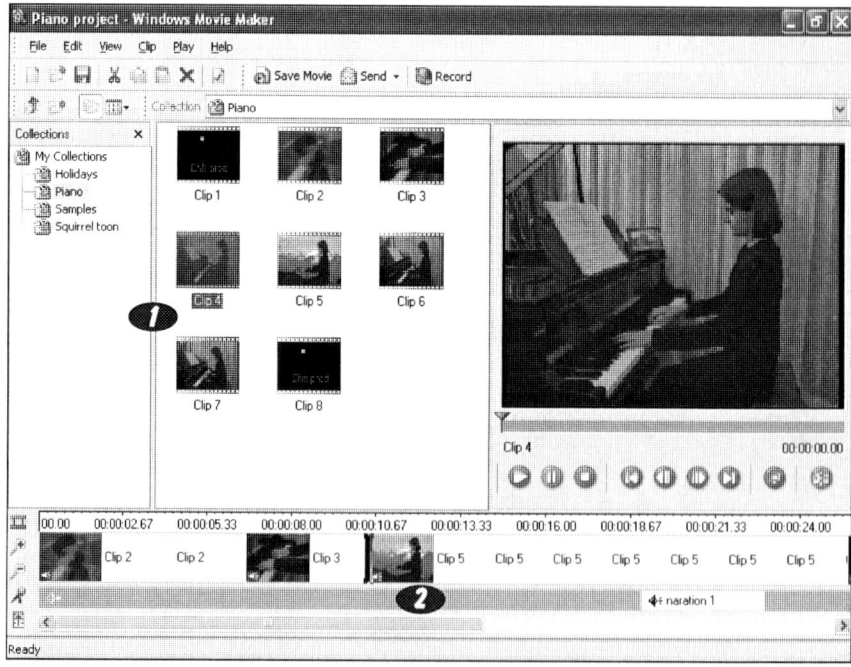

In this example, the vertical bar in the workspace indicates that the selected clip (Clip 4) is being dragged between Clip 3 and Clip 5.

1. Click the name of the collection that contains the clip you want to add to the project then select the clip concerned. To add several clips at once, `Shift`-click to select them if they are listed consecutively, or `Ctrl`-click to select them if they are not.

2. Point to the selected clip(s) and drag it/them into the workspace. Drag video clips or still pictures onto the first bar and drag sound clips onto the second bar (audio bar).
Release the mouse button when the blue vertical bar reaches the position in the project where you want to insert the clips (in front of the first clip, after the last or in between two clips).

Video clips and still pictures are displayed in the first bar in the workspace, whereas sound clips appear on the second bar, known as the audio bar.

If you want to use only part of a clip in your project, you can trim away the rest. You can remove material from the beginning and/or the end of a clip. This operation has no effect on the source material, which remains intact.

TRIMMING A CLIP

▨ If necessary, display the **Timeline** view of the workspace using the **View - Timeline** command or by clicking the ⊞ button in the workspace.

▨ In the workspace, click the clip you want to trim (if necessary, do not hesitate to magnify the **Timeline** using the button to make it easier to read).
The clip appears on the monitor.

▨ To trim away the beginning of the clip, point to the slider on the monitor's seek bar (▨), drag it to the end of the section you want to remove, then use the command **Clip - Set Start Trim Point** (or `Ctrl``Shift``←`): the material from the beginning of the clip up to the position of the cursor is trimmed off.

▨ To trim away the end of the clip, point to the slider on the preview screen's seek bar, drag it to the beginning of the section you want to remove, then use the command **Clip - Set End Trim Point** (or `Ctrl``Shift``→`): the material from the position of the cursor to the end of the clip is trimmed off.
You can trim the beginning of a clip, the end of a clip or both.

Windows Movie Maker

If you change your mind about trimming a clip, you can cancel all the trim points set: select the clip and use **Clip - Clear Trim Points** (or Ctrl Shift Del).

To trim away the beginning of the clip, point to the start trim marker in the workspace (a grey triangle at the left of the clip) and drag it to the end of the section you want to remove. To trim away the end of the clip, point to the end trim marker in the workspace (a grey triangle at the right of the clip) and drag it to the beginning of the section you want to remove.

You may want to split a video or sound clip, to insert another clip within the split sections or to use only part of a particular clip.

SPLITTING A CLIP

- In the workspace or in the collections area, select the clip that you want to split.

  If you are working in the workspace and not in the collections area, it is better to activate the Timeline view.

- Point to the slider on the seek bar and drag it to the position where you want to split the clip.

- Use the **Clip - Split** command or click ▦ under the monitor screen or press Ctrl Shift **S**.

  If you split a clip in the workspace, the clip in the collections area remains intact and vice-versa.

Applications & multimedia

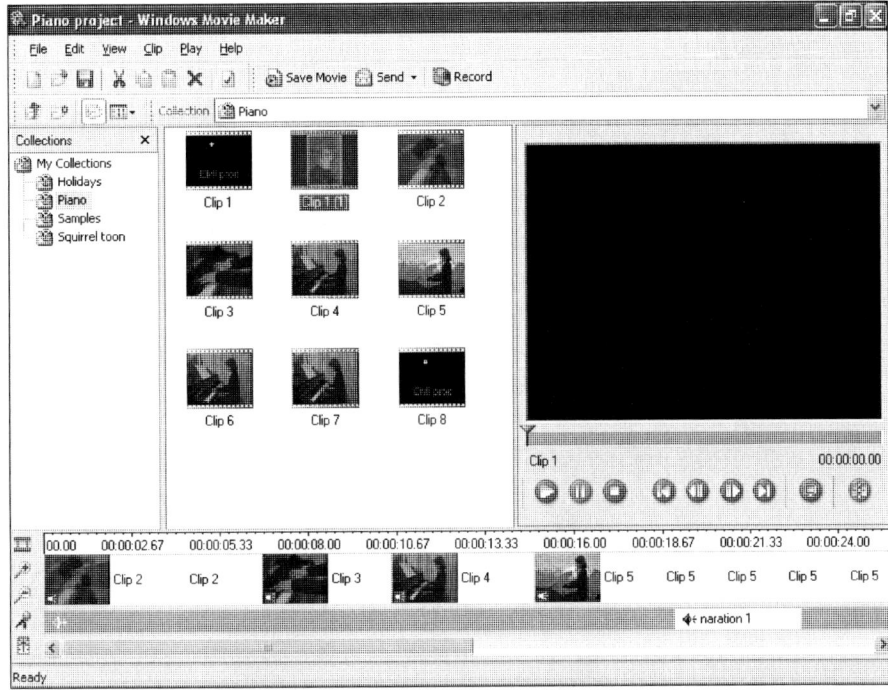

*In this example, **Clip 1** from the **Piano** collection has been split. The first clip keeps its original name, while the second clip uses the same name followed by a number.*

You can also combine two or more clips to create a single clip. Select them in the workspace or the collections area and use the **Clip - Combine** command or ⌨ Ctrl ⌨ Shift **C**. The new clip adopts the name and properties of the first clip in the group you combined.

 To delete the beginning or end of a clip, you can also activate the **Timeline** view in the workspace then drag the trim markers (grey triangles situated at both ends of the clip).

Windows Movie Maker

A transition is an effect that is visible when one clip (video or still picture) replaces another during the video sequence. When a transition is applied between two clips, the frames of the first clip disappear gradually while the frames of the second clip appear.

APPLYING TRANSITIONS

▨ Display the **Timeline** view of the workspace using the **View - Timeline** command or by clicking the ▦ button in the workspace.

▨ In the workspace, select the second of the two clips between which you want to create a transition.

A blue border appears around the clip.

▨ Drag towards the left so that the second clip overlaps the first clip.

▨ Release the mouse button when this icon appears: ◣.

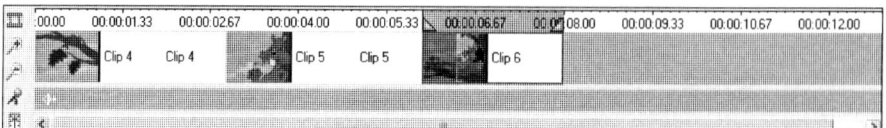

The shaded area in the left part of Clip 6 represents the transition period: the wider the area, the longer the transition.

▨ To change the length of the transition, make sure that the two clips involved are displayed in the workspace and select the second (the overlapping clip on the right). Drag it towards the left to make the transition longer or towards the right to make it shorter.

As you carry out this operation, the following icon appears next to the clip: 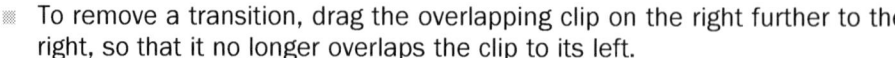.

▨ To remove a transition, drag the overlapping clip on the right further to the right, so that it no longer overlaps the clip to its left.

Applications & multimedia

Once you have inserted clips, applied transitions and made other changes, you will be eager to see the result! You should preview your clip(s) or the entire project before saving your movie.

PREVIEWING A CLIP/PROJECT

▨ Select the collection or open the project containing the clip(s) you want to view.

▨ To preview a clip, or a set of clips, select them in the collections area or, if they have been added to a project, select them in the workspace then use the **Play - Play/Pause** command or ⬭ or the ⌧Space⌧ key.

▨ To preview all the clips in a project, use **Play - Play Entire Storyboard/Timeline**.

▨ To stop the preview, use **Play - Stop** or click the **Stop** button (⬤) below the monitor.

▨ To pause the preview, use **Play - Play/Pause** or click the **Pause** button (⬤) below the monitor.

The simplest way to start the preview again is to click ⬭.

▨ To display the preview full-screen, open the **Play** menu and choose either **Play/Pause** or **Play Entire Storyboard/Timeline** then use the **Play - Full Screen** command or press ⌧Alt⌧⌧↵⌧ or click the ⬤ button underneath the monitor. To close the full screen window and return to the usual preview, press the ⌧↵⌧ key or click in the full screen window.

You can use the ⬤ and ⬤ buttons to display the **Previous Frame** and **Next Frame** of the clip in the monitor and the ⬤ and ⬤ buttons to show the last screen **Back** and the **Next** screen of the project.

Windows Movie Maker

When your project is complete, you can save it as a movie, which you can then view on your computer (using a player such as the Windows Media Player), attach to an e-mail, transfer to a Web server or even copy onto a CD-ROM.

SAVING A MOVIE IN A FILE

▨ Create or open the project you want to save as a movie.

▨ **File - Save Movie** or `Ctrl` **M** or Save Movie

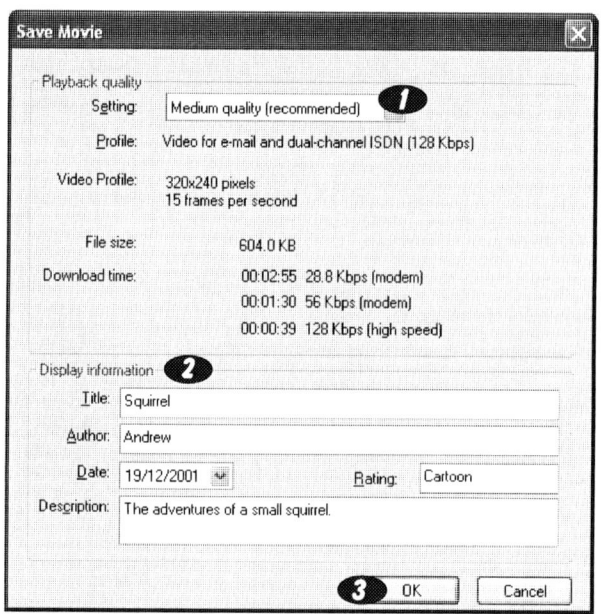

1. Open the **Setting** list then click the quality you want to apply. You must not choose a quality setting greater than that you used when you recorded the source material. You should choose a quality setting that is supported by the computers on which the movie will be viewed.

2. Use the text boxes in the **Display information** frame to fill in the information you want to display when the file plays.

3. Click the **OK** button.

▨ In the **Save in** box, select the drive and the folder in which you want to save your movie. Give a name for the movie in the **File name** box and click the **Save** button.

Applications & multimedia

The dialog box that appears shows you how the creation of the movie is progressing. It provides a button that allows you to cancel the operation, if necessary.

After that, there is a message telling you that the movie has been saved successfully and giving you the opportunity to play it.

▨ Click the **Yes** button to play the movie in Windows Media Player or the **No** button to return to the Windows Movie Maker window.

▨ When you have finished playing the movie, click the  button on the **Windows Media Player** window.

▨ If you chose to save your movie on a CD-ROM, start your CD writer, as you would normally (cf. Copying folders or files to a CD-ROM).

 Movie files have .WMV name extensions.

*When you have recorded your movie, you can view it with **Windows Media Player**, directly from your **Windows Movie Maker** application.*

VIEWING A MOVIE

▨ To view a movie with **Windows Media Player**, use the **File - My Videos** command to display the contents of the **My Videos** folder (movies and projects).

▨ If the movie you want to view is not contained in the **My Videos** folder, use the **Folders** explorer bar to select the folder concerned.

▨ Double-click the video or audio sequence you want to view.

▨ When you have finished viewing, click the  button to close the **Windows Media Player** window.

Windows Movie Maker

In a single operation, you can save a project as a movie and send it to a contact via e-mail (providing you have an e-mail program and an Internet connection).

SENDING A MOVIE BY E-MAIL

▨ Create or open the project that you want to save as a movie and send to one or more of your e-mail contacts.

▨ **File - Send Movie To - E-mail**

▨ Open the **Setting** list and click the quality you want to apply (cf. Saving a movie in a file).

▨ Use the text boxes in the **Display information** frame to fill in the information you want to appear when the file plays then click **OK**.

▨ **Enter a file name** for your movie in the text box provided in the **Name of file to send** dialog box (this file name can contain only letters and numbers) then click the **OK** button.

The movie is saved as a Windows Media file with the .wmv name extension. When you are saving a movie to send by e-mail, the movie file is saved in **C:\Windows\Temp** by default.

▨ From the list, select the e-mail application you are going to use then click **OK**.

The e-mail application's window appears on the screen. The file containing the movie has been inserted as an icon.

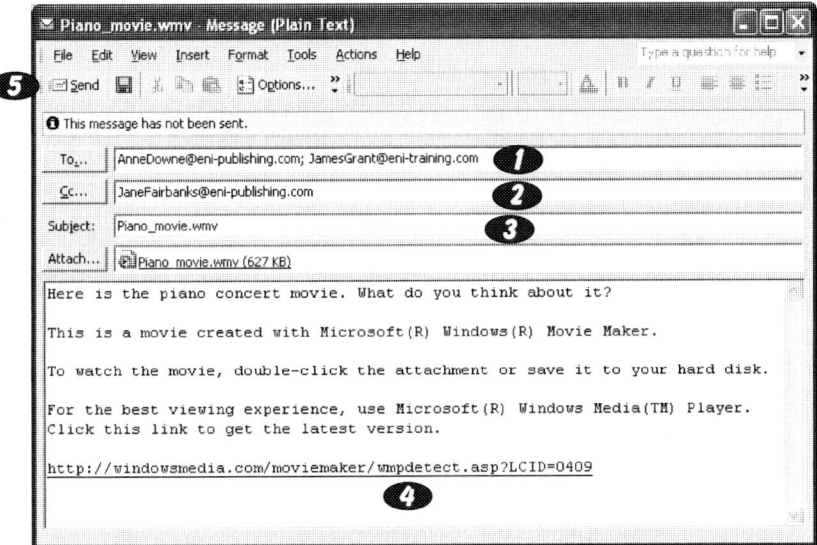

This window will look different from one e-mail application to another (this example shows Outlook 2002).

1. Type the address of the recipients in the **To** box. If you are entering several addresses, use semi-colons to separate them.

2. Use the **Cc** box to enter any addresses to which you want to send a carbon copy of the message.

3. Enter the subject of your message in the **Subject** box.

4. Use the large text box below to write any message you would like to send with your movie. This box already contains a default message, which you can modify or delete as you require.

5. Send the message. In Outlook 2002, click the ⌐≡ Send button.

To view the movie in the Windows Media Player, the message recipients must open the message then double-click the icon representing the file.

To view your movie, the recipients' computers must have **Windows Media Player**.

Windows Media Player

The Microsoft Windows Media Player can read a large number of audio and video file formats from your computer or from the Internet. You can use the Windows Media Player to listen to radio stations from anywhere in the world, read and copy CDs, read DVDs (if you have a DVD drive) or look for available videos on the Internet; it will even manage customized lists of all the digital multimedia files stored on your computer.

DISCOVERING THE WINDOWS MEDIA PLAYER

▨ To open this application, click the **start** button then **All Programs - Windows Media Player**.

these two buttons close the window

click to hide or display the taskbar

▨ The **Windows Media Player** window contains:

- title bar and menus (a): this area appears automatically when you point to the **Playlist Selection** area (b). To keep this bar on the screen or make it disappear again, click the ⬤ button on the **Playlist Selection** area.

- player display area (c).

- **Playlist Selection** area (d): you can use the buttons in this area to choose a playlist or another type of element or to display play and playlist tools.
- **Features Taskbar** (e): this bar contains seven or eight buttons; each button runs a specific feature; you can also access these features using the **View - Taskbar** menu option.
- **Playback Controls** area, which offers the following controls:
  - (f)   pauses a video or audio sequence,
  - (g)   stops what you are currently playing,
  - (h)   mutes or re-establishes the sound,
  - (i)   adjusts the sound volume,
  - (j)   goes to the next or last track,
  - (k)   rewinds and winds fast forward,
  - (l)   seeks (drag the cursor).

- If your Internet connection is open when you start the **Windows Media Player**, it will display the contents of the WindowsMedia.com site in its monitor, automatically. If you have an on-demand connection (via a modem for example) click the **Media Guide** button then confirm your request to access the network to obtain the guide's contents. If you do not request a connection, the reader display area stays black.

- Select **View - Skin Mode** or $\boxed{\text{Ctrl}}$ **2** or $\boxed{}$ to give your **Media Player** a skin appearance and select **View - Full Mode** or $\boxed{\text{Ctrl}}$ **1** or double-click $\boxed{}$ to restore your **Media Player** to its normal appearance.

*When you play an audio CD, **Windows Media Player** provides an attractive interface, including an effect called a visualization, whose look you can alter to suit your taste.*

PLAYING AN AUDIO CD

- If it is closed, open the **Windows Media Player** application (**start - All Programs - Windows Media Player**) then insert an audio CD in your CD-ROM drive.

Windows Media Player

If you insert an audio CD before starting the **Windows Media Player** application, Windows XP may show you this window:

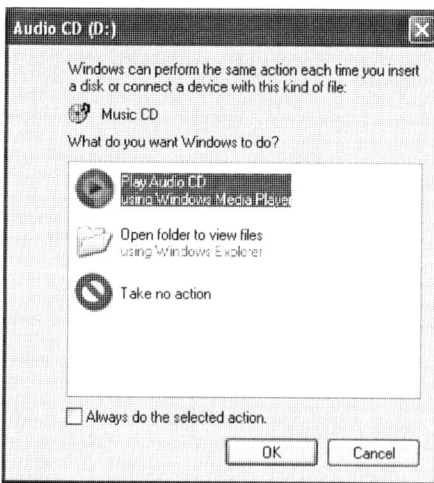

- If this happens, click the **Play Audio CD using Windows Media Player** option and click **OK**; this will activate the Windows Media Player and start playing the CD.

- If necessary, click the **Now Playing** button on the **Features Taskbar**.

- In the **Playlist** pane, click the required track then click the button on the **Playback Controls** area to start playing the track (once you activate it, this button changes into).

- Once it starts playing, use these commands to manage the playback options:

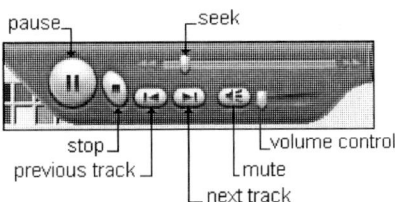

The track currently playing appears in green in the Playlist pane and the length already played is shown at the bottom right of the window.

- To change the visualization that appears in the centre of the player in the **Now Playing** page, use the **View - Visualizations** command on the menu bar then activate the required view.

You can also click the button at the bottom left of the player and choose one of the options offered. There are not as many options here as in the Visualizations menu.

If the Windows Media Player does not recognize your CD, it will show "Artist Unknown".

To play a DVD, your computer must have, not only a DVD drive, but also a DVD decoder program (such as WinDVD (InterVideo Inc.) or PowerDVD (CyberLink Corp.)).

MEDIA PLAYER AND DVDs

Playing a DVD

- Insert the DVD in the DVD drive.

Windows Media Player

Windows Media Player may start automatically. However, if your computer has several DVD playing applications and the Media Player window is not open, the following dialog box appears so that you can choose the application you want to use:

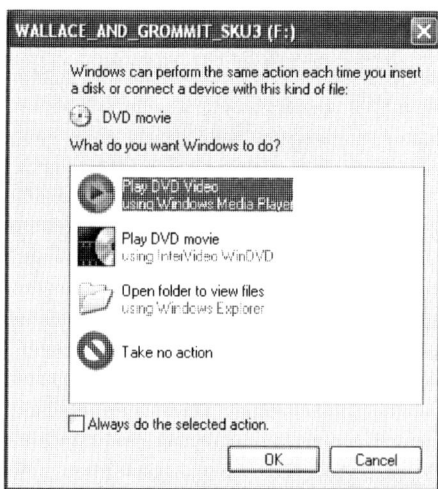

▨ Click the **Play DVD Video using Windows Media Player** option.

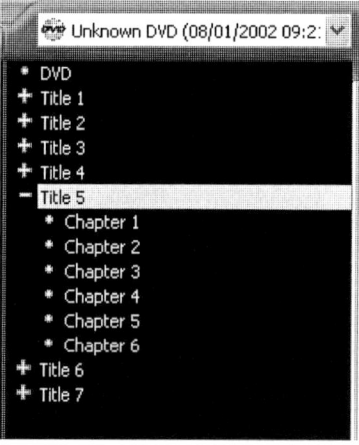

The contents of the DVD appear in the Playlist pane. In the example above, the DVD contains 7 titles and each title contains one or more chapters.

▨ To view the chapters for a title, click the + sign to the left of the title concerned. To hide the chapters for a title, click the - sign to the left of the title concerned.

Applications & multimedia

※ To play a DVD manually, open the **Play** menu and use the **DVD or CD Audio** command, or open the  list and click the name of the DVD you want to play.

※ In the Playlist pane, click the title or chapter of the DVD you want to play.

※ To view your DVD in full screen mode, select the **View - Full Screen** command or press [Alt] ↵ or click the button.

When you switch to full screen view, the Player controls appear briefly before disappearing again.

※ To restore these controls to the screen, move your mouse or press any key.

Before you start playing a DVD, it is advisable to deactivate the screen saver. For this purpose, select the **Tools - Options - Player** tab then deactivate the **Allow screen saver during playback** option.
To specify any **Parental control** or **Language settings**, select **Tools - Options - DVD** tab and choose the required options.

Activating the Now Playing Tools

※ **View - Now Playing Tools**

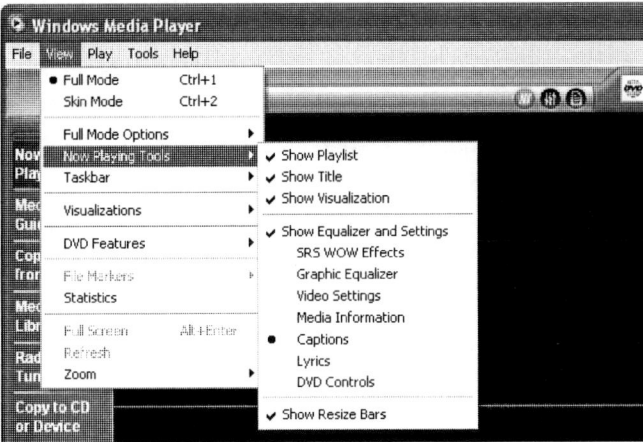

In the submenu the active DVD tool is preceded by a dot.

※ Click the tool you want to activate.

Windows Media Player

The items associated with the active option appear towards the bottom of the screen.

▨ To activate another option, click the 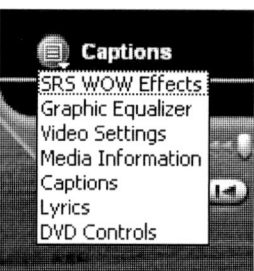 button then select the option you want.

You can also use the **View - Now Playing Tools** command and click the required option.

▨ To hide the playing tool, use the **View - Now Playing Tools** command and click the **Show Equalizer and Settings** option to deactivate it.

Capturing a still picture from a DVD

▨ Play the DVD concerned.

▨ **View - DVD Features - Image Capture**

The **Image Capture** command will be available only if your graphics card and your DVD decoder support this feature.

▨ If necessary, select the folder in which you want to save the image then enter the **File name**.

▨ If necessary, change the **Save as type** option.

▨ Click the **Save** button.

Before you copy the tracks from an audio CD onto a blank CD, you must add them to the Media Library.

ADDING TRACKS FROM A CD TO THE MEDIA LIBRARY

▨ If it is closed, open the **Windows Media Player** application (**start** - **All Programs** - **Windows Media Player**) then insert an audio CD in your CD-ROM drive.

▨ If necessary, click the ▣ button to stop playing the CD.

▨ Insert a CD into the CD-ROM drive and click the **Copy from CD** button.

▨ If necessary, deactivate any tracks that you do not want to copy (by default, all the tracks are activated).

You can click the ✔ box at the top of the list to activate or deactivate all the check boxes.

▨ Click the **Copy Music** button.

If author copyright protection is activated the first time you use the **Copy Music** button, a message appears to remind you that you cannot copy protected (or licensed) tracks copied from a CD onto another computer. Click **OK** or deactivate the **Do not protect content** check box and click **OK**.

By default, the selected track(s) are copied into the **My Music** folder and classified in the **Media Library**. The **My Music** folder contains subfolders carrying the name of the artist or the name **Various Artists**, if several different artists feature on the album. You can ask Windows to save your music files in a different folder if you wish.

To add a file from a computer or an Internet site, open the **File** menu then click the **Open** option (if the file you want to copy is on your computer or a workstation in your network) or the **Open URL** option (if the file is on an Internet site). Locate and select the file you want to add then follow the file copying procedure described previously.

Windows Media Player

You can create a series of tracks called a playlist, that you can then use in various ways: you can write music onto a CD, for example.

CREATING A PLAYLIST

▨ If it is closed, open the **Windows Media Player** application (**start - All Programs - Windows Media Player**).

▨ On the **Features Taskbar**, click **Media Library** then the **New playlist** button.

▨ **Enter the new playlist name** in the text box of the same name then click **OK**.

The new playlist is included automatically into the **My Playlists** category in the Media Library.

▨ If you want to add a single file to the playlist, in the left-hand pane, select the category that contains the file then, in the right-hand pane, click the file you want to add; if you want to add several files to the playlist, Shift-click to select adjacent files or Ctrl-click to select non-adjacent ones.

▨ Click the **Add to playlist** button.

▨ Click the name of the playlist into which you want to add the selected item.

▨ Add as many items as you wish, although you should keep a check on the total volume of the playlist, if you are going to copy it later onto a CD.

Applications & multimedia

You can add only items from the Media Library to a playlist.

 To delete a playlist, right-click that playlist's name in the Media Library then click the **Delete** option.

*You can use the Windows Media Player to copy tracks (.**wma** (Windows Media format), .**mp3** and .**wav** files) stored in your Media Library onto a CD. However, you cannot copy live incoming data, such as a radio station transmission. You can carry out the actions described in this section, only if you have a CD writer and some blank CDs (CD-R or CD-RW).*

COPYING FILES ONTO AN AUDIO CD

▧ If it is closed, open the **Windows Media Player** application (**start - All Programs - Windows Media Player**).

▧ Click the **Copy to CD or Device** button on the **Features Taskbar** or use **File - Copy - Copy to Audio CD**.

The **Select music to copy** window is divided into two parts, the **Music to Copy** list on the left and the **Music on Device** list on the right.

Windows Media Player

▓ Click the  button on the **Music to Copy** pane then choose the playlist or track category that you want to copy from the **Media Library**.

The number of items selected and their total length appears at the bottom of the **Music to Copy** pane:

▓ If necessary, deactivate the check boxes of any tracks that you do not want to copy.

▓ Insert a CD-R or a CD-RW into your CD writer.

▓ If you have several writers, click the ☑ button in the **Music on Device** pane then select the CD writer containing the blank CD.

▓ Click the **Copy Music** button at the top right of the window.

Before starting to write onto the CD, Windows checks the tracks and converts them to the file type that suits the CD.

Look in the **Status** column in the **Music to Copy** pane to see how the conversion or copying process is progressing:

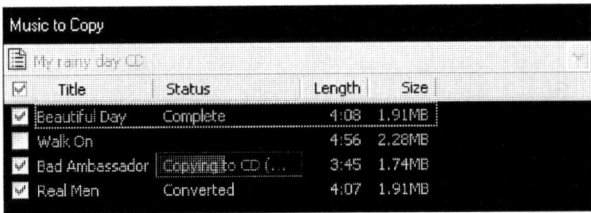

 You should avoid carrying out other actions while you are writing a CD, as this can cause the CD writer to stop.

You can listen to some national and international radio stations over the Internet: this is made possible using a continuous broadcasting process. For the user, the main advantage of this is that he or she can listen to the radio without waiting for sound files to be loaded, avoiding a "chopped" sound effect. To carry out the following actions, your Internet connection must be open.

LISTENING TO THE RADIO

Looking at the Radio Tuner

- If it is closed, open the **Windows Media Player** application (**start** - **All Programs** - **Windows Media Player**).

- Click the **Radio Tuner** button on the **Features Taskbar**.

Windows Media Player

By default, the Windows Media Player displays the radio information available on the WindowsMedia.com Web site:

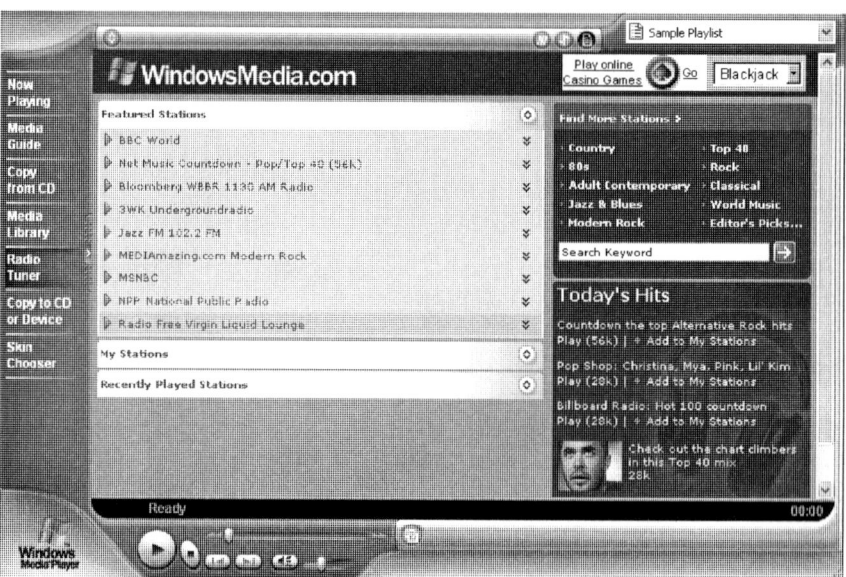

The Player window shows link to radio stations, classified into three categories: **Featured Stations, My Stations, Recently Played Stations**.

- To show or hide the contents on any of these categories, click the corresponding ◇ button.

Finding a radio station

- If it is closed, open the **Windows Media Player** application (**start - All Programs - Windows Media Player**). Click the **Radio Tuner** button on the **Features Taskbar**.

- To make a station search, click one of the required radio types located in the right pane of the screen, or enter in the appropriate text box a keyword representing the station you want to find. If you enter a keyword, finish by clicking the ➡ button.

Applications & multimedia

WindowsMedia.com lists the stations that correspond to your search and also allows you to qualify your search request with more criteria:

- To make a combined search using a **Genre** and a **Keyword**, fill in the **Browse by Genre** box and the **Search** box then click the  button to the right of the **Search** box, to start the search.

  The **Zip Code** search criterion is valid only in the USA.

- To return to the previous page, click the **Return to My Stations** link.

Listening to a radio station

- If it is closed, open the **Windows Media Player** application (**start** - **All Programs - Windows Media Player**). Click the **Radio Tuner** button on the **Features Taskbar**.

- If the radio station to which you want to listen is not in any of the three categories offered, make a search to view it (cf. Finding a radio station, above).

- Click the link corresponding to the radio station concerned to see some details about it.

Windows Media Player

▓ Click the **Play** ▷ button to listen to the selected station.

You can also listen to a station by clicking the ▷ button just to the left of its name.

Windows may ask you to install some characters so it can display the Player window correctly in a given language with certain written characteristics:

▓ If this occurs, click the **Install** button and follow the installation instructions.

Note that each time you start listening to a radio station, your PC's Web browser (such as Internet Explorer) opens and displays the active station's home page: additional advertising screens, called pop-ups may also appear. You can quickly get swamped by these! If you wish to see or close a pop-up, you may first have to activate it by clicking its button on the taskbar.

▓ To stop the radio, click the ⬛ button in the **Playback Controls** area.

Applications & multimedia

Adding a station to your list of favourite stations

This feature lets you add shortcuts to one or more radio stations for easier access.

⬚ If it is closed, open the **Windows Media Player** application (**start** - **All Programs** - **Windows Media Player**). Click the **Radio Tuner** button on the **Features Taskbar**.

⬚ If the radio station to which you want to listen is not in any of the three categories offered, make a search to view it (cf. Finding a radio station).

⬚ Click the link for the radio station in question to display the details about it.

⬚ Click the **Add to My Stations** ✚ button.

⬚ To see the list of your favourite stations, open the **My Stations** category by clicking the corresponding ◇ button:

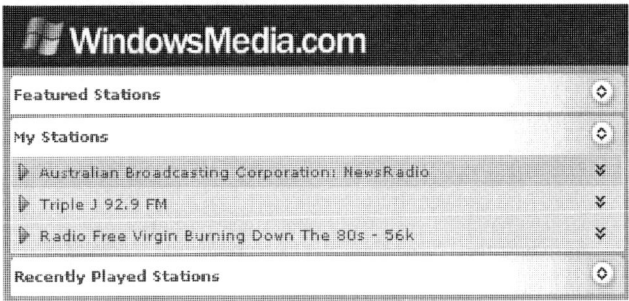

You can change how your Windows Media Player looks by applying different "skins" (or presentations) to it.

CHANGING THE LOOK OF THE WINDOWS MEDIA PLAYER

⬚ If it is closed, open the **Windows Media Player** application (**start** - **All Programs** - **Windows Media Player**).

⬚ Click the **Skin Chooser** button on the **Features Taskbar**.

Windows Media Player

1. Click one of the skins offered: a preview of your selected skin appears in the right part of the window.

2. To apply the selected skin to the Windows Media Player, click the **Apply Skin** button.

The Windows Media Player takes on the selected appearance. This is always divided into two sections:

To return to **Full Mode** view, double-click the ▨ symbol or press `Ctrl` **1**.

To adopt the **Skin Mode** again, click the  button or take the **Skin Mode** option in the **View** menu or press ⌊Ctrl⌋ **2**.

To download other skins from the WindowsMedia.com site, click the **More Skins** button (your Internet connection must be open) and download one of the skins on offer by clicking the appropriate link.

Digital photos

You can use many different types of device to load photos (pictures) into your computer: scanners, digital cameras, MultiMediaCard readers and so forth. You can even download pictures from the Internet. You can store your photos (pictures) in the My Pictures folder that Windows XP provides. You can also create other folders for this purpose.

SETTING UP A FOLDER TO CONTAIN PICTURES

▨ If you use a pictures folder other than **My Pictures**, make sure that your folder is either the **Pictures** type or the **PhotoAlbum** type, so that Windows XP will associate specific image processing commands with them. For this purpose, right-click the folder concerned, click the **Properties** option, click the **Customize** tab and open the **Use this folder type as a template** list.

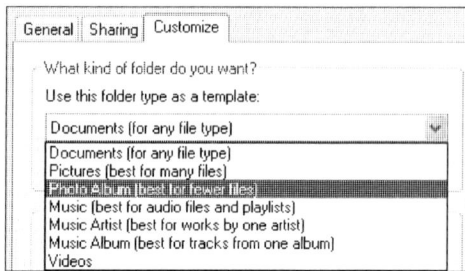

▨ Click the **Pictures** option or the **Photo Album** option, then click the **OK** button.

As with other types of folder, you can change the view of Pictures and Photo Album type folders. In addition, you can view such folders as slide shows.

VIEWING A PICTURE

▨ Click the **start** button then the **My Documents** option.

▨ Double-click the name of the folder that contains your pictures: this could be your **My Pictures** folder or another folder that you use for this purpose.

▨ If required, change the view by choosing one of the six view options that the **View** menu provides.

The Filmstrip and Thumbnails views provide previews of the pictures that the folder contains.

▨ In addition, you can view the pictures in your folder as a slide show. For this purpose, click the **View as a slide show** link in the **Picture Tasks** box in the left-hand pane of the folder window.

If you select no pictures, or just one, the slide show will display all the pictures in the folder, one after the other. If you select at least two pictures in the folder, the slide show will include only those pictures you have selected.

⬚ Use the tools on the following bar to start or pause the slide show, to go to the previous or next picture, or to close the slide show view:

If this toolbar is not visible on the screen, move the mouse pointer to the top right of the screen.

Windows offers a Photo Printing Wizard to help you print your pictures using different layouts.

PRINTING A PICTURE

⬚ Click the **start** button then the **My Documents** option.

⬚ Double-click the name of the folder that contains your pictures: this could be your **My Pictures** folder or another folder that you use for this purpose.

⬚ Click the **Print pictures** link in the **Picture Tasks** box in the left-hand pane of the folder window.

⬚ In the **Photo Printing Wizard** window that opens, click the **Next** button.

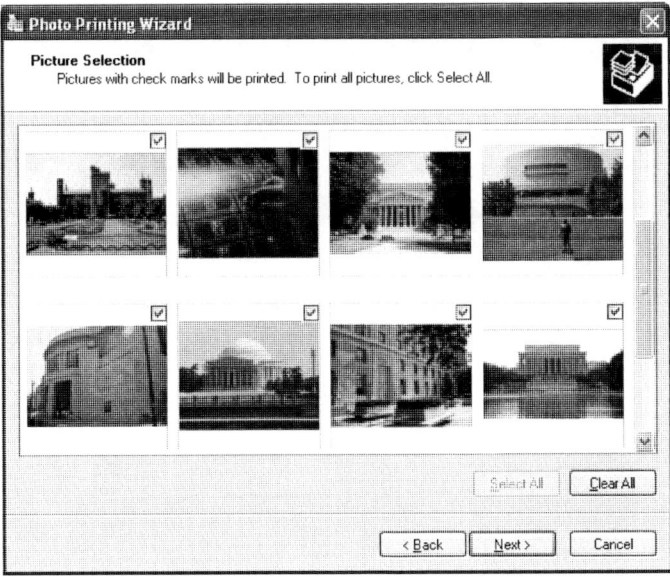

Selected pictures are ticked in their top right-hand corners.

Digital photos

▨ To deselect all the pictures, click the **Clear All** button.

▨ To select all the pictures, click the **Select All** button.

▨ To select or deselect a specific picture, click the check box in the top right-hand corner of the picture concerned.

▨ When you have selected the pictures you want to print, click the **Next** button.

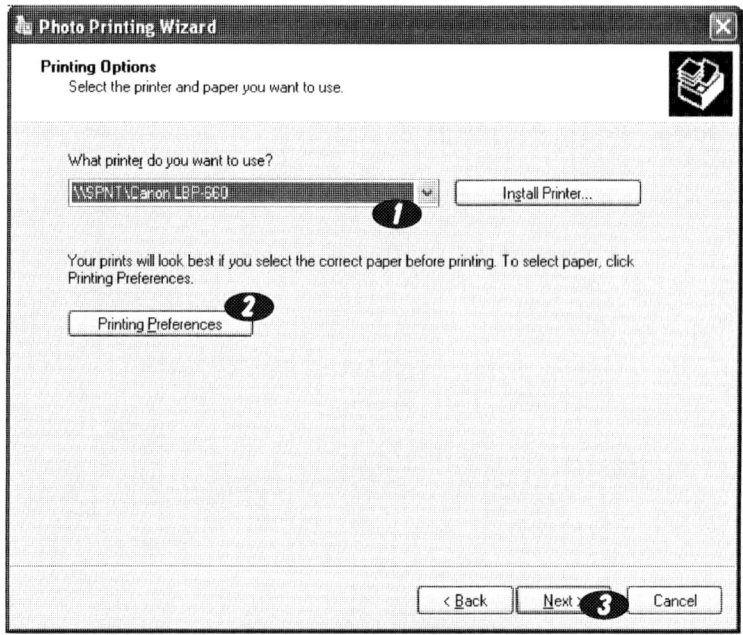

1. Open the **What printer do you want to use?** list and choose the printer you require.

2. Click the **Printing Preferences** button to define settings such as the paper orientation: these settings will vary according to the printer you are using.

3. Click the **Next** button.

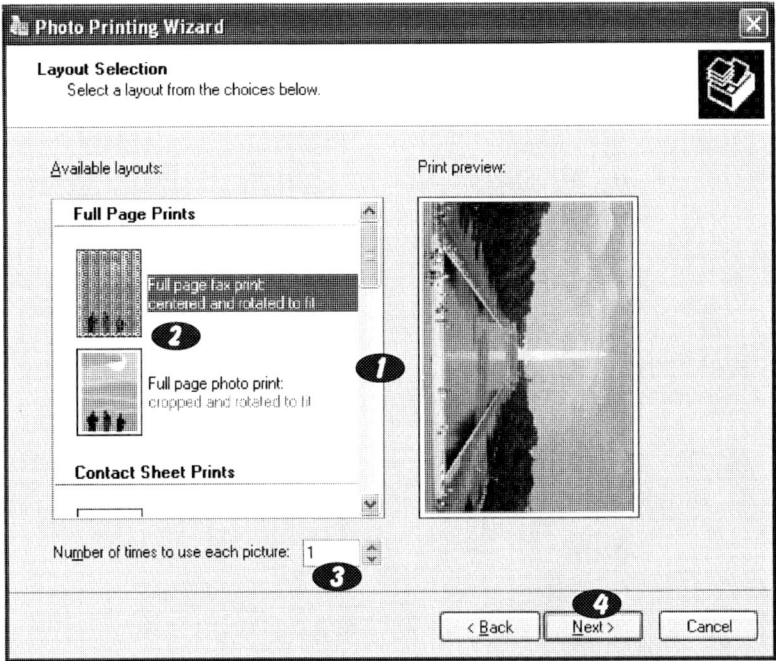

In the left hand pane, the wizard offers a variety of **Available layouts** in a list box.

1. To view the different layouts available, use the vertical scroll bar.

2. Click the layout you require.

3. Specify the number of copies you require in the **Number of times to use each picture** box.

4. Click the **Next** button.

⬚ Click the **Finish** button.

Windows Messenger

You can use the Windows Messenger application to exchange messages with other users in real-time.
Your correspondents can be on your local network or on the Internet and they must have:

- an Internet connection

- a Microsoft .NET Passport (cf. Managing users - Creating a Microsoft .Net Passport),

- the Windows Messenger application installed on their computers (Windows XP installs this application automatically).

To use Windows Messenger, you must first set up your Microsoft .NET Passport. You can then sign in to Windows Messenger and communicate with other users who are also signed-in to Windows Messenger (after they have also set up their Microsoft .NET Passports).

SIGNING IN AND SIGNING OUT

▨ Click the **start** button followed by **All Programs** and **Windows Messenger**.

The **Windows Messenger** window opens:

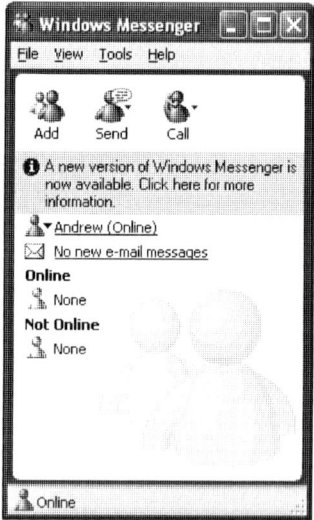

When you use Windows Messenger for the first time, it indicates that you have no contacts.

▨ To hide this window, click the ✖ button or select the **File - Close** command.

Windows Messenger informs you that it will continue to run even though you have closed its window. In this way, Windows Messenger is able to notify you as soon as you receive a message, provided that your Internet connection is active.

Applications & multimedia

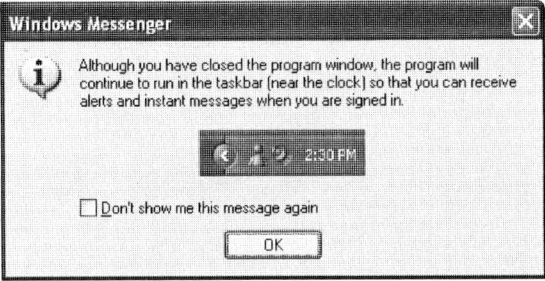

Click the **OK** button.

The  icon on the right of the taskbar symbolises the active Windows Messenger application.

To sign out of Windows Messenger, right-click the icon on the right of the taskbar then click the **Sign out** option.

If the Windows Messenger window is open you can also sign out using the **File - Sign out** command.

To reopen the Windows Messenger window, double-click the icon on the right of the taskbar (alternatively, you can click this icon to open its shortcut menu then click the **Open** option).

To converse directly with other users from the Windows Messenger window, you must first add them as contacts so that this window will show them.

ADDING A CONTACT TO YOUR LIST

Sign on to Windows Messenger or open the Windows Messenger window.

Click the Add button in the **Windows Messenger** window.

There are two ways of adding a contact to your list, according to whether or not you know your contact's e-mail address.

Windows Messenger

You know your contact's e-mail address

How do you want to add a contact?

⊙ By e-mail address or sign-in name

○ Search for a contact

▧ Activate the **By e-mail address or sign-in name** option then click the **Next** button.

▧ Enter the full e-mail address of the person you want to add as a contact, in the text box provided for this purpose.

▧ Click the **Next** button.

Windows Messenger checks whether or not the contact you want to add has a Microsoft .NET Passport.

Your new contact has a Microsoft .NET Passport:

▧ When Windows Messenger has checked that the contact has a Microsoft .NET Passport, it adds him/her to your list.

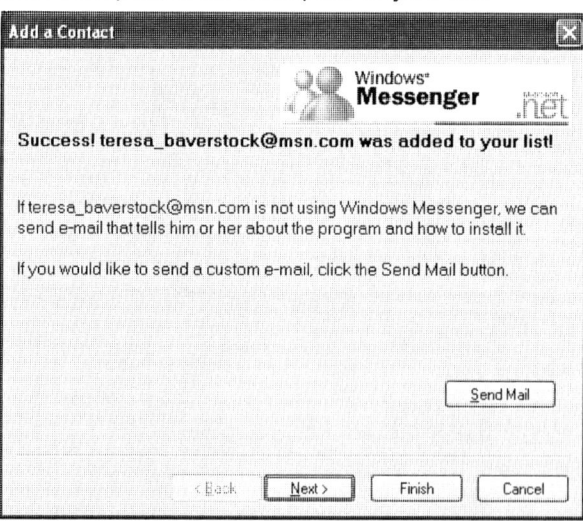

*Use the **Send Mail** button to send a message to this new contact.*

▧ Click the **Finish** button to confirm the addition of your new contact to your list.

Applications & multimedia

Your new contact does not have a Microsoft .NET Passport:

▨ Windows Messenger informs you that it is unable to add your new contact to your list because he/she does not have a Microsoft .NET Passport.

▨ To close this dialog box, without sending a message to this person, click the **Cancel** button. To send a message, in order to suggest that he/she might like to create a Microsoft .NET Passport, click the **Next** button.

▨ If you click **Next**, the following dialog box appears:

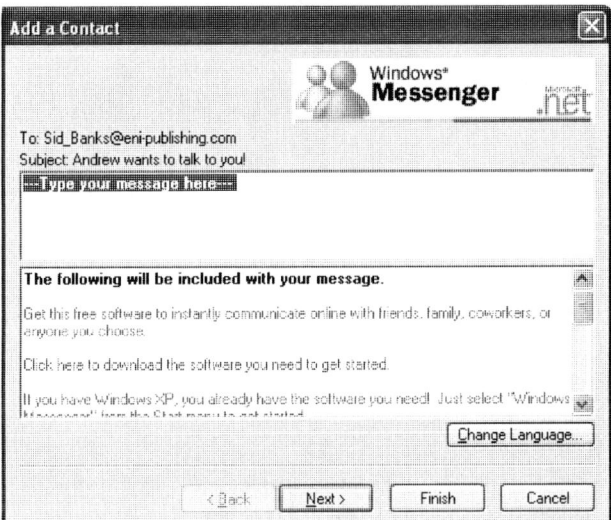

You can use the Next button to add another contact.

▨ Enter your message where **Type your message here** appears then click the **Finish** button.

You do not know your contact's e-mail address:

▨ Activate the **Search for a contact** option then click the **Next** button.

▨ Enter the **First Name**, the **Last Name** and possibly the **Country/Region** of the contact you want to add.

▓ If necessary, open the **Search for this person at** list and choose to look for the person in the **Hotmail Member Directory** or in the **Address Book on this computer** then click the **Next** button.

Windows Messenger shows its search results in a dialog box.

▓ Select the name of the person concerned then click the **Next** button to check whether or not the person has a Microsoft .NET Passport.

▓ If the person has a Microsoft .NET Passport, Windows Messenger offers to send him/her a message to explain how to install Windows Messenger and contact you.

In this case, click the **Next** button to send the person a message or click the **Cancel** button if you decide you do not want to add this contact to your list.

▓ If the person concerned does not have a Microsoft .NET Passport, you can send him/her a message in order to start exchanging messages with him/her (via Windows Messenger).

 You can add up to 150 contacts to your list.

If you no longer want to communicate with one of your contacts, you can remove him/her from your list.

DELETING A CONTACT FROM YOUR LIST

▓ Sign on to Windows Messenger or open the Windows Messenger window.

▓ Right-click the name of the contact you want to remove from your list then click the **Delete Contact** option (or press the ⌷Del⌷ key).

 Windows Messenger users who are not on your contacts list can still contact you, unless you block them to prevent them from doing so.

When you block a contact, you prevent him/her from contacting you directly. However, you may still find yourself in a conversation with this person if another user invites both of you into a conversation.

BLOCKING A CONTACT

▓ Sign on to Windows Messenger or open the Windows Messenger window.

▓ Right-click the name of the contact you want to block then click the **Block** option.

▓ To unblock a contact, right-click the name of the contact you want to unblock then click the **Unblock** option.

 A blocked contact appears as follows: ⊗ l.rice@eni.com (Blocked).

You can send an instant message to anyone in your Windows Messenger contact list.

SENDING AN INSTANT MESSAGE TO A CONTACT

▓ Sign on to Windows Messenger or open the Windows Messenger window.

▓ Right-click the name of the person you want to contact, who can be either **Online** or **Not Online**.

▓ If the person is **Not Online**, Windows Messenger asks you to confirm that you want to send him/her mail by clicking the **Yes** button. In this case you can carry on creating your message. This procedure will vary according to your mailbox (such as msn.com, yahoo.com, excite.com, for example).

Windows Messenger

If the person is **Online**, the **Conversation** window appears:

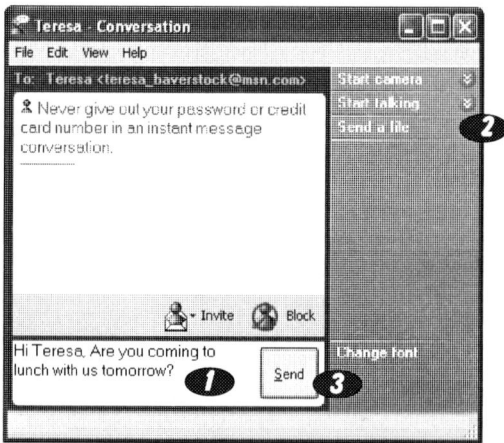

1. Enter your message (of up to 400 characters) in the lower pane of the dialog box.

2. To send a file with your message, click the **Send a file** link, select the file you want to send then click the **Open** button.

3. Click the **Send** button.

The message you entered moves to the upper pane of the dialog box.

During your conversation, the status bar at the bottom of your dialog box tells you when your contact is entering a message:

or the date and time of the last message you received:

Last message received on 26/12/2001 at 15:43.

Applications & multimedia

You can also send an instant message to someone who is not in your contacts list.

SENDING MESSAGES TO A PERSON WHO IS NOT IN YOUR CONTACTS

▨ Sign on to Windows Messenger or open the Windows Messenger window.

▨ Click the ⬛ Send button then choose the **Other** option.

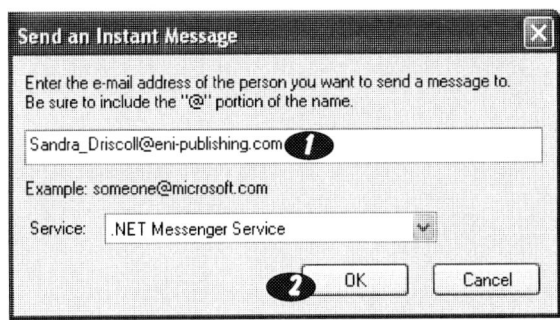

1. Enter the e-mail address of your correspondent (who must have a Microsoft .NET Passport).

2. Click **OK** to confirm.

The **Conversation** window opens.

▨ Enter your message then click the **Send** button.

Windows Messenger informs you if it is unable to contact your correspondent:

> 🐾 The following message could not be delivered to all recipients:
>   Can we fix a time to discuss our new project?

This part will explain how you can manage your folders and files using a folder window. You will learn how to create folders to store your files, how to delete files that you no longer need, how to copy a file to a floppy disk to give to a friend and how to find the different files you have created.

3rd Part

My Documents window

Discovering the environment

For each user of your computer, Windows XP creates an individual folder called **My Documents**, in which the user can store all his/her files (letters, workbooks, pictures etc.). By default, the **My Documents** folder contains two subfolders: **My Pictures** and **My Music**. These subfolders contain sample pictures and music. Naturally, each user can create other subfolders in his/her **My Documents** folder (cf. Managing folders and files - Creating a folder).

If you wish, you can allow other computer users to access your personal (**My Documents**) folder and its subfolders or you can make these folders private by forbidding all other users from accessing your personal data. If several users can access your computer, Windows XP identifies the different personal folders according to the name of the user concerned. For example, suppose a computer has two users, Beatrice and Benedick: when Beatrice is logged on to the computer, her personal folder is called **My Documents**, while Benedick's personal folder appears under the name of **Benedick's Documents** (Beatrice can view Benedick's personal folder in the **My Computer** window by choosing **start - My Computer**). Windows identifies the **My Pictures** and **My Music** folders in the same way: when Beatrice is logged on to the computer, Benedick's **My Pictures** and **My Music** folders appear under the names of **Benedick's Pictures** and **Benedick's Music**, respectively.

DISCOVERING THE MY DOCUMENTS WINDOW

▓ To open the **My Documents** window, click the **start** button on the taskbar then click the **My Documents** option.

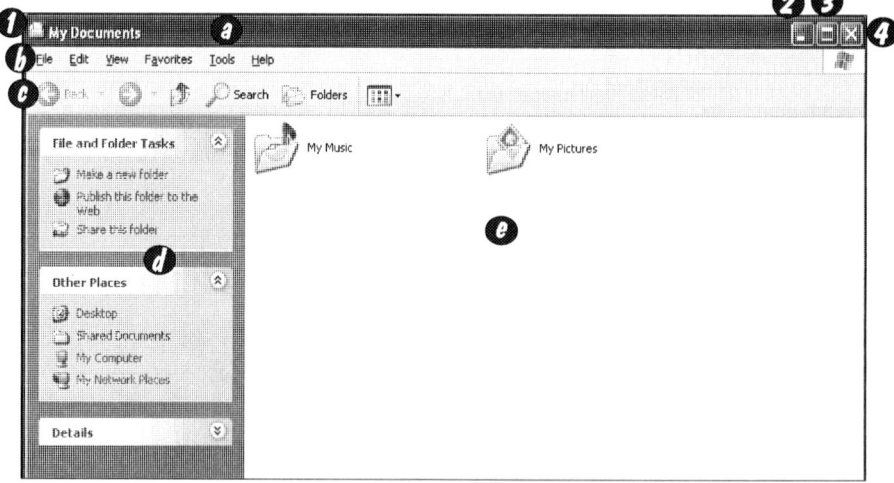

By default, the **My Documents** window contains only the **My Pictures** and **My Music** subfolders. You can create other folders in the **My Documents** folder and thereby add them to this list of existing subfolders.

The **My Documents** window contains the following items:

- **Title bar** (a): contains the **Control** menu (1), which allows you to manage the **My Documents** window, followed by the name of the selected folder (the **My Documents** folder in this case). On the right-hand end of the title bar, the **Minimize** (2) and **Maximize** (3) buttons collapse the window into its scroll bar button and enlarge the window to the full screen size, respectively, while the **Close** button (4) closes the window.

- **Menu bar** (b): contains the different menus for managing the contents of the window.

- **Standard Buttons** toolbar (c): contains tool buttons to carry out certain actions quickly.

- The left-hand pane (d) contains several list boxes showing options that carry out certain actions when you click them. Five types of list boxes may appear: **File and Folder Tasks, Other Places, Picture Tasks, Music Tasks**, and **Details** . These boxes will offer different options according to the window item you select. If you cannot see the options that a box contains, click the ⊗ button on the right of the box's title bar. Similarly, to hide a box's options, click the ⊗ button, which appears in the same position.

- The right-hand pane (e) shows all the folders and files in the folder concerned (this example shows the contents of the **My Documents** folder).

You can view additional information on the item(s) you have selected in the status bar at the bottom of the **My Documents** window (to display the status bar choose **View - Status Bar**).

Discovering the environment

*When you open a folder window, by default, Windows displays a frame containing a set of boxes and each box offers a set of options that allow you to carry out various actions. You can replace this pane by one of five explorer bars. For example, the **Folders** explorer bar shows your computer's folder hierarchy (the full set of folders and files that your hard disk contains) and allows you to copy, move, delete, rename or search for folders and files.*

DISPLAYING AN EXPLORER BAR IN A FOLDER WINDOW

▨ Open the folder window in which you want to display an explorer bar (for example, the **My Documents** folder window, or the window of a subfolder of the **My Documents** folder).

▨ Click the **View** menu and point to the **Explorer Bar** option.

▨ Click the name of the explorer bar you want to display:

- the **Search** bar allows you to search for folders, files, people or other computers in your computing network. It also allows you to search the Internet.

- the **Favorites** bar lists all your favourite pages (whether they are on the Internet or not). You can add new page items to the list in this bar to make it easier to access these pages in the future. You can group your pages according to common themes by organizing them into different folders.

- the **Media** bar allows you to read music, video and multimedia files from the same folder window. It also provides access to the different media that the computer offers, such as Internet radio stations, for example.

- the **History** bar shows the pages (Web pages, Windows Help pages, documents and so forth) that you have visited today or in preceding days or weeks.

- the **Folders** bar displays the hierarchical structure of your computer's files, folders and devices and allows you to manage these items (by copying, moving, deleting, renaming and finding your files and folders, for example). You can also display this bar using the **start - All Programs - Accessories - Windows Explorer** command).

▨ To close an explorer bar, click the ☒ button in the top right-hand corner of the bar.

You can hide, lock or move the toolbars that you can see in a window.

MANAGING TOOLBARS

▨ To display or hide toolbars, click the **View** menu, point to the **Toolbars** option then activate or deactivate the option corresponding to the toolbar you want to display or hide.

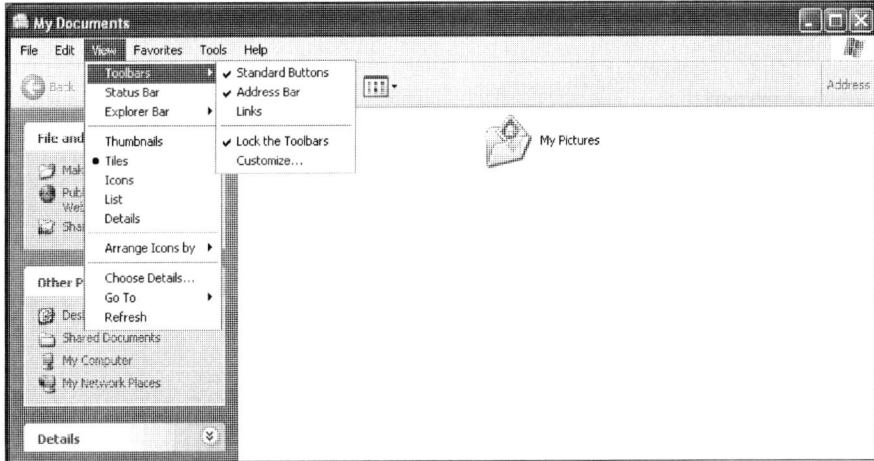

A tick to the left of a toolbar name indicates that the toolbar is currently visible.
*The **Links** bar offers rapid access to certain Internet sites*
(providing you have an Internet connection).

▨ To change the size of the buttons on the **Standard Buttons** toolbar, choose **View - Toolbars - Customize**.

Open the **Icon options** drop-down list then choose **Small icons** or **Large icons**.

Click the **Close** button to validate your action.

▨ You can lock or unlock the locations of your toolbars, according to whether or not you want to move them. For this purpose, click the **View** menu, point to the **Toolbars** option then activate or deactivate the **Lock the Toolbars** option (by default, the toolbar locations are locked).

Discovering the environment

To move a toolbar, first check that the **View** - **Toolbars** - **Lock the Toolbars** option is deactivated (you can move a toolbar only if the toolbars are unlocked). Next, point to the dotted vertical line (move handle) on the far left of the toolbar then drag above, below or on the same level as an existing toolbar.

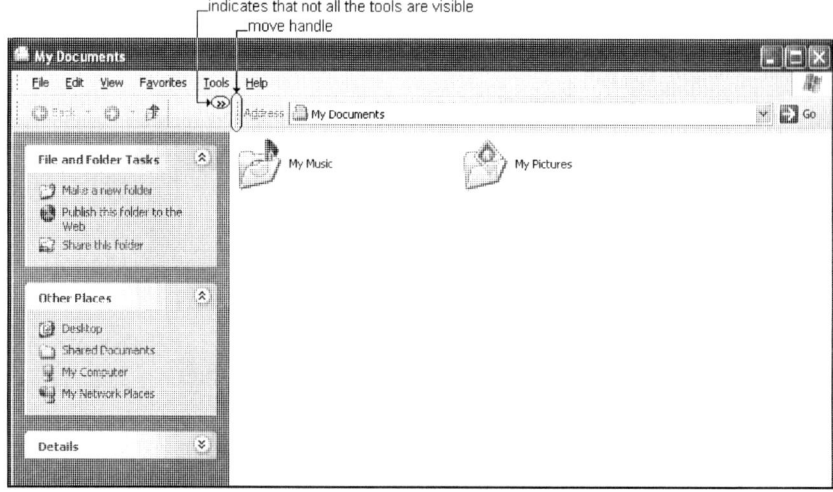

*In this example, the **Address** toolbar has been placed to the right of the **Standard Buttons** toolbar. As a result, certain buttons on the **Standard Buttons** toolbar are no longer visible.*

When two toolbars are placed side-by-side, you can drag the move handle (dotted vertical line) of the right-hand bar to change the relative lengths of the bars.

If you need to use a button that is not visible on a toolbar, click the ⏵⏵ button at the extreme right of the bar to view the tool button then click this tool button to carry out the required action.

My Documents window

*Although it is recommended that you work in the **My Documents** folder, you may still need to access folders other than those your **My Documents** folder contains. For example, you may need to access another user's folders, or another drive such as a floppy-disk or a CD-ROM. For this purpose, you can use the **Folders** explorer bar, which displays the complete hierarchy of your hard disk.*

ACCESSING A DEVICE OR A FOLDER

▓ Open the folder window of your choice.

▓ Display the **Folders** explorer bar either by using the **View - Explorer Bar - Folders** command or by clicking the **Folders** button on the **Standard Buttons** toolbar.

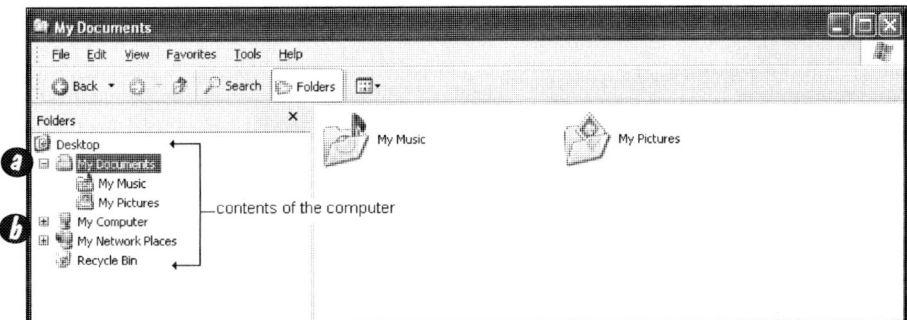

The right-hand pane displays the contents of the item selected in the **Folders** bar. In this example, the right-hand pane shows the contents of the **My Documents** folder, which is selected in the **Folders** bar.

▓ In the example below, the **Folders** bar shows the different items of the desktop as a hierarchy: some branches of the hierarchy are expanded (a) to show the folder objects they contain, while other branches are collapsed (b). A minus sign (-) indicates an expanded branch, while a plus sign (+) indicates a collapsed branch. To expand or collapse a branch just click the + or the -. To expand a branch fully, click the folder concerned then press the * key (on the numeric keypad).

In the **Folders** bar, click **My Computer** to display the items it contains.

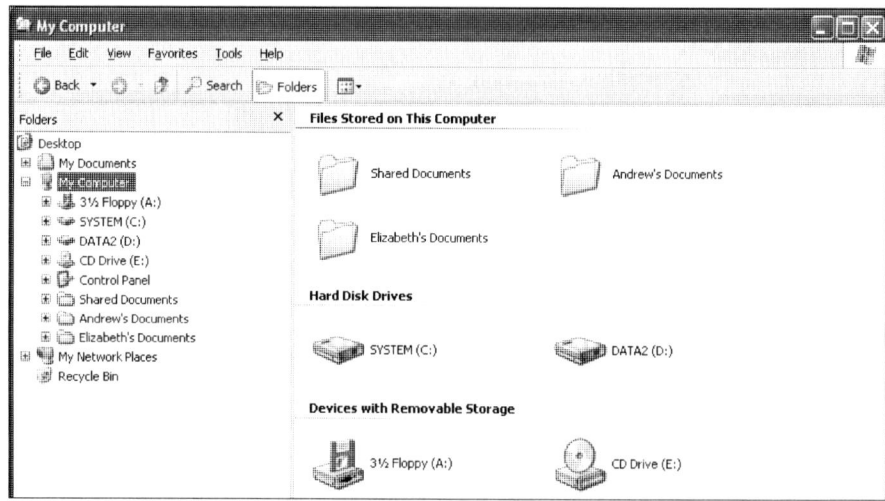

The items contained in **My Computer** will vary according to the installation. However, they are generally grouped into the following categories:

- **Files Stored on This Computer** groups the folders that contain your working files.
- **Hard Disk Drives** group your computer's hard disk drives (this example shows two hard disk drives: C: and D:).
- **Devices with Removable Storage** groups drives on your computer into which you can insert and withdraw storage units, such as floppy-disks and CD-ROMS.

Notice that different categories use different icon styles to portray their items.

To view the contents of a folder or a device, click the folder or the device in the explorer bar or double-click its icon in the right-hand pane.

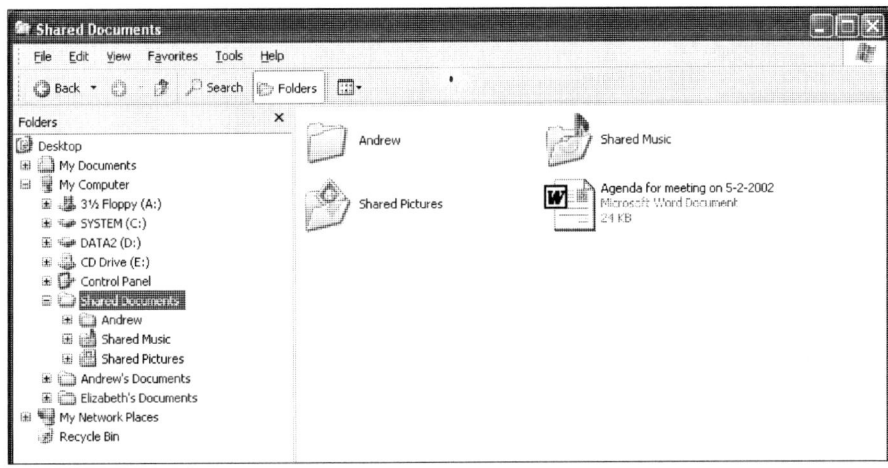

In this example, **Shared Documents** was clicked to show all the folders and files that this folder contains in the right-hand pane.

To help you to distinguish a folder from a file, remember that a folder is used to store subfolders and files. A folder works in a similar way to a physical folder, which may contain dividers ("subfolders") with documents ("files") between them. A folder is always represented by this style of icon: 📁. On the other hand, the icon for a file will vary according to the application that created it.

A folder that is not preceded by a + or - sign indicates that the folder does not contain any subfolders. However, the folder may still contain files.

When you open (expand) a folder, its icon changes (as with the **Shared Documents** folder in the example above).

▨ To access the folder on the next level up (the parent folder) you can run the **View - Go To - Up One Level** command. Alternatively, you can click the 🔼 button on the **Standard Buttons** toolbar or press the backspace ⬅ key.

In the example above, clicking the 🔼 tool button will display the contents of **My Computer**.

▨ To go back to the folder or device you viewed previously, you can run the **View - Go To - Back** command. Alternatively, you can click the **Back** 🔙 button on the **Standard Buttons** toolbar or press the Alt⬅ shortcut key.

▨ To go forward again to the folder or device you viewed before you last went back, you can run the **View - Go To - Forward** command. Alternatively, you can click the ⊙ button or press the `Alt` `→` shortcut key.

▨ To view again one of the folders or devices you viewed since you opened the folder window, click the down-arrow on the **Back** ⊙ or the ⊙ tool button then click the name of the folder or device you want to view again.

When a folder or drive appears in the right-hand pane, you can double-click it to view its contents.

 To refresh the contents of the window so that it will take into account any changes that have occurred since you opened the window, use the **View - Refresh** command or press the `F5` key.

By default, a folder window shows the name of each file along with its size, its type and an icon representing its type. You can change this display, for example, to view only the icon or the name or each file or to view a thumbnail (miniature) of each file.

CHANGING THE PRESENTATION OF THE FOLDER/FILE LIST

▨ Select the folder whose presentation you want to change.

▨ Open the **View** menu or click the ⊞▾ button.

▨ You can choose from one of six options:

Filmstrip available only for picture folders, this option presents each picture as a thumbnail along with its name, in a single line. When you select a picture, a larger scale preview appears in a pane above.

Thumbnails presents a miniature version and the name of each file in the folder. Pictures appear as thumbnails, while other types of file appear as the logo of the application that created them.

Tiles shows the name of each file along with its type and an icon representing its type.

Icons shows only the name of each file underneath an icon representing its type.

List shows only the name of each file beside an icon representing its type. The files appear in the form of an ordered list in one or more columns (in alphabetical order by default). You cannot move the files to different positions in the list.

Details lists the files in a single column showing an icon representing the type of each file along with other information including its name, its size, its type and the date and time it was last modified.

The example below shows the contents of the **Correspondence** folder in **Details** view.

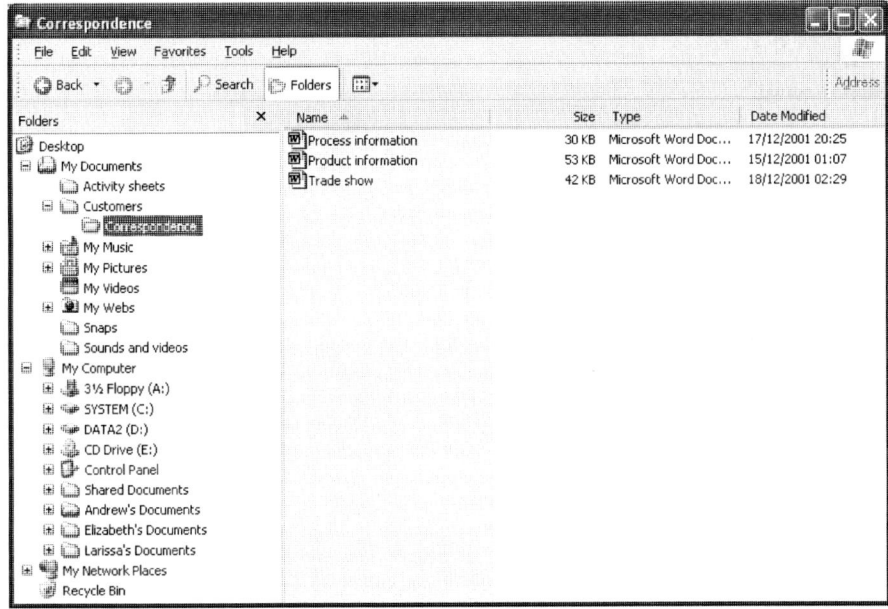

This view shows the size of each file in **kilobytes (KB)**: a byte is the space that one character occupies. The type of a file is associated with its format, which depends on the application that created the file. The icon preceding the file also depends on the application that created it, as does the filename extension (this is a set of three characters that appears as a suffix to the filename: by default, the filename extension does not appear in the folder window). The date and time of the last modification shows the system time when the file was last modified (your computer has an internal clock, which it uses for this sort of information).

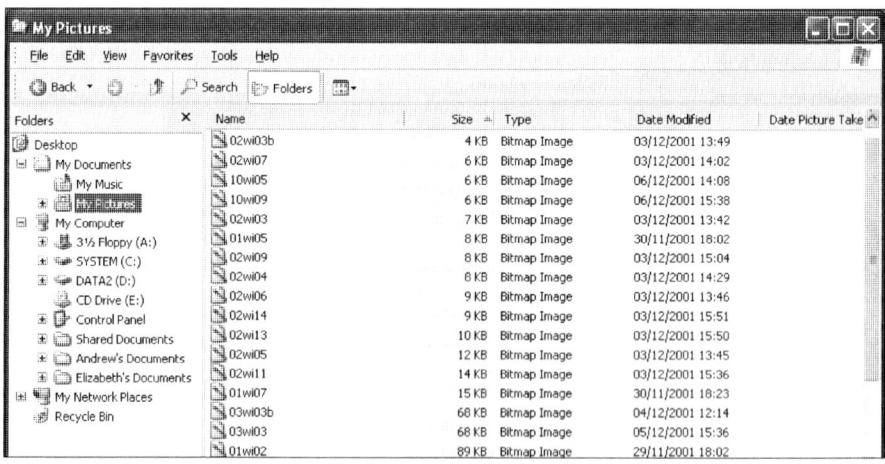

※ If any information in a column is not entirely visible, an ellipsis (…) appears at the end of the content (as in the **Type** column, in the above example). To view the content of a column in its entirety, you must widen the column concerned. You can do this by dragging the vertical separator line that appears to the right of the column header (for example, to the right of the **Type** header, above).

Whatever the view mode you choose, by default, the folder window shows the folders followed by the files, sorted in alphabetical order. You can sort your files on other criteria: for example, to view the most recently modified files at the top of the list.

SORTING A FILE LIST

※ In the **Folders** bar, select the folder whose file list you want to sort.

※ **View - Arrange Icons by**

※ Activate an option according to how you want to sort: for example, by **Name**, by **Size**, by **Type** or by date of last modification (**Date Modified**).

The **Arrange Icons by** list will vary according to the folder you select. For example, if you select a picture folder, you can also choose the **Pictures Taken On** or **Dimensions** option.

*This example shows the contents of the **My Pictures** folder sorted by file size.*

When your files appear in **Details** view, you can simply click the header of the column on which you want to sort. For example, clicking the **Date Modified** header will sort your files according to the date and time they were last modified: click once to sort in ascending order; click again to sort in descending order.

Managing folders and files

*Even if you have just bought your computer, your hard disk will not be empty: it must contain the files of the Windows XP operating system. These files are grouped together into folders. Your personal folder is present on the hard disk under the name of **My Documents**. This folder is there to accommodate the files you will create. When you have created a certain number of files, you may have trouble finding a specific document. To avoid long searches, it is recommended that you store your files in different folders that you can create for this purpose within your **My Documents** folder. Each of these folders can represent a certain theme or contain a certain type of file. For example, you could store all your files concerning your budget in a folder called **Budget**, or you could store all your letters in a folder called **Correspondence**. To draw an analogy from everyday life: it is better to store your clothes on different shelves in a wardrobe, than to keep them all together in a trunk.*

CREATING A FOLDER

▧ To create a new folder in your **My Documents** folder, open the **My Documents** folder directly. For this purpose, click the **start** button followed by the **My Documents** option.

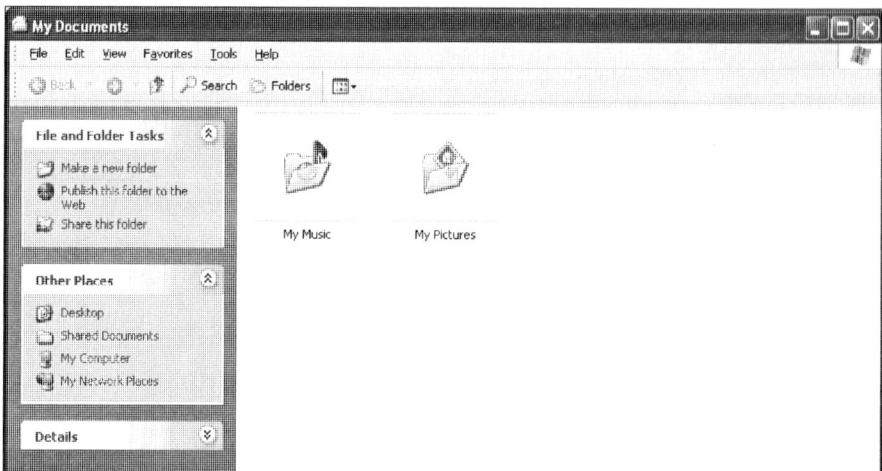

The **My Documents** window appears on the screen. Its left-hand pane offers a number of options in the form of hyperlinks.

▧ To create a folder in your **My Documents** folder (on the same level as the **My Music** folder and the **My Pictures** folder) do not select any folder or file in the **My Documents** window.

To create a subfolder of an existing folder, double-click the folder concerned (for example, the **My Pictures** folder).

Click the **Make a new folder** link in the **File and Folder Tasks** box in the left-hand pane (if the options of this box are not visible, click the button first). If your **File and Folder Tasks** box does not offer a **Make a new folder** link, you must have already selected a folder or file in the window. Deselect this folder or file by clicking in the white area of the right-hand pane that is not occupied by any particular folder or file.

Alternatively, you can right-click an empty space of the right-hand pane then choose the **New** option followed by the **Folder** option.

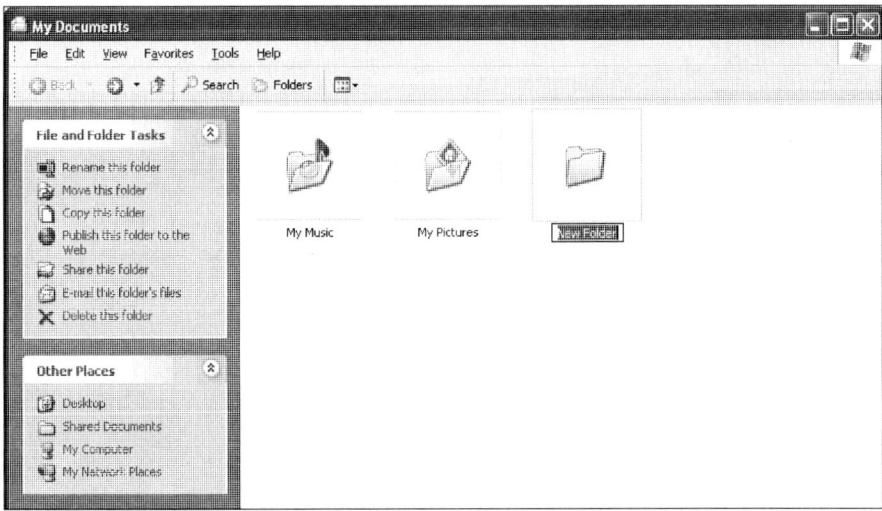

A new icon appears in the right-hand pane. This folder is called **New Folder** for the moment: this name is highlighted and the insertion point blinks at the end of it, indicating that you can change it.

Enter the name of your new folder: your name can be up to 255 characters long, including spaces; you can use uppercase or lowercase letters, or both, but you cannot insert the following characters: \ / ? : * " < > or |.

Press the key to validate the name of your new folder.

Windows creates your new folder empty.

Managing folders and files

Whatever you want to do with your folders or files (for example, to copy, move or delete one or more of your folders or files) you must start by selecting the folder(s) or file(s) concerned.

SELECTING FOLDERS AND FILES

▨ Open the folder window that contains the folders or files you want to select.

▨ If necessary, change the presentation of the file list using the ⬚▾ button and/or sort the file list using the **View - Arrange Icons by** command.

▨ To select several adjacent files in the list, point to an empty space just to the right of the first name you want to select then drag the mouse so that the dotted rectangle that appears surrounds the names and icons concerned then release the mouse button.

Be careful: if the mouse pointer appears as a black circle with a diagonal bar across it and the file names move with the mouse pointer, release the mouse button immediately and start again.

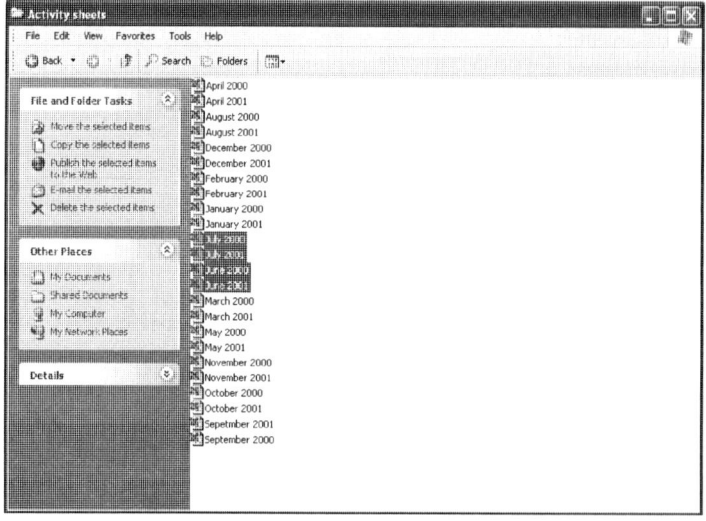

Four files have been selected in this example.

▨ To extend your selection of adjacent files to include other files further down the list, press the ⌷Shift⌷ key then click the document name you would like to appear at the end of the list.

For instance, if you want to include the **March 2000** and **March 2001** files in the example selection above, press the ⌷Shift⌷ key then click the **March 2001** file name.

- To include another group of adjacent files or folders from the open folder (that is not adjacent to the existing group), press the Shift key then drag the mouse so that the dotted rectangle that appears surrounds the names and icons of the new group you want to include in your selection. When you are satisfied with your new selection, release the mouse button followed by the Shift key.

- To include another single file or folder from the open folder (that is not adjacent to the existing group), press the Ctrl key then click the name of the file or folder concerned.

  For instance, if you want to include the **December 2001** file into the example selection above, press the Ctrl key then click the **December 2001** file name.

- To select all the files and folders contained in the open folder, use the **Edit - Select All** command or press the Ctrl **A** key combination.

- To invert your selection, use the **Edit - Invert Selection** command.

 **When you have selected a group of folders or files you can right-click your selection to view the menu options you can apply to your selection (this is called a shortcut menu).**

If you select one or more folders or files by mistake, you can withdraw them from your current selection without canceling your whole selection.

CANCELING THE SELECTION OF ONE OR MORE FOLDERS OR FILES

- To deselect several folders or files, hold down the Ctrl key and drag the mouse so that the dotted rectangle surrounds the names you want to withdraw from your selection then release the mouse button followed by the Ctrl key.

Managing folders and files

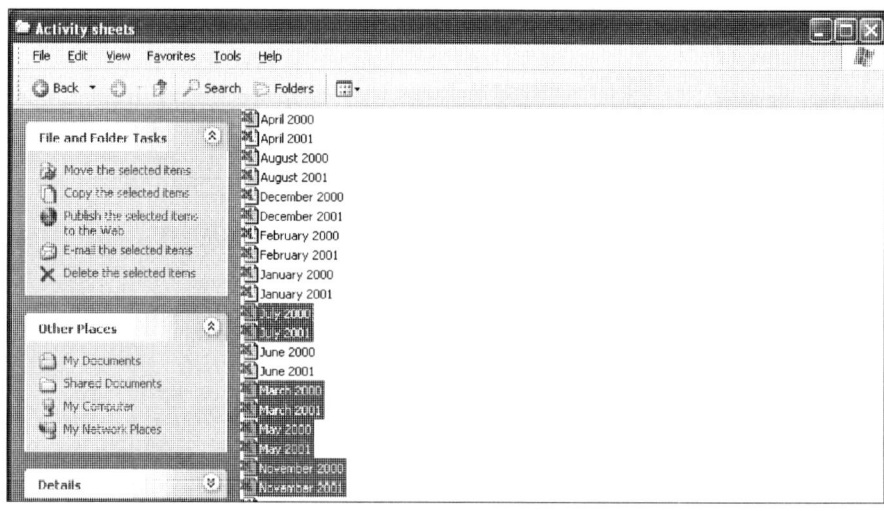

In this example, the *June 2000* and *June 2001* files have been withdrawn from the selection.

▨ To cancel the selection of all the folders and files, click anywhere in the right-hand pane of the folder window (except on a folder or file name).

To select files, you must first access the folder that contains them. If you do not know the name of the folder that contains your files, you can search for your files in all the folders on your hard disk.

SEARCHING FOR FILES ACCORDING TO THEIR NAMES

▨ Click the **start** button on the taskbar then click the **Search** option.

Alternatively, if a folder window is active, you can click the **Search** tool button in this window to display the **Search Results** window.

▨ If necessary, click the button in the **Search Results** window to display this window in full-screen mode and view all the options that the **Search Companion** offers.

By default, a little dog called **Rover** animates the **Search Companion** pane.

Click the **Documents (word processing, spreadsheet, etc.)** option.

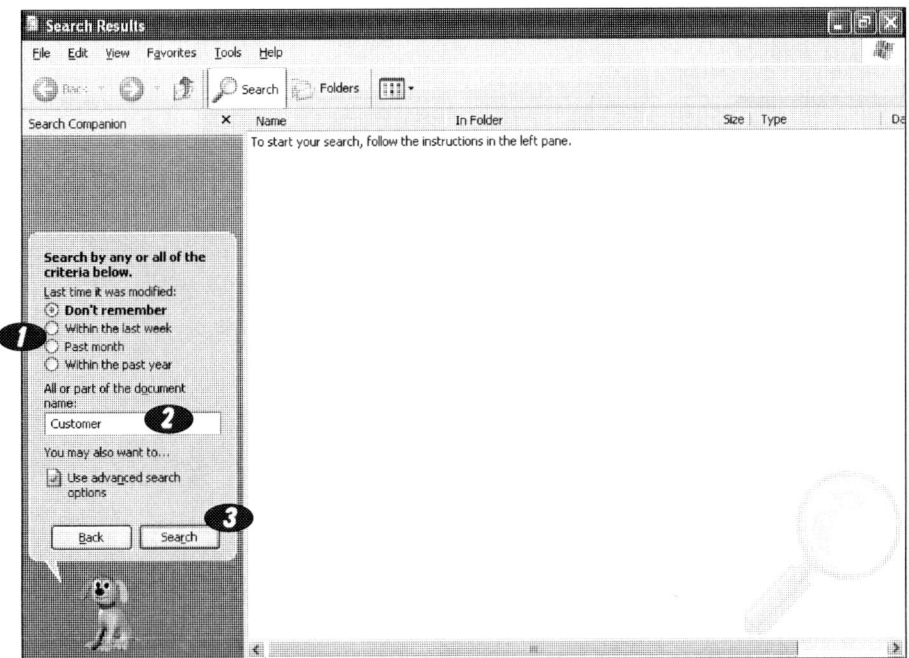

Windows will search for folders and files whose names contain the text you entered
*(**Customer**, in this example).*

1. If you know when the file you seek was last modified, activate one of the three other options. Otherwise, leave the **Don't remember** option active.

2. Enter the name or part of the name of the document you seek. If you are not sure of the exact name of the document, you can use the * and ? wildcard characters: use the asterisk (*) to represent zero or more characters: (for example if you enter **cap***, you will find files called **cap, cape, caption, capture** and so forth); use the question mark (?) to represent one character (for example, if you enter **cap?**, you will find the **cape** file but not the files **cap, caption , capture** and so forth).

3. Click to start the search.

Managing folders and files

When Windows has finished the search, it displays the items it has found in the right-hand pane.

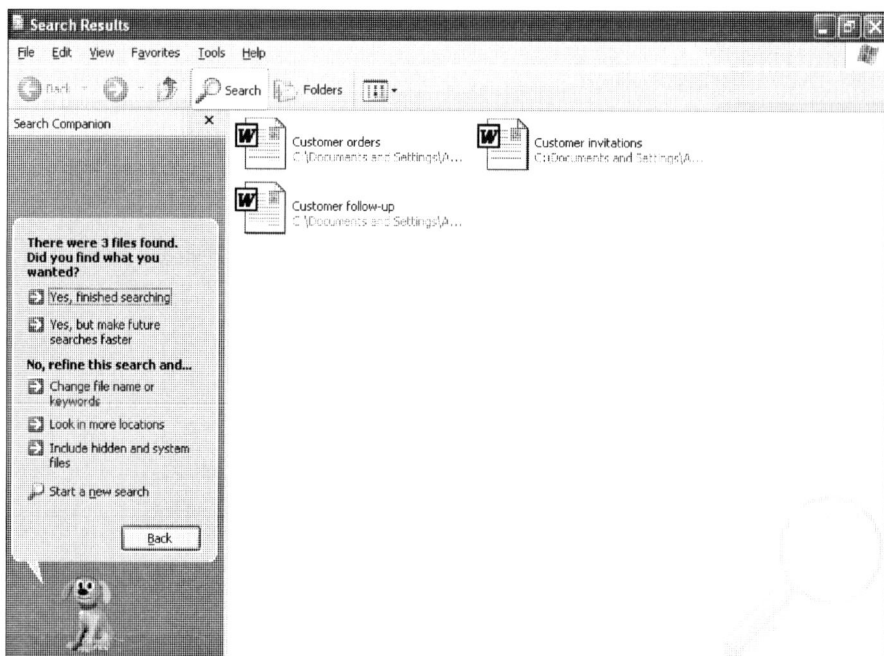

- To view a brief description of one of the files found, point to its name: a description appears in a ScreenTip showing the file's type, author, size and so forth.

- To open one of these files, double-click its name (or its icon): the file opens along with the application that created it.

- To carry out another search, click the **Start a new search** link.

- To close the **Search Companion**, leaving the **Search Results** window open, click the **Yes, finished searching** link.

- To close the **Search Results** window, click the ⊠ button.

My Documents window

To duplicate a folder or a file, you can make a copy of it and possibly rename the duplicate file.

COPYING FOLDERS AND FILES

▒ Click the **start** button then click the **My Documents** option to open your personal folder.

▒ In the left-hand pane of the folder window, select the folder(s) or file(s) you want to copy.

▒ In the **File and Folder Tasks** box of the left-hand pane, click the **Copy this file** link or the **Copy this folder** link or the **Copy the selected items** link, according to what you selected for copy (if none these options are visible, click the ⊗ button in the **File and Folder Tasks** box).

▒ In the **Copy Items** dialog box that appears, click the name of the folder into which you want to copy. If this destination folder is not visible in this dialog box, click the + sign preceding the name of the parent drive or folder.

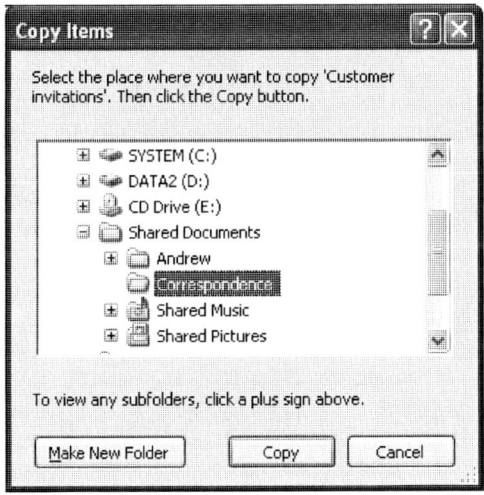

*This example is copying the **Customer Invitations** file into the **Correspondence** folder of the **Shared Documents** folder.*

▒ Click the **Copy** button.

▒ If necessary, close the folder window.

Managing folders and files

 As its name suggests, the **Make New Folder** button on the **Copy Items** dialog box allows you to create your destination folder.

You can also copy folders or files in a folder window, by displaying the **Folders** explorer bar and using the **Copy** and **Paste** commands in the **Edit** menu.

You can duplicate a folder or file by copying it to a floppy disk. You can then give your floppy disk to another person so that he/she can copy it onto his/her computer.

COPYING FOLDERS OR FILES TO A FLOPPY DISK

▦ Check that your floppy disk drive contains a formatted floppy disk (cf. the Formatting a floppy disk section at the end of this chapter).

▦ Open the folder window that contains the folders or files you want to copy to your floppy disk.

▦ Select the folder(s) or the file(s) concerned.

▦ **File - Send To**

▦ Click the option corresponding to your floppy disk drive: this is often called **$3^{1/2}$ Floppy (A)**.

A **Copying** window indicates how the copy is progressing. The noise of the floppy disk drive and its green light also indicate that the copy is underway.

 A standard floppy disk cannot contain more than **1.44 MB (1.44 Megabytes)** or **1474 KB (1474 Kilobytes)**. If the file is too big, Windows displays a message to indicate that it is unable to copy your folders or files to the floppy disk.

My Documents window

If your computer is equipped with a CD writer, Windows XP can copy your files onto a CD-ROM: either a CD-R (Recordable CD-ROM) or a CD-RW (ReWritable CD-ROM). You start by selecting the folders and files you want to copy to your CD. Windows automatically stores your selection in a temporary file and allows you to modify your list. When you are satisfied with this list of items, you can start writing your CD.

COPYING FOLDERS OR FILES TO A CD-ROM

Preparing the CD writer and the computer

▨ Insert your CD-ROM into the CD writer.

▨ Click the **start** button then the **My Computer** option.

▨ Click the icon for the CD writer. This icon generally appears under **Devices with Removable Storage**.

▨ Select the **File - Properties** menu option (or right-click the CD writer icon and choose the **Properties** option).

Note that a standard CD has a capacity of around 650 Megabytes (MB) and that a high-capacity CD can store up to 850 MB.

▨ Under the **General** tab, check how much **Freespace** there is on your CD then click the **Recording** tab.

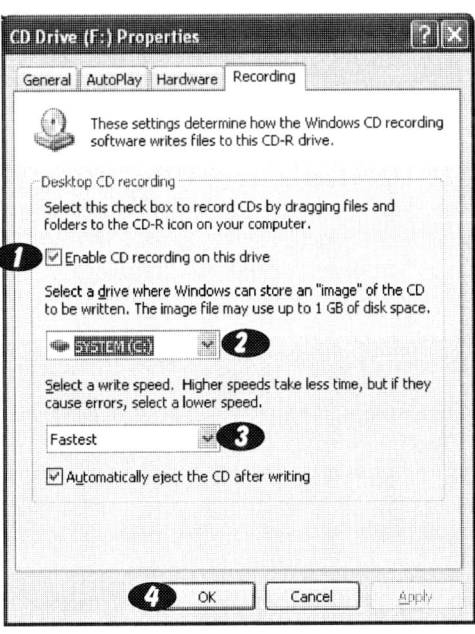

1. Check that this option is active.

2. Select the drive on which Windows can store its temporary file that will contain an image of the items you want to copy.

The size of this file can vary, according to whether your CD has a capacity of 650 MB or 850 MB: Windows will reserve up to 700 MB in the first case or up to 1 Gigabyte (GB) in the second case.

3. In the second drop-down list, select the recording speed. The speed you choose will depend on the type of CD writer you are using.

4. Validate your settings.

Selecting the folders or files you want to copy

▥ Open the folder window for the folders or files you want to copy to the CD-ROM.

▥ To copy a set of files contained in a folder, double-click the folder to open it then select the file(s) concerned. To copy an entire folder, click its name to select it.

▥ If the files are contained in a pictures folder or a video folder (such as **My Pictures** or **My Videos** for example), click either the **Copy to CD** link (if you selected one or more files) or the **Copy all items to CD** link (if you did not select any files, in which case Windows will copy the entire contents of the folder). Windows will then automatically copy the files to its temporary file, ready to be written to your CD.

▥ If the files are contained in a music folder (such as **My Music** for example), click either the **Copy to audio CD** link (if you selected one or more files or folders) or the **Copy all items to audio CD** (if you did not select any file, in which case Windows will copy the entire contents of the folder). Windows will then automatically copy the files to its temporary file, ready to be written to your CD.

▥ In all other cases, when you have selected the file(s) or folder(s) you want to write to your CD, click the **Copy this folder** link or the **Copy this file** link (if you selected only one item) or the **Copy all the items** link (if you selected several items). In this case, the **Copy Items** window opens: click the name of your CD writer then click the **Copy** button.

The files are copied to the temporary file, ready to be written to the CD.

My Documents window

Managing the contents of the temporary file

▨ Click the **start** button then the **My Computer** option.

▨ Double-click the name of your CD writer.

The Files Ready to Be Written to the CD appear:

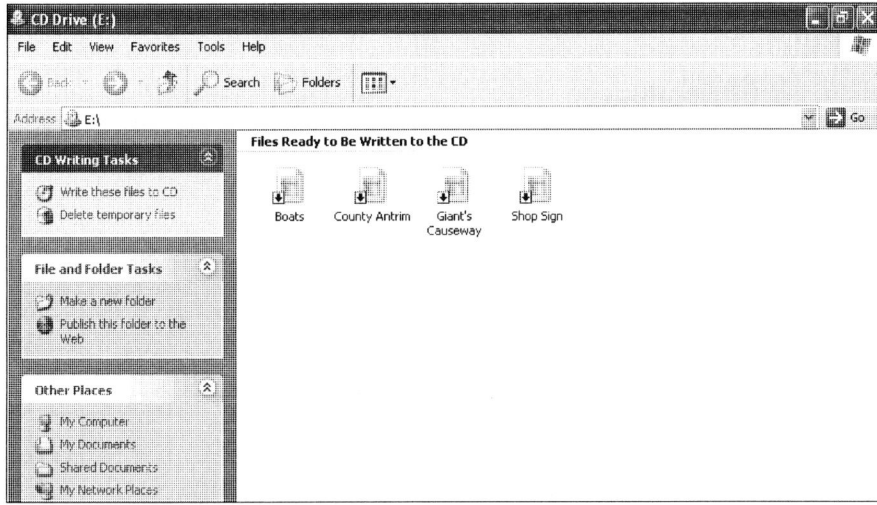

▨ To delete the contents of the temporary file, click the **Delete temporary files** link (this action will not affect your original files).

▨ To delete one of the temporary files, click it then press the Del key and confirm your action by clicking the **Yes** button.

Alternatively, you can click the **Delete this file** link in the **File and Folder Tasks** box of the left-hand pane.

▨ If necessary, click the ⊠ button to close this window.

Writing the files to the CD-ROM

▨ Click the **start** button then the **My Computer** option.

▨ Double-click name of your CD writer.

▨ Check the list of files that are ready to be written to the CD and modify this list if necessary (cf. Managing the contents of the temporary file, above).

It is advisable to check that the volume of the files you want to copy to your CD does not exceed the available space on the CD (cf. Preparing the CD writer and the computer, above). For this purpose, go into **Details** view (by selecting **View - Details**).

Managing folders and files

▓ Start writing to the CD-ROM by clicking the **Write these files to CD** link.

   The **CD Writing Wizard starts.**

▓ In the wizard's first dialog box, if necessary, change the **CD name** (by default, Windows uses the current date for this name).

▓ Click the **Next** button.

   The CD writing software prepares your files then writes them to the CD. The time this process will take depends on the number and size of your files and the characteristics of your CD writer. A progress bar tracks the process.

   The wizard informs you when it has managed to copy your files correctly:

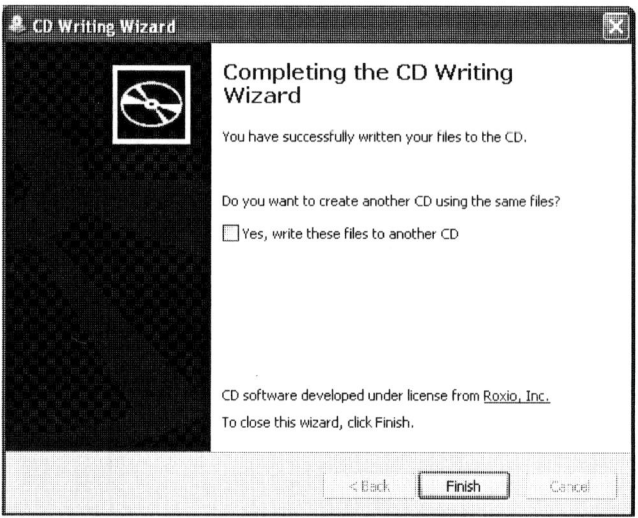

▓ If you want to write another CD, activate the **Yes, write these files to another CD** option.

   In this case, the **Finish** button is replaced by a **Next** button.

   Remove the first CD from the CD writer then insert a new one.

   Click the **Next** button.

   The wizard repeats the process of preparing your files and writing them to the CD.

▓ When you have finished writing your CD(s) click the **Finish** button.

You are strongly advised to check the contents of each CD you write. For this purpose, insert the CD in the CD writer and Windows will display the contents of the CD automatically. If the CD'is already in the CD writer, open **My Computer** (select **start - My Computer** option) then double-click the name of your CD writer. Windows displays the **Files Currently on the CD**.

When you have created a folder or copied a file, you can always change its name.

RENAMING A FOLDER OR A FILE

Click the **start** button then the **My Documents** option to open your personal folder window.

Select the folder or the file whose name you want to change.

Under **File and Folder Tasks,** click the **Rename this folder** link or the **Rename this file** link, according to whether you selected a folder or a file.

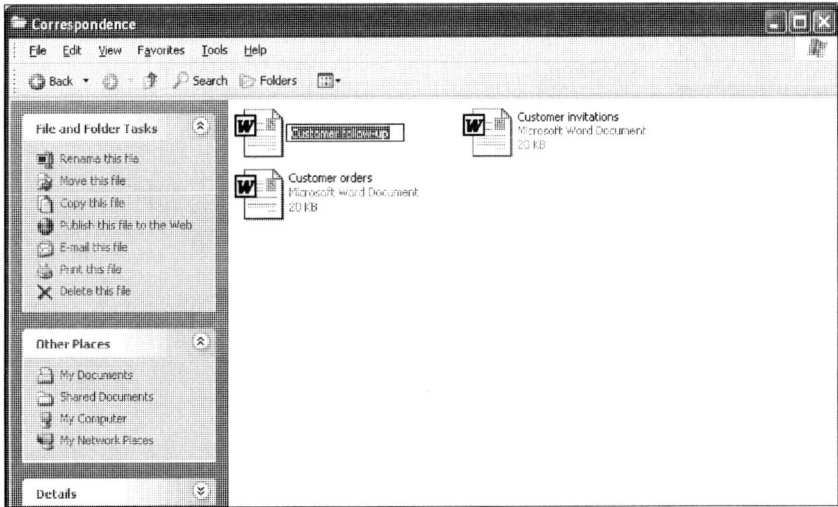

The name of the folder or file appears highlighted and the insertion point blinks to indicate that you can change the text.

You can use the arrow keys to move the insertion point around in the name.

Managing folders and files

Remember that you cannot insert the following characters in the name: \ / ? : * " < > or |.

▨ Validate your new name by pressing the ⏎ key.

Windows changes the name as required, provided that your new name is valid and that an item of the same name does not already exist in the folder.

When you have created your folders, you can store appropriate files or folders in them. You can always copy these files into your new folders, but this approach will use more space than necessary and needlessly complicate your file management. It is generally a much better idea, simply to move your folders and files from one folder to another.

MOVING FOLDERS AND FILES

▨ Click the **start** button then the **My Documents** option to open your personal folder window.

▨ Select the folder(s) or the file(s) you want to move.

▨ Under **File and Folder Tasks** in the left-hand pane of the window, click the **Move this folder** link or the **Move this file** link (if you selected only one folder or file) or the **Move the selected items** link (if you selected several folders and/or files).

▨ In the **Move Items** dialog box, click the name of the folder into which you want to move your folders or files. If this destination folder is not visible, click the + sign preceding the device name and the parent folder.

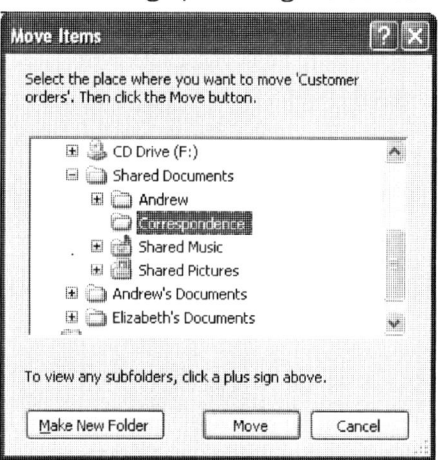

This example shows the Cus-tomer orders document being moved to the Corres-pondence subfolder of the Shared Documents folder.

- Click the **Move** button.
- If necessary, close the folder window.

As its name suggests, the **Make New Folder** button in the **Move Items** dialog box allows you to create a new destination folder.

*To tidy up your hard disk, you can delete files you no longer need. However, deleting a file by accident can cause hours or even days of extra work. To safeguard against such handling errors, Windows allows you to delete your files in two stages: first, Windows copies these files to the **Recycle Bin**. The files no longer appear in your folder, but they are still present on your disk and you can recover them at any time. To remove your files permanently from your hard disk, you must delete them from the **Recycle Bin**.*

DELETING FOLDERS AND FILES

- Click the **start** button then the **My Documents** option to open your personal folder window.
- Select the folder(s) or the file(s) you want to delete.
- Under **File and Folder Tasks** in the left-hand pane of the window, click the **Delete this folder** link or the **Delete this file** link (if you selected only one folder or file) or the **Delete the selected items** link (if you selected several folders and/or files).

   Alternatively, you can press the [Del] key or use the **File - Delete** command.

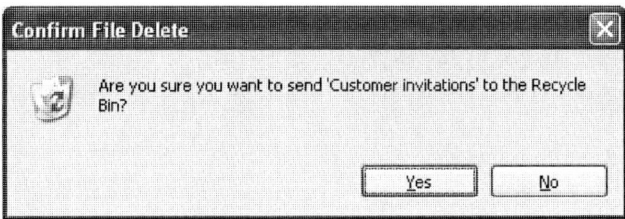

- Click the **Yes** button to confirm that you want to send the folder(s) or file(s) to the Recycle Bin.

Managing folders and files

Almost immediately, the folder(s) or file(s) disappear from the folder window. **When you delete a folder, you also delete all the files and any subfolders it contains**.

This deletion is not final: the documents you have deleted are still present on the disk although they are no longer visible in your folder window.

To delete files permanently and free the disk space they occupy, you must either delete the files in the Recycle Bin or empty the Recycle Bin.

Important note: if you delete items from a drive other than your computer's hard disk (for example, from a floppy disk or from a drive on the network) Windows does not use the Recycle Bin and you will not be able to recover these files later.

 If the files you want to delete are contained in several folders, you can run a search for them then select them in the **Search Results** window before deleting them.

 To delete a file permanently from your disk without using the Recycle Bin, select it and press the [Shift][Del] keys instead of the [Del] key alone. Do not use this key combination unless you are absolutely sure that you want to delete the files you have selected.

When you have deleted a file you can still view it in, and recover it from, a special folder called the **Recycle Bin**.

MANAGING FOLDERS AND FILES IN THE RECYCLE BIN

▦ To view files you have deleted, double-click the **Recycle Bin** icon on your desktop to open this folder.

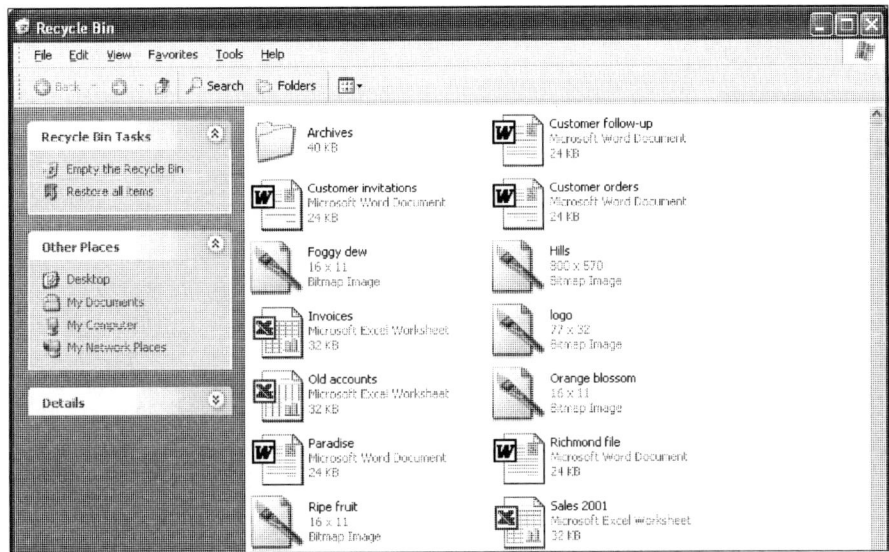

The folders and files contained in the Recycle Bin appear. You can manage this list as you would manage the list of items in any other folder: the options of the **View** menu allow you to define its presentation.

To recover one or more files or folders from the Recycle Bin, select the items concerned in this window then, under **Recycle Bin Tasks** in the left-hand pane of the window, click the **Restore this item** link (if you selected only one folder or file) or the **Restore the selected items** link (if you selected several folders and/or files).

The files and/or folders disappear from the Recycle Bin. Windows restores each item to the folder from which it was deleted, recreating this folder if it no longer exists.

To restore all the items in the Recycle Bin to the folders from which they were deleted, make sure that no folder or file is selected and click the **Restore all items** link under **Recycle Bin Tasks** in the left-hand pane of the window.

To delete permanently one or more folders and/or files and thereby free the disk space that they occupy, select the folders and/or files in the Recycle Bin window then select **File - Delete** or press the ⎡Del⎤ key. Confirm your action by clicking the **Yes** button.

- To delete permanently all the folders and files in the Recycle Bin, click the **Empty the Recycle Bin** link under **Recycle Bin Tasks** in the left-hand pane of the window. Confirm your action by clicking the **Yes** button.

After you have emptied your Recycle Bin, it will remain empty until you delete other folders or files.

 To delete permanently all the folders and files in the Recycle Bin, you can also right-click the **Recycle Bin** icon on your desktop and choose the **Empty Recycle Bin** option.

When you compress an item, such as a file, folder or program, you reduce its size and thereby reduce the amount of disk space you need to store it. In addition, when a file is compressed, it takes less time to transfer it to another computer.
When you compress items, you create a specific folder to store them in their compressed state.

COMPRESSING FOLDERS AND FILES

Compressing into a compressed (zipped) folder

- Open the folder window in which you want to create the compressed folder.
- Do not select anything.
- Create a new compressed folder by opening the **File** menu, pointing to the **New** option then clicking the **Compressed (zipped) Folder** option.

Windows creates a new compressed folder and highlights the default folder name it provides to suggest that you change it.

- If necessary, change the default name that Window provides then confirm your new name by pressing the ⏎ key.

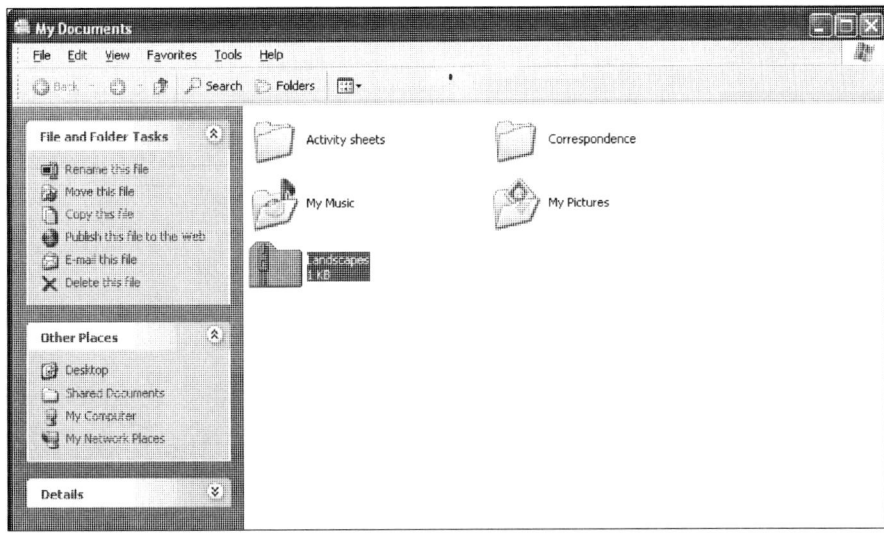

*In this example a new compressed folder called **Landscapes** has been created in the **My Documents** folder. Notice the special symbol on the icon, in the form of a zip.*

▓ Open the folder window that contains the folders and or files you want to compress. If this folder is not visible in the active window, use the **Folders** explorer bar to select it (click the **Folders** [image] tool button to show the **Folders** bar).

▓ Select the files and/or folders you want to compress.

▓ Right-click your selection to display its specific shortcut menu.

▓ Click the **Copy** option.

▓ If necessary, close the **Folders** bar by clicking the **Folders** [image] tool button.

▓ Click the **Back** [image] tool button once or more, until you view the compressed folder.

▓ Right-click the name of the compressed folder then click the **Paste** option.

Windows automatically compresses your files and/or folders.

▓ If necessary, close the active folder window by clicking the ☒ button.

Managing folders and files

You can copy a compressed folder to another computer on the network or to another folder on your hard disk. A user on the destination computer will be able to manage the compressed folder provided that the destination computer runs a program that handles the zip format.

To send a compressed file as an e-mail attachment, you must send the compressed folder that contains the file.

Decompressing a compressed folder

▓ Open the folder window that contains the compressed folder that you want to decompress.

▓ Double-click the name of the compressed folder concerned.

▓ Click the **Extract all files** link under **Folder Tasks** in the left-hand pane of the window.
   The **Extraction Wizard** opens.

▓ Click the **Next** button.

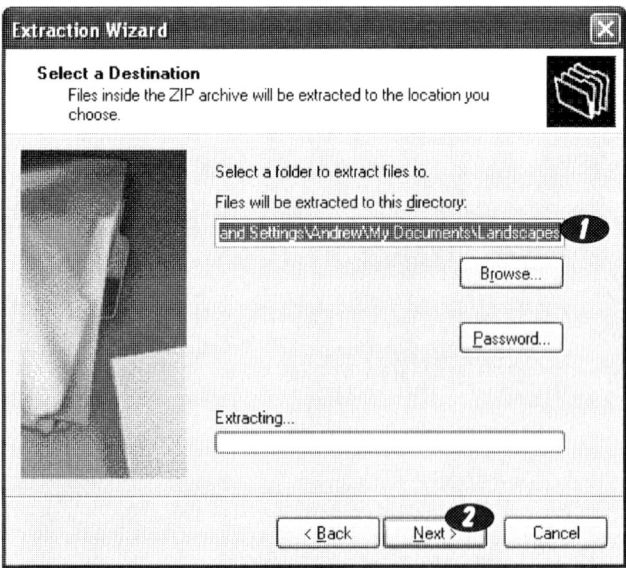

My Documents window

1. Enter the address of the folder you want to receive the extracted files or click the **Browse** button to select a folder on your computer.

2. Click the **Next** button.

- To view the extracted files, activate the **Show extracted files** option.

- Click the **Finish** button.

- If necessary, close the compressed folder window and the folder window that contains the extracted folders and/or files.

If your computer has an e-mail application (for example, Outlook 2002) and an Internet connection (via a modem, for example) you can send copies of your documents to other people who also have e-mail addresses.

SENDING FILES BY E-MAIL

- Open the folder window that contains the file(s) you want to send by e-mail.

- Select the file(s) concerned.

- **File - Send To**

- Click the **Mail Recipient** option.

  Windows automatically starts your default e-mail application (Outlook 2002, for example).

- Specify the recipients and the subject of your message together with any covering note you require then send your message, as you would send any other message with your e-mail application.

  The files you selected will be sent as attachments.

Managing folders and files

Although most commercially available floppy disks are preformatted, you may some-times need to format or to reformat a floppy disk. This operation allows your operating system to organise the floppy disk according to the characteristics of your computer's floppy-disk drive (in particular, it determines the capacity of the floppy disk).

FORMATTING A FLOPPY DISK

▓ Insert the floppy disk in your floppy-disk drive.

▓ Open the **My Computer** window using the **start** - **My Computer** command.

▓ <u>Right-click</u> the icon for your floppy-disk drive, which is often called **3 $^{1/2}$ Floppy(A:)**.

▓ Click the **Format** option.

The capacity of the floppy disk is ex-pressed in Megabytes (MB) or in Kilobytes (KB). Remember that a byte is the space required to store a character. The informa-tion 3.5" refers to the physical dimension of the floppy disk.

1. If necessary, define the **Capacity** of the floppy disk according to its physical characteristics: for a High Density floppy disk, choose **1.44 MB**, for a Low Density floppy disk, choose **720 KB** (most modern floppy disks are High Density disks).

2. If required, specify the name you want to give your floppy disk. This name cannot be longer than 11 characters (for FAT file systems).

3. If your floppy disk has already been formatted, activate the **Quick Format** option to allow Windows to delete the contents of the floppy disk, without checking the sectors on the disk.

4. Click the **Start** button to start formatting.

A message appears to warn you that the formatting operation will delete all the files on your floppy disk.

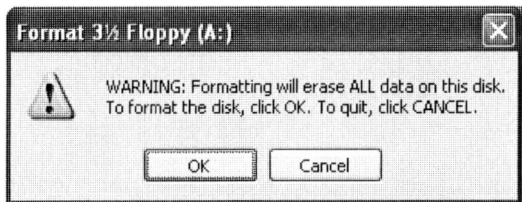

Click the **OK** button to confirm that you want to format your floppy disk.

At the end of the operation, click the **OK** button in response to the message informing you that the formatting is complete.

Click the **Close** button in the **Format 3** $^{1/2}$ **Floppy (A:)** dialog box.

If you try to use a floppy disk that has not been formatted, Windows will display an error message indicating that the floppy disk has not been formatted and offering to do it for you.

This final part describes features you can use to customize your environment and to install or uninstall an application.

4th Part

Changing the environment

Managing users

With Windows XP several users can work on the same computer. Each user has his/her own environment, characteristics and permissions. For example, you can define one working environment for yourself, and for your children, another working environment in which you restrain certain features, such as access to the Internet or to important documents that you want to protect.

USERS OVERVIEW

▨ Windows XP offers three <u>types</u> of user account, with varying permissions:

Computer administrator account can:

- create and delete user accounts,
- change account settings (such as the picture, the password and the type),
- manage network passwords, create a reset password disk and set up his/her own account to use a .NET Passport.

This type of account is for people who need to make system level changes to the computer, to install applications and to access all non-private files of the computer. Only a Computer administrator user has full access to all the other user accounts on the computer. There must always be a Computer administrator account on a computer.

Limited account can:

- not usually install applications or hardware components, but can generally access applications that have already been installed on the computer,
- can change the picture associated with his/her own account and password,
- not change the name or type of his/her account,
- manage his/her network passwords, create a reset password disk and set up his/her own account to use a .NET Passport.

This type of account is for people who must not be able to change most computer settings or delete important files.

Guest account is similar to a **Limited** account, except that **Guest** accounts do not have passwords.

This type of account is for users who do not have personal accounts on the computer.

To find out the type of your account, open the **User accounts** window by selecting **start - Control Panel - User Accounts**: the type of your account appears next to your account picture, beneath your user name.

If you have just bought your computer, it probably has just one user account: that of a Computer administrator.

If someone else must work with your computer, you can create (add) a new user account on your computer so that the user can work in his/her own environment. For this purpose, you must be logged on with a Computer administrator account.

ADDING A USER ACCOUNT TO YOUR COMPUTER

▨ Click the **start** button, followed by the **Control Panel** button.

▨ Click the **User Accounts** link.

▨ Click the **Create a new account** link.

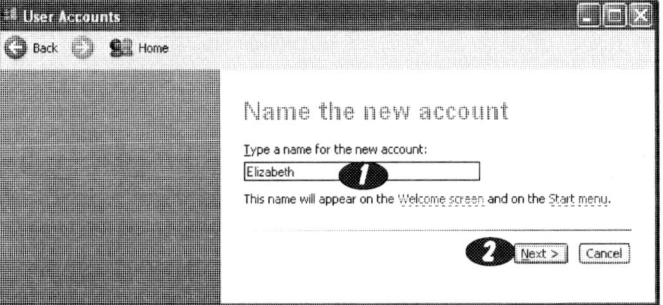

This example adds an account to the computer's list of existing user accounts, for Elizabeth.

1. Enter the user name.

2. Click the **Next** button.

▨ Specify the type of account this user must have, by activating the **Computer administrator** option or the **Limited** option.

When you point to one of these options, you view a list of actions that a user with this account type can carry out.

▨ Click the **Create Account** button.

Managing users

▨ Click the ⊠ button in the **User Accounts** window followed by the ⊠ button in the **Control Panel** window.

When you have defined several users, you can access the working environment of a specific user.

LOGGING ON AS ANOTHER USER

▨ To log on as another user, click the **start** button followed by the **Log Off** button.

▨ To log on as a new user, without logging off the current user, click the **Switch User** button (⬍); to log on as a new user after logging off as the current user, click the **Log Off** button (🔑) and save any open documents, as necessary.

Changing the environment

The Windows XP welcome screen or the **Log On to Windows** dialog box appears.

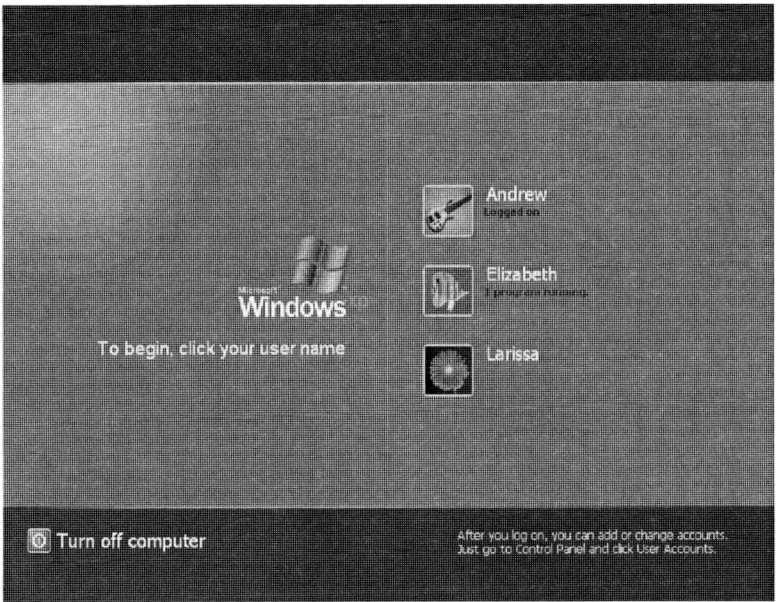

In the Windows Welcome screen, open sessions are indicated by the **Logged on** message or by the number of programs that are currently running. In the above example, two users are logged on: Andrew and Elizabeth.

On the Windows Welcome screen, click the name of the user as whom you want to log on then enter the user's password, if required. If the **Log On to Windows** dialog box appears, enter the user name and any password required then click **OK**.

If you did not log off the previous user, he/she stays logged on in the background. To reactivate this user account, use the **start - Log Off** command again.

Managing users

Several users can be logged on at the same time only if you activate the **Use Fast User Switching** option (**start - Control Panel - User Accounts - Change the way users log on or off**). If this option is not active the **start - Log Off** command will display the following dialog box:

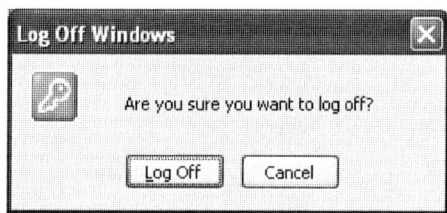

In this case, you must log off as one user to be able to log on as another user.

If you do not want other people to use your account, you must set a password for it. If you are the only user of your computer who has a Computer administrator account then you must set passwords for Users who ask you to do so.
*Remember that a **Computer administrator** has full permission to change user accounts (for example, a Computer administrator can associate a password with his/her own account and also with those of the other users) while a **Limited** user has partial permission to change user accounts (for example, a **Limited** user can change the password associated only with his/her account).*

ASSOCIATING A PASSWORD WITH A USER

▨ Open the **User Accounts** dialog box (**start - Control Panel - User Accounts**).

▨ If you are logged on as the Computer administrator, click the name of the user to whom you want to give a password in the **or pick an account to change** list (this can be your own account).

If you are using a **Limited** type of account, you will not be able to access other user accounts: your own will be activated automatically.

▨ Click the **Create a password** link.

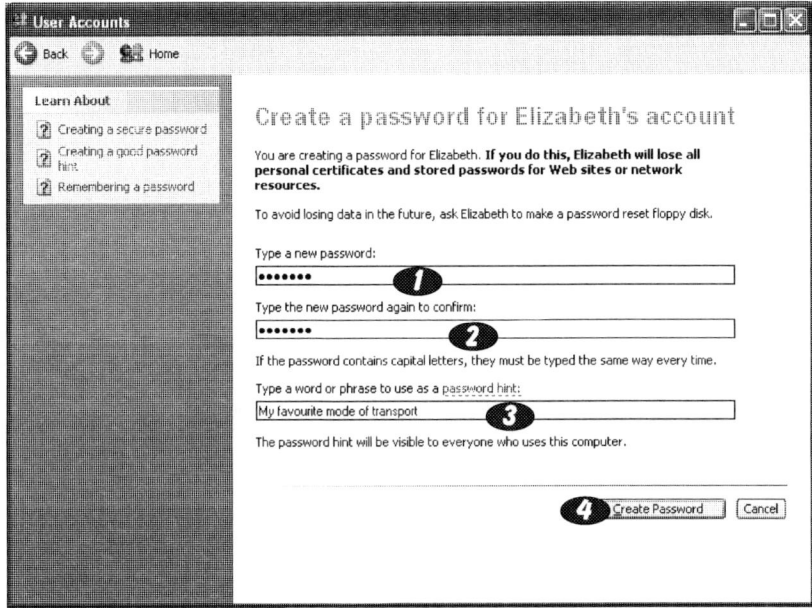

1. Enter the password: the characters you enter appear on the screen as dots, since the password must stay invisible.

2. Enter the password a second time to confirm it.

Windows takes into account the character case: that is, it differentiates between capitals and lowercase letters.

3. If you are afraid of losing your password, enter a word or a phrase that will give a hint to what your password is: this text will help you to remember your password if you have forgotten it.

4. Click the **Create Password** button.

If you are logged on as the Computer administrator, Windows XP will ask if you want to make your files and folders private.

Managing users

▨ To prevent other users from accessing your folders or files (despite the password protection), click the **Yes, Make Private** button. Otherwise, click the **No** button.

For more information on private folders, see the Protecting your personal folders section.

▨ Click the button in the **User Accounts** window followed by the ⊠ button in the **Control Panel** window.

 To display the **Password Hint** when you are entering the password in the Windows XP Welcome screen, click the ❓ button.

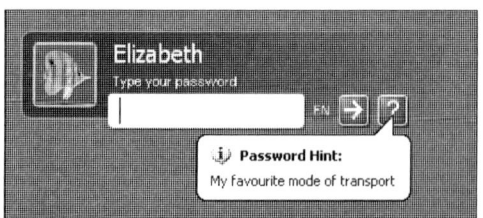

You can change your password at any time. If you have a Computer administrator account, you can change other users' passwords as well.

CHANGING A PASSWORD

▨ Open the **User Accounts** dialog box (**start - Control Panel - User Accounts**).

▨ If you are logged on as the Computer administrator, click the name of the user account whose password you wish to modify in the **or pick an account to change** list (this can be the name of your own account).

If you are using a **Limited** type of account, you will not be able to access other user accounts: your own account will be activated automatically.

▨ Click the **Change my password** link, if you are changing your own account or the **Change the password** link, if you are working on someone else's account.

▨ Enter the password required to log on in the first box.

▨ Enter the new password in the second box.

- Enter the password a second time to confirm it in the third box.

- If you are afraid of forgetting your password, enter a word or a phrase in the last box that will give a hint of what your password is: this text will help you to remember your password if you have forgotten it.

  Changing the password erases the old password hint automatically. If you wish to keep the same password hint, you will have to enter it again.

- Click the **Change Password** button.

- Click the 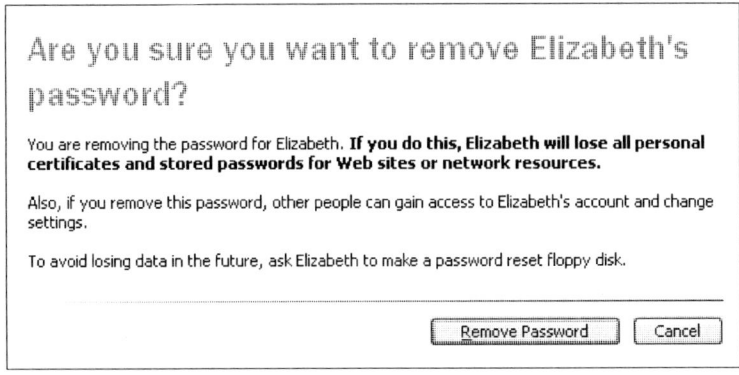 button in the **User Accounts** window followed by the ⊠ button in the **Control Panel** window.

You can delete your password at any time. If you have a Computer administrator account, you can delete other users' passwords as well.

DELETING A PASSWORD

- Open the **User Accounts** dialog box (**start - Control Panel - User Accounts**).

- If you are logged on as the Computer administrator, click the name of the user account whose password you wish to remove in the **or pick an account to change** list (this can be the name of your own account).

  If you are using a **Limited** type of account, you will not be able to access other user accounts: your own will be activated automatically.

- Click the **Remove my password** link, if you are changing your own account or the **Remove the password** link, if you are working on someone else's account.

- If you are removing a password for an account other than the active account, Windows XP points out the consequences of removing the password:

Are you sure you want to remove Elizabeth's password?

You are removing the password for Elizabeth. **If you do this, Elizabeth will lose all personal certificates and stored passwords for Web sites or network resources.**

Also, if you remove this password, other people can gain access to Elizabeth's account and change settings.

To avoid losing data in the future, ask Elizabeth to make a password reset floppy disk.

[Remove Password] [Cancel]

Managing users

▓ When you have read the message, click the **Remove Password** button, if you still want to remove the password, or if you have decided not to, click **Cancel**.

▓ If you want to delete your own password, Windows reminds you what effect this will have and asks you to identify yourself:

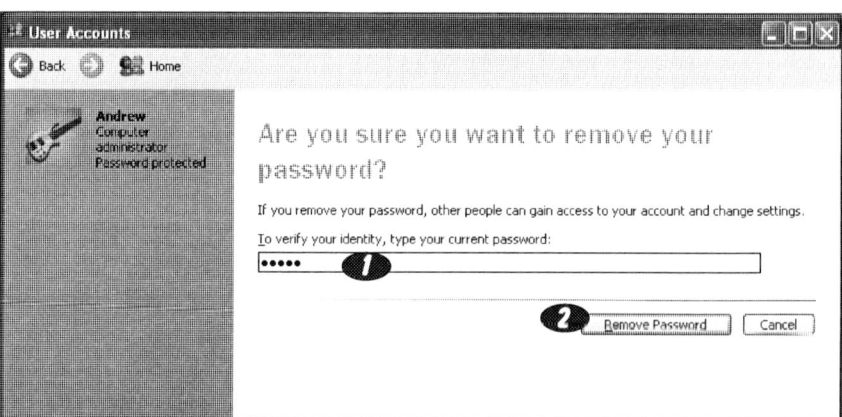

1. Once you have read this message, enter your password to identify yourself.

2. Click this button if you still wish to remove your password; otherwise, click the **Cancel** button.

▓ Click the ⊠ button in the **User Accounts** window followed by the ⊠ button in the **Control Panel** window.

Remember that the Computer administrator can change anything on a user account, but a Limited user can change only certain settings. If you are logged on as a Computer administrator, you can change your user name or that of another user of your computer (for example, if the name is no longer suitable for any reason).

CHANGING A USER NAME

▨ Open the **User Accounts** dialog box (**start - Control Panel - User Accounts**).

▨ In the **or pick an account to change** list, click the user name that you want to modify (this can be your own account, if you wish).

▨ Click the **Change the name** link (or the **Change my name** link if you are working on your own user account).

▨ Enter or change the user name in the **Type a name for** text box and click the **Change Name** button.

▨ Click the ☒ button in the **User Accounts** window followed by the ☒ button in the **Control Panel** window.

If you use the Windows XP Welcome screen to log on, you will have noticed that a picture is associated with each user. If you no longer want the current picture, you can choose another picture that Windows offers or use another one from your hard disk.

CHANGING A USER'S PICTURE

▨ Open the **User Accounts** dialog box (**start - Control Panel - User Accounts**).

▨ If you are logged on as the Computer administrator, click the user name concerned in the **or pick an account to change** list (this can be your own account, if you wish).

If you are using a **Limited** type of account, you will not be able to access other user accounts: your own will be activated automatically.

▨ Click the **Change the picture** link (or **Change my picture** if you are working on your account).

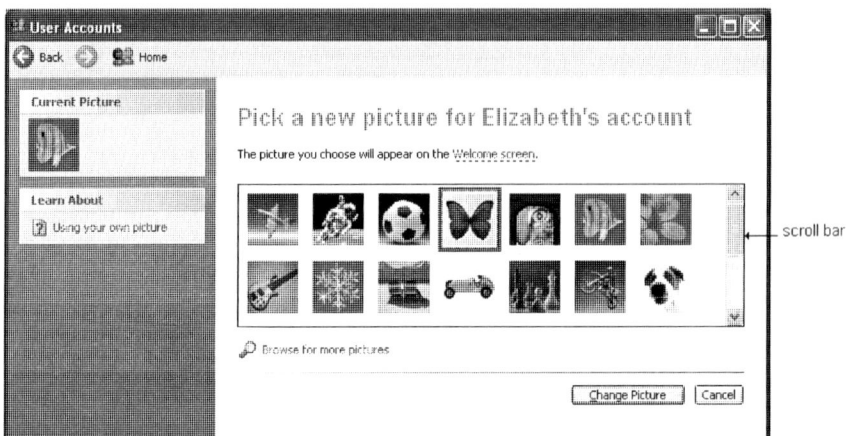

The title of this window becomes **Pick a new picture for your account** if you are changing the picture for your own account.

▓ To use one of the pictures suggested by Windows for the user in question, scroll through them with the vertical scroll bar and click the one you require. Confirm your choice by clicking the **Change Picture** button.

▓ To **Browse for more pictures** other than those offered by Windows, click the corresponding link then, using the **Open** dialog box, select the required picture file (by default Windows looks for bmp, gif, jpg and png files). Click the **Open** button to confirm your choice.

▓ Click the ☒ button in the **User Accounts** window followed by the ☒ button in the **Control Panel** window.

Changing the environment

As the Users overview section of this chapter described, a user will have different permissions according to whether he/she has a Computer administrator account or a Limited user account. If a user's account type is no longer appropriate, you can change it. Only Computer administrators can use this feature.

CHANGING THE USER ACCOUNT TYPE

▦ Open the **User Accounts** dialog box (**start - Control Panel - User Accounts**).

▦ In the **or pick an account to change** list, click the user name whose account type you want to modify (this can be your own account, if you wish).

▦ Click the **Change the account type** link (or **Change my account type** if you are working on your own account).

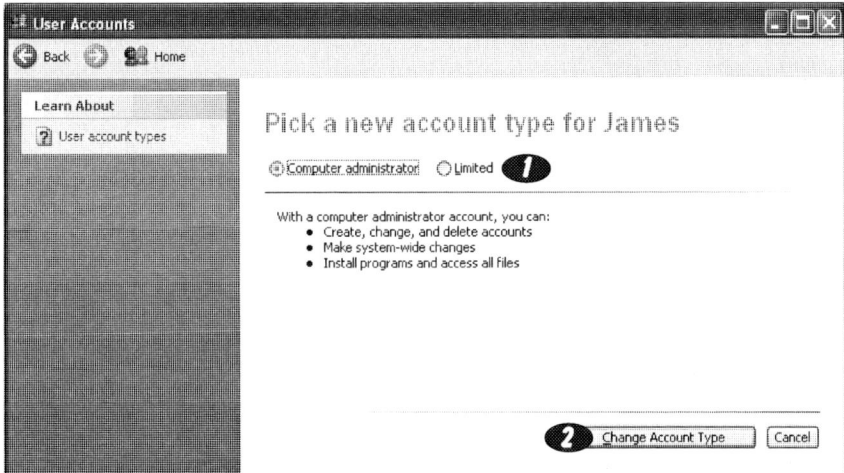

1. Activate the required account type.

2. Click this button.

▦ Click the ❌ button in the **User Accounts** window followed by the ❌ button in the **Control Panel** window.

Managing users

When a user no longer wants to work on the computer, you will want to delete his/her account. Only Computer administrators can use this feature.

DELETING A USER ACCOUNT

▨ Open the **User Accounts** dialog box (**start - Control Panel - User Accounts**).

▨ In the **or pick an account to change** list, click the user name whose account you wish to delete.

▨ Click the **Delete the account** link.

This example is deleting James' user account.

▨ To delete the account along with its folders and files, click the **Delete Files** button.
To delete the account, but keep the user's folders and files, click the **Keep Files** button.

▨ When Windows asks you to confirm that you want to delete the account (along with its folders and files if you requested this action), click the **Delete Account** button.

▨ Click the ⊠ button in the **User Accounts** window followed by the ⊠ button in the **Control Panel** window.

Changing the environment

*To prevent other users from accessing your personal folders, you can make them "private". Your personal folders are those included in your user profile: your **My Documents** folder (and the subfolders it contains, such as **My Pictures** and **My Music** for example), your desktop, **start** menu, Cookies and Favorites.*

PROTECTING YOUR PERSONAL FOLDERS

For this feature to be available, your hard disk must have been formatted as NTFS.

▨ Click the **start** button followed by **My Computer**.

▨ Double-click your hard disk drive on which Windows is installed: this is generally the C: drive.

▨ If the contents of the drive do not appear, click the **Show the contents of this drive** link under **System Tasks** in the left-hand pane.

▨ Double-click the **Documents and Settings** folder.

▨ Double-click your user folder.

Your "user profile" folders appear.

▨ Right-click the folder you want to protect then click the **Properties** option followed by the **Sharing** tab.

▨ Tick the **Make this folder private** option to protect this folder then click the **OK** button.

If your user account does not have a password, Windows displays the following message to point out that even if you make this folder private, if you do not have a password, anyone can log on in your name and access this folder.

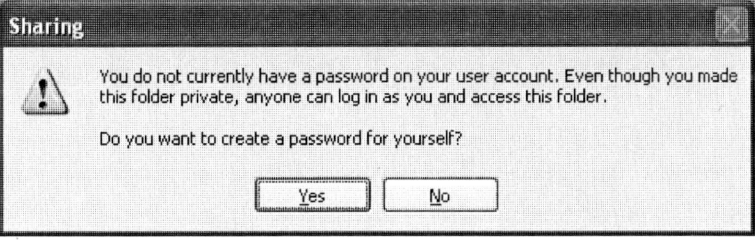

▨ If required, click the **Yes** button to create a password for your user account and make your folder private or click the **No** button to make your folder private, without creating a password for your user account.

▨ Click the ▨ button in your user folder window.

Managing users

With Microsoft .Net Passport you can use the same user name and password to access all Passport-enabled services and Web sites (this concerns all the Microsoft.com sites plus those of other organizations who have entered into a commercial or partnership agreement with Microsoft). Your personal data are encrypted in your "Passport profile" for which Microsoft guarantees total confidentiality. Microsoft also ensures that all Passport information is removed from the computer when you disconnect: this allows you to use public or shared computers safely. If you already have an account with MSN Explorer or Hotmail, this account will act as a passport.

CREATING A MICROSOFT .NET PASSPORT

▨ Check that your Internet connection is active.

▨ Open the **User Accounts** dialog box (**start** - **Control Panel** - **User Accounts**).

▨ If you are logged on as a Computer administrator, click your user name in the **or pick an account to change** list.

If you are logged on as a **Limited** user type, your account is active automatically, as you cannot access other user accounts.

▨ Click the **Set up my account to use a .NET Passport** link.

The **.NET Passport Wizard** starts.

▨ Click the **Next** button.

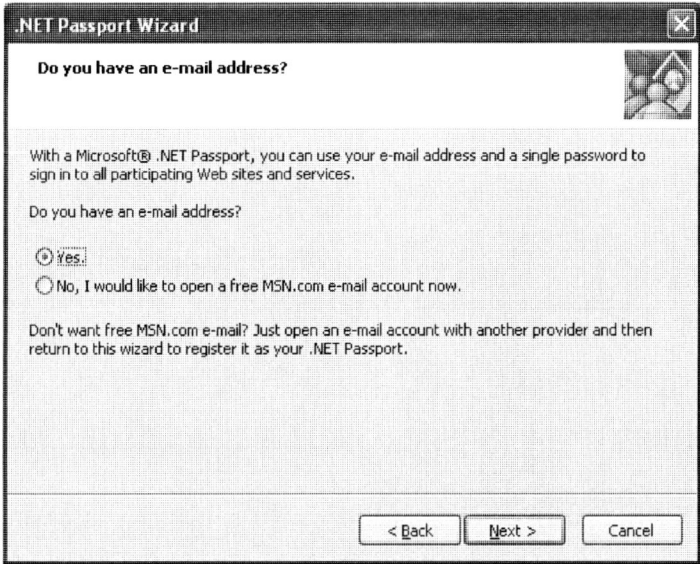

Windows suggests either that you use your existing e-mail address for your new Passport or that you create an e-mail account on MSN.com (Hotmail.com) to use for your Passport.

You want to use your existing e-mail address for your Passport

▓ Activate the **Yes** option then click the **Next** button.

▓ Enter your **E-mail Address** in the text box then click **Next** .

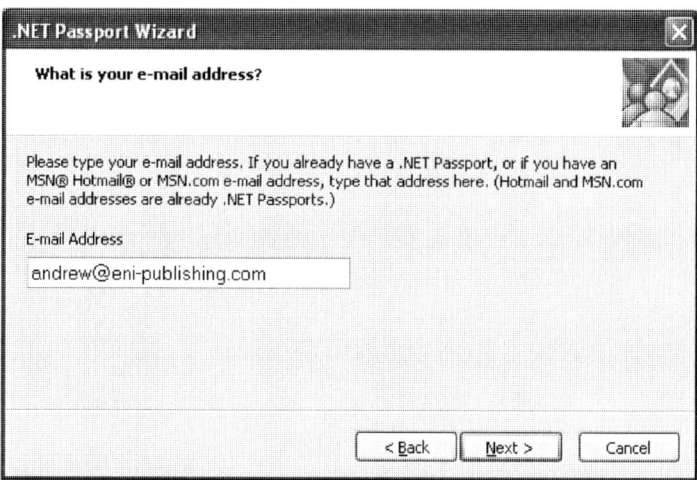

- If you enter a Hotmail or MSN.com e-mail address, Windows asks you to enter your password for this account.

  If you did not enter a Hotmail or MSN.com e-mail address, enter a **Password** for your account then confirm your password by entering it again in the **Retype Password** box.

- Click the **Next** button.

- Carry on creating your Passport account as described in the "You want to create an MSN.com account" section.

You want to create an MSN.com account

▦ Activate the **No, I would like to open a free MSN.com e-mail account now** option then click the **Next** button.

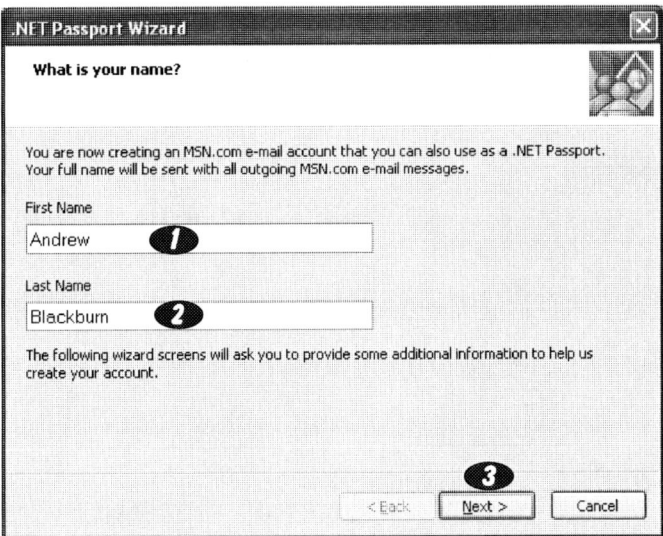

1. Enter your **First Name**.

2. Enter your **Last Name**.

3. Click the **Next** button.

▦ In the **Where do you live?** dialog box, fill in the **Country/Region, State, Zip Code** and **Time Zone** boxes then click the **Next** button.

This window shows the conditions and privacy statements you must accept to use Hotmail and .NET Passport.

▦ To continue creating the account, activate the **I accept the agreement** option then click the **Next** button (otherwise, if you do not want to accept the agreement, click the **Cancel** button, to stop the creation process).

▦ In the **Tell us a little more about yourself** dialog box, fill in the **Birth Date** and **Occupation** boxes then click the **Next** button.

The next step asks you to create your e-mail address:

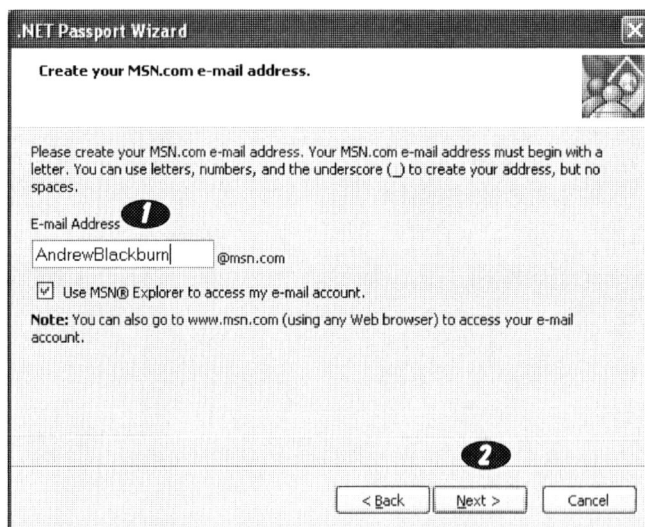

In this example, the full e-mail address would be: AndrewBlackburn @msn.com.

1. Enter the name you want to use for your e-mail address. This name must begin with a letter and can contain letters, numbers and the underscore character (_): for instance, the above example could have used **andrew_blackburn, andrew.blackburn** or **ablackburn**.

2. Click the **Next** button.

Enter a **Password** for your account then confirm your password by entering it again in the **Retype Password** box.

Your password must contain at least six characters: it can contain uppercase and lowercase letters, numbers and standard symbols; on the other hand, it must not contain spaces or extended characters; you may not use the name part of your e-mail address, either.

Click the **Next** button.

As an additional security measure, Windows asks you to choose from the **Secret Question** list then to enter an **Answer** to this question.

With this approach, if you forget your password, before you can create a new one, you must give the exact answer to your question (your favourite film, for example).

Click the **Next** button.

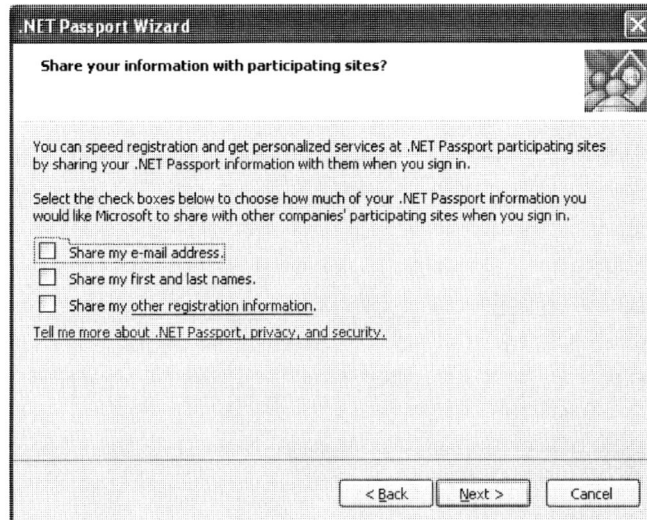

Remember that .NET Passport participating sites include Microsoft sites and sites of other organizations who have entered into commercial agreements and/or partnerships with Microsoft.

▓ You can choose to let other sites that participate in .NET Passport know your **e-mail address**, your **first and last names** and/or **other registration information** that you are using to set up your passport. For this purpose, activate the corresponding option(s). Click the **Next** button.

▓ To be listed in the **Hotmail Member Directory**, activate the corresponding option then click the **Next** button.

Windows tells you that your Windows XP account can now use the .NET Passport you have just created.

▓ Click **Finish** to validate your passport.

Customizing the desktop

The desktop and the taskbar are the two basic elements of the Windows environment. You can create icons (known as shortcuts) on your desktop for rapid access to applications, folders or files. After a while your desktop may become cluttered and your icons may overlap: if this happens it may be time to reorganise your desktop.

REORGANISING THE DESKTOP

▨ To move an icon, point to it, hold down the mouse button and drag it to its new position.

▨ To sort the icons on your desktop, right-click an empty area of the desktop and point to the **Arrange Icons By** option.

▨ Click an option according to how you want to sort your icons: by **Name**, by **Size**, by **Type** or by the date they were last **Modified**. The **Auto Arrange** option aligns your icons horizontally and vertically.

The folder icons appear first on your desktop, followed by the other icons, sorted according to your chosen criterion.

A shortcut represents an object such as a drive, a folder, a file or an application. You can include a shortcut on your desktop to make the drive, folder, file or application readily available.

CREATING A SHORTCUT ON THE DESKTOP

▨ Open the **My Documents** folder (**start - My Documents**) then click the **Folders** button to display your computer's hierarchy.

▨ If necessary, reduce the size of the window by clicking the button to show part of your desktop in the background (you may also need to resize the window by dragging its borders).

▨ Right-click the icon of the drive, folder, file or application for which you want to create a shortcut then click the **Create Shortcut** option.

▨ Drag the shortcut that you have just created from the folder window onto the desktop.

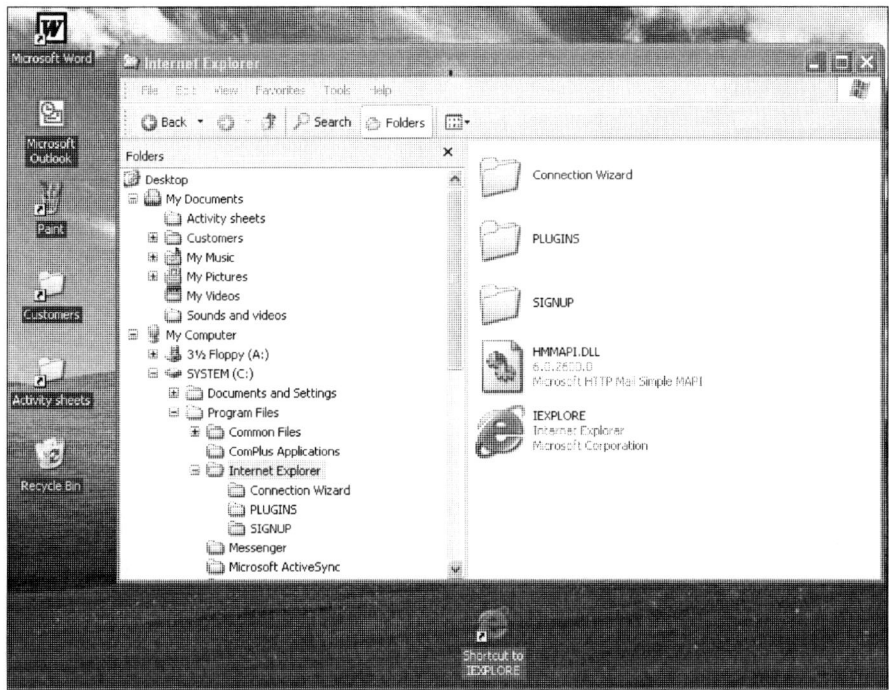

To install a shortcut to the Internet Explorer browser, access the folder that contains
*this application and drag the **IEXPLORE** icon onto the desktop.*
A little arrow appears on the shortcut icon.

- Click the ⊠ button to close the folder window.
- To rename your shortcut, right-click it, click the **Rename** option and enter the new name then press ⏎ to confirm.
- To run the associated application or open the associated drive/folder/file, double-click the shortcut on the desktop.
- To delete a shortcut, right-click its icon and click the **Delete** option. Confirm your action by clicking the **Yes** button.

Customizing the desktop

By default, the Windows XP desktop shows a landscape scene. You can change this image to suit your taste by choosing another background that Windows offers or even by using a photo of your family or one from your holidays last summer, for example.

CHANGING THE DESKTOP BACKGROUND

▓ Right-click an empty space on the desktop then click the **Properties** option.

▓ If necessary, click the **Desktop** tab.

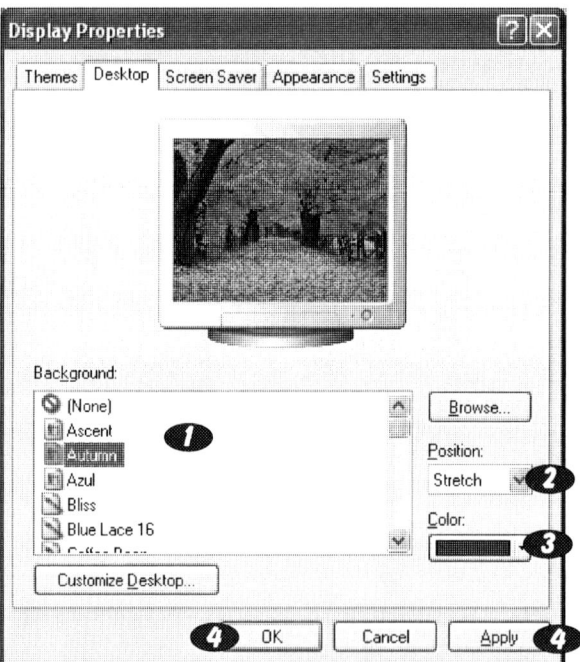

You can preview the settings you choose, in the upper part of the dialog box.

1. Select the file that contains the image you want to appear in your desktop background. If you want to use one of your own pictures, click the **Browse** button then select the corresponding file. The format of this file must one that the Paint application supports; either a bit-mapped format (.bmp or .gif) or a jpeg format (.jpg).

2. Indicate how you want your picture to appear:

Center to centre your picture on the screen.
Tile to repeat your image as necessary to fill the screen.
Stretch to enlarge your image so that it fills the screen.

These options have no effect when the picture already fills the screen.

3. If you chose the **Center** option, you can display a colour around your picture: open the **Color** list then click the colour you want to appear or click the **Other** button to create a custom colour.

4. Validate your settings by clicking **OK** (you can also use the **Apply** button to view the picture on the desktop without closing the **Display Properties** dialog box).

You can also use the desktop display properties to specify a screen saver: a screen saver is an animated image that appears on the screen when the computer has been idle for a certain time. The screen saver hides items that normally appear on the screen, but its main purpose is to preserve the monitor's cathode ray tube by ensuring that a fixed image does not stay on the screen.

DEFINING A SCREEN SAVER

▨ Right-click an empty space on the desktop then click the **Properties** option.

▨ Click the **Screen Saver** tab.

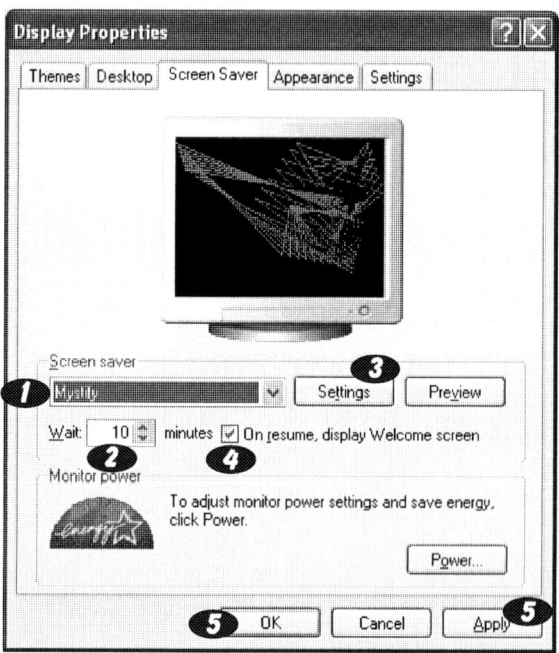

A miniature preview of your chosen **Screen saver** appears in the upper part of the dialog box. To see a full-screen preview of your screen saver, click the **Preview** button (to return to the **Display Properties** dialog box, just move your mouse).

1. Select a screen saver.

2. Specify the amount of time the computer must be idle before the screen saver starts.

3. Click this button to define the settings for your selected screen saver (if you chose the **3D Text** screen saver, for example, click this button then, in the **Custom Text** box, enter the text you want to use).

4. Activate this option if you want Windows to show the Welcome screen when you start using the computer again.

5. Validate your choices by clicking **OK** or use the **Apply** button to view the picture without closing the **Display Properties** dialog box.

Changing the environment

By default, the title bar in each window is blue, the desktop (without the background picture) is blue and the application background is grey. To brighten up your environment, you can change the colours of these different items.

DEFINING THE APPEARANCE OF WINDOWS AND DIALOG BOXES

- Right-click an empty space on the desktop then click the **Properties** option.
- Click the **Appearance** tab.

1. Select the style you want to use for **Windows and buttons** from this list.

2. Select the **Color scheme** you want to use.

3. Select the **Font size** you want to use in your windows.

4. Click the **Effects** button to define visual effects for menus, icons and fonts then validate these settings by clicking **OK**.

5. Click the **Advanced** button to customise the appearance of the windows, menus, fonts or icons.

Customizing the desktop

- To change the colour of one of the desktop items, first select the item concerned from the **Item** list then select the colour(s) you want to apply using the **Color 1** and/or **Color 2** lists.
- To change the size of one of the desktop items, first select the item concerned from the **Item** list then choose its new size in the **Size** list.
- If the item you choose has text, you can modify the text's **Font**, **Size**, **Color** and attributes: bold characters (**B**) and or italics (*I*).

- Click the **OK** button in the **Advanced Appearance** dialog box.
- Click the **OK** button in the **Display Properties** dialog box.

You will have noticed that the current time appears on the right of the taskbar: this is part of the system date and time. You can insert the system date and time as a variable in the documents you create (such as an Excel table or a letter you are writing in Word, for example): Windows will update this parameter to reflect the current system date and time.

CHANGING THE SYSTEM DATE AND TIME

Only users with Computer administrator accounts can change the system date and time.

▩ Click the **start** button, followed by the **Control Panel** option. Click the **Date, Time, Language and Regional Options** link (in Category view) then click the **Date and Time** link.

Alternatively, you can double-click the time on the taskbar.

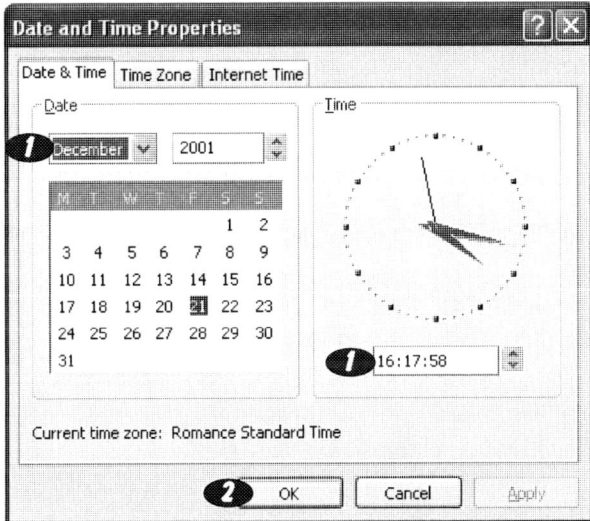

1. Specify the date and the time using the corresponding list and text boxes.

You can set the time zone for your locality under the **Time Zone** tab; you can also choose to **Automatically adjust clock for daylight saving changes** on this page.

2. Click **OK**.

▩ Click the ⊠ button to close the **Date, Time, Language and Regional Options** window.

Customizing the desktop

 When you point to the time on the taskbar the current date appears in a ScreenTip.

*At the bottom of the desktop the taskbar appears: the taskbar contains the **start** menu, which provides access to all the applications on your computer. As with most items in the Windows environment, you can customize this bar.*

MANAGING THE TASKBAR

▓ You can unlock or lock the taskbar, according to whether you want to move it or not: right-click an empty area of the taskbar then click the **Lock the Taskbar** option. A tick to the left of this option indicates that the taskbar is locked; no tick means that the taskbar is not locked and that you can move it.

▓ To move the taskbar, first check that it is not locked. Next, point to an empty area of the taskbar, hold down the mouse button and drag the taskbar to another side of the screen.

▓ To change the height (or width) of the taskbar, point to its top border (or to its right, left or bottom border according to the taskbar's position) then drag.

▓ To manage the display of the taskbar, right-click an empty area of the taskbar then click the **Properties** option.

Changing the environment

The **Taskbar** page of the **Taskbar and Start Menu Properties** dialog box opens.

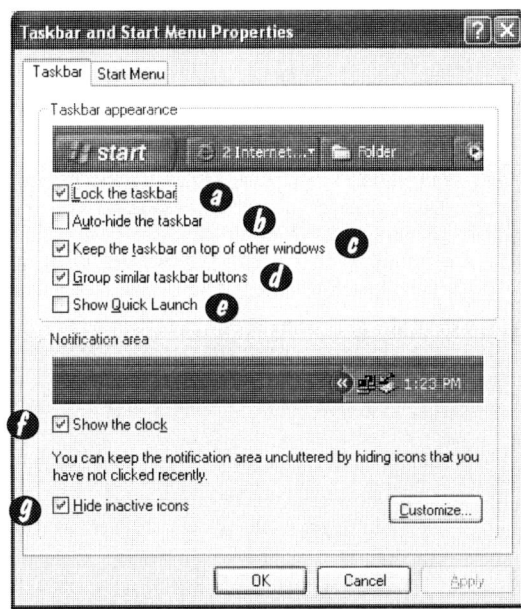

▨ Activate (or deactivate) the following options to suit your requirements:

(a)   activate this option if you do not want to be able to move the taskbar.

(b)   activate this option to reduce the taskbar to a thin line at the bottom of the screen: the taskbar will reappear when you point to this line.

(c)   activate this option if you want the taskbar to stay visible when an application runs in full-screen mode.

(d)   activate this option to group all the buttons for files of the same application: if the taskbar gets too cluttered, this option represents all files of the same application by a single button. Click this type of button to open its list and choose the file you want to view.

(e)   activate this option to display the **Quick Launch** bar in the taskbar: you can show the desktop or start an application directly from this **Quick Launch** bar.

(f)   activate this option to show the time in the **Notification area** to the right of the taskbar: when you point to the time, the current date appears in a ScreenTip.

(g) activate this option to hide unused icons in the **Notification area** (to the right of the taskbar): the 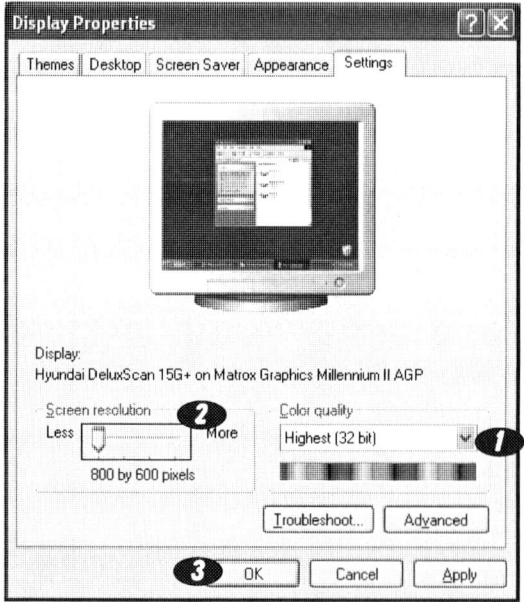 button displays these hidden icons.

▧ Validate your settings by clicking the **OK** button.

Some applications require specific settings before they can run correctly. For example, when you start a game from a CD-ROM you may see a message indicating that the application requires 256 colours and a screen resolution of 640 x 480, to run correctly. To meet such requirements you may need to change the desktop settings.

DEFINING SCREEN SETTINGS

▧ Right-click an empty space on the desktop then click the **Properties** option.

▧ Click the **Settings** tab.

1. Select the **Color quality** level from this list (it is better to specify the highest quality level available, unless the application you are running requires limited colour quality).

Changing the environment

2. If necessary, modify the **Screen resolution** by dragging this slider to the right or to the left. Nowadays, the standard resolution is 800 by 600 pixels: this setting specifies the number of pixels (points) the screen displays horizontally and vertically. The higher this value is, the more items your screen will be able to show (the more rows you will see in a table, for example) but the smaller these items will appear. The range of available values depends on the characteristics of your computer's graphics card.

3. Click the **OK** button.

Windows reminds you that you have reconfigured your desktop:

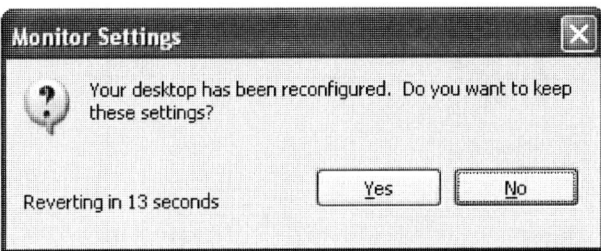

Click the **Yes** button to keep your new settings or click the **No** button to revert to your previous settings.

You can use small sound files to mark events, such as closing Windows, or to notify you of problems, such as a jammed printer.

ASSIGNING SOUNDS TO EVENTS

Click the **start** button, followed by the **ControlPanel** option. Click the **Sounds, Speech, and Audio Devices** link (in Category view) then click the **Change the sound scheme** link.

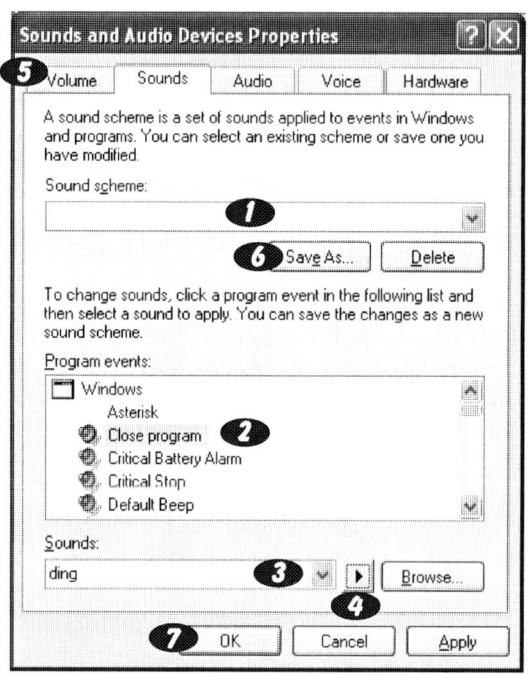

The dialog box that appears lists the program events to which you can apply sounds.

A 🔊 icon next to an event name indicates that a sound has been applied to that event.

1. If necessary, select a **Sound scheme** from this list.

Windows comes with a sound scheme called **Windows Default**. This scheme contains a set of sounds assigned to different events. You can modify this sound scheme or create a new one.

2. From the **Program events** list, select the event to which you want to apply a sound.

3. From the **Sounds** list, choose the sound file that must run when your chosen event occurs, or choose the **None** option so as not to apply a sound to this event. You can click the **Browse** button to select another sound file that is not in this list.

4. If you select a sound, you can click the ▶ button to listen to it.

5. To change the sound volume, click the **Volume** tab then drag the **Device volume** slider, as required.

6. If you have modified the sounds that are applied (or not applied) to the events but you want to keep the former sound scheme, click the **Save As** then use the **Save this sound scheme as** box to save your new sound scheme under another name and click the **OK** button.

7. Click the **OK** button.

 To delete a **Sound scheme**, go into the **Sounds and Audio Devices Properties** dialog box, select it in the **Sound scheme** list and click the **Delete** button.

The general look of your desktop (including its background, screen saver, windows, buttons, fonts and sounds) is called its theme. Windows XP provides a Windows XP theme and a Windows Classic theme. You can use these standard themes as a basis for creating new themes.

CREATING YOUR OWN DESKTOP THEME

▓ Right-click an empty space on the desktop then click the **Properties** option.

▓ Under the **Themes** tab, look in the **Theme** list and select the option you want to use as a basis for your new theme.

▓ Choose the different options you require under the **Desktop**, **Screen Saver**, **Appearance** and **Settings** tabs to define the general look of your desktop.

▓ If necessary, include a sound scheme in your new theme (cf. Assigning sounds to events) and/or a different mouse pointer (using **start - Control Panel - Printers and Other Hardware - Mouse**) keeping the **Display Properties** dialog box open.

▓ If any other dialog boxes you have opened to define your new theme are hiding the **Display Properties** dialog box, you can redisplay this dialog box by right-clicking an empty space on your desktop and clicking the **Properties** option.

▓ If necessary, click the **Themes** tab.

Customizing the desktop

In the **Theme** list, the name of the standard theme you chose appears followed by the word (Modified).

▓ Click the **Save As** button.

The **Save As** dialog box appears.

▓ If necessary, change the folder that must contain your new theme (by default, Windows stores your themes in your **My Documents** folder).

▓ To replace an existing theme, enter its exact name in the **File name** box. To create a new theme, enter a name that does not already exist.

▓ Click the **Save** button.

Changing the environment

If you chose to replace an existing theme, Windows asks you to confirm your action.

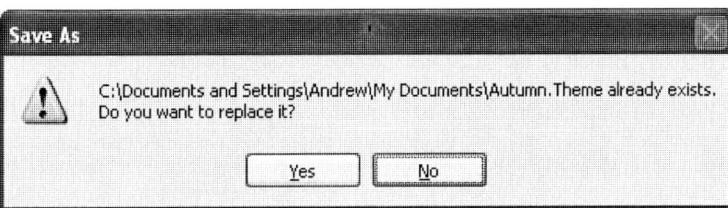

- Click **Yes** if you want to replace the existing theme; otherwise click **No**.
- Click the **OK** button in the **Display Properties** dialog box.

 To delete a theme you have created, display the **Display Properties** dialog box (by right-clicking an empty space on your desktop and clicking the **Properties** option) select the theme you want to delete from the **Theme** list under the **Themes** tab then click the **Delete** button; you cannot delete the standard **Windows XP** and **Windows Classic** themes.

Installing

If your computer came with a printer, you must install this device physically by connecting it to your computer via a cable, according to the manufacturer's instructions. When you run a print command, Windows sends instructions to the printer. However, each printer needs specific instructions that it can understand. For the printer to be able to understand the instructions Windows sends, your hard disk must contain a special file, called a driver. This driver provides a link between Windows and the printer. The Windows XP CD-ROM contains a large number of drivers and it probably includes one for your printer. However, if the Windows XP CD-ROM does not provide a driver for your printer, you will find one on the CD-ROM or floppy disk supplied with your printer.

INSTALLING A PRINTER

▩ Click the **start** button followed by the **Control Panel** option.

▩ In Category view, click the **Printers and Other Hardware** link followed by the **Add a printer** link.

The Add Printer Wizard starts.

▩ Click the **Next** button.

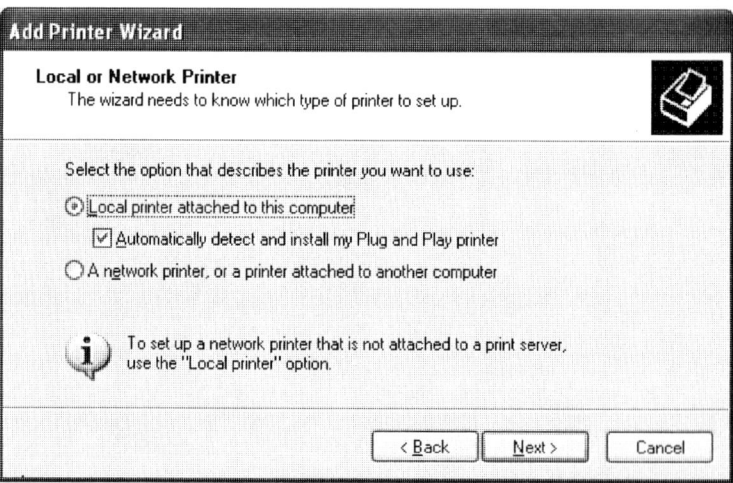

▩ If you have only one computer, activate the **Local printer attached to this computer** option. In addition, if you leave the **Automatically detect and install my Plug and Play printer** option active, Windows may be able to detect your newly connected printer and install it automatically.

Changing the environment

▨ If your computer is part of a network and the printer is connected to another machine in the network, activate the **A network printer, or a printer attached to another computer** option.

▨ Click the **Next** button.

▨ If you are installing a network printer, leave the **Browse for a printer** option active, click the **Next** button then select one of the printers in the **Shared printers** list and click the **Next** button.

▨ If you are installing a local printer and the **Automatically detect and install my Plug and Play printer** option was not active in the previous screen, you can change the output port in the **Use the following port** list, if it does not correspond to the port to which you connected your printer. Click the **Next** button.

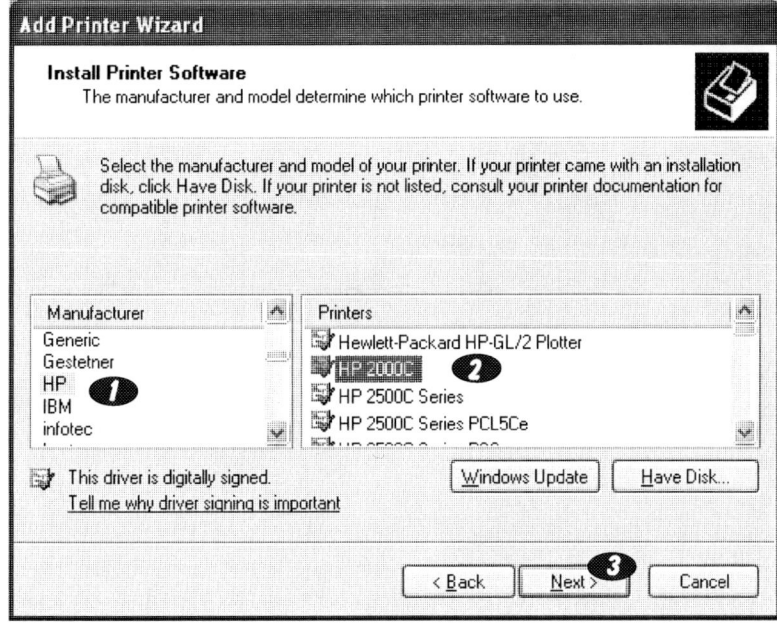

Add Printer Wizard

Install Printer Software
The manufacturer and model determine which printer software to use.

Select the manufacturer and model of your printer. If your printer came with an installation disk, click Have Disk. If your printer is not listed, consult your printer documentation for compatible printer software.

Manufacturer	Printers
Generic	Hewlett-Packard HP-GL/2 Plotter
Gestetner	HP 2000C
HP ➊	HP 2500C Series
IBM	HP 2500C Series PCL5Ce
infotec	

This driver is digitally signed.
Tell me why driver signing is important

[Windows Update]   [Have Disk...]

[< Back]   [Next > ➌]   [Cancel]

1. Select the make of your printer.

2. Select your printer model: if the exact model of your printer is not in the list, select the nearest model or insert the CD-ROM or floppy disk that contains the driver into your computer then click the **Have Disk** button: check that the correct drive is selected in the **Copy manufacturer's files from** list then click the **OK** button and select the name of your printer.

3. Continue with the installation procedure.

⬚ If you are installing a local printer, specify the **Printer name** in the corresponding box, if necessary.

⬚ Specify whether or not Windows applications must use the printer by default then click the **Next** button.

⬚ According to your computer configuration, the wizard may ask you whether or not you want to share your printer, at this stage. If your printer is only for users of your computer, leave the **Do not share this printer** option selected; otherwise, select the **Sharename** option and enter a share name for your printer. Click the **Next** button.

⬚ If you are installing a local printer, specify whether or not you want to print a test page then click the **Next** button.

⬚ Click the **Finish** button.

⬚ Click the ☒ button in the **Printers and Faxes** window to close it.

 To install on your computer, hardware devices such as scanners, printers or digital cameras, start the **Add Hardware Wizard**: select **start - Control Panel - Printers and Other Hardware - Add Hardware** link (in the **See Also** box) then follow the installation procedure.

After you have bought a software application on a CD-ROM or a floppy disk, you must install it on your hard disk before you can use it (installing an application consists of copying the application files onto your hard disk and defining settings to make the application work). You would generally carry out this operation using an installation wizard, which asks you certain questions as the installation progresses (such as on which drive you want to install and whether you want to install the full version or a limited one).

INSTALLING A PROGRAM

You need to use a Computer administrator type of account to install some programs.

▨ If your application is on a CD-ROM, insert the CD-ROM in your computer's CD-ROM drive.

Most applications on CD-ROM offer an Autorun feature, which installs the application automatically.

▨ In this case, click the **Install** button to start the installation process and follow the instructions that appear on the screen (these instructions vary from one application to another).

▨ If your application does not install itself automatically (or if your application is on a floppy disk) access the **Control Panel** (**start - Control Panel**) then (in Category view) click the **Add or Remove Programs** link.

The dialog box that appears lists the applications installed on your hard disk.

▨ Click the **Add New Programs** button followed by the **CD or Floppy** button.

▨ Insert the application's CD-ROM or first floppy disk in the appropriate drive of your computer, as Windows asks you to, then click the **Next** button.

Windows searches your CD-ROM or floppy disk for the application's installation program then displays its name in the **Open** box. You can use the **Browse** button to look for your installation program manually.

▨ Click the **Finish** button to start the installation procedure.

Windows copies the files it needs to install the application.

▨ Follow the different steps of the installation program, until the end.

When you have installed an application its name appears in the **start - All Programs** menu, which is common to all the users of the computer: you can run your application from this menu.

Installing

When you no longer need an application it is better to uninstall it. Rather than simply deleting the folder that contains the application's files, you are strongly advised to follow the uninstall procedure set out below.

UNINSTALLING A PROGRAM

Before you attempt to uninstall a program, check that you are logged on alone with a Computer administrator type account (since you cannot install some programs with a Limited type of account).

▓ Access the **Control Panel** from the **start** menu.

▓ Click the **Add or Remove Programs** link (in Category view).

▓ Click the **Change or Remove Programs** button in the left of the window.

▓ In the **Currently installed programs** list, click the row corresponding to the program you want to remove.

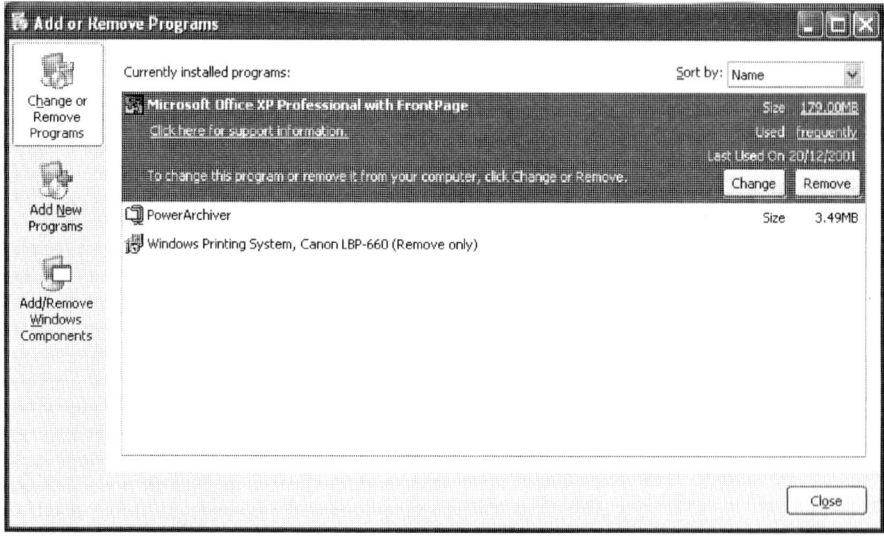

According to the application concerned, Windows may provide a **Change** button and a **Remove** button or a single **Change/Remove** button.

▓ Click the **Remove** button or the **Change/Remove** button.

Windows asks you to confirm your action.

▦ Click the **Yes** button.

Windows removes all the application files you no longer need.

▦ When Windows has finished the uninstall procedure, click the **OK** button.

▦ Click the **Close** button in the **Add or Remove Programs** dialog box.

▦ Click the ▣ button to close the **Control Panel**.

Shortcut keys

GENERAL SHORTCUT KEYS

F1	Display an application's **Help** window.
Alt F4	Leave an application.
Ctrl Esc	Open the **start** menu.
Alt ⇆	Activate an application that is already open.

DESKTOP AND WINDOWS EXPLORER

F2	Rename a folder or document.
F3	Display the **Search** explorer bar.
Ctrl X	Cut the selection.
Ctrl C	Copy the selection.
Ctrl V	Paste the selection.
Del	Delete a folder or document.
Shift Del	Delete a file without sending it to the Recycle Bin.
Alt ↵	Display the selected object's properties.

MY COMPUTER AND FOLDERS WINDOW

F5	Refresh the window.
Ctrl Z	Undo the last action.
Ctrl A	Select all.
Alt →	Display the previous page.
Alt ←	Display the next page.

FOLDERS EXPLORERS BAR

+	Expand a branch.
-	Collapse a branch.
→	Expand branch or, it is already expanded, select the first subfolder.
←	Collapse branch or, it is already collapsed, select the folder above.

Appendix

—Index

—Index

—Index——————

—Index——————————————

—Index

M

—Index—

—Index

—Index————————————————

—Index

W

WINDOW

WINDOWS MEDIA PLAYER

See MEDIA PLAYER

WINDOWS MESSENGER

See MESSENGER

WINDOWS MOVIE MAKER

See MOVIE MAKER

WINDOWS XP

Z

ZIPPING

See COMPRESSING